UNKNOWN SCENT

WEREWOLF SERIES - BOOK TWO

by

Gina Marie Long

Black Rose Writing
www.blackrosewriting.com

© 2011 by Gina Marie Long

All rights reserved. No part of this book may be reproduced, stored in a retrieval system or transmitted in any form or by any means without the prior written permission of the publishers, except by a reviewer who may quote brief passages in a review to be printed in a newspaper, magazine or journal.

The final approval for this literary material is granted by the author.

First printing

All characters appearing in this work are fictitious. Any resemblance to real persons, living or dead, is purely coincidental.

ISBN: 978-1-61296-019-7

PUBLISHED BY BLACK ROSE WRITING

www.blackrosewriting.com

Printed in the United States of America

Unknown Scent is printed in Times New Roman

ACKNOWLEDGMENTS

I would like to sincerely thank the following who have helped make this second book a reality: my husband for his support and motivating me to keep writing; my parents for their time and suggestions while reading the first draft; my sister-in-law for devoting her time, proofreading skills and ideas; my friends and fans for their encouragement and praise; Kennett Photography for my professional author's photo; and my publisher, Reagan Rothe, of Black Rose Writing for accepting *Unknown Scent* for publication.

"It is necessary to write, if the days are not to slip emptily by. How else, indeed, to clap the net over the butterfly of the moment? For the moment passes, it is forgotten; the mood is gone; life itself is gone. That is where the writer scores over his fellows: he catches the changes of his mind on the hop."
—Vita Sackville-West

FOREWORD

Werewolves…I had grown comfortable in their presence. That fact alone should cause worry, but that's not the half of it. Throw into the supernatural mix a vampire, a coven of witches and a demon. I sunk deeper and deeper into their unknown or hidden existence from *most* of the real world. In a little over a month my old, familiar life had been stripped away. My new boyfriend was a werewolf named Daniel. It was an unusual relationship, but I had chosen it, and I loved him. To complicate things, another competed for my heart. Dominic: a human psychic - like me. His discovery of my psychic power brought all of us together. I wanted to use my special abilities to help others, human or not, whenever I could. It felt right and it gave my life a greater meaning. If the good guys failed to band together, we could be killed or tortured by the evil ones. Who knew how far and fast evil could spread? This had become my new life; my way to survive. The Liaison team remained strong, but was forced to adapt to a tidal wave of shocking ordeals. We opened our minds to all possibilities, utilized our senses for any situation and honed our individual skills. We forged stronger bonds between our members and found new allies to help defeat the enemy. I have to admit that it's hard to catch my breath before the next harrowing experience consumes me. But nothing stays the same forever. Changes are inevitable. Come on…we all know that. And you can't please everyone. Choices and decisions have to be made… one way or another…

CHAPTER 1
CHRISTMAS EVE

"Daniel, do NOT wreck this car! Get us away from the lake! I can't believe this is happening HERE!" I shrieked as my hands had a death grip on the dashboard of my new Dodge Challenger. With great generosity, just three weeks ago Eli had presented the car to me on my 21st birthday. It was now Christmas Eve.

I promised my parents we would visit them for the holidays and properly introduce them to Daniel. But, we hadn't planned on the nine inches of snow mixed with sleet. At a turtle's pace, Daniel progressed past Silver Lake on Route 143 towards Marine, Illinois. I breathed a sigh of relief once we were beyond the danger of sliding off the road and taking a nosedive into that cold lake. I'd recently experienced that exact life or death situation and didn't want to revisit it again. Shivers ran up and down my spine. Only four miles to go…

…And the car started fishtailing. It appeared we were the only idiots inching our way down the icy, snow-packed road, so there was no fear of colliding with another vehicle. The car slid partially off the road, narrowly missing someone's mailbox. Without a second thought Daniel jumped out of the car. Using his core werewolf strength, he shoved the car back onto the road as if it were nothing.

We managed to identify the El Kay Meadows subdivision sign through the snow and darkness. Since it was only twenty feet away, Daniel made the decision to get us off the main road before we ended up in a much worse situation. The car skidded sideways as he attempted to make the right turn into the subdivision. Brakes were useless as we waited for the car's momentum to finally come to a complete stop. We were safe, the car didn't get a scratch and there we sat staring through the windshield. It was 6:00 p.m. At that time of the year the darkness reigned. Swirling, drifting snow added to our blindness.

I turned to Daniel, "Now what? We are so close to making it to Mom and Dad's house...this is ridiculous! It's not like I can call Dad and tell him to come get us. He'd get stuck, too!"

"Didn't you tell me before that The Liaison's underground hideout is nearby? Couldn't we take cover there?" Daniel asked. He had a brilliant idea, but I didn't know if I could gain access to the facility. About half a mile back at the lake, in a heavily wooded area, there was a hidden hatch door that led down into the tunnels. Zac used that entrance after he rescued me during the lake incident. Once inside the tunnels, four-wheelers were conveniently positioned to take you to the facility's main headquarters several miles away. Eli, scientist/founder/Mr. Money-Bags of our secret Liaison team, bought the old, closed down military base.

"Give me a minute to mentally link up with Dom to see if he can help us get inside. And I'm not positive on the exact location of the door," I explained. Daniel's eyebrows lifted as he smirked with that male rivalry flaring up. I rolled my eyes at him. Daniel and Dominic were friends, but could just as easily flip and become enemies. If that were to happen, they knew it would devastate me. Since both cared so strongly for me and didn't want to hurt me, they maintained a friendly bantering.

Daniel shook his head and argued, "Why don't you just use the cell phone instead of taxing your brain right now?"

"What? And miss out on all this fun? Nope, this is a great opportunity to experiment," I pleaded my case.

I focused on Dominic, my best friend, with all my energy. *Dom, it's Kara.* I closed my eyes, concentrated on his face and envisioned creating a telepathic connection. *Dom, can you hear me? Please, I need your help. Beam me in...hellooo...are you out there?*

Gradually I felt a familiar presence seep into my mind. Dom and I had practiced our long distance telepathy only a few times since the team had left Hamlin, Kentucky. It was difficult to hold the mental link at such great distances, but we were able to communicate this way if we didn't have any major distractions. The farther apart we were from each other made the experience similar to a bad cell phone connection. Dominic happened to be visiting family in Arizona so this was considered a monumental accomplishment.

Kara, hold on...I'm walking to a private area so I can focus... What's wrong? Are you hurt? Dom's concern for my well-being was quite evident. He worried about my relationship with Daniel and choices I might make in the future. Dom wished I would choose a life with him instead of Daniel.

Don't panic. I'm okay. Daniel and I are a couple of miles from my parents' house. The roads are covered in snow and ice so we pulled off into a subdivision. We're afraid the car will slide off the road if we keep going. Silver Lake is very close. Can we open that hatch door to the hideout and get inside?

I could hear and almost feel Dominic groan in despair. *Nooo...I didn't give you a key yet. My fault. Although with Daniel's strength, he could probably rip the hatch open, but then the tunnels are exposed to the weather and to being discovered by someone.*

I was allowing Daniel to listen in on the psychic communication that Dom and I shared since this problem involved our safety and well-being. During specific situations in the past, I had created mental blocks that prevented Daniel from hearing my thoughts. When Daniel heard Dom mention his strength, he poked me in the arm and said, "Hey, you realize I *can* get us to your parents' house? It's dark outside; no one would see me if I shape shifted into beast form and carried you on my back the last few miles. If we can't or shouldn't break into the underground hideout, then this is another viable option. Unless, of course, you really want to knock on someone's door out here on Christmas Eve to ask for help? We have to make a decision. We can't stay in this car all night. I would be fine, but it will quickly become too cold for your body to handle."

"Mom and Dad are probably wondering why we haven't made it to their house yet. I really wanted to make it there for Christmas Eve," I pondered.

Dom responded, *I hate to say this, but he's right. Layer up, throw a blanket around his upper body and let him carry you piggyback across the fields until you get closer to Marine. He can transform back to human form then. Get the car tomorrow once it's daylight and the roads have been cleared. I'll be back there in two days. Get going and be careful.*

I replied with a smile on my face, *Oh, I didn't know for sure if you'd be around here or not. Can't wait to see you, Dom. Bye.*

We dissolved the mental link. Daniel cleared his throat to bring my attention back to him. He smiled at me with male confidence and that tough-guy attitude. He was entirely ready to be the hero of the day...or night, as it happened to be. He didn't even have to *try* to look tough; he exuded power, authority and devotion to my welfare.

"I'll put some of our personal items in the duffle bag and sling it over my shoulder like a backpack. I suppose if you're transforming, then the clothes you're wearing now better go in there. It would be rather inappropriate to arrive naked at my parents' house, don't you think? I doubt that would make a very good first impression," I gave him a wicked smile.

Daniel chuckled at my remark, visualizing the shocked expressions on my parents' faces if he actually pulled that stunt. He replied, "Well, let's get going. I have a feeling our arrival without the car is going to look strange. The average person would not hike four miles in weather like this. Get prepared for their questions and ready to tell them another lie...er, uh, story, I mean."

I frowned and nodded in agreement. I hated the constant string of lies I kept creating. But I couldn't exactly come out and say that Daniel was a werewolf...and, oh yeah, I've also met an ancient vampire who recently warned us about a resurgence of evil witches out east. My parents would faint. The least outrageous of all these astonishing revelations would be telling them of my newfound psychic skills: how I'm able to read minds and manipulate the thoughts of others. I would then have to admit to implanting positive thoughts into their heads during the past few months which kept them calm and lessened their suspicions over my abrupt departure from home. The guilt over this deception weighed heavily in my mind and heart. Should I tell them the truth?

"I'm going to call and tell them we're running behind because of the snow," I visualized my parents peering out the front window and pacing the floor. In actuality, we were already an hour late. We had planned on arriving at 5:00. I briefly chatted with Mom on the cell phone, explaining we would be there soon; obviously, I left out our new method of arrival.

I grabbed the duffle bag from behind the driver's seat. We exited the car and walked to the trunk. I contemplated what bare essentials we would need for the overnight stay at my parents' house and stuffed those items into the bag. I removed my coat, added another sweatshirt, and bundled up again making sure I had my scarf and gloves on securely. I looked like I was ready to tackle a hiking expedition in Alaska. Daniel found this amusing as I found it rather uncomfortable.

"You're next, Mr. Cold Weather Doesn't Bother Me. Strip down," I said bluntly, smirked and attempted to cross my arms with the many layers of clothing. Daniel bared it all in the winter weather without a single complaint. I grumbled in exasperation while stuffing his clothes into the duffle bag and trying not to stare at his nakedness. He reached inside the trunk for a blanket to cover himself. The blanket would provide some added protection from the cold weather since he did have four miles to hike. Plus, it helped to conceal his werewolf form of the beast from anyone who might catch sight of him.

"Kara, remember that seeing me as a beast is not something you're at ease with yet. I've only transformed into that shape a few times in front of you. Don't forget to stay away from my mouth and teeth as I carry you on my back. My bite, a nip or a scratch from my teeth could convert you into a werewolf while I'm in this shape. We don't need to deal with any accidents like that tonight," Daniel warned me.

He proceeded to lock the doors and give the car a quick security check. He glanced at the position and angle the car was parked in. The rear-end was jutting out too much onto the street due to sliding as we attempted to stop. Someone could easily hit the back or side of the car in the dark. In a mere three seconds, he lifted and maneuvered the rear-end of the car further to the side of the road, straightening it out.

Looking quite satisfied with the placement of the car, Daniel said, "Time to go. Talk to me with your mind. You've witnessed it's difficult for me to speak in beast form. And stay away from my teeth!"

Daniel, in all of his handsome (and naked) glory, transformed into a fearsome, lethal beast. The transformation occurs so fast that the human eye and brain have a difficult time comprehending what it sees. Every time I observed the shape shifting in any form it seemed so magical and mystical. Instinct forced me to take two steps backward. I couldn't help myself. It was terrifying seeing him like that. I knew it bothered him as I stood there with immediate fear emanating from my entire body. I felt guilt for stepping away from him. The only part of this beast that still resembled Daniel was his eyes. Whether he took the shape of a beast or a wolf, his penetrating dark eyes always remained the same. Human. Perhaps the correct expression would be those of a man, as I knew he was no longer human but a werewolf.

I took one timid step forward as he reached his hand (or claw as it was) towards my face. I touched at his mind ever so gingerly and felt reassured it really was *my* Daniel. He slowly ran the back of his knuckles across my cheek. He kept his sharp, dagger-like fingernails curled away from my face to avoid scratching me. I smiled and rubbed his furry arm in a manner that an animal would enjoy. Daniel was indeed a very powerful cross between an animal and a man at that moment. It was best to keep him at ease and comfortable with his surroundings. Not that he would intentionally hurt me, but I didn't want to take any chances, especially with those teeth of his. I had not made a final decision on whether I wanted to become what he was – a werewolf – and I didn't want that decision to be made for me because of being reckless.

The blanket had fallen to the ground during his shape shifting. He reached down and snatched it up. I watched him as he slung it over his shoulders. The sinewy muscles rippled through his fur as he went through the rugged movements. Graceful, flowing motions were not part of this creature's fine points. But when he was a wolf or a man, those traits returned in full force. I placed the duffle bag over my shoulders. Then Daniel turned his back to me, squatted and gestured for me to climb on. I had a feeling this was going to be some ride.

I kept my arms tucked well under his jaws, clenched around his neck. My legs firmly encircled his waist as he tried to grasp them with his claws in a way that wouldn't rip through my jeans. He stood up to his full height. Boy, the world looked different from this vantage point. He assessed his footing and balance on the snow and ice. His feet were now a cross between human feet and paws. He had much better traction in this shape, although the ground was still a bit slippery. My weight had to affect his balance, too. And, of course, I was clinging to his back which was something of a different sensation for him.

I felt as if I was strangling him. I whispered in his ear, "Am I choking you?"

I swear it sounded like he laughed at me. Something between a cough and a gurgle. I dove into his mind for his response. Daniel answered, *Are you kidding? You choking me?! I don't think so. But your warm breath sure feels nice on my ear!*

Wonderful. I sighed. He was enjoying this too much.

Daniel embarked on the four mile trek attentive to the slick conditions. I buried my face into the blanket that covered his shoulders. His body heat radiated through the material like my own personal furnace. Thank God. I hated winter and being cold and worrying about the stupid weather. I wondered how long it would take to get to my parents' house. I estimated about 40 minutes but with Daniel's faster pace and longer strides it would shorten that timeframe. Regardless, I had to craft another story to tell Mom and Dad concerning how in the world we managed to walk all the way to their house from El Kay Meadows subdivision in a snow and ice storm. Or I could just tell them the truth. That idea crept into my thoughts frequently.

As Daniel made his way over the fields and through the snow, he was forced to let go of my legs and use his arms in various ways to keep us from falling down. At times, he was hunched over almost walking on all fours like a wolf. It was not comfortable for me trying to hang on. My arms were tired and my body ached from being jostled around. If this was only a half mile hike, I probably would have considered it to be fun. We had two more miles to go yet. Ugh.

Even though we stayed away from the main road, it was inevitable that we still had to cross a highway. There was no way around it. Daniel remained in the shadows, away from the overhead lights, surveying the situation. A large truck with a snow blade crept past us, unaware we stood in the shadows watching it clear the road as it drove by. Daniel waited a moment for the taillights to disappear and tentatively stepped onto the highway. No other vehicles approached from either direction. The coast was clear for our crossing such a well-lit area. We did not want anyone to see us as it would reveal Daniel's beast form. It was best to avoid creating rumors of strange creatures stalking the area.

We made it across the highway without any incident. As we gloated in our good fortune of remaining concealed and traversing through the elements, Daniel's footing failed him. Looming before us was a deep trench. We went down. Daniel was terrified he would crush me as he fell. To protect me, he clutched my legs and rolled his body towards the snow. That way, I was on top of him instead of under him. I wasn't crushed, but one of his claws sliced through my jeans. The whole scene played out in five seconds.

The moment we stopped sliding, Daniel released my legs and immediately realized what happened. He swung around to examine me and saw the cut in my jeans. Then the wound started to bleed. It wasn't a severe cut. No stitches needed, at least I didn't think so. I would easily survive this. If this was summer and I had shorts on without the protection of pants, I would have been in a much worse condition.

Due to the circumstances, Daniel transformed back to human shape. He applied pressure to the wound and crouched over my leg, shaking his head from side to side.

"Kara, I'm so sorry. Are you okay? I thought I was keeping you from harm and yet I still hurt you!" Daniel was mortified that he had cut my leg. In his mind, this was completely unacceptable.

I grabbed his arm and soothed him, "Daniel, I'll be fine. I just need a bandage. It's not that bad. Look!"

He removed his hand that was applying pressure and took another glance at the wound. I looked, too. Thank goodness it really wasn't bleeding much at this point. He dug around in the duffle bag and found a shirt that could be constructed into a nice bandage which he carefully wrapped around my leg. All was right in the world once again.

Daniel looked into my eyes and expressed, "This was too close of a call, Kara. Luckily my claws can't convert you into a werewolf or we'd have quite a mess on our hands. And on Christmas Eve…when

I'm supposed to meet your parents for the first time. This is crazy!"

"Come on. Let's get going. Change back to your furry self and get me out of this ditch! I'm freezing!" I brought us back to our current situation and the need to keep moving. Daniel shook his head once again, still upset with himself. He leaned forward and gave me a gentle kiss.

He pulled away with concern and said, "You *are* cold. Your teeth are chattering."

Daniel stepped away for my safety and transformed back into the beast. He knelt down and I clambered onto his back. He clawed our way up and out of the trench to flat ground. With determination and absolute conviction, he was going to get us to our destination.

I clung to Daniel. I kept my eyes closed as the cold air made them burn and form tears. My injured leg felt numb from the cold air, which was a good thing. I remained silent both in speech and telepathic communication with Daniel. He needed all his senses to be alert and focused. It was dark and cold. He was in unfamiliar territory stomping through snow and patches of ice. He was carrying me on his back and we needed to appear invisible to wandering eyes. Many minutes passed…possibly ten? fifteen? He halted and asked, *Can you tell me if I'm going in the right direction?*

Daniel's anxious voice in my head immediately jolted me back to reality. I had been zoning out, letting my mind wander. I was running through the different scenarios of what I would tell my parents upon our arrival at their doorstep. He had never been here before and I should have realized he would not know which way to go. He had no clue exactly where my parents' house was located. During the trek to Marine, he followed as close to the main road as possible without being detected. I glanced around and recognized the outer edges of town. It was probably best that he transform back to human shape before we continued.

"Oh, yes, you're my hero! Take us to that thick line of trees by the field over there. Let's get you back to looking human and dressed again," I pointed to the area where I thought he could discreetly make his change.

Daniel made the transformation and speedily pulled on his clothes. Since we still had several blocks to walk, he gave me a piggyback ride once again. I was fully alert, anxious and longing for the warmth of my parents' house.

We arrived. Daniel was practically sweating in the freezing temperatures. It was a sight I wouldn't forget. First, he was incredibly nervous about meeting my parents. Second, his body did not need all the pieces to the winter garb that he was wearing. In order to look normal, he had to wear layers and a coat. Before we could say a word to each other, the front door flew open and Mom pulled us inside. Show time!

CHAPTER 2
SHOW TIME

"Where have you been? Did you get stuck somewhere?" Mom prodded for information as she hugged the life out of me. "And this must be Daniel!" She hugged him next.

Dad stood a little distance away letting Mom bustle around us. I was surprised and proud when Daniel reached forward to shake Dad's hand to introduce himself. I should have already initiated the greetings and failed.

"Sir, I'm Daniel and am very pleased to meet you."

Dad nodded and commented, "How's it going?"

They firmly shook hands in a cordial manner but Dad looked like he was ready to give Daniel the "third degree". Dad held the undaunted eye contact with Daniel longer than necessary. I decided to step in to break the staring contest by giving Dad an overly-enthusiastic hug.

I interjected with, "Ahh…Shame on me. I forgot to do the proper introductions! Let's start again. Mom, Dad, this is Daniel Taylor. Daniel, this is my mom, Tanya and my dad, Adam. You may have seen each other during that October trip we took to Daniel's resort."

I promptly turned to answer Mom's previous question, "And, yes, we more or less got stuck. The car kept sliding around and we decided to park it and walk the rest of the way. That's why we're so late getting here."

Dad noticed my makeshift bandage and asked, "What happened to your leg?"

"Oh, I slipped on an icy spot and fell down. Tore my jeans and got a little cut. No big deal but we covered up the tear so my leg wouldn't get cold," I tried my best to brush it off. Both parents were giving me the scrunched-up eyebrow look which meant they thought my story was a wee bit off.

I went on, "So, have you been keeping the food warm all this time? Or did you go ahead and eat?"

Mom replied, "No, of course we didn't eat without you! It's ready to go whenever you are."

"First, can we use the bathroom to freshen up? Then we can eat. I'm starving!" I was making my best attempt to keep on the subject of it being Christmas Eve, a great meal and spending time visiting. I had no idea how I was going to avoid the inevitable questions they would start asking. I could use my ability to manipulate their thoughts and implant ideas about what had happened on our journey here. I could calm their emotions and place positive images in their minds. I could…give up and tell them the truth. I was tired of playing this deceptive game.

Without a sound, my parents' lovable dog, Nicky, suddenly appeared in the room. He stood still for a moment staring at us. When he made the realization it was actually me, he dashed over, barking and jumping with maximum enthusiasm. Since he only weighed fifteen pounds, I scooped him up in my arms and gave him a kiss on his nose.

"Nicky! How are you doing, my little buddy?" I proceeded to baby talk to him as I rubbed him vigorously. Daniel smiled and nodded in approval.

I mentally sent Daniel a tease, *Oh gee, you're not jealous of Nicky?!* He just chuckled.

I noticed my parents looked at each other as if they missed out on something. I put Nicky back down on the floor and he turned instantly to face Daniel. He took a playful bow with a wild wagging of his tail and exuded a bark that indicated he wanted to have some fun. Daniel squatted to get closer and gazed into Nicky's eyes, tenderly scratching him behind his ears. They were communicating. My dog was in awe of Daniel. It was adorable. Nicky rolled over on his back and Daniel gave him a soothing belly rub. After a few seconds, Nicky popped up and ran to get his toy ball for Daniel to throw. So cute!

You were just talking to him, weren't you? I inquired of Daniel.

Daniel responded in my mind, *Yes, I'd say we've bonded. Oh, he thinks I'm pretty cool. Now if your parents will just think the same of me.*

Daniel and I took turns using the bathroom. I removed the shirt/bandage from my leg and thoroughly inspected the area. I cleaned the cut with hydrogen peroxide from the closet. As I guessed, it really wasn't anything to worry about since my jeans had taken the brunt of Daniel's razor-sharp claw. It was a rather long cut but not very deep. The bleeding had stopped from applied pressure, the bandage and time passing. I stuck a neat line of four Band-Aids over the length of the cut. Then I changed into different jeans that were stuffed in the duffle bag hoping my parents would forget about the injury if it wasn't visible.

The rest of the evening was manageable. Food, more food, idle chit chat about mundane things, basic questions pertaining to Daniel's resort. Nothing that I couldn't handle. Most families have a traditional gift exchange at Christmas but we had unanimously agreed two years before to stop buying presents for each other. No one knew anymore what to purchase and hated to spend money on something that could end up being unused or useless for the receiving person. Still, my parents didn't completely hold true to that agreement…Mom handed small envelopes to Daniel and to me. Inside was cash to do with what we wanted.

I sensed my parents knew my brain was frazzled from the precarious drive up from Kentucky and the remaining hike to get to their house. They chose not to pressure me for answers to their imminent questions. At least not yet. Each one of us vowed to have a nice Christmas Eve…and I was just plain tuckered out.

* * * *

It was Christmas morning. I stretched out on my childhood bed. Daniel was in a spare bedroom next to mine. I felt refreshed and ready to conquer the day. I mentally prepared for the onslaught of questions from Mom and Dad. I had a real battle I needed to win. It was difficult to be at complete ease around my parents, knowing I kept a secret from them. Let's get real - there were numerous multifaceted secrets.

I shuffled out of my room as Daniel made his appearance at the same time. We could smell sausage, bacon and eggs wafting through the house. Breakfast was delicious but I spoke little while we ate. I lightly tapped into Mom's mind, trying to get a heads up on the dreaded questions that inevitably would be asked. I wasn't picking up her inner thoughts as easily as I knew I was capable of doing. I poked around in Dad's head but he was focused on reading the newspaper. Was Mom shielding her mind from me? Now how could that be… unless she already knew something about this whole insane situation?

As we finished eating, Dad walked to the sliding glass door to let Nicky go outside. Nicky was only out there a few seconds, when Daniel abruptly rose up from his chair at the kitchen table. He rushed to the door and jerked it open, almost popping it off its track. I heard a barely audible growl coming from deep within Daniel's throat. Dad, Mom and I followed Daniel outside to see what all the commotion was about.

In the backyard a mangy coyote had defenseless, little Nicky cornered forty feet away by the lawn shed. A coyote meandering into town was not a normal occurrence but this one was obviously not well. He was foaming at the mouth and had a crazed look to his face. With a savage snarl he appeared ready to take a bite out of my dog's neck. At that moment the coyote sensed another predator had entered the picture and snapped his head up. My Daniel was the other predator. The coyote forgot about Nicky in an instant as he twisted around and made eye to eye contact with Daniel.

I wasn't worried about Daniel. He wouldn't be harmed. The coyote, on the other hand, was no match against Daniel's strength, speed, agility and innate skills. I had witnessed Daniel in action and knew he could handle himself. The animal's outward signs indicated it carried rabies. Not good. It would have to be put down. And Daniel would be the one to carry out this deed. I accepted the sad fate of this animal.

Daniel was coaxing the coyote to him by using soft, verbal sounds and mental persuasion. The rest of us were afraid to move or say a word. Mom's hand went to her mouth as if she were holding back a scream. I read Dad's mind. He was about to reach inside the door and grab his rifle. He kept one leaning in the corner for easy access just for possible situations like this or protection against intruders.

No! Don't move a muscle! I pushed into Dad's mind. He looked at me trying to determine if I had said that out loud or not.

I jumped to Mom's mind next. *Mom, please don't move. Don't say anything. Daniel is in control of this.* She didn't flinch, but her insightful eyes darted right at me. I had a feeling I knew where all this would end up now that I had blown my cover and exposed my psychic ability.

The feral creature ambled within reach of Daniel. It seemed dazed and weary. Out of the blue, the silence was broken by a snow plow blasting down the roads. The coyote shook its head after hearing the noise and resumed an attack position. His head lowered and with one final growl, it sprang at Daniel.

The snapping of its neck resonated in our ears. I grimaced from the sound. The whole episode was terrifying and sad at the same time. Daniel had no choice. Heck, Dad would have shot the coyote if given the chance. After all, it had rabies and was about to kill my dog!

But, the blatant facts remained dangling before us...Daniel had just mesmerized this animal and then killed it with his bare hands. As he placed the dead creature on the snowy ground, another quite visible detail emerged; his hands were partially transformed werewolf claws. Oh boy. I couldn't cover that one up.

Daniel kept facing away from us, realizing my parents were absorbing the facts of what they had witnessed. As he crouched down, Nicky streaked over to him. Nicky showed no fear whatsoever towards Daniel; in fact, I sensed gratitude for saving his life. Daniel's arms reverted back to human. Purposely displaying affection for my parents to see, he scooped Nicky up into his powerful arms, rubbing him behind his ears. Daniel turned to face us. It was such a sweet sight. I think I about cried at that moment.

I sighed at Mom and Dad, "I guess I've got some explaining to do."

Daniel continued to hold Nicky, staying at a distance. At least he had walked several feet away from the carcass. He let me take the reins at that point. He didn't know what to say or do and wanted to avoid freaking out my parents any more than they were already.

Dad spoke, "Everyone back inside. It's too cold to discuss this out here."

We filed into the house with Daniel bringing up the rear, still carrying Nicky. I think Daniel holding Nicky made him appear less frightening and more human. It helped instill a notion that he couldn't be all bad…that he wasn't a monster. Telepathically I sent Daniel a thought, *Good move on your part playing the "gentle giant" with Nicky.* I made sure to send him feelings of confidence and peace to help lessen his growing anxiety.

Once we arranged ourselves around the kitchen table, I decided to jump in feet first and not drag out the punch line of my story. My mouth felt dry and my back started to ache. I quelled the panic attack that was building within my body. I needed to focus on getting the truth out in the open and deal with my parents' reaction whatever it might be.

I began, "Well…um…I'm telepathic, psychic. I can read minds and speak to people within their minds. I can manipulate thoughts and emotions. And Daniel's situation is a bit more complex. In case you haven't figured that one out, he's a werewolf."

Mom exclaimed, "I knew it! I knew something was up the whole time you've been gone, Kara! Every time our phone conversations ended, your father and I always felt like we were partially drugged or drunk. You were messing with our minds, weren't you?"

"Yeah, well, I suppose you could call it that. But if I hadn't, you would've called the cops and stirred up all kinds of trouble for us!" I countered. "Wait a second. Aren't you in shock with what I just told you? I just announced I'm psychic and even crazier - Daniel's a werewolf! You saw what he just did outside. You saw his arms partially transform!"

"Kara," Mom cleared her throat and explained, "you happen to descend from a long line of psychics on my side of the family; although, sometimes the ability skips a generation. Some of our relatives have had unbelievable powers and others perhaps only tiny blips of intuition. I don't have anywhere near the telepathic ability like you displayed. I *do* have a little of that sixth sense that helps once in a while. But it's not reliable. Otherwise, I should have gotten that feeling that Nicky was about to be attacked. It's very sporadic for me, especially if I'm involved or distracted working on other things.

"Ever since you were born, we wondered if you might wake up one day and discover you were different…that you were capable of doing things that the regular person couldn't do. Once you became an adult, I thought maybe the psychic gift had skipped you. After all, here you were 20 years old and nothing too weird had occurred that indicated telepathy. Also, since I, myself, had so little skills maybe the ability was fading out through the generations."

Dad piped in stating, "For your information, I do NOT have any supernatural or paranormal oddities. This is all on your mother's side. Anyway, we had our suspicions from the time you ran off. Obviously, Kara, you were controlling our thoughts and emotions to some degree which probably prevented us from total hysteria. But, everything about that situation pointed to the 'signs' we had been looking for. Also, the family trip you suggested we take to Kentucky Lake a month before you left seemed unusual. When you told us you were staying at that exact same resort with Daniel, we suspected something was up with him, too.

"I guess we just let this thing play itself out and didn't push the issue…you *were* influencing our thoughts. Plus, you're an adult now and we realized you had newly discovered skills to deal with. I remembered Daniel from his resort as being a decent guy and that calmed our nerves. He wasn't some deadbeat idiot. But, I have to say, Daniel, I am shocked that you are an actual *werewolf*. I wasn't expecting that one. It's been quite a few years since we've encountered one of your kind." Dad sat contemplating what to say next.

"WHAT?!" I screamed. "What are you talking about? You mean to tell me that you already knew about all this stuff? Aren't you freaked out that my boyfriend is a werewolf?"

I stood up from my seated position at the kitchen table, frantically gesturing with my arms while I started to pace the room. My mind was trying to comprehend the fact that this was good news. If my parents were aware that werewolves exist, then they should more readily accept Daniel. But would they accept him with open arms or with a wary eye? What else did they know? Great. Christmas was no longer going to be centered around the festive holidays as I had hoped. Instead, it was time for all the secrets to be exposed. Fresh knowledge to be absorbed for all parties involved.

I stared at my parents and began again, "Okay. I suppose I feel left out of the loop. You should have told me about my ancestors and prepared me for what could happen."

"But if the psychic ability had actually skipped you, then we would've had you all worked up for nothing." Mom clarified. "You would have become paranoid waiting and wondering if or when something odd was going to happen. And if we told you werewolves existed, you would have thought we had lost our minds or you'd be living your life always looking behind your back - on guard. Maybe, just maybe, during your lifetime nothing paranormal would have crossed your path. So, we were trying to shield you. What you didn't know, couldn't hurt you. Yes, yes…and I realize knowledge is power. So, you're damned if you do and you're damned if you don't."

Dad took on the protective parental role and stated, "Daniel the Werewolf. The Boyfriend. Hmm…This creates complications if my memory on werewolf lore serves me right. Kara, you're human. I'm assuming the two of you have had this discussion. This is very serious. Being around Daniel so much, you could accidentally get converted into a werewolf."

"I've heard this over and over. We know about the dangers and the precautions we must take," my answer was defensive. Dominic, for one, harped on me about this all the time.

Mom shrieked, "Your leg! It has a cut on it. Were you honest when you told us it was from a fall?"

She was good. "Yes. Daniel and I did fall down on the snow. He was carrying me piggyback and slid down into a trench. It was a deep ditch. I need to mention that Daniel was transformed at that time in the shape of the beast. I assume you know they can take three forms, right? Human, an in-between shape of a beast and the last form, of course, a wolf. Normally, only the older and highly skilled werewolves can master and maintain the beast form," I paused to take note if they knew this information.

"Your grandmother had spoken of that phenomenon. I'm curious to see that transformation! By the way, Daniel, how old are you?"

Mom was going for the details.

Daniel had been quietly sitting at the table holding Nicky. "I'm 26 human years old." He gulped. My parents slowly nodded, eyebrows knitted together.

Daniel continued, "Um...Add on to that number the years I've been a werewolf and that makes me 342 years old." He gulped again.

Mom and Dad sat very still. Their eyes blinked many times. Complete silence. If there were any crickets around, you would have heard them chirping.

To keep them from fainting, I carried on, "Getting back to your original question about my leg...when we fell down, Daniel was in beast form. When he takes that shape, his hands turn into claws as you witnessed outside. Since he was carrying me on his back, he grabbed at my legs during the fall. His claws are super sharp and ripped my jeans. My leg was cut. All I needed was a Band-Aid. No teeth involved. I haven't been converted. You can breathe now."

Mom seemed relieved with my answer then asked, "Daniel, where did you live when you were younger? Before you became a werewolf?"

"Salem, Massachusetts," Daniel answered politely.

Mom's mouth fell wide open. She whispered, "Oh my...That's where our ancestors came from. What time frame? What years?"

Daniel nervously glanced at me. I mentally said, *All this needs to come out in the open. Hang in there. Answer their questions. Calm down.*

"We left there in 1693," he answered.

"Why?" Mom grilled him.

"Well, I will try to summarize the incident. My brother and a friend and I had been hunting for this clan of witches. There was proof that their sorcery was pure evil and wicked. One night we stumbled upon their location. They were ready for us and in no way were they going to be hauled off to jail. So, they cast what is called the Lycaeonia Curse upon the three of us. It turned us into werewolves. In our ignorance, we accidentally converted several family members and friends. We tried to lay low, but the townspeople were starting to suspect my family and close friends of engaging in witchcraft not knowing our existence had been cursed to become werewolves. During that time in history, you were hanged if found guilty of witchcraft. That's what happened to my wife, Mary. They hung her. I left immediately after that along with the other werewolves. Eventually, over many years, we ended up in Kentucky."

Mom's eyes were brimming with tears. She spoke up, "You do know that not all witches practice black magic, right? There are many witches who dabble in spells or create charms that are quite useful and helpful."

"Oh, yes!" Daniel replied with assurance. "I agree with you. Just like with werewolves and vampires…you're aware of vampires?" Mom and Dad nodded yes. Daniel gratefully continued, "There are the good ones and there are the bad ones. I hope it registered with you that I am a GOOD werewolf!"

Mom smiled and Dad broadcasted, "If we thought you were bad, I'd have already shot you. And I do recall *where* to shoot to make it fatal."

Gee, that was blunt. Dad started snickering. I lightly touched at his mind to make sure he was teasing Daniel. I didn't want Daniel blindsided from a shot to his head or other major organ the moment he turned his back. I read Dad's thoughts and he was truly getting a kick out of razzing Daniel. It was a little mean, but I could deal with Dad's teasing.

I asked, "Mom, why are you concerned about the witches? I heard you say our ancestors were also from the same area as Daniel… which is definitely a coincidence."

"Yes, it is eerie. I think it must be fate that the two of you met. Not only have there been psychics throughout our lineage but many have also been witches," Mom declared.

Daniel straightened up in his chair. Mom had his full undivided attention. If he was in wolf form, his fur would have bristled. I prayed we were the good witches…not the evil ones. Not descendents from the black magic witches that put the curse on Daniel. He would despise us and probably want revenge for all that he, his family and friends had endured over the years.

I pursued, "Mom, please tell me we come from the good witches."

"Of course we do! What do you think I was getting at when I

mentioned the good spells that some witches whip up?! But, during the point in history when Daniel was cursed, our ancestors were alive and well and living in his village. I'm positive our relatives were NOT involved in black magic, though. From stories passed down over the centuries to researching old diaries to even the conversations that your great grandmother had with another werewolf (seriously) – all validate we come from good witches. We did not have dealings with any who practiced evil sorcery.

"I know it can be such a fine line when we're dealing with witchcraft. Most people hear that word - witchcraft - and automatically assume the evil version of it. What is considered 'bad' by one person may not be by another. Daniel, do you understand?" Mom pleaded her case with Daniel. The entire conversation about witches had created tension in the air and made Daniel edgy. Everyone noticed his apprehension.

Daniel relaxed in his chair and realized we were not the bad guys out to get him. He regained his composure and inquired, "Yes, I do understand. I believe you. Just for a moment I feared that your family had put this curse on me. I'm so thankful we're all on the same side. By the way, had you heard about the resurgence of a clan out east, around the Salem area? We've been told they are heavy into black magic. And we have trustworthy evidence that they *are* direct descendants from the witches who put the werewolf curse on me."

Mom looked worried and answered, "No, I'm sorry, but I don't keep up to date with news out east. Ever since my mother, Kara's grandmother, died last year we rarely hear from anyone. And when we do, the topic usually doesn't cover paranormal happenings. My mom lived in Lawrence, Massachusetts. We moved here when Kara was a baby because Adam had a job transfer. Most of the family, which isn't very large, is spread out across the United States. My mom had lived in and around that region her whole life and steadfastly chose to remain there. Everything that I know about psychics, witches, werewolves, vampires all came directly from her. She kept me clued-in on the subject up until the time she died. At the time, nothing seemed unusual about her death. But you've got me wondering now…"

I decided it was time to take a break. The morning was rapidly disappearing and everyone still needed to get cleaned up for the day. After an hour or so, we converged back in the kitchen. I asked Dad if he could drive us out to where my car was stranded.

Dad asked, "Sure! Where did you park the car?"

"El Kay Meadows subdivision," I replied, knowing full well his reaction.

"You walked all the way from there in a snow storm?!" He was astounded.

Daniel beamed, "Actually, if you recall, I did the walking. Kara got a piggyback ride. The cold weather doesn't bother me much, especially in full beast form. A benefit of being a werewolf, I suppose."

I rolled my eyes and sighed, "Come on, let's go!"

"Wait! Before the three of you leave...Daniel, I've got a special favor to ask of you," My mom was acting like a kid in a candy store. She exclaimed, "My curiosity has gotten the best of me. Can you turn yourself into the beast and the wolf for us?" She gestured to herself and Dad.

Daniel's distressed face suddenly broke into a mischievous grin. "Let me grab a blanket off the couch. Stay here. I'll be back."

He walked into the living room while Mom, Dad and I waited in the kitchen. I silently prayed that he wouldn't knock over a lamp or destroy something during his shape shifting episodes. My mental link with Daniel informed me that he had stripped down and was wrapping the blanket around his mid-section. He transformed into the beast and made his grand entrance. The fuzzy, warm blanket was a comical contrast to his horrifying, monstrous appearance.

Daniel held up one of his razor sharp fingers and attempted to say, "One moment, please."

I had to translate the garbled words to my parents. He started laughing while in his beast form and the sound was a mixture of a howl and yawn with a dash of gurgling. It was Christmas Day...I suppose a little fun was in order.

In a flash, he shifted into the enormous black wolf right in front of their eyes. What a show off! Daniel was the center of attention and soaked it in. My parents, especially Mom, were tickled pink watching his transformations. Nicky barked his head off and ran circles around

Daniel nudging him with his nose. Daniel grabbed the blanket off the floor with his wolf's jaws and shook it hard as canines liked to do. Nicky chased the blanket and followed him back to the living room where Daniel shifted to human form and dressed.

As I stood reveling in the unique relationships that bound us together, a distinctive tap-tap popped in my mind. Dominic mentally relayed he would arrive the following morning and drive directly to the Liaison's underground facility. Daniel and I would meet him there. I was looking forward to reuniting with my best friend, even though it had only been a few weeks since I'd last seen him.

Daniel rejoined us in the kitchen and my parents couldn't stop gawking at him. To observe up close some of his transformations amazed, shocked and thrilled them. He commented that he should bury the coyote. It wouldn't take him long or be any trouble with his super speed and strength. Dad agreed that something needed to be done with the animal and told Daniel to help himself to a shovel in the garage. He was out the door without another word.

By the time I had put my boots and coat on, Daniel had already returned, boasting, "Done."

The roads were cleared of snow and it was time we retrieved my car. It was parked where we left it and unharmed. When we returned, Daniel and I took turns skimming through the previous month's adventures. The afternoon dissolved into evening. Christmas Day ended on a good note. Secrets had been revealed. And for the most part, we chose discussions over remaining freaked out. We sifted through the facts, pondering what to do next. I was relieved that my parents and Daniel managed to co-exist without strangling each other. Mom and Dad developed a sincere respect for Daniel and his past. They couldn't deny their concerns about our future, though. I squirmed away from the subject as much as possible.

I didn't sleep well that night. I couldn't remember the dreams, but I sensed they were not pleasant. My instincts were warning me that trouble was approaching.

Chapter 3
Reconnect

Dominic landed at Lambert Airport in St. Louis early in the morning. We needed to give him time to drive to the Liaison's underground facility. Base camp. Command center. A defunct military base. The description varied depending on who was referring to it.

I didn't have a key to get inside or Dom's telekinetic ability that could unlock the door. Mid morning Dom called the house using an actual phone instead of his mind.

"Hi, Kara! What's up? I made it." Dom's voice garbled in my ear.

"Amazing. You still remember how to use a phone. The connection is scratchy. We'll head over there now," I nodded to Daniel to grab the car keys.

Dominic explained, "I wanted to check the quality of the phone lines to see if they even worked. Someone needs to do maintenance around here. Not fun. Anyway, the door will be unlocked when you get here. See ya'."

My parents knew what our plans were for the day. We'd be back for supper and I asked if Dom could eat with us, too. I didn't want him to make a meal and have to eat alone. Although he loved cooking, I doubted he had time to go grocery shopping before arriving at the command center. Dom was originally from Arizona, but definitely took up residency here. He considered it job relocation. The other members of The Liaison were scattered around visiting family for the holidays. Eli was in St. Louis and Zac and Tessa were out east.

The main entrance to the facility is located several miles in the opposite direction of Silver Lake's hidden entry. Eli had the money and power to purchase the old military base. Several tunnels traveled out from the main command center for miles stopping at dismantled missile silos. Eli, Dominic and Zac did renovations to suit their immediate needs. And interior decorating wasn't at the top of the list.

Daniel and I planned on staying another day or two with my parents. I'm positive Dominic would have visited longer with his family out in Arizona if we hadn't made the trip up to Marine. He wanted to see me again. And he only had a few days to reconnect before I left - before Daniel and I left, that is. With or without my psychic gift I knew his intentions and his concern about me and my safety.

The main roads had been cleared of snow. One small part of our jaunt was on a country road that had snow-packed surfaces. I pointed to Dominic's tire tracks that turned down a private lane into a wooded area. Daniel followed the path until we saw Dom's car parked.

Daniel ventured to say, "Well, so far, I like these woods. This fits my style."

"Uh, huh," I stated, "Wait till you get inside. I hope you're not claustrophobic."

The creaky steel door was unlocked as Dom promised. Down the steps into the dungeon and at the bottom was door number two. Upon swinging it open, there stood Dom smiling from ear to ear. An attempt was made by Dom to elbow Daniel out of the way to get to me. Daniel merely shook his head and moved to the side. Dom bear-hugged me until I couldn't breathe.

"Good to see you, too," Daniel teased.

Dom realized his total disregard of Daniel. He turned, extended his hand to shake and coolly remarked, "Hey, how's it going? I imagine you'd like a tour of this place. Follow me."

After the complete tour, which took a whole two minutes, I told Dom he was invited to my parents' house for supper. Daniel and I would spend the day with him at base camp. He seemed pleased.

With a sly look on his face, Dom asked, "Daniel, how good are you with fixing stuff?"

The next thing I knew, Dom promoted Daniel to be "Mr. Fix It Guy". He sent Daniel on patrol to the opposite end of the command center (where we had entered) to check on the intercom system. Dom and I stayed in the kitchen, which was the last room on the tour, to test our end of the intercom. It was obvious two people were needed for this chore. Each one had a few tools to tinker with the electronics in their designated work spots.

"-an y-- hea- me?" Daniel's voice crackled. The reception was unacceptable.

Dom and Daniel took turns speaking a few times. Both ends of the transmission were a mess so they agreed to attempt making a few adjustments. I had a feeling Dominic was up to something other than just routine maintenance. And then it came...

"Kara? Are you set on staying with Daniel? You've been with him for several weeks now and seen his lifestyle. I hope your common sense kicked in and you realize what challenges you're up against," poor Dom pleaded with me. "I so wish you'd stay with your parents. We could run the command center under Eli's authority and go on more covert missions together!"

You had to give him credit. Dom doesn't accept failure with grace. No matter how many times I explained my feelings for him (best friend) and for Daniel (boyfriend), he kept hoping that my heart would flip in his direction and I'd choose him. He'd be waiting for me with open arms. He stopped tinkering with the intercom and gazed into my eyes. I could feel waves of emotion flowing out of Dom and surrounding me with love. With his free hand he tucked some stray hairs around my ear.

I turned away, looked down at the floor and sighed. I was prepared to give my response. My reaction alone indicated the answer would not be what Dom wanted to hear. He leaned against the wall, tilted his head back and closed his eyes. He tried to keep tears from slipping out. At times like those, I had to admit, Dominic tempted me to rethink my future. I almost felt as if he could sway me in his direction...perhaps I had deeper feelings for Dom than just being my best bud. I loved Daniel, though, and didn't question those feelings one iota. But, the undying commitment, openness and endearing nature of Dom tugged at my heart. Very complicated situation.

My peripheral vision noticed Dom pull away from the wall as if something caught his attention. Oh no...It dawned on me that I had not blocked him from reading my thoughts! And that is exactly what just happened. Not good. He knew everything I had been pondering in my confused little head! I threw up the mental block in full force at that moment, but the damage was done. A glimmer of hope crept onto his face. He felt there was a chance, a possibility that he could win me over now.

We looked at each other. I chewed my lower lip. Dom went to reach for me again when Daniel's voice startled us as it bellowed through the intercom - loud and clear.

"Hey! How's it sound now?" Daniel asked.

I pressed the button and responded, "It's clear. No more crackling. How do I come through?"

"Better than before, but not perfect."

After he replied, a sudden dizzy spell overcame me and I fell forward into Dominic's arms. My brain felt a rather sharp jab that knocked my balance off. I slid down to the floor with Dom's help. In the span of a few seconds, Daniel was kneeling over me. Our mental connection was so strong that during my immediate distress he realized something strange had happened and with super werewolf speed came to my aid.

Daniel lifted my chin and questioned, "What was *that*? Are you okay?"

He glared at Dom, ready to throw the blame onto him. Dominic blasted, "I didn't do anything! Kara finished speaking on the intercom to you and then zoned out."

I slurred, "Josiah. It's Josiah."

Josiah was Daniel's long time ally. And a vampire. I met him a few weeks back at Daniel's resort. Not many werewolves and vampires could stand to be around each other. Their relationship was unique. They shared similar views on life and had fought together against evil beings in the past.

My head cleared and I regained control of my speech. "Wow! Josiah really packed a punch with his telepathy. We'll need to practice more so he doesn't blow my brain out of my skull."

Daniel was ticked off at Josiah for taking such a risk with my human well-being. He stated, "He won't live long enough for that after I get done with him. That was too dangerous. He should know better by now to monitor his strength when communicating with a human…with you."

"Take a chill pill," I stood up and walked to a chair. "I'm fine now." Josiah fizzled out of my head when he realized I had about passed out. "Dom, Josiah is the vampire I was referring to when we talked the other week, just shortly after hearing the news of the witches. I need to settle down and link back up with him at my own pace. I sensed his news won't be cheery."

I relaxed as best as I could on the hard chair. Daniel and Dom each grabbed a chair, too. Between the three of us, we had varying degrees of psychic ability. Daniel's telepathic skills were quite limited but Dom and I possessed several types of psychic talent. I would be the catalyst to mentally hook up with Josiah. Daniel and Dom would "listen in" through me by holding my hands. We had performed this act of communicating before with success.

I concentrated on Josiah, mentally calling his name, forming a connection. He had patiently waited for me to re-establish contact. This time he entered my mind with the utmost caution, testing the waters as he did so, making certain he wasn't causing any harm. I made him aware that Daniel and Dom were listening to the conversation and he appeared impressed with the linking that we created. I gained a tremendous amount of Josiah's respect and approval…being that I was a mere human.

Kara, I am sorry for shocking your system a few moments ago. I was hasty in my need to talk to you and regret the abrupt, forceful method I used. Daniel is correct in stating I should have known better. By the way, well done on the telepathic bonding! Josiah stated in that Old World style of his. He sounded so professional and proper, although he tried not to be too obvious about it. It tended to draw unwanted attention to him when in public.

I responded, *So, you're able to read Daniel's thoughts, too? We haven't practiced this multiple linking up with you before, but we have with others in our group.*

Daniel focused on his thoughts with all his energy and chewed Josiah's butt for almost hurting me. I cut him short, and reminded everyone how draining a multiple linking conversation could become. Although I did not get the impression Josiah would be tired out at all. His power was immense and telepathy was a vampire specialty.

It was time to get to the point of this whole affair.

Josiah began, *I'm in Winchester, Massachusetts. That's not far from Boston. And Daniel's original hometown, the ever-famous Salem, isn't too far away, either. I chose to dig deeper into this witch problem before it exploded out of control. It's worse than I imagined. Some of the witches <u>are</u> descendants of the evil-doers that cursed you, Daniel. They are filled with greed and hunger for power. They are preparing a resurrection of sorts.*

What or who is being resurrected? I dared to ask.

Josiah sighed (even that could be recognized through our mental link). He continued, *A demon, I think. They are using black magic. A few in the coven have developed their witchcraft to levels rarely seen or heard of since ancient times. Some are psychic and sensed my presence in the area. A spell was cast preventing me from reading their minds. Even with my power, I hesitate to attack them alone. This demon resurrection will occur soon...but I gathered we have a little time yet.*

Dom remained quiet during the majority of this little session. He made a suggestion. *I need to call Eli. This whole Liaison idea was his baby and he should know what's going on. He may not go out in the field like we do, but we can't keep him in the dark. He <u>does</u> fund this operation, supplies us with almost anything we need and financially supports Kara, Zac, Tessa and me. And he has a ton of knowledge and contacts. What does everyone think?*

All agreed Eli needed to be brought into the loop. Even Josiah who did not know Eli personally, but had heard about him, felt it was the right thing to do. He understood our commitment to and trusted our judgment of Eli. We dissolved the mental link to allow Dom to call Eli and would re-connect as soon as possible. Josiah was standing by on alert for my psychic call. His strength in helping uphold these mind melds eased the strain we would normally have experienced. Two people reading each other's minds wasn't that taxing, but when more entered the connection, it sapped your energy level. Dom and I acknowledged this revelation of Josiah's power as he reached for the phone.

Daniel and I sat listening to Dominic recount the events to Eli on the speaker phone. Eli had a few questions then decided it was time to take action. We had officially been assigned a new mission. He offered to call Zac and Tessa and ask if they could drive over to Winchester, Massachusetts, where Josiah was. The city was about four hours from where they had gone for the holidays. Another coincidence, but a lucky break, too. Eli wanted them to meet up with Josiah at a location of Josiah's choice and to do surveillance as a team. I was concerned about how Zac and Tessa would react to working with a vampire. Eli promised he would diplomatically explain that Josiah is a good vampire, like Daniel is a good werewolf. And they were able to work with Daniel just fine with no complaints.

Eli confirmed what we suspected. No more covert field missions for him as he was getting too old and too slow. He was 60 something years old and looked great for his age. The problem was much of what we dealt with seemed to require a great deal of physical output. He didn't want to keel over from exhaustion at a critical time that might endanger the rest of The Liaison.

Daniel wondered if Eli had any plans on where he might stay next. His living quarters tended to vary from the command center to his real house located in the area. If it was not necessary for Eli to stay here, Daniel asked if he would consider hanging out at his resort and work part time to keep it open. We could not run the resort if we were gone on a covert operation out east. Daniel planned on inviting his brother, Isaac, along on this trip for additional muscle. That meant another werewolf from his pack would be absent and not able to help with the daily operations at the resort. We did have one advantage. It was the dead of winter. Very few people rented any cabins during this time of the year.

Eli got a little choked up with the invitation to stay at Daniel's resort. The werewolves respected and welcomed him into their lives. Not many humans were allowed to know about the existence of their species (or others). Eli cared about the wolves' welfare and they never doubted his loyalty. He was a doctor, scientist and wonderful mediator in resolving problems.

Eli accepted and thanked Daniel for the offer. Another issue Eli would address while at the resort: one of the werewolves, Rachel, was pregnant. Female werewolves had terrible difficulty getting pregnant. No offspring had been born within the pack in many years. Now that there was an actual pregnancy, being a physician, he wanted to keep an eye on her progress. He had theories on this subject that needed more research. Hopefully he'd stumble upon the explanation one day.

Time to get back to Josiah. The phone call to Eli rambled on too long. At least it was a decent connection. The earlier labors on the communication system, by Daniel and Dom, managed to work out the kinks. We ended the call with a promise to stay in touch.

The three of us sat in our chairs and duplicated the previous telepathic scenario of holding hands and letting me call out to Josiah. Once again, he was cautious with mentally linking up with me. I asked him if he could just read my mind and pluck out that particular phone call with Eli. Wouldn't that be faster than "telling" him everything word for word?

Josiah replied, *I am capable of sifting through memories. The physical distance does make this feat a bit more difficult; whereas before it was just like talking to each other; interacting back and forth - using words as if we were truly speaking with our mouths. If you permit me to do this, we must focus only on that conversation with Eli. Daniel and Dom should do the same so there are no distractions. I won't have to hunt for the memory if it's being thrown at me. I'll instantly absorb the incident.*

Do it, I told Josiah. Daniel's hand jerked my hand. He was uneasy with my memories being accessed. Even Dom tightened his grip on the other hand. This intrusion into my mind was not being taken lightly. Josiah was not simply reading current thoughts in my head, but had the capability to reach deep into all my memories and grasp anything he chose to.

I reassured Daniel and Dom by squeezing their hands and stated, *Focus on the conversation with Eli.*

Josiah's voice dropped an octave. His tone was mesmerizing, slow and determined. *Daniel, Dominic - don't fight me. She gave her permission.* Josiah felt their resistance.

*Kara...let me in...*Josiah's whisper felt soothing in my head. *Let the walls come tumbling down...we are remembering the phone call with Eli...Relax and have faith in me...Ahh - I've got it!*

I smiled. Well, that was painless and fast. The guys visibly relaxed. Josiah was aware of the new plans. He did suggest that Zac and Tessa meet him in a neutral location. Let *them* choose it. He didn't want them to feel threatened by him (he IS a vampire!) during this initial meeting. It was unquestionably important to establish trust if they were to watch each other's backs. He anticipated our arrival in a few days and gave us the address of a rental house he had nabbed up in Winchester. We should drive directly to his house and set up base camp there.

We decided to end the psychic chit chat with Josiah. If anything critical happened on either end, we'd make contact.

The day had disappeared. It was the middle of the afternoon and we were starving. The kitchen was no longer stocked with perishable foods. A few leftover bags of snacks sat on a shelf and we devoured them. It didn't matter if Mom was preparing a meal for us in a few hours. We had to finish off those snacks right then and there. Daniel and Dom wrestled over the chocolate chip cookies. Of course, Daniel won the scuffle. I tossed Dom a sweet and salty almond breakfast bar. We hit the jackpot - there was a full box! I loved those things.

Daniel called his brother, Isaac, and filled him in on all the latest chaos. He told Isaac we could use his muscle and the benefit of having a bigger team. Isaac didn't hesitate a second to jump at the chance to come along. He was bored to death during the winter months. The werewolves generally did not travel. Anywhere. They feared detection and kept secluded to the little Hamlin area. To take the risk and venture out into society was a thrill ride Isaac wasn't about to pass up.

Daniel, Dom and I planned to leave the next morning. We were cutting our holiday visit short by one day. Mom and Dad would understand - hopefully. We'd swing down to Hamlin, pick up Isaac, re-pack for the trip and drive non-stop to Winchester, Massachusetts.

Dom followed us back to my parents' house and the normal introductions were made. During supper, I explained to Mom and Dad the day's events and our plans to leave the next morning. They frowned and looked worried. I was 21 years old and they could no longer tell me what I could or couldn't do. This was the path in my life I chose to walk down. I felt needed, useful and that I was serving a greater purpose with my newfound psychic skills. I had encouragement and support from The Liaison and the werewolves; I embraced my abilities with enthusiasm. I was terrified at times, but I couldn't turn away from my new discoveries.

Mom let out a long sigh, glanced at Dad and said, "If you are diving into the lifestyles of the 'unknown', then it's time I give you something that belonged to your grandmother. Maybe it can help you. I'm not able to use it and there's no point in it sitting around gathering dust."

She walked over to an old, cracked cookie jar and reached inside. What could Mom have inherited from Grandma that could help me? Let's not forget, she *was* a psychic witch. I sure hoped it wasn't some sacred dead animal part I'd have to stuff into my back pocket. My heart pounded with anticipation.

Chapter 4
Gift

The large stone sparkled from the overhead kitchen lights. It was as long as my little finger. A medium length silver chain looped through one end of the crystal. As I studied the unusual antique necklace sitting in my palm, a soothing sensation washed through my body. My eyes widened in astonishment and my jaw dropped.

Mom nodded in approval, "You can feel it, can't you?"

Bewildered, I asked, "What is it? I feel...energy."

Daniel and Dominic teetered on the edges of their chairs. Dad relaxed knowing there was no danger. With a timid hand, Dom reached out to touch my arm, but first paused to confirm with me that it was okay to do so.

I smiled with encouragement and threw into his mind, *Oh my God! Dom, can you feel this, too?*

He placed his hand on my arm and focused on any power the necklace emitted then bobbed his head up and down. Not to feel left out, Daniel grasped the opposite hand to check if he felt anything. He tilted his head to one side and closed his left eye.

Daniel really concentrated and mumbled, "Kara, I can feel a tiny difference. Like an electrical charge...a healthy boost of power. The animal - werewolf - part of me is able to sense that in you. Dom's psychic strength is much stronger than mine and more sensitive to this phenomenon."

Mom proceeded to explain. "What you're looking at is a natural quartz crystal. It amplifies energy and increases your psychic awareness, which includes telepathic traveling. The stone has healing abilities and eliminates negative vibes. In case you're wondering, there is nothing special about the chain. But the quartz has a tremendous mystical value to a witch or a psychic who is able to harness its abilities. I wouldn't be flashing it around. When you get a chance, experiment with it...but keep it tucked away."

"Thanks, Mom," I said while rubbing my fingers over the stone. "I think this could be helpful in many ways."

We lounged in the living room for the remainder of the evening. My parents did not normally entertain visitors in their home. For the most part, they were hermits and didn't have a long list of close friends. They deserved a blue ribbon for their involvement in this escapade and for not losing their cool.

My dog, Nicky - well, their dog now - was enjoying all the extra attention as he ran from person to person. At one point, Nicky was darting around Dad's legs as he walked into the kitchen. Dad returned carrying five glasses filled to the brim with iced tea.

Well, Dad's hospitable attempt to serve us was duly noted. Nicky was just in the wrong place at the wrong time. Or maybe Dad was... either way, Dad tripped over Nicky and the tea-filled glasses started flying through the air. Luckily, we had been observing the precarious situation unfold as Dad emerged from the kitchen. Dominic was trigger-ready with his telekinetic skills. He contained the disaster within an invisible force field. Inside that magic bubble, he righted the glasses and guided the ice and tea back into each glass. Slowly, he lowered the drinks onto the end table, thus averting a sticky mess. And Daniel, with his werewolf reflexes, played his part by catching Dad before he crashed onto the floor. Quite the show! My two heroes saved the day! Nicky appeared to agree as he continued to bound about, barking his little head off, and continuing to get under foot.

Another hour passed while we talked about the impressive skills of our team. My parents reminded us to keep aware of our surroundings. Stay alert. They insisted on extra details concerning the east coast trip and we filled them in.

It was time for bed. I needed to calm their nerves before they drove us bonkers. I felt a little guilty doing it, but I dove into Mom and Dad's minds. I implanted reassuring, confident thoughts. Daniel and Dom snickered, knowing full well what I had done.

Dom headed back to the command center to spend the night. The rest of the household staggered off to bed, hoping to get a good night's sleep.

* * * *

In the early morning, Daniel and I met Dominic at the Liaison's underground facility. We made a thorough sweep of the rooms, preparing for departure. We decided to travel together in my car, leaving Dom's car on the premises. Once we were back at the resort, we'd switch vehicles and take Daniel's extended cab truck to Winchester, Massachusetts.

A few hours into the drive, I withdrew the quartz necklace from inside my shirt. I wore it proudly around my neck but kept it concealed as Mom suggested. I placed my hand over it resting on my upper chest. My thoughts drifted…

"I wonder how the quartz would react if I became a werewolf?" I pondered out loud. I didn't necessarily expect anyone to give me an answer. Well, this being a sore subject with Dom, he came unglued. He wasn't about to let this slide without commenting.

Dom's words burst from his mouth like a volcano exploding. "How 'bout you try NOT to find out! So, in the midst of everything we're dealing with, you wanna go play experimental lab rat and turn into a different species?! Gee, let's have the still-developing psychic turn into a newborn crazed werewolf running around wielding an unfamiliar mystical stone! Oh, yeah, that's a real good idea. Mm-hmm."

In turn, Daniel reacted to that statement, which didn't surprise me. Dom's comments were harsh. Since Daniel was driving at the time, he swerved the car over onto the shoulder of the road and slammed on the brakes. I was sitting in the passenger seat; Dom sat on the backseat. Daniel jumped out and jerked the seat forward. He reached inside, grabbed Dom by his arm and pulled him out of the car. Dom stumbled, landing on his hands and knees on the road. Daniel roughly lifted him to his feet and brought him to my side of the car. At least any oncoming traffic couldn't hit them now.

I flew out of my seat and watched in fear as I noticed Daniel's rage growing with each passing second. He shoved Dom backwards several feet. Somehow Dom managed to stay on his feet without falling in the ditch.

Daniel roared at Dom, "Kara is quite capable of making her own choices. Don't bully her into what *you* want her to do or wish her to be."

Daniel could hurt or kill Dom without breaking a sweat. Dom took it for granted that Daniel would never go that far. They were friends, right? But...I happened to be the center of the debate. That made things tricky.

"You really think changing her into a werewolf is the right thing to do? You're willing to take a chance that she'll survive the transition and new lifestyle totally unscathed? And her family and friends...I guess she'll just stand by, watch them age and die while she stays looking the same forever," Dom yelled.

Daniel fired back, "I'm not forcing her or bribing her in any way. But if she turns to me and with complete conviction asks me to convert her into a werewolf, I will. Isn't it possible this is meant to be? She's the one that came to me first and made the connection. And you hounding her about this has gotten very old. I've told you before - back off!"

He took a few steps in Dom's direction and rammed into a shield Dom threw up to protect himself. Daniel pounded his fists on an invisible wall. Neither one was ready to give up the fight. Dom took advantage of the situation. He spotted a fallen tree branch and using his mind whipped it at Daniel's backside. Daniel stood right in front of the shield and the force of the branch pushed him against it. Besides looking surprised, no damage done.

Daniel bristled, "So, you want to play unfair, huh? My turn."

I noticed Daniel's hands slowly transform into claws. We were out in the open and it was daylight. Someone might drive by and witness Daniel if he went through the full transformation. This had to stop before it attracted attention and (most likely) Dom getting injured.

"Daniel, please calm down," I begged and seeped into his thoughts, attempting to flood him with calm, loving feelings. "You can't cause a scene out here."

"He's really gotten under my skin this time, Kara. The criticism, sarcasm and basically cutting down what I am..." Daniel didn't move and continued to stare at Dom. At least the transformation paused with only his claws exposed.

Dom stared back, holding his ground. He stressed, "Don't hurt her. Let her go."

Daniel snarled, "I'll always protect Kara; I have no intentions of ever harming her, you idiot! And I'm not keeping her chained to my leg. I can't mesmerize and use mind control on her like a vampire or cast a love spell like a witch could. She *chooses* to stay with me."

After that statement, Daniel swiped at the invisible shield and this time his claw sliced through it. Both sets of eyes blinked wide. Dom obviously let his guard down, feeling defeated by Daniel's words. I squirmed in between the two before any further brawling ensued. Daniel's claws returned to human hands again. He darn well wasn't about to carelessly slash me with his sharp as razor nails. Dom would throw that right back into his face as proof Daniel could definitely hurt me.

"Enough!" I pushed at both of their chests; Dom's shield had dissolved. I separated them further apart. "Quit fighting over me and about me! You guys must be able to get along with each other if we're diving into a new mission. Remember the witches' agenda? Resurrecting a demon?" I huffed. "Unbelievable. Everyone back in the car!"

Daniel and Dom glared at each other but actually started to follow me back to the car. Huh. And thank God. Could that quartz around my neck have dispelled some of their negative energy? I *had placed* my hands on both their chests and felt a rush of emotion to get them to chill out. They didn't want me to be mad at them. They knew how important it was to me that they remain friends.

With a teasing (albeit risky) push to Daniel's shoulder, Dom sighed, "Sorry, man. I should've known better. I needed to vent and I worry. A lot. You still got my back?"

Daniel put Dom in a playful headlock stating, "Sure thing. After all, I know you've got *my* back - the tree branch?! Good one. You realize I would've kicked your butt back there, though."

What was it with men? One minute they're ready to beat each other to bloody pulps and the next minute they act like nothing happened or that the incident was no big deal. I tended to have a bad habit of holding a grudge…forever.

We had another few hours to travel until we hit Hamlin. Daniel took over the driving again. I loved that car but preferred not to be the driver. I could never handle a job as a delivery person. The conversation centered on witches and reviewing travel details. Time flew by.

Approximately thirty miles from the resort, I felt a strange sensation ripple through me. No one was trying to use telepathy to contact me. I was sure of that. It wasn't painful or a sick feeling, either. It felt like I crossed a line drawn in the sand entering new territory. A light pulse of power feathered over my body. I told Daniel and Dom about the experience.

Daniel grinned and replied, "Let's try it again." He turned around in a driveway, backtracked about a mile, whipped a quick U-turn in the middle of the road and drove the route for the second time.

"There! I felt it again!" I blurted. "Dom, did you sense anything?"

Dom suspected foul play was in the works. Daniel kept glancing at him with a smug look, watching for a reaction.

"I'm not sure," Dom evaluated the moment. "Something seemed off at that spot. The feeling is gone now. I would never have noticed anything if you didn't call attention to it, which made me focus on any paranormal activity."

Dom and I looked to Daniel for an explanation. In silence, we kept staring at him. Waiting.

"Okay, okay…" Daniel loved suspense. "We crossed an area where a boundary spell was cast. Kara, I'm assuming that quartz necklace you're wearing gave off a warning. Remember what your mom said? It amplifies energy and can cleanse away negative energies. And your psychic awareness increases, giving you more insight into your surroundings."

I asked, "Why is there a boundary spell here?"

Daniel cleared his throat. "Since we, the werewolves, chose to live here permanently, we knew after several years the public would start getting suspicious when we never aged. Imagine if I had a neighbor that looked the same age as me, then fast forward thirty years and I haven't changed a bit while he's gotten bald and wrinkled.

That would get the locals talking. And all we wanted to do was blend in, not send up flares in our direction."

"So this spell blurs the fact you don't age," Dominic completed the explanation.

"Precisely put, Dom," Daniel stated. "The boundary spell affects everyone entering this area. It is harmless; it only makes people forget the oddity of us not aging."

"Wait. I'm confused. How come the spell doesn't work on Kara and me?" Dom had a great point.

"Because you already know I'm a werewolf. You are aware of and understand what we are. You, Kara, The Liaison aren't sitting around speculating what is making us appear unusual or why we haven't aged. You *know*. The townspeople *don't know* we're werewolves. The spell keeps their minds off the fact we don't age, which in turn, keeps them from suspecting we aren't human and takes the spotlight off of us. So, if someone discovered I'm a werewolf, the spell is broken on that person. See?"

I pressed on, "Did witches cast the spell?"

Daniel definitely had a spotlight on him right now. He fielded questions left and right from Dom and me.

He responded, "No, not exactly. There's a little story to tell. Almost 180 years ago, Josiah and I met for the first time. Perhaps "met" is too nice of a word. We crossed paths in the woods around Hamlin. As we faced each other, I knew he was a vampire and he knew I was a werewolf. Normally the two species are enemies. We went into full attack mode and both of us sprung into action. I hate admitting this, but he put me in my place and held me down to the ground. Thankfully, he sensed I wasn't evil or looking for a fight. He scanned my mind. I was only defending myself. Our meeting was an unlikely event, but we agreed it was pure coincidence.

"Anyway, he was following the trail of a rogue vampire. Even in those days, Josiah was one of the good guys. He wasn't alone, though. Two other vampires, Mizar and Serena, were searching the area. The three companions traveled around the country and hunted and killed anything evil. I introduced them to my pack...a delicate, balancing act to say the least. As I mentioned before, vampires and werewolves generally do not socialize with one another.

"To jump to the punch line, both species agreed to a truce - to work on the same side. Everyone wanted this rogue vampire destroyed, so we tracked the sadistic creature before he could do anymore harm in the villages. And yes, he killed many people but didn't turn any of them. So we killed him. The End," Daniel paused with a firm nod of his head.

I looked at him sideways and said, "I bet there's more to that story."

Daniel admitted, "There always is. We'll have to get together with Josiah so he can add his flavorful side of the story. Back to your question...since we, the werewolves, assisted with that kill (although the vampires were so powerful they didn't need our help) the vampires inquired if there was anything they could do for us. This was their way of thanking us since they had invaded *our* territory and we didn't fight them. Their offer to aid us in some way or another strengthened the truce. We talked about several problems we dealt with as werewolves. One issue was living in the same place for many years and humans noticing we never aged. I joked with Josiah that if they could help us blend in, take away people's suspicions, it would be a wish come true. I remember laughing after that statement, not at all serious.

"But the vampires were *not* laughing. Serena flat out stated she could grant my wish. Before she had been turned into a vampire, she was a powerful witch. Not bad or wicked, but she knew her witchcraft. After her conversion into a vampire, her talent with creating and controlling spells became superior. Serena cast the boundary spell in this area. We owe her a great deal of gratitude," Daniel ended with a smile.

"Wow." That was all I could mutter.

Dominic spit out a few words in his awe, "Are they still alive?"

"Serena and Mizar? I don't know," Daniel shrugged. "I assume they've survived the years. Josiah would know...I should ask him. After that first confrontation with me about 180 years ago, he visited a few times to stay in touch. I'm glad he showed up again. We'll need his ancient skills and power to fight those east coast witches."

Another few miles to go until we arrived at Daniel's resort. Enough time to squeeze in one more question.

I asked, "Did werewolves or vampires have anything to do with the naming of Blood River?" This river was an inlet of Kentucky Lake. The resort was situated on the lake side, but Blood River bordered the opposite side of the little peninsula.

"My pack wasn't living here yet," Daniel tried to be brief. "Back in the late 1700's, Indians inhabited this part of the country. White people were attempting to take over their land and the Indians fought back. Many people were killed. Eventually, more whites moved this direction, destroying the Indians or driving them out. The name Kentucky is from an Indian word signifying the river of blood. All the slaughter would equate to a "river of blood", if you think about it. I'd have to confirm with Josiah, but I recall a story about a few vampires initially fighting on the side of the Indians. The vampires would have created a bloody mess, too, possibly adding credibility to the naming of the river. At a certain point, they must've realized there were too many whites to fight and moved on. And so, I believe that's the history on the name Blood River."

I swear that trip to the resort was like another history lesson. I never was a big history buff, but when it pertained to the paranormal and my life, I soaked up the knowledge like a sponge.

We arrived at Daniel's resort and unloaded my car. The rest of the afternoon and that evening we prepared for the mission to Massachusetts. Daniel had a meeting with all the werewolves to explain our intentions and what should be done in his absence. Besides the weapons and gadgets brought from the command center, Daniel included his own array of protection. We planned to leave first thing in the morning and pick up Isaac who'd be waiting at his own resort.

During the overnight hours, I was jerked out of a restless dream, drenched in sweat. I sat on the edge of the bed fanning myself. The clock displayed 3:36 a.m. Daniel reached out, "Baby, what's wrong?"

I didn't get a chance to answer him. The phone started ringing.

CHAPTER 5
LOSS

A phone call around 3:30 in the morning is never a good thing. I let it ring twice and snatched it off the night stand.

"H-hello?" My voice faltered.

"Kara? It's Zac..." he struggled for air. He was sobbing. "Tessa... she...she's *dead!* They killed her!"

Daniel's acute hearing caught Zac's words. He was on his feet staring at me within half a second. I stood up, almost dropping the phone because my hand shook so violently.

I cried, "WHAT?! No, no, NO! What do you mean? Oh my God, Zac, what happened?"

"The witches did it. I couldn't do anything to save her. Just get here soon..." Zac cried out and hung up. That was it.

My trembling fingers fumbled with the keypad attempting to call him back. My heart was thumping way too fast and loud in the deafening quiet of the bedroom. I could hear it beating in my brain; which was reaching critical mass to the point of exploding. It went to his voice mail. I didn't leave a message as he would see the caller ID and know I tried to reach him. Tears poured down my face.

"What are we going to do now?" I shrieked and looked to Daniel for guidance.

"Call Dominic. Tell him to get over here," he directed. Dom slept next door in one of the empty cabins.

Dom, wake up. WAKE UP! I mentally screamed to Dominic with enough force to wake a whole army.

Gee whiz, Kara, I about fell off the bed from your blast to my brain. Did I forget to set the alarm? Is it time to get up already? Dom complained.

Meet us in the kitchen ASAP. I have something very bad to tell you. And then I slammed down my mental block. Dom pushed hard at my mind, trying to get in. With the few words I psychically sent him, he sensed my panic and sadness. I wouldn't dream of letting him read my thoughts that Tessa had been killed. Telling him face to face was the only, proper way.

Daniel and I ran from our bedroom to the kitchen to wait for Dom. I tried Zac's number again with little hope that he would pick up. No answer.

"I can't believe this, Daniel. This is insane," I blubbered through my tears and runny nose.

Daniel was trying to keep his body under control. A stressful, tragic and emotional situation, as we were experiencing, could trigger a primal instinct within him to transform. The physical reaction was a type of self-preservation mode or a fight or flight response. Shifting into the beast or a wolf at that time wouldn't be beneficial at all. During other more appropriate situations, Daniel's different forms are quite valuable, but totally uncalled for when we were knee-deep in making life and death decisions. Tessa was his friend, too, and her death had a profound effect on him. He pulled me away from the kitchen counter that I had propped myself against and wrapped his muscular arms around me. He nuzzled my neck, planting a few kisses and breathed in my scent to help calm his nerves. I felt Daniel's teardrop moisten my skin.

Dominic arrived seconds later. I told him exactly what Zac said, which wasn't much. The words echoed in the air. One of our friends, part of our team had been killed. He staggered to the sink in disbelief. I unglued myself from Daniel and went to Dom to give him a heartfelt hug. Too bad if Daniel didn't like me consoling Dom. If I noticed a jealous streak over this, I would personally punch him. We needed to be there for each other. Dom had no one here but us to turn to in desperate times.

Daniel broke the silence first, "We *will* find the murdering witch who did this. And I have no problem with dishing out the punishment myself."

Dom let go of me and nodded in agreement with Daniel. He

clenched his teeth while his fists curled into tight balls. Dom's mental state fluctuated from despair to confusion to shock and to anger. Tessa was dead. Zac had to be flipping out. Without warning, Dom's powers of telekinesis overcame him - several cabinet doors flew open, two chairs crashed against the wall and a coffee mug near his arm scooted off the edge of the counter. Daniel's lightning fast reflexes managed to catch the mug before it hit the floor. Dom hadn't deliberately meant to act out his frustrations, especially in Daniel's home. He closed his eyes to regain his focus and composure. Using his psychic ability, he shut the doors and set the chairs upright, putting things back in place.

"Sorry. I didn't mean to do that..." Dom apologized, embarrassed with his behavior. "Kara, did you try to contact Zac with telepathy? Maybe that would work. We need to talk to him and find what went down. And you could mentally manipulate his thoughts so he doesn't take off on a killing spree...and wind up on the witches' doorstep and on their chopping block."

I had my doubts that I could enter Zac's mind. He was hundreds of miles away, he had zero psychic power (which put all the exertion on me to link up), he didn't *want* to be contacted after the phone call and both of us suffered intense turmoil. It would be a monstrosity of a challenge and a miracle if I did get through to him. But I tried. Then I grabbed Daniel and Dom's hands and tried again. All three of us focused on Zac. Dom's skills alone should have boosted my chances. I momentarily felt Zac's essence, his familiar trail in my mind. I couldn't grab a hold of it. Zac flipped a switch in his brain and all communication ceased. I dropped to the floor bawling. We had no clue what kind of trouble Zac was involved in and no way to immediately be there for him.

Daniel belted out, "Try Josiah. Remember that Josiah, Zac and Tessa were going to meet somewhere and go spy on the witches. If that's the case, then Josiah and Zac should be together in the same place."

Why hadn't Josiah already contacted me by now? Why would Zac have bothered calling us on the phone if Josiah was right there? Were they at a hospital? A morgue? Or still standing over Tessa's dead body? Had Zac been hurt? What about Josiah? He's so powerful, how come he wasn't able to protect Tessa? Was Zac seeking revenge and waging war against the witches on his own, at that very moment?

"Kara, reach out to Josiah. Stop jumping to conclusions," Dom handed me tissues as he had read all of my thoughts. His bloodshot eyes were rimmed with tears. Several escaped, trailing down his cheeks. Pulling the front of his shirt to his face, he wiped them away.

Daniel scooped me off the kitchen floor, carried me to the lounge area and plunked my butt on the couch. Dom followed, dragging his feet. The fireplace sizzled with what remained of the wood. Quickly, Daniel threw more logs on to create a relaxing ambiance, hoping that it might help comfort us. He knew how I loved the crackling, warm fire. Possibly it could enhance my telepathic abilities.

"Hey! Are you wearing your grandmother's quartz?" Daniel's light bulb popped on.

I bopped my head with my hand. "No. It's on the dresser. I didn't even think about using that." Daniel raced to the bedroom and back before I attempted to get up. I felt stupid and careless that I failed to use all the resources around me. The quartz necklace sparkled as if it was calling to me. I secured it around my neck vowing to wear it at all possible times. Instantly a tingling sensation coursed through my body. There was no denying the magic it possessed. I just needed to figure the darn thing out and how best to use it. It's not like it came with an instruction manual.

We arranged ourselves on the couch in our usual fashion. I was in the middle with Daniel and Dominic sitting on opposite sides holding my hands. I suspected I would be able to contact Josiah without their added power, but "a meeting of the minds" was needed where everyone could share information right away. We agreed our séance method was a winner.

I breathed slowly through my mouth, concentrated on our vampire comrade and whispered, "Josiah…"

Seconds passed…*Kara, I'm here. I feel the link with Daniel and Dominic, too. You've already heard from Zac. I'm sincerely sorry for the loss of Tessa.*

I mentally pleaded, *But Josiah, he didn't explain anything; just that she was killed and he hung up. We don't know what happened.*

Josiah was distracted and hesitated. *Zac is struggling to stay calm so I need to be near him in case there's an issue. We recently returned* to my house from the city morgue. He called you from the bedroom he's residing in here. I'm trying to give him some privacy. Earlier this evening, I met Zac and Tessa as planned. We discussed tactics while getting familiar with one another. They followed me to the house that belonged to an evil witch who frequently had other witches over. We separated to surround the house for better surveillance. I feared Zac and Tessa didn't comprehend the danger in dealing with black magic...Josiah trailed off for a few seconds.

He picked up his pace and explained, *After a few hours, Tessa lost patience and made a risky decision to move in closer and peer through a window. The witches must've cast a spell around the house to alert them of trespassers. Tessa triggered it and immediately started choking. We ran to help her as the front door flew open and a witch threatened that if we didn't leave, Tessa would die. We began to retreat but heard an awful snap coming from Tessa's body. We looked down at her and she was dead. Her neck was broken. I'm not sure the witches meant to kill her or if they lost control over the spell and it was an accident. I'm sorry. I couldn't help her. And I didn't want to risk Zac's life, too, and decided it was best to leave.*

To be honest, Josiah boasted, *I could probably kill all of them before they'd even know what hit them. But, is that what The Liaison wants? I don't think so. They are all human. Witches, but human. No vampires, werewolves or demons-yet. I will admit: their black magic skills are strong. One in particular vibrated with power but did not show herself. It wouldn't hurt me to have back-up. And if we attack as a group, we have numbers on our side plus added distractions to throw at them. We'd have various types of skills and power, the advantage to attack from more angles, and could watch each other's backs.*

Just lay low till we get there, Daniel recommended.

My face was drenched from crying. Josiah had obviously thought this through like a master strategist. I quizzed, *Didn't the person working at the morgue look at you guys with suspicion when you came waltzing in carrying Tessa's body?*

No. Josiah elaborated, *I placed false memories in the man's mind of the incident. He doesn't suspect anything strange. He won't remember that we brought her in. His reports will tell a different* story. Don't worry.

We are heading out within the next few hours, Daniel promised.

I wiped at my tears. *Josiah, I can't make contact with Zac. Will you watch him for me?*

Yes, I will keep my eyes on him. I sensed Josiah's reassuring smile. *Zac needs time alone. He doesn't want to talk now. I expect he'll go to the funeral home later today to make arrangements. Don't dawdle getting here.*

Dominic wanted his thoughts heard, too. *I don't really know you, Josiah, but thank you for being there for Zac. He's my good friend... and I won't let Tessa's...* Dom held back sobs trying to get the word out... *murder be ignored.* I rubbed my fingers over Dom's hand.

One last observation... Josiah seemed to be zeroing in on me. Nothing too intrusive, but it felt more intimate than he'd ever tried before. *Kara, something is different with your psychic energy. You feel...like a charge of electricity.*

Daniel bristled. *That's enough with your charms. Let go of her!*

Even with the terrible news we'd been dealt, I half smiled at Daniel's jealousy and remarked, *Well, I hope it is a positive voltage and not negative.*

Josiah stated, *You're on the plus side. But what did you do or what do you have?*

I knew this could be a long story, so I kept it short. *My grandmother was a psychic witch and I recently inherited her mystical quartz necklace. She wasn't evil.*

Ahh...yes. I think Josiah was tapping his chin, pleased. *I am aware of the power that certain stones contain. Very good. Keep it with you. I need to check on Zac. We'll see you soon.*

With a tiny poof, he ended the session. The three of us sat in silence for another minute staring at the floor. An alarm clock went off in the bedroom, startling us out of our stupor. I wished that alarm was waking me up from a bad dream. But, no, I was living and breathing a nightmare.

We ate a light breakfast then finished last minute preparations for our departure. My duffle bag was stuffed with clothes that could survive a nuclear blast. Not that I owned much along the lines of girly feminine clothes in the first place. I tied my hiking boots to the bag, letting them dangle, as my fingers stroked over the leather. They were a gift from Zac and Tessa on my birthday. I had to keep moving or else I'd start bawling again.

I glanced up and caught Daniel watching me as he stood in the bedroom doorway. I reached my arms out to indicate I wanted him to come to me. He gave me a warm hug and kissed the top of my head. Daniel announced that he and Dom would be ready to leave in about an hour. I quickly packed my personal items - bare essentials only. I passed the mirror, not wanting to see myself, but glanced up anyway. What a mess. Red, puffy eyes and I couldn't breathe through my stuffed nose. I looked beaten.

To win this battle, or at the least to have the upper hand, I needed to roll with the punches. People depended on me. I had my cry and now it was time to regroup. I wished I could work a little emotional manipulation on *myself* instead of just on others. Too bad Dominic didn't have that psychic gift so he could ease my grief over Tessa.

I found him filling up bags with food and drinks; the less stops the better on our long drive. We lugged our over-flowing assortment of bags out to Daniel's truck. I heard a "ruff" and immediately jerked my head in the direction of the sound. Several months ago, I would've panicked being in a wooded area and having an animal vocalize itself to me. But I recognized it was a wolf and one I knew well. It was Daniel…he trotted over to us.

When Daniel transformed into a wolf, he was much larger than the average wolf and anyone who didn't know what was going on would be terrified to encounter such a creature. Dom knew it was Daniel, too, and relaxed knowing that he would not hurt us. Although seeing Daniel like this could momentarily throw you off balance. To my shock, Dom reached out to scratch Daniel on the back, gave him three firm buddy pats on his side and walked back into the resort. Well, we did need each other's support and Dominic was a compassionate man, after all. Even if he wished I'd leave Daniel and go running directly into his arms instead.

I dove into Daniel's mind wondering why the shift to wolf form. He had finished preparing for the trip and wanted to go for a quick run in the woods before we left. Over the years he learned that the best way to release any stressful emotions was to turn into a wolf, go for a run and be one with nature. I leaned over to wrap my arms around his neck and bury my face in his soft, warm fur. The early morning sunlight made the coal-black color shine like lip gloss.

"I'm getting a whiff of your cologne," I told Daniel, smiling. I was intrigued the scent still lingered on his wolf body.

And then Daniel licked my face which kind of grossed me out. He knew it would. I was smiling at the time, thinking about his musky cologne when his slobbery, huge tongue lapped up the front of my face, catching my upper lip, and leaving behind a trail of wolf spit. Yum. He politely sat on his rump, cocked his head to the side and panted.

He gave me that innocent look that said, "What?"

I wiped the gummy-goo from my face as Daniel decided to sprint off into the tree line. Dominic marched by and tossed his last bag into the back of the truck. He gave me a quizzical look then identified what I was doing.

"That's gross," he stated. I thought he might vomit the way his face got all scrunched up. He sat on the bumper.

Dom tested me, "So, is anyone approaching the resort?"

I already knew Eli was due to arrive, so it wasn't much of a test. "It's Eli. Have you had a chance to tell him what happened to Tessa yet?"

"No. I wanted him to get here safely and not wreck the car after hearing the news," Dom informed me. I agreed that something of this magnitude should be discussed in person not over the phone or especially by psychic means.

We waved to Eli as he drove up the lane and parked his car near the truck. He knew we planned to leave early and he had chosen to drive down to the resort in the wee hours of the morning to catch us before we left. But we didn't think he had any idea Tessa died during the night. Dom and I did a quick mind read on Eli to determine if he had any notions about Tessa. Nothing there. Zac obviously had not called him. Eli gave me a hug and Dom a handshake/hug as a greeting and made a few brief comments about his trip down.

Dom and I stood in awkward silence with somber expressions. I probed, "I guess you haven't heard from Zac during your drive, huh?"

We didn't need to stand around in the cold air relaying this horrific story to Eli. We went to the lounge, sat down and proceeded to pour out the important details. Dom was up front and didn't keep Eli in suspense that Tessa was killed. Poor Eli. He felt guilty for calling Zac and Tessa at Christmas time, asking if they would go on this reconnaissance since they were only a few hours away.

I sent Dom a quick mental message, *Should I try to relieve some of his sadness? Implant happier thoughts?*

Putting happy images in his mind isn't the right move. But if you can soothe him and take the edge off...try that, Dom suggested.

I discreetly worked my psychic magic on Eli while he and Dom went over our finances during the stay in Winchester, Massachusetts. We needed a source of money for living expenses and Eli had been our own private "bank", but he wasn't going on this mission. Between credit cards, ATMs and cold hard cash, we were set.

Daniel appeared in the lounge, looking refreshed from the wolf run. He saw Eli and shot me a look equivalent to: "Why didn't you alert me he was here?" He apologized to Eli for not being at the resort to initially greet him and acknowledged with proper respect the loss of Tessa.

Daniel gave Eli a few instructions on handling his resort while we were away. There were no visitors checked in to worry about at that time. Daniel explained that a few of the other werewolves would be rotating between his resort and Isaac's to help out, mainly Anthony, Sarah and Phillip. Eli was familiar with all the wolves and breathed a sigh of relief knowing he would have assistance if visitors or problems arose.

Daniel, Dom and I had to get a move on. Time was of the essence and we lost about an hour of it talking to Eli. Not to say that the conversations weren't important, because they were. But we still had to pick up Isaac. No doubt he was frantically pacing in front of his own resort. I realized I could telepathically send him a message to clue him in. Over the last month I had enough interaction with him that would allow me to enter his thoughts with ease.

*Isaac? It's Kara...*I attempted a light touch at his mind so as not to freak him out. *Isaac, can you hear me?*

Well, so much for the light touch. *Ahhh!* I envisioned Isaac tripping as he gasped and tried to regain his coolness. *Whoa! Kara, I* am still not prepared for how clear you come through and with no forewarning! Where are you guys? You're late. Can I blame my brother this time?*

Even with the gloomy news, I chuckled. Isaac's personality tended to be easy-going, carefree, the funny guy type, but not necessarily needing to be the center of attention. *Yes, Daniel is slowing us down. Eli is here. We'll be there in ten minutes. Don't worry - we couldn't possibly forget you!*

I poked Daniel's arm, reminding him we needed to leave. And fifteen minutes later, we had Isaac claiming his seat in the truck after casually tossing his one lone piece of luggage into the back. Our smiles were grim and he could see that something was dreadfully wrong. Isaac focused his attention on me. My face spoke volumes as the crying spell I had earlier over Tessa's death left me with bloodshot, puffy eyes for hours.

Isaac reached for my arm, "What in the world happened?"

That seemed to be the question of the day.

CHAPTER 6
JOSIAH

Thirty minutes later, bombarded with numerous questions from Isaac, we brought him up to speed on the dire situation in Winchester. He pledged his allegiance to The Liaison and would do everything in his power to help us. Isaac was only four years younger than Daniel and both became werewolves at the same time - cursed by black magic witches in 1693. Over many, many years, Daniel and Isaac learned to control the aggressive nature of their species. They managed to keep evil from manifesting itself and spreading inside their minds and bodies. And with their own free will, they could transform into the beast or large wolf and maintain human thinking patterns. Needless to say, if you were going into battle, it would be handy to have them on your side.

The trip would take about two days. I hoped my brain would survive as I was stuck in a vehicle filled with raging testosterone. I dealt with three males amped up on adrenaline who talked non-stop about strategy, kicking ass, razzing each other and showing off. Even Dominic held his own against Daniel and Isaac. Dom may not be a werewolf but with his psychic talents, especially telekinesis, it elevated him to a well-respected level with the two brothers.

Each of the guys took a shift driving. No one asked if I would drive, which was fine with me. We debated whether to stay one night at a motel or drive straight through to Josiah's house. It was a unanimous vote: get rooms so we could take showers, eat a decent meal and sleep in an actual bed. I won't bore the reader with the road trip details as it was thankfully uneventful.

Daniel volunteered to drive the last few hours. It was dark outside when we finally arrived, which Josiah would appreciate as he vastly preferred tending to activities at night. (More details on vampires to come.) Daniel barely had a chance to turn off the truck, when I glanced out the window and gasped as Josiah stood outside my door. If I thought werewolves had super speed, well, vampires blew them out of the water.

Josiah opened my door and offered his hand to assist me out of the truck. Desperate to escape from my confinement, I eagerly grabbed Josiah's hand and looked back at the boys with a huge smirk. I heard snorts, jeers and sensed tinges of jealousy over Josiah's proper, gentlemanly ways and the fact he touched me with such familiarity.

"Hello, my darling Kara. I am glad you made it here in one piece," Josiah raised his eyebrows at the men sitting in their seats and then bent to kiss my hand. "I wish the circumstances for your visit were of a different nature."

All three emerged from that truck so fast you'd have thought a time bomb was ticking, ready to blow. They realized I stood defenseless in the dark against a vampire of immense power, who had his hands on me. I'll admit it: Josiah, to some degree, mesmerized me at that moment.

I heard Daniel's deep growl which broke the temporary enchantment I felt. I knew Josiah wouldn't hurt me, at least never intentionally. I hoped. He wasn't trying to use mind control, just some good old-fashioned flirting. And he was getting a kick out of Daniel's reaction in more than one way.

"And that type of raw, dedicated emotion is what we're going to need to fight these witches," Josiah expressed with enthusiasm as he stared at Daniel; and not at all what we expected him to say. "Just make sure to concentrate on the *real* enemy and don't get distracted by actions that may be harmless."

"Let go of her hand," Daniel glared back, but he did give Josiah an understanding nod that surprised me. Josiah let my fingers feather out of his hand.

"Good to see you, too, Daniel. Isaac. Dominic. You are welcome in my home," Josiah announced. He recommended we unload our luggage and acquaint ourselves with the surroundings.

Josiah had rented this house many weeks ago. It was in the

vicinity of another house that he believed belonged to one of the witches. That house seemed to be a popular meeting place and Josiah kept tabs on it the best he could. The witches discovered or suspected he was spying on them and erected a spell to prevent him from reading their thoughts. He still surveyed the property but until we arrived, he didn't want to infuriate the witches any more than necessary. No point in putting a big spotlight on his head, drawing unwanted attention.

As we stepped up to the door, it opened and there stood Zac. Talk about grief with a capital "G". Josiah insisted on carrying my bags, so my hands and arms were free to immediately give Zac a hug. I was never much of a hugger when I was younger, but something changed over the last few months. I now hugged whenever I could. He stood for a moment without returning the greeting, one hand on the door, the other arm hanging at his side. I gave it a few more seconds, and then he broke down sobbing. His arms gripped around me like I was a life preserver that he was afraid to let go of, afraid of drowning. He stepped back inside the house, still holding onto me, and the others walked in.

The physical contact I had at that moment with Zac did not bother the other men. There were no feelings of jealousy, possessiveness or a need to protect me. They felt awkward, unsure of what to say to Zac and not sure what might set him off. Having me as a buffer took some pressure off of them being forced to acknowledge Tessa's death and to give their condolences.

Josiah leaned against the living room wall, giving us time to adjust and talk with Zac. The funeral arrangements had been made. Tessa's body would be cremated. He concocted a story to tell their families: an undercover assignment "went bad" and Tessa was caught in the crossfire…he would attend the memorial service for her then return here to complete the mission. Zac opened up better than I would have guessed. Besides a few hours dealing with the families and the funeral home, for the most part, he only had Josiah to turn to. And they had just met hours before this awful turn of events. I imagined it had been difficult to talk in depth with Josiah, a stranger and a vampire. Zac probably kept most of his thoughts bottled up inside until he saw us and then let everything pour out.

After an hour, Josiah commented that we needed to choose rooms or places in the house to sleep. He gave us a quick tour of the house, pointing out his and Zac's sleeping quarters. Josiah was in the basement (gee, what a shock there) and Zac had a bedroom on the first floor. Isaac chose to sleep on the couch. Dom nabbed a tiny bedroom on the second floor and Daniel and I shared the larger bedroom, also upstairs. We decided not to unpack all our belongings in case of needing to perform a hasty escape.

Earlier that day Zac had stocked the kitchen with tons of food when he heard we would be arriving that night. Dominic took over as chef, a pastime he thrived on, and whipped up a meal that had us salivating from the aromas wafting through the house.

Josiah informed us after we had settled in, "The witches abandoned the house that they had used for meetings. I thought one of the witches owned the house, but perhaps it was merely a rental. We have to start from scratch searching for their new location."

"Maybe we need to go on a scavenger hunt tonight," Daniel volunteered. "Isaac and I have excellent tracking skills and finely-tuned werewolf senses that might give us some clues."

"I agree. I will take you and Isaac to the witches' old house and anywhere else I consider suspicious. Let's wait a few hours until more of the city is sleeping. We don't need to cause a panic with the three of us venturing out in the streets...we are rather intimidating," Josiah bared his teeth and gave us a cocky smile. "It would be a bonus to keep your arrival here unnoticed from the witches for as long as possible. We'll leave around midnight."

Zac added, "Yeah, too bad as mere humans we actually need to sleep once in a while. You vamps and wolves can go a lot longer without sleeping and don't seem to need much when you do."

"Ah, that is true, my new friend! But both our species do need to rest and rejuvenate at some point. If we can keep nourished, it helps to extend our awake time and our alertness. And on that note, I must depart for a bit, but will return shortly," Josiah turned from Zac and stared at me before whizzing out the door at super speed. His hunger pulsated right through me...which was weird. He needed blood and left to find it.

I had my grandmother's quartz necklace on and the moment

Josiah flew by me, the stone tingled then went cold, then tingled and stopped reacting. I suspected it was confused trying to figure out Josiah's temperament. He's a vampire and many vampires are evil but in his specific case, he's not. He's one of the good guys. I couldn't remember if the quartz had a similar reaction the first time I wore it around Daniel or Isaac. If it did, I probably thought I was imagining things at the time. Then again, neither of the werewolves was likely to suck my blood as Josiah could, which made him come off as a threat to the quartz (and me).

I headed to the truck to fetch the AC adapter for my laptop. Daniel had placed it into the glove compartment during the trip. As I began walking back to the house, I sensed Josiah was nearby. He wasn't directing his thoughts at or to me, but his surge of power and elevated emotional state could not be ignored. Curiosity got the best of me, and I found myself walking half a block down the sidewalk. My peripheral vision caught a small movement under a tree and I jerked my head in that direction.

It was dark outside and I had a heck of a time narrowing my vision in on what I was really seeing. Josiah's presence was intense and beating at my brain. It had to be him. But I saw *two* people pressed against each other tightly. My quartz necklace was once again debating whether I was in peril or not. I drew in a sharp breath because I realized what was happening in front of me. Of course. He had just told us about needing nourishment. Freaked out and intrigued, I witnessed Josiah drinking blood from a woman's neck. She didn't fight him. She didn't say a word.

His eyes looked up at me while his mouth remained on her neck. He kept drinking her blood for a few more seconds then he licked the pinpricks with his tongue. He grasped her by the shoulders and gazed deep into her eyes. I tried mentally eavesdropping on what must have been mind control or a type of compulsion. Ow! Josiah closed off his mind to me with a push that actually made me stagger backwards.

The lady turned away from Josiah and returned to the sidewalk. She gave me a vacant smile and walked to her car. She unlocked the door, got in, fired it up and drove down the road, conscious of her surroundings, and no longer in a daze. She didn't have any memory of a vampire sucking the blood out of her neck!

In a flash, Josiah appeared at my side. I inhaled sharply. One of his fingers touched my lips and he whispered, "Shhh...I'm not going to hurt you, Kara. What are you doing out here alone?"

I stuttered, "I, I'm, you... I felt you were near and you gave off such interesting...vibes that I followed your trail...I'm sorry I saw you..."

Josiah held back his laughter but couldn't stop the grin which turned into a full-fledged, toothy smile. No protruding fangs, at least, and he had beautiful, white teeth. They weren't all black and gnarly like you'd expect. "I'm assuming our telepathic link we forged together allows you to home in on me with relative ease. And don't deny that I have a...shall I say..."an effect" on you? I'll have to monitor whether I should mute or dampen your access to my mind as you might not feel comfortable with my behaviors...yet. We'll see. As far as what you saw...I need blood to survive. You know that. I would have preferred that you not catch me in the act of feeding, but since you did, what are your thoughts?"

Well, that was down-right silly. I told him, "You can read my thoughts about anything. I don't need to say a word. You're very mesmerizing."

"Kara, I don't always want to read thoughts all the time, day in and day out. It's nice to have a normal conversation..." Josiah explained as he bent his head down and seductively breathed out the rest of the sentence over my lips, "by using our mouths."

He straightened his body, took my arm and hooked it around his, just like in the olden days. Wow. I didn't know what to think about that! We began walking back to his house. My quartz necklace was calm. That was a relief! I didn't feel threatened but instead I sensed affection and protection from his touch.

I blurted out, "If I hadn't stumbled upon the scene, would you have killed her? Drained her dry? Turned her into a vampire? Is she your servant now that you've drank her blood?"

"Slow down, Kara! First, I would NOT have killed her. Remember, I'm fighting on the good side? Let's get back to the house. The men are wondering what's taking you so long. With your psychic abilities, you should be able to hear them questioning that issue," Josiah chastised me. "You apparently don't know many details about my kind. During my visit to Daniel's resort a few weeks ago, I should have elaborated on vampire characteristics for you. A few of the others could use a refresher course on vampires, too. Shame on Daniel and The Liaison for not teaching you pertinent information."

Speaking in defense for Daniel, The Liaison members and for my own ignorance, I argued, "Well, I know *some* things! When you visited us, I learned a little from you...but now that I think about it, most of the talk was on witches... And as far as The Liaison is concerned, Eli and the others said they didn't want to bombard me with too much at one time. All I had to do was ask questions when I was ready. Kinda like a need to know thing," I chattered.

Josiah opened the front door for me and stated, "I do believe this *is* a need to know thing, my dear."

Daniel rushed to my side, glaring at Josiah with a threatening look that questioned any underlying motive he might have tucked up his sleeve. He pulled me under the possessive security of his shoulder then turned and asked, "Are you okay? I thought you were only going to be gone a few seconds."

Everyone looked at me for my response. I had to remind myself I was the only girl in this group and the men would naturally be protective of me.

"I'm fine. Can everyone chill out? I wandered down the block because I sensed Josiah was near and I was nosy. The next thing I realize, I'm watching him suck blood out of some lady's neck," I confessed.

Josiah took the reins, "Kara flooded me with questions and I decided it would be best to bring her back to the house. I would like to disclose some facts about vampires and I'd appreciate it if the entire team was present."

We scattered around the living room, although I chose to stay as close to Josiah as possible. Daniel promptly plopped down next to me. Of course. Dominic sat on the opposite side of Josiah and Isaac and Zac rounded out the circle. Now all we needed was a bonfire and marshmallows with a full moon overhead and people telling scary stories.

Daniel informed Josiah, "I told Kara and Dominic about how we first met and the boundary spell placed around our home territory."

Josiah seemed pleased but skimmed over the story quickly for Zac's sake since he did not know this information. Zac nodded with understanding and thought the spell was ingenious in keeping the local people from gossiping about Daniel and his bunch never aging.

Daniel asked if Mizar and Serena were still alive. Those were the vampires who traveled with Josiah 180 years ago. Serena had been a powerful witch before she was turned into a vampire and had been the one to cast the boundary spell for the werewolves. Josiah believed both were indeed alive but not positive on where they currently resided. He paused a moment and appeared to make a mental note as if he wanted to research this at a later date.

I leaned forward, pressing my elbows into my knees with fascination, and asked, "How old are you, Josiah? Daniel gave the impression you were much older than him."

Without skipping a beat, he replied, "886 years old. I was born in 1123."

"You were *born* a vampire?" I squeaked in amazement. Josiah had the group's full undivided attention. He stood throughout his tell-all which added to the enthrallment.

"Yes. Vampires are a species. We are not the undead or walking dead as portrayed in some books and movies. My heart beats. Now ghouls and zombies are another thing altogether. They *are* dead. Or the walking dead, if you prefer. Vampires are either born a vampire or have been turned into a vampire by a blood transfer." Josiah's voice permeated the room.

It was the kind of voice perfect for commercials. Heck, he could be the star in commercials. Viewers would either run to the store to buy whatever he was pushing or totally forget what he was trying to sell and only remember Josiah for being so sexy in it. I might love Daniel but that didn't mean I was blind to everyone else around me! And a little flirtation was healthy for the soul.

"Did I lose you, Kara?" Josiah raised a curious brow at me. I felt his presence slip out of my mind. That knucklehead had read my thoughts. About him. The sparkle in his eyes indicated his satisfaction with his discovery. Thankfully, Daniel and Dom had been absorbed in Josiah's speech. They had not linked into my dreamy thoughts about Josiah which could have started a brawl. Anyway...

I blinked several times, shook my head and sharply replied, "No, you didn't lose me. Can't a girl be still and listen?"

All the men erupted in laughter at my statement. I scowled at each and every one of them for making fun at me.

To get the ball rolling again, I asked, "The lady that I saw you drink blood from…is she your servant now?"

Josiah explained, "No. I do not choose to keep human servants. What I will do is put a temporary compulsion on a person to behave a certain way and I implant false memories. And you wonder why I would do such things? Usually to protect the human or to hide my existence from them."

Daniel piped in, "Yes, as everyone recalls, the werewolves recently had an issue with a few of our own, Stephen and David, who risked their exposure to society. Keeping the unknown species or beings hidden from the general public remains a challenge."

"Exactly the reason why I utilize mind control methods," Josiah confirmed.

"How exactly does a human become a vampire?" I was dying to know. Hmm…maybe that was not the right word choice - dying. Dom narrowed his eyes at me and teetered on butting into the conversation, but instead sent me a mental jab that meant to get the idea of converting into *anything* out of my head.

Josiah picked up on the exchange between us and cleared his throat to bring the focus back to him. "As I mentioned, a blood transfer is required to be converted into a vampire. In layman's terms, I bite your neck, I drink most all your blood, I slash my wrist and you drink a significant amount of my blood. Over a period of two days, and excruciating pain, the human will be converted to a vampire."

I jumped in, intrigued, "So the conversion is not instant. Okay, another thing…I noticed that you don't burst into flame from the sun, but I sense you do prefer the nights."

"Correct observation, my dear Kara," he continued, "Vampires have difficulty with the sun but it doesn't kill us. Oh, I suppose if an enemy kept us tied up outside for a few days, it would kill the majority of my kind. Depending on the length of time in the sun, we receive varying degrees of sunburn, much like humans, just more susceptible to burning than the average human. Our main disadvantage during sunlight hours is our diminished supernatural powers. We are weaker during the day."

I couldn't hold back the question any longer. It was plainly obvious that it needed to be brought up considering the direction the discussion was moving in. "Josiah, how do I kill you - a vampire?"

CHAPTER 7
KNOWING

He winced from my abrupt, harsh words as if I had slapped him in the face. Josiah was a vampire, after all, and I should have expected his reaction. I had flat out asked how I could kill him. Well, maybe not him in particular, but any evil vampires that savored causing anarchy and harm, especially if they're coming after my neck. No pun intended.

Josiah's intense dark eyes turned solid black as he glared at me; the whites of his eyes had disappeared. Total silence and stillness saturated the room. His lips twitched and grew tight in an attempt to keep his pearly fangs concealed, but I still caught a glimpse of them. They had appeared with his anger and instinct for self-preservation. That was the second time in one night I had seen his fangs exposed; the first time, feeding off of a woman. An unnerving hiss escaped his mouth as his own mortality was questioned.

Daniel moved to the edge of his chair, placing his hand on my knee. The atmosphere in the living room tensed as the rest of the men looked ready to pounce on Josiah if he attacked me. If needed, Dom was ready to throw an invisible force field around me with his psychic skills. He held back his kneejerk reaction to just go ahead and do it only because Josiah could mistake it as Dom making the first move to fight. Everyone allowed Josiah the opportunity to take a breather and reassess the situation.

I nibbled on my bottom lip, realizing I had been disrespectful and callous with my question. I knew better. And for some strange reason, I wasn't afraid. He had a right to be angry, but I felt no evil presence flowing from him. And my quartz necklace only slightly tingled. I would have hoped if I were truly going to be attacked, it would be blaring a warning sign in some form or fashion.

"Josiah, I am so sorry!" I pleaded, trying to break the uncomfortable silence. After the initial spoken apology, I put up a mental block to keep the others that could read my mind from hearing the rest. I wanted this to be private.

I interjected telepathically to him, *I really am sorry! Please don't be mad at me for my stupid choice of words. What if no one is around to protect me and a bad guy vampire decides it's the perfect time to attack? I have to know <u>what</u> to do and what my choices are! You said earlier that I needed to know all I could about you and other paranormal stuff.*

Kara, Josiah sighed and visually relaxed to everyone's relief. His eyes returned to "normal" and the fangs disappeared. The men immediately presumed that Josiah and I were having a conversation in our minds. I sensed that Daniel and Dom, having the ability to read my mind, tried to eavesdrop but couldn't get through my mental block. They didn't like it. Too bad.

Josiah continued, *I apologize, too, for my threatening appearance. I do not mean you any harm. You are very dear to me... more so than other humans I interact with and have known in a very long time. I...I was hurt and shocked by your words when you so bluntly asked how to kill me. And defensive instincts will kick in during those times. I recognize the honesty of your question and why, of course, you need to know the answer.*

I added, *Josiah, it was cruel the way I asked you, though. What's wrong with me? Maybe being around all these macho men has roughened me up. And with all the changes I'm dealing with in my life...and crazy witches and Tessa's death and trying to figure out this mystical quartz necklace...I feel pressure to be like Cat Woman!*

I squirmed in my chair, frowning and wringing my hands. Daniel's eyes went from me to Josiah and back to me. His head was cocked to the side like a dog trying to figure something out. If he was in wolf form, his ears would have been standing at attention. I didn't give off any signs of distress so he waited, although somewhat impatiently, figuring that Josiah and I were working out our misunderstanding.

Josiah reached for my mind and responded, *Kara, there is nothing wrong with you. We are all dealing with a stressful situation. I have an idea...I possess the same ability as you do with using mental manipulation in various ways. Would you like me to soothe your anxiety?*

I...I'm not sure, I stuttered. It was so tempting and yet I wanted to be in control of myself and my actions. I couldn't afford to have my intuitions dampened down to the point I might become careless and put myself or others in danger.

He read those thoughts, of course, and said, *Yes, I understand your concerns with wishing to stay alert. But, if you ever need or want any of my services, just ask.*

Oh, now that sounded like an open-ended invitation to more than just one method of relieving my stress! Gee, he started out wanting to throttle me and ended up offering to...ah, wait a minute - he was reading my mind again!

Thanks, Josiah. And again, I'm sorry, I wrapped up our mental chat. I knew in my heart that he wouldn't hurt me. He might get ticked off at me from time to time, but I felt secure with him and safe from him.

An affectionate smile popped up on my face as I gazed into Josiah's mesmerizing eyes. Quickly, I diverted my smile to those around the room, reassuring the group that I had managed to settle everything with Josiah. Lighthearted comments erupted to lighten the mood. My attention whipped back to Josiah when a slight caress grazed my cheek and a gentle, overall nurturing sensation washed through my body. He played innocent and didn't confirm or deny in any way what I had just experienced. I don't think I imagined it but couldn't seek out his thoughts as he locked up his mind to me at that moment.

"So, Josiah, back to my question. Let me word it so as not to offend you," I ribbed him on purpose. "How does one kill an evil, blood-thirsty, murdering, savage, vile, living on the dark side with no hope for redemption, and considered for the most part to be immortal, vampire? Which, as everyone in this room agrees, is the complete opposite of what you are. Except for the part of being an immortal vampire."

The entire room once again held their breath in stark silence. I giggled. Josiah shook his head and looked at the ceiling trying hard not to show emotion. And then he started to chuckle, too. Everyone was laughing within seconds. Rarely did Josiah tolerate anyone pushing his buttons or being openly teased about sensitive matters and yet I was granted special permission to get away with it. Most of the guys hooted with approval when Josiah had loosened up and surprised us by actually laughing.

"Kara, that was indeed descriptive of the type of vampire you need to know how to kill," Josiah was amused and appreciated the distinction I made between a bad vampire and a good vampire.

He dove into the grisly details for my benefit, as the others already knew this information. "A stake in the heart, whether it's wood or not, immobilizes a vampire but will not kill one. Keep in mind that immobilizing us is still excellent strategy until a better opportunity presents itself to go for the kill. It takes enormous effort to move any part of our bodies in that paralyzed state. To destroy a vampire you must completely set us on fire, burning our bodies to ashes or cut off our heads or dismemberment. Cutting off an arm or a leg will not be enough to kill us. Also, we regenerate and heal almost instantly. We can live for thousands of years. And we never look older than perhaps 35 to 40 years old."

I sponged up that information as fast as it left his lips. The last statements answered more questions than I had intended to ask, at the time, but it was interesting to know. He might have been snooping inside my head, knowing what I was curious about, and decided to fill in the blanks while he was on a roll speaking.

"Do you turn into a bat?" I jumped in with a spur of the moment thought that sounded a little childish.

"I can but I prefer other forms as bats do not have the most agile bodies while in flight to carry out certain activities. I am able to shape shift into several different animals."

"Such as?" I queried.

"Well, let's see...a bat, as I mentioned, plus an owl, leopard, wolf, python, shark, oh, and I can transform into something that is not an animal. Mist. I do have to practice if I'm trying out something new, though. I've tried to incorporate different animals for all kinds of travel," Josiah matter-of-factly stated with an air of superiority.

I leaned back in my chair in awe trying to comprehend how he could turn into mist. Strange how his ability to turn into other animals didn't seem to cause my bewilderment, but the mist thing had me stumped. Seeing Daniel and his pack transform into wolves or the half man - half wolf creature over the past months had allowed my mind to accept shape shifting and I assumed Josiah would have this ability, too. But he could pick and choose from a repertoire of animals and throw in mist as an added benefit for protection or to be used as a weapon!

To demonstrate his ability and I'm sure to impress me, his body dissolved on the spot. He became a thick fog that swirled through the group like a tiny twister and then disappeared. I learned later that he spread out his molecules to the point that he wasn't visible to the eye and considered that to be a type of mist. He was definitely still there though, as he snaked his way around and up my legs, which invoked a muffled shriek from me as I felt the sensation. Daniel instantly figured out Josiah's sneaky trick and snarled at the outright flirtation. And then without further ado, Josiah reappeared where he'd been standing before his shockfest. His arms were folded over his chest, feet planted in a wide stance and he flaunted a huge, smug grin. It *was* an awesome display of supernatural skills even if he was showing off!

"All right, hotshot," Daniel started in. "Let's test your tracking and hunting capabilities against werewolf super-heightened senses. It's nearing midnight and you said we'd scope out suspicious locations for witch high jinks. While we're gone, Kara, Dom and Zac should get some sleep." The male competition remained fierce…and I saw no sign of it ever dying down.

I knew Daniel was right and didn't argue as my exhaustion set in hard and fast. I had an idea Dom and I would be out in full force early the next day doing our share of spying and research while our non-human counterparts slept in. Well, I supposed they needed to sleep at some point if they planned on roaming the city during the rest of the night. The werewolves immensely enjoyed the evening hours but didn't experience any problems with the sunlight so they didn't *have* to sleep during the day. And I was comforted to learn that Josiah *could* move about in daylight without bursting into flames even though his power was significantly reduced making him more vulnerable to his enemies. Plus he'd get a nasty sunburn as a side effect.

The boys and I stood up and stretched from having sat so long while Josiah waited at the front door, primed for the sensory challenge against the werewolves. Daniel hugged and kissed me with a mighty show of possession for all to see. He playfully swatted my butt and headed outside with Josiah and Isaac. The game was on.

I yawned which caused a domino effect as seconds later Dom yawned followed by Zac which included a rather obnoxious belch to top it off.

* * * *

"Hey baby, wake up. We're back," Daniel whispered in my ear.

I groaned, not attempting to hide it. "How many hours did I get to sleep?"

"Ahhh...that's the first thing you want to know? Five hours, maybe a little more. Get up, get up!" He lifted me off the bed with no physical strain whatsoever and proceeded to sit down in my nice warm spot on the sheets with me on his lap. His muscular arms surrounded my sleepy body as I burrowed my face on his chest. Oh, I really wanted to sleep longer.

Daniel prodded me, "Isaac is waking up Dominic and Zac. We need to have a meeting about what we found out. It's close to the time you'd get up for the day anyway."

I asked, "Who won?"

"What?"

"Who won the battle of the bad-ass hunters last night...or rather, early this morning...in tracking down anything to do with the witches? The brawny werewolves or the mighty vampire?"

He frowned making it clear I was missing the point. "Our competitive nature pushes us to use all resources that are available to our advantage. We discover tiny details, scents, evidence and trails that offer insight into unraveling the mystery. The past few hours were not necessarily meant to be a contest between werewolves and vampires."

I brought my gaze to his eyes and teased, "Yeah, right. It didn't sound like that when the three of you left. Quit acting elusive. Who won?"

"It was fairly even, if we were being judged. If you must know, Josiah might have had a bit of an edge over Isaac and me," he admitted with clenched teeth. "Well...he *is* a very old vampire so he should be well endowed! And I'm referring to his skills...[agitated growl from Daniel]... as in supernatural skills, nothing sexual!"

Daniel kept digging himself deeper into a hole. I giggled as I brought his face closer and kissed him to bolster his confidence and his mood. Daniel had a jealous streak in him a mile wide and Josiah had not been one to conceal his interest in me, let alone that Josiah's significant power could be very daunting. Personally, I was more intrigued than intimidated.

Using my psychic talent to implant thoughts, and drawing energy from Grandma's mystical quartz necklace that I wore, I flooded Daniel's mind with love, comfort and desire. I felt the intense surge of emotions release from me as if they were direct-wired into Daniel's brain. It reminded me of static electricity created from shuffling across a carpet with your socks on in winter...then touching something and getting zapped. Whoa...I hadn't planned to overwhelm him like that. Some people could've interpreted what I did as a jolt of shock treatment or even mind control since I didn't give him any room for other thoughts to enter. Daniel was submerged with a single driving motive and that's what his focus zeroed in on. Thanks to me.

He straightened his back, pulling away from my face for a second, and shook his head. Then he tossed me onto the bed, straddling my mid-section and leaned down until he was nose to nose with me. Daniel's dark eyes gleamed with excitement and need as his wolfish grin was proof positive that my stunt worked. His breathing was labored, his heart rate had increased and wild ideas ran unbridled through his head. I know because I read his mind. He felt empowered and on top of the world knowing how much I loved him. He grabbed his shirt and jerked it over his head almost crushing me in the process.

"Oops!" I managed to squeak out. "I double-whammied you big time with good vibes. I figured you should know what triggered all of...this. I'm guilty."

Daniel paused to comprehend what I had done. A battle raged deep within his soul, pulling him in opposite directions: keep going on the intended path or stop now before things went too far. We could never let ourselves forget that I was still human and he was a werewolf. Somehow he regained his composure and reeled in his physical distress. A bead of sweat slid down his nose and dripped on my chin. Since he had maneuvered out of his shirt, I couldn't help but gaze dreamily at his glistening chest. Werewolves have a warmer body temperature than humans and add to that the stimulation I had blasted into his mind, well, needless to say he was burning up.

"Girl, you are going to drive me crazy!" He rolled off of me onto his back and stared at the ceiling. "I have to be in control! What if I get too rough because some natural instinct takes over? Or worse, if I partially shape shifted into the beast and my teeth scratched you or I bit you? You haven't decided whether you want to become a werewolf yet, or *when* if you do, and my teeth could convert you when I'm in wolf or beast form! That was a tad dangerous putting those thoughts into my head while I was already kissing you! And what was that about a 'double-whammy'?"

"The quartz."

"Oh…yes, I'd say it definitely enhanced your psychic talents," he groaned and rolled on his side to get a better look at me. He poked my arm and announced, "Okay, let's go. You managed to distract me long enough. Although I will say it was a nice distraction, to take my thoughts off of what we have to tell you."

I quizzed him, "It's not good news, is it? Otherwise, why would we be here? I could pluck it from your mind, but I won't. I'll wait till the whole gang is together."

Daniel gave me a few clues as we headed down the stairs. "As you know, Josiah, Isaac and I investigated some witch hot spots. They had been clever and careful covering their tracks and so we kept coming up empty-handed. We continued to prowl around until we finally had a lead. It was unmistakably the smell of death and lingered heavily in the air. We followed the scent of the dead…"

"What does that mean?" I didn't like the feeling of dread overcoming me. We made our way into the living room, where the others were waiting for our arrival.

A bleak expression spread over his face. Disgusted, he explained, "Slaughtered dogs. We found ten large dogs drained of their blood or close to being drained. The bodies were tossed in a side alley. It sickens me. The witches will use the blood as a sacrifice in the ritual to summon their demon."

Chapter 8
Infiltrate

I foraged for the remote control to the television, turned it on and started searching for a local news channel. It was almost 6:00 in the morning and by now someone had to have stumbled upon the dogs in the alley and called the police. Reporters and their cameramen would've swarmed to the location to film or provide live coverage on such a gory, hot story. Sure enough, I found a station broadcasting the tragedy as its latest developing headline. Thankfully, the police covered the bodies of the deceased dogs with sheets. I assumed that the crime scene was too gruesome for the public to view on the news station. As it was, my stomach knotted up and tears poured out of my eyes just thinking of all those poor dogs that were viciously killed.

Daniel and Isaac felt a great deal of outrage and grief concerning the murdered dogs. Since wolves are related to dogs, they shared a kinship with them and the number of deaths had been a shocking blow.

The news channel moved on to other topics, but the grave truth behind the slayings hit a nerve with everyone in the room. The witches were preparing for the resurrection. Soon. Perhaps that very night. Or could they have already performed the ritual within the last few hours? If so, did it work? Did we have a newly awakened demon to deal with plus his witches to fight?

Dominic stomped off to the kitchen to make breakfast while the rest of us quickly got ready for the day.

When I returned an hour later, I flopped down in front of the television set with my cold meal and asked if there had been any updates on the news. Isaac said that a local Humane Society reported a break-in over night. And guess what? Ten dogs were missing. The same ten found killed in the alley.

I looked at Dom and he nodded. We'd do our diligent detective work and check out the Humane Society.

Zac had already left to drive home and tend to Tessa's memorial, which was arranged for that day. He had other related things to take care of, which we completely understood, and wouldn't return until the next evening.

Daniel, Josiah and Isaac needed their turn to sleep and would be more or less out of commission until later that day. All three incessantly reminded Dom and me that if anything at all came up where we found ourselves in trouble we should use our telepathy to call for help and to forcibly wake them up. And whatever the time happened to be when we arrived back at the house, to alert them to our findings. Their behavior reminded me of worried, hesitant parents allowing their kids to drive the car for the first time.

Josiah gave us directions to a magic shop as a second place to investigate during the day. He believed Dom and I had the ability to slink into the mind of whomever worked there and look for anything suspicious. His previous attempts to ferret out any information had failed. In fact, he wasn't even able to enter the shop. With all the mystical goodies available in one spot, the witches used that to their advantage in casting mega-powerful spells to keep out supernatural beings. And that included vampires, of course. Josiah's frustration was evident; after all, he was an incredibly strong and ancient vampire who normally didn't encounter obstacles in getting whatever he wanted. But, he wasn't up to par with spells and black magic. He didn't deny it and loathed this weakness, this crack in his armor. I realized the exact same weakness held true for the werewolves.

As I prepared to leave, Daniel approached and gently forced me to turn and face him. He spoke quietly, which was ironic because a few of the guys could read his mind or hear him speak with their heightened hearing. That is, if they wanted to eavesdrop on our conversation.

"Kara, I shouldn't have to tell you to be careful. Pay attention to your quartz for any warnings it's trying to give you. I'm not thrilled with the idea of you traipsing through this unfamiliar city without me by your side and crazed witches on the loose," Daniel broadcasted.

I'll stay close to Dom. No one knows who we are. Yet. I mentally responded. *We have an advantage with his telekinesis skills and did you so quickly forget how I can sway a person's thoughts?* I teased him with the memory of what I did to his mind just a few hours earlier in the bedroom.

He snickered with mixed emotions then grew serious again. *Don't leave Dominic's side. Stay within his range of sight. I know he'll do anything in his power to protect you. But don't get too chummy with him and you know what I'm referring to.*

Daniel side-glanced at Dom, sensing that Dom probably overheard our private mind chatting, and came to the conclusion that if he did listen in, all the better. Dominic gave nothing away if he was or wasn't snooping around in our minds...my guess would be he did because after a few seconds Daniel turned his head away from him, and Dom immediately looked at me and winked.

Daniel snatched his truck keys off the counter, tossed them at Dom and barked, "Catch! You can take my truck. Be sure to take care of her - both Kara and the truck!"

"My pleasure, O' Great Furry One. I promise to fulfill my duties," Dom mocked Daniel and bowed to him.

Coming from different areas in the house, I could hear laughter from Isaac and Josiah. Daniel bristled from the remark at first but relaxed when he realized we were having a playful team moment. And all of us needed that coming-together feeling to release the tension.

After a few more rounds of bickering, Dom and I were on our way to the Humane Society, hoping that the police and reporters had left the premises by the time we arrived. Luckily, the building had cleared out except for the manager and another employee.

I decided to formulate a cover-up story for our timely appearance. Dom and I needed to give these people a meaningful reason to even bother talking to us. We weren't there to adopt a pet. We were there to pick their brains. The two workers saw us approach and they tried to shake off their doom and gloom expressions. I spoke with honest compassion and pushed that emotion firmly into their minds.

"Excuse me...I know this may not be the best time...I'm so sorry about the dogs that were taken and what happened to them. We've been researching similar cases around the country and to have such an incident occur right under our noses, well, we had to investigate. Over the years, there have been outbreaks of dog abductions where it's believed the animals are sold to laboratories for use in experiments or to puppy mills for breeding purposes," I paused to let this sink in. The manager listened intently. He was a round, middle aged man with gentle eyes. The employee was a tall, slim lady in her thirties, and looked like she could vomit from all the commotion.

I continued, "I'm sure you've heard of such things before..." They nodded in agreement. The woman's eyes glistened with tears. "Well, we are on a mission to uncover the evil-doers. We want to hunt them down and rip apart their operations!" Boy - I was on a roll. And the ironic thing about it - most of what I declared was the actual truth. It was important to get these people on my side and willing to work with me.

The lady sniffed and asked, "But if the dogs were being used for experiments, why was their blood drained? They were stolen, killed and dumped all in the same night. You'd think they'd be taken to a lab somewhere...I don't understand."

I had to think fast or the story I concocted would start to unravel. With complete conviction I surmised, "That's just it! Heck, the crazy scientists probably told the psychos they hired that the blood is all they actually needed for their latest experiment. Why keep the dogs locked up in their lab, taking up space, needing constant care, when perhaps a large amount of the dogs' blood would do the trick?! I just can't imagine ten dogs killed for a sacrifice...um...for those scientists to look upon it that way for their research. Truly disgusting!"

Dominic gave me a look to tone down the drama. My little white lie was becoming too similar to the real incident with the witches. He turned to the employees and pried, "Do you remember anyone visiting here who seemed odd or acted suspicious? Maybe walking through the building, checking doors, the cages, locks, the hours this place is open to the public? Their focus would've been on the larger dogs."

The manager closed his eyes to think. The lady paced the floor and muttered to herself trying to recall the recent visitors. Dom and I knew this was our chance to dive into their thoughts and grasp any images that jumped to the forefront of their rattled minds.

Between the two employees, they recounted the majority of the past week. Humane societies usually don't deal with a huge flow of foot traffic and it wasn't too difficult for them to go through each day and recall the individuals who stopped in. The lady's face flared to life when she remembered two young women who fit Dom's description of acting "suspicious". I nabbed the images from her, but of course I didn't know these people, so the mental photographs really didn't mean a thing to me. She proceeded to describe what they looked like.

"Do you know them? Do you have their names or phone numbers?" I pushed.

"No, I don't," her frustration escaladed. "We don't write down any personal information unless they adopt a pet. They weren't here for very long, either. They did a walk through, looking at everything, and were definitely interested in the larger dogs. They were undecided on whether to adopt or to view them first and decide later. That's what one of them said. I remember one placed her hand over some of the cage locks...like she was marking them or something...which did seem weird at the time. Oh My God! You know what? Those were the exact cages the missing dogs came out of...I'm sure of it! Those women had to be the same people who broke in here. And since they'd already scoped out the place earlier, they knew in advance which dogs to steal."

She started crying again. The manager held her in his arms to keep her from dropping to the floor. I tried to ease her grief over her realization of the recent events by psychically dampening the emotions but I couldn't remove the memories. What we were discussing was the entire reason why Dom and I were there. My mental manipulation tactics to implant other thoughts didn't fit the situation, either. I couldn't put the idea in her mind of vacationing in Bermuda (to calm and distract her from the current sad state of affairs) and then suddenly strike up a conversation with her pertaining to that sunny visualization. It would only be temporary and everyone would think she'd gone bonkers.

I politely requested if I could take a look around. I knew I had created a mutual respect with them and gained their support in providing any information to help stop the suspected scientists and hired cronies. Dominic kept them occupied while I wandered through the building. Visually, there was nothing unusual due to the break-in. A small, broken window could be associated to the intruders; a common characteristic for gaining access. Then simply unlock the back door and waltz outside for easy removal of the dogs.

    I approached one of the empty cages while dogs barked all around me. I placed one hand on Grandma's quartz hanging from my neck and the other hand on the cage lock. Instantly, the quartz tingled and felt warm in my hand. I moved to another cage that contained smaller dogs and touched the lock. Nothing. The quartz didn't react. Once again, I walked to an empty cage that had kept one of the big dogs and grabbed the lock. The quartz flipped back to warm and tingly.

    I firmly believed that the lady who worked there unknowingly made an accurate guess about the locks being "marked". They literally *were* marked. She thought it was your average thieves doing the dirty work. My little experiment confirmed what we suspected - it was witches. I didn't know enough about witchcraft, yet, but because the witch had touched certain locks, it was probably a trigger of sorts for the locks to easily open for them when they returned to take the dogs. I pictured a witch waving her hands in the air and - poof - all the "marked" locks opened at once, making a quick escape with the dogs. Maybe the locks didn't magically open for them, but I definitely knew she had touched the cages of the dogs that were now gone.

    I squatted in front of a cage to rub some of the dogs prancing about inside. I felt sad seeing them. This was not a no-kill facility and after a certain length of time, dogs and cats would be euthanized. It's just the way it was. And probably another reason the witches chose this place, knowing full well that many of the animals would be killed anyway. I had to work hard to control myself from being overcome with emotions as all the many dogs kept up a never-ending chorus of barking and whining. The cats were in another large room and here and there I heard their meowing.

    I looked behind me and saw the two employees resuming their duties as Dom approached where I knelt on the floor, still petting the dogs. The lady glanced up, met my tear-filled eyes with her own and smiled. She didn't doubt Dom or me and our good intentions. I smiled back but had to look away quickly to avoid a meltdown.

Dom was in my head and silently heard my anguish. He squatted next to me and stuck his hands through the bars to play with the dogs, too. After a few minutes, we got up and moved to another cage and thrust what we could of our hands through the bars to rub a different group of dogs. I noticed one dog had a collar on that was rather tight and that glaring fact bothered me a great deal. I guessed it had been left on after taking the dog for a quick walk. And the collar wasn't choking him by far, just snugger than I would have buckled it if it was on Nicky. As sweet and caring as these people were, I was positive the too snug collar was unintentional, probably placed on him in a hurry. I whispered to Dom and pointed to the dog's neck. I couldn't fix the problem with limited access to the dog; my fingers fumbled and failed. My aggravation was growing by the second.

Dom nudged me and said, "Watch this. *I* can fix it."

Using only his telekinesis power, the collar unbuckled, released one notch and then buckled itself back together. The movements of the collar made you think an invisible man was performing the good deed. I reached for the dog once more, rubbed him on his nose, and stood up at the same time Dom did then gratefully hugged him for his thoughtfulness. He, of course, was thrilled with any extra attention I gave him and hugged me back with probably more intensity than the moment called for.

We thanked the Humane Society workers for their help and promised to do everything within our powers (more than they could comprehend) to find the culprits who committed this awful crime.

The next stop was the magic shop. Witchcraft central. It was on the far side of the city which allowed us plenty of drive time to talk. And that meant an opportunity for Dom to have me all to himself. He had a captive audience as I was stuck in the truck with him. In Daniel's truck, let's not forget. I sensed the onslaught was coming, so I constructed my mental block just in case Daniel was awake and thought to touch my mind with his. Daniel didn't need to hear Dom's pleas to me, again; begging me to leave Daniel and run off into the wild blue yonder with him instead.

I mumbled loudly enough for Dom to hear, "Here it comes. Go ahead. Get it out of your system, Dom."

He frowned, wrinkling his forehead and brows as his eyes narrowed. He confronted me head-on. "I want you…I mean, I wish you weren't so hung up on Daniel and would break off the boyfriend/girlfriend thing. Move away from him. Come back to me-- uh, Highland, your parents. It's so dangerous what you're doing. The more contact you have with the werewolves, the higher the chances of getting accidentally converted into one of them. Hell, just living in their world, and with Daniel's constant influence, you could be persuaded to irrationally *ask* for the conversion. And I'm not saying that we couldn't all still work together on future missions. We could."

Dom tenderly squeezed my left leg while he kept his eyes on the traffic. He wasn't shy about his affection for me and since Daniel was nowhere in sight, he had an advantage. I knew, he knew, Daniel knew; Dominic sincerely cared for me. Well, Dom loved me and had told me so. I loved him, too, but it felt more like a best friend relationship… most of the time…

I sighed but grabbed his hand anyway and squeezed it back. My mixed emotions, actions and thoughts (many he had read) over the past week had given him a tiny drop of hope that maybe, perhaps, it was conceivable, I might jump ship (Daniel's) and climb aboard The Dominic Enterprise! An enormously optimistic smile spread across his face…as he read my thoughts, again. Ahh!! I hated to lead him on and give him false impressions.

Dom turned his attention to maneuvering the streets as I continued to read the directions. We parked half a block down the street from the small shop. Anyone inside could not simply look out the window to see what type of vehicle we had and would have to peer outside to identify our truck.

Dominic and I had anonymity on our side which was to our advantage with infiltrating the tightly knit group of witches. We had just arrived in town, no one knew us and the association between Dom and I and Josiah and Zac (and Tessa) had not been figured out as yet. Josiah and Zac were now considered enemies of the witches. Perhaps all of the witches had not directly seen Josiah and Zac, but I'm sure enough of them did and had burned the images in their minds.

We agreed to erect solid mental blocks in case those in the magic store had mind reading abilities. An eerie feeling washed through me as I crossed the threshold and I casually smiled at Dom. He nodded in agreement with my internal reaction. We felt a psychic awareness of the many magical items and supernatural influences on and in the store.

"Hi! Can I help you find anything?" A peppy welcome addressed us from a young, well-groomed girl who was stocking shelves. She appeared normal to the average person, although I picked up tremendous power radiating from her aura, both psychic and what I would guess to be witchcraft influence. And there was something else...mostly good vibes but an overshadowing of evil. Like she bordered or wavered from one side to the other. Underlying her outward friendliness, she was ridden with guilt and confusion. She wasn't trying to block us; most likely she thought there was no need or danger and chose not to put in the effort to even try. As long as we played our cards right and didn't expose ourselves for who we were, she was ripe for the picking and we'd be able to gain some information from her mind.

I approached her and inquired, "My boyfriend and I recently moved here from out west." Dom was startled that I referred to him as my boyfriend but he recovered instantly as his face beamed. "We're into witchcraft and wondered if you could recommend a local group to join."

"Well..." she stammered.

"I don't broadcast what I'm about to tell you, but we *are* in a magic store, for goodness sakes. Um...I like to dabble in some black magic, too," I announced with a giggle as I touched her arm. That physical contact served two purposes: my psychic sensitivity to her increased and it provided that much-needed human connection. And now we shared a secret, albeit a lie on my part, that I hoped would create a bond and gain her trust.

With extreme caution to not give anything away, she said, "The owner of this store has a group that practices witchcraft...among other things. I'm a member and could find out if we're accepting new recruits."

"That would be great!" Dominic chimed in. "Do you meet here in the shop? It seems like it would be crowded unless you have a back room with more space."

"We get together at another place. This is definitely not roomy enough for what we do," the girl explained with a faraway look in her eyes. She was replaying events in her head.

I tried to dance around topics without blurting out what I really wanted to say. For example, how about the slain dogs drained of blood that was to be used for a resurrection of a demon!? And I had to keep up a solid mental block in case she got suspicious of our questions and decided to read *our* minds. As it stood, we were absorbing oodles of images out of her unguarded mind and so far, she was clueless.

I manipulated a wee bit more information, "Hopefully this place you're referring to is in the general area as we're still not familiar with the city yet. We haven't had a chance to drive the streets, checking things out."

"Hey, did you hear about those dogs drained of blood last night? *There's* a sacrifice in the making! It was all over the news." Dom put on a good act of innocence. I was shocked that he raised that question and the look on the girl's face obviously told us she thought it was too coincidental him asking such a thing. It dawned on me our undercover work could be blown sky high so with a great deal of stealth to remain undetected in her thoughts, I trickled emotions of trust, faith and assurance into her thought patterns. It worked, although she seemed edgy.

She responded, "Yeah, I heard it on the news, too. Not a pretty sight." She kept tight-lipped. But Dom and I got what we came for. We needed to stop prying while we were ahead of the game and before we got caught in our deceit.

To break up the awkwardness and to relax the tension in the room, I offered, "Oh, by the way, my name is Kara and this is Dom."

"I'm Lexy."

"This is really a nice shop! I'll have to check my supplies and see what goodies I want to buy. We'll drop by in about a week to see what you found out about us joining your witchcraft group. Okay? We'll let you get back to work. Thanks, Lexy!" I graciously thanked her, pouring on the sweetness, and after a few more farewells, Dom and I were out the door.

We had plucked from her mind a plethora of useful data. Dom and I shared everything we discovered such as the image of the building where the ritual was to take place. We did not have an exact address but caught the name of the street plus other visuals and clues. That street could be a very lengthy street, though, and we would have to narrow down the correct building before raiding it.

And the night before, when the dogs were drained of blood, the witches *had* actually made an attempt to resurrect their demon. They failed, thank goodness. The ritual had been rushed through, for whatever reason. The main significance and discovery was that dogs' blood won't work. At least, that's what we gathered from Lexy's thoughts. She wasn't involved in the capture of the Humane Society dogs or the slaughter for their blood but she was present at the ritual. Using the dogs for a sacrifice sickened her which placed her loyalty to the coven of witches on shaky ground.

We also learned the witches wanted to try the resurrection ritual again and this time the sacrifice would come from a different source. Blood remained the required offering needed to bring their demon to life. Whatever type of life that could be; I shivered from the possibilities.

Dom and I rushed back to Josiah's house so we could update our team with our findings and create a battle plan.

There wasn't much time…according to what we gathered from Lexy's mind, the next ritual to raise a demon into our world was scheduled for the following night.

CHAPTER 9
CURSE

Dom and I arrived back at Josiah's house in the late afternoon. Zac was still gone until the next night dealing with Tessa's memorial. We needed to rouse the supernatural powerhouses from their naps. Isaac had flopped on the couch, Daniel was in our upstairs bedroom and Josiah slept in a spare bedroom in the finished basement. Dom wanted to change out of his heavy shirt and offered to wake up Daniel since the rooms were right next to each other.

As Dom went upstairs, I realized neither of us chose to enter the basement to wake up Josiah. Surely he'd hear all the footsteps and show himself in a second. Or maybe he felt extra secure resting with the addition of the werewolves in the house. And Dom and I weren't a threat to him. The mere fact that we had returned might not automatically rip him out of his deep sleep since we weren't the enemy.

Feeling gutsy and curious, I crossed the threshold leading down into the basement, to Josiah's sleeping quarters. I found myself creeping down the steps, quiet as a mouse, and tiptoed to his room. His door was wide open, which surprised me. Perhaps he didn't like the feeling of being trapped or contained behind a closed door. And he was not sleeping in a creepy coffin like I'd seen in so many movies. I stood inside the doorframe and stared at him in amazement.

Josiah was stretched out on his back, eyes closed. His tall body barely fit on the single bed. No blankets were needed as he could regulate his body temperature. He didn't wear pajamas (could you really picture a vampire in pajamas anyway?!) but wore old, faded, holey jeans and a sleeveless, white tank. Of course, he oozed with the essence of coolness and looked hot all at the same time. He probably considered those his slumming clothes compared to his active clothes of choice: everything all black including the long trench coat that billowed in the wind. Very gothic, but served his purpose for blending into the night.

I moved closer to observe him in this state of relaxation and vulnerability. It wasn't quite dark outside yet and he had said that during the daylight hours his supernatural powers were significantly diminished. I could see now, as he slept in front of me, why an enemy would seek out a vampire's lair during the day to kill him. A vampire wouldn't have his full strength and chances were high he'd be sleeping. The slayer would have a definite advantage in making a quick kill. I wasn't so sure with Josiah…he could be quite active during daylight hours and still retained a great deal of his strength, as far as vampires go.

Then why wasn't he waking up? I didn't like that instant realization. I almost felt angry at Josiah for allowing himself to become such an easy target. What the heck was wrong with him? Shouldn't he be guarding himself better? Heck, I just walked right up to him. What with the witches knowing what he was, we didn't need any of them sneaking in here and chopping his head off. It was one thing to visualize killing an evil vampire in his vulnerable state and feeling satisfied to rid the world of any of his future sadistic acts of violence. But Josiah was not that creature. He was not evil. I wanted him to stay alive.

Josiah had explained to me that I should never hesitate waking him up whenever I needed him…just another few seconds…to look at him…to appreciate this being for what he was. He seemed so human and at peace lying on the bed.

These supernatural creatures, both vampires and werewolves, all had physically fit bodies that would make most athletes cry with jealousy. It was part of the package deal, their biological make-up, the way and the reason they lived so long, their mysterious chemistry. Werewolves didn't physically age beyond about 30 and vampires stopped around 35, maybe 40 years old. Their bodies constantly regenerated, which understandably created healthy, strong, sexy, muscular physiques. Basically perfect.

My fingers automatically reached out to touch Josiah's face but I pulled back before making the contact. My hand just hovered in the air, not sure of what direction to take, then moved to feather my fingers down the length of his arm. I wanted to awaken him gently, carefully, compassionately...

Well before I even finished that thought, I was flat on my back, on Josiah's bed. He had one hand wrapped around my neck and the other holding my arms above my head as he straddled me. I wasn't able to move anything but my legs and decided it was best to be still and not fight.

I closed my eyes and focused on my quartz necklace...but it remained neutral. It wasn't giving off a warning. I was just attacked by a vampire - but nothing emitted from the quartz. I felt confused, opened my eyes and Josiah smiled at me with such a cocky attitude I wanted to hit him.

In my mind I heard Josiah say, *Kara, Kara. As your thoughts are not easily hidden from me, I must say I'm impressed with your observations, grateful for your concern and want to thank you for all the compliments I received, indirectly, from you.*

You weren't sleeping? I mentally threw back at him.

He took his hands off my neck and wrists, but continued to hold me down by my shoulders. *I <u>was</u> sleeping until you entered my room. But your mind was blasting out such interesting thoughts, I decided to listen. Plus I wanted to teach you a valuable lesson.*

I was still confused. I asked, *Why didn't my quartz react to you? I thought it helped to protect me? To keep negative energy away?*

Josiah spoke out loud and with heartfelt conviction. "You already know the answer...I am not evil. The quartz senses that. I won't hurt you. I promise I will do all I can to keep you from any type of harm. But that doesn't mean I can't have a little fun. I am a vampire, after all. You truly are special and I care a great deal for you. Don't worry...I'm not trying to lure you away from Daniel. I don't think I could have a relationship like the two of you do, although I do have odd pangs of jealousy once in a while about it. And so, I enjoy flirting with you... pushing the limits a bit. This is such a unique opportunity for me to play, to tease, to feel emotions as I do when I'm around you. Is that so bad? To have a human, you - Kara, know what I am without having to alter your memories to make you forget, to engage in conversation with you and have mutual respect for each other, to fight together on the same side against evil. None of those things are meant to hurt you."

Josiah's eyes burned into me as he attempted to get his point across and he no longer boasted a cocky expression. He bent to my ear and whispered, "I've lived a very long time and life can become dreary. To have you be some part of it now keeps me grounded and it gives me more purpose, Kara. I find you intriguing. Keep in mind, I do like to play. Just a little."

Before he released me, he kissed my neck, lingering right where my pulse throbbed in violent beats and where I imagined it was the sweet spot for vampires to have their little drink. He moved off of me and grabbed my hand to pull me to my feet. Someone was approaching and he didn't want a conflict with being caught sitting on top of me on his bed. I engaged in conversation to help cover the awkwardness.

"What was the lesson you wanted to teach me?" I quizzed him. I doubted his confession had anything to do with this lesson he had yet to explain to me.

Daniel waltzed right into Josiah's room without a second thought. "Hey, is everything okay?" He looked back and forth from Josiah to me.

"We're good," I confessed. Well, it was the truth. "I had just asked Josiah a question, though, about learning a lesson."

Josiah took his cue. "Yes, two lessons actually. Lesson One: strive to better shield your mind, although it's doubtful you'll ever completely keep me out, but I should at least feel some resistance from you. You are an open book, which I find rather alluring, but the witches, or other mind-readers, could find it useful if they'd discover who you're working with. If your mental block is weak, they could cast some nasty spells on you, too. Lesson Two is to never assume a vampire is such a deep sleeper that he's not aware when somebody enters his lair, especially a human being. We can smell your delectable blood from a distance before we even see you. I will admit in my particular situation that since the premises were rather secure in the first place, and I know you are no threat to me, I internally toned down my alarm system until you walked through my door. Then, as I said earlier, your thoughts were so darned entertaining, I faked sleeping for a while longer to simply listen."

I scowled at Josiah while he tried to keep from laughing. Daniel looked at us like he'd missed the punch line to a joke. He decided to bring the attention back to what Dominic and I had learned for the day during our jaunts to the Humane Society and the magic shop.

The team assembled in the living room and I dove into describing the sensation I felt and the reaction of the quartz when I had touched certain cages at the Humane Society. Confirmation in the involvement of witches. Dom and I took turns relaying the story about the magic shop, Lexy and our invaluable readings we snatched from her thoughts.

Tonight was New Year's Eve. There would be no ringing in the New Year for any of us. Instead, we discussed what to do next and laid out our plans. Zac wouldn't return until the next night and we'd have to fill him in on the spot. Dom reminded us that Zac was an ex-Navy SEAL and should be able to instinctively adapt to his surroundings and to whatever was thrown at him.

In a little over 24 hours the next attempt at the resurrection would be performed.

* * * *

The next morning we jumped into Daniel's extended cab truck to start scouring the buildings located on the street Dom and I had seen flash through Lexy's mind. We made sure to share these images with Daniel, Josiah and Isaac so they could "see" what we had seen and everyone could be on the lookout. I sat squished in between Daniel and Dominic on the front seat. Since Josiah had sensitivity to light, he stayed on the back seat with Isaac.

We cruised down the street allowing Lexy's mental snapshot of the area to guide us to finding the exact building. Confidence was high. She had no idea Dom and I were psychic and could read her mind. Prompting her about a local meeting place for the witches automatically triggered her to think of their newest location. Our minds viewed this information as if we were holding a real photograph, taking quick glimpses and comparing that to what our eyes actually were seeing on the street.

It didn't take long. I think everyone spotted the building at the same time, pointed and blurted, "That's it!"

We couldn't scope it out any further for fear of either being seen, caught in the act of breaking and entering, leaving evidence that we had been there or even setting off some black magic alarm system alerting the coven we had sniffed them out. If the witches knew we were onto them and we were planning to raid their resurrection party, they'd look for another location. We'd have to start from zero all over again. If our cover was blown, I doubt we'd get so lucky to figure out their next move instantaneously and the level of danger would increase.

So, there we sat, about half a block away, gawking at the very old, vacant structure with the "For Sale or Lease" sign hanging at a forty-five degree angle in the window. We guessed the witches were either temporarily renting the building or more likely had used witchcraft to unlock a door at the back entrance and were trespassing on the property, like squatters.

Daniel drove around the block twice, slowing but never stopping when we were adjacent to the store, giving us the opportunity to memorize or take note of anything important for the upcoming raid. It was New Year's Day, the traffic was light and we didn't want to stick out like a sore thumb driving around and around the block. We didn't think any of the witches were in the building at that time. None of us felt any strange vibes or evilness in the air. Dom and I believed the ritual would be held at or around midnight. We had the entire day to dwell and plot over this ordeal.

Daniel sighed and said, "We might as well go back to Josiah's house until later tonight. We can't let the witches know that we know what their intentions are. Zac should be back by supper and we'll have to bring him up to speed. It's going to be rough on him and I hope he'll be able to concentrate on the mission. I can't get over that Tessa is gone…dead. And poor Zac jumping right back into this mess a day after her memorial."

I offered, "Maybe it would help if Dom and I linked our minds with Zac's when he gets back? And then we could relay to him the important images of the building and any discussions we had throughout the day."

"That's an excellent idea," Josiah approved. "I will offer my assistance, too. If Zac gives his permission, I will help familiarize him with what we observed today. I was with him when Tessa was killed and watched him suffer extreme grief and anger during and after her death. Strange… it feels like a type of bond I have with him."

Everyone sat in silence for the remainder of the drive to Josiah's house, except for a stray sniffle here and there, most of which came from me.

Once back inside, talk fired up on how to best go about ending this insane resurrection ritual without the witches turning on us. We did not want a reenactment of what happened to Tessa to happen to one of us. Josiah had explained she had triggered some kind of perimeter spell that alerted the witches to intruders and the next thing they knew, Tessa's neck was broken. Josiah believed the witch who actually broke her neck had not meant to take it that far but didn't have her black magic power under control. That witch had only wanted to threaten and scare, not to murder anyone, as the expression on her face revealed before a door was slammed in Zac and Josiah's faces.

Either way, these particular witches were dangerous, especially if they were messing with black magic and didn't know how to contain it. Daniel quickly brought up his concern about that fact and three humans would be involved on this raid: me, Dom and Zac. Daniel, Isaac and Josiah, the supernatural beings, weren't *as* susceptible to the spells as humans; they had built-in warning systems and could usually block out spells or move fast enough to stop the witch mid-spell before completing it.

"Dealing with this black magic is making me nervous," Daniel thought out loud. "This is very different than tackling another werewolf or a vampire. It seems so unpredictable. What happens when we stroll in tonight and that one witch...what's her name? Lexy? Well, what happens when Lexy recognizes Kara and Dominic from the magic shop? Don't you think she's going to feel betrayed and want immediate revenge? I'm sure she knows Kara and Dom are human and could be ensnared in some twisted spell faster than a werewolf or vampire could be. And several witches would remember Zac and Josiah from the last run-in days ago when Tessa was killed. Keep in mind; several of these witches descend from the actual coven that cast the werewolf curse onto Isaac and me. Who says they might not pull that trick out of their hats and turn the humans into wolves tonight? And do we even know *what* kind of demon is being resurrected?"

"If I'm turned into a werewolf tonight then so be it," I blurted.

Every head turned to look at me in complete shock and horror.

I babbled on, not completely sure of myself, but tried to sound brave. "Well, everyone knows I've been considering that option. You know, being converted into a werewolf!? No bite necessary, Daniel. If I'm *cursed* to be a werewolf, then no decision has to be made on my part to do it or not…to have you turn me. I won't have to make up my mind; it will be made up for me by the witches at that point. Right? And the crazy witches will think "ha ha"- they showed us because they whammied me with the werewolf curse. But they don't know I had been toying with the idea anyway, so maybe in some sadistic way, they would've done me a favor."

"Stop! Stop talking that way! You don't realize what you're saying and how *you're* the one sounding crazy!" Dominic shouted at me. He was ticked off with my nonchalant attitude.

Daniel shook his head in disbelief. His teeth clenched and he looked away from me for a few seconds. Then he stomped right up to me and firmly grabbed my shoulders, lifting me up onto the tips of my toes. All the men kept their eyes on Daniel and had taken protective positions to come to my aid if Daniel became violent. He was aware of being the center of attention and lessened his hold on me so my feet could touch the ground.

To prove a point in front of everyone, Daniel proclaimed, "Kara, I love you and this is not how I want this decision to be made. I don't want it forced on you. It is your choice, as I've said all along, and have never tried to push you in one direction or the other on whether you want to be converted into a werewolf. I can tell, everyone here can tell, you are simply not making sense. You are making light of an extremely serious situation. Have you forgotten about Dominic and Zac? They are human. If these witches have the ability to cast the Lycaeonia Curse, then they, too, would be cursed along with yourself.

Do you want that for them?"

I started to cry and leaned into Daniel's chest. The guys shifted uneasily in the room, recognizing Daniel was not going to hurt me after all, and glanced away from us.

"No, I don't want Dom and Zac to be cursed or for anything stupid to happen," I stopped crying and wanted to explain. "I'm sorry. I just don't want anyone to be worried about me, especially since I'm the only girl, and then end up screwing up whatever it is they *should* be focused on and get hurt themselves in the end. But it still holds true that I'm considering the conversion…and everyone here *does* know that."

"Baby, I know," Daniel hugged me and in a low voice, which everyone heard regardless, he spoke sweetly next to my ear, "But if that's what you decide, to become a werewolf, I don't want it to happen at the hands of an evil witch who cursed you. I want you to come to me and tell me that is what you want. If or when *you* are ready, at a time and a place that *you* are comfortable with. I want to be the one who converts you."

I bobbed my head up and down and snuck in a quick kiss. I was impressed that Daniel had let everyone see this show of affection and surprised that he hadn't waited till we were alone. Of course, this was also a show of possession to the other men. I had seen it before with Daniel. It was part of his animal side; a natural, protective instinct for his mate.

"I'm going to puke if I have to see or hear anymore of this between you two," Dom stated. "Look - we are speculating wildly about what the witches may or may not do. Let's go over the building layout and plan some strategic moves."

By evening, Zac made his entrance. We did not linger on the topic of how things went with Tessa's memorial, how he had to deal with both families or the time he spent taking care of some of her belongings and paperwork. Zac's behavior indicated he needed to immerse himself into this mission and get this situation with the witches resolved. He would return home at a later date to finish up anything further pertaining to Tessa's death.

Zac allowed, without any flinching or hesitation, Dom, Josiah and me to psychically show him images of the building and to relay most of the tactical discussions of the day. He was charged up and ready for action. Daniel and Josiah had made the decision that it might be best to have Zac play the role of a sniper as he had experience in this area. He would remain in the shadows as much as possible and only emerge if absolutely necessary. His job was to shoot anyone that physically attacked our team or attempted to use witchcraft directly on our team. Shoot to maim, but if anyone on our team was in lethal danger, then shoot to kill. And if a resurrection managed to raise a flesh and blood demon, Zac's order was to take the thing out without even thinking about it.

Daniel looked at Dom and me. "The two of you are to stay in the shadows, completely out of sight of those witches. And I mean that. Hopefully that will keep you out of danger from their spells. If they don't realize you're there, then they shouldn't direct any spells at you and it won't blow your cover with Lexy. Use your psychic abilities whenever and *if* you can, but do so discreetly to avoid being caught in the act."

It was nearing midnight. We had to time the raid just right.

I mustered together every ounce of willpower and kick-butt determination. "Let's roll, boys."

CHAPTER 10
RISING

The resurrection needed to be almost complete in order to permanently kill the demon. We could not attack until it fully materialized, but had not yet reached its full strength; therefore, it was safer and easier to slay. Once the threat from the demon was eliminated, Dom and I planned on popping out of the shadows, and along with Josiah's compulsion ability, make our move with a little mental manipulation on the witches. We'd try to change their perspective in dealing with black magic and the harm it can cause. If they felt the urge or need to use witchcraft then whip up some good, constructive spells but chill out with the evil stuff. Obviously, *that* would be the ideal scenario…

If we arrived too early, we speculated the witches would stop the resurrection, engage us in a show of power and hastily make their escape. All that would do is delay the resurrection for another time and place and we'd have to start all over tracking down their next, newest location. The witches weren't going to give up, and seemed almost obsessed in their conviction to successfully bring this demon to life. For what reason they wanted a demon stomping about, we had yet to discover. Josiah guessed it related to gaining ultimate power and control. Greed. This scenario was *not* the ideal outcome.

If we arrived too late, and the resurrection ritual succeeded, then we'd have a demon unleashed on the world. We'd be unaware of what type of power, supernatural or otherwise, it possessed and what kind of damage it could do until it engaged us in battle. Who knew if the witches would be able to contain and control this demon? Highly unlikely…and if they could, they'd sic the demon on us so we'd be out of their way…dead. This scenario was absolutely, positively *not* the ideal outcome!

Daniel's extended cab pick-up truck was our mode of transportation as it was roomier than Zac's SUV or Josiah's sports car. But cramming six bodies into the vehicle did not agree with Josiah so he chose to transform into an owl and would meet us at the final destination. Not one of us acted shy about watching him make the transformation and no one was disappointed in the show. Even Daniel and Isaac, who were quite familiar with transforming into wolves, were impressed with the swiftness and grace of Josiah's shape shifting, and his confidence in his ability as he flew away into the night. He would beat us to the location with the advantage to fly straight there with no traffic lights or other distractions. We hurried into the truck and took off, not wanting to make Josiah wait too long for us plus hoping to time our raid on the witches for the optimum results.

We parked across the street from the old building. Josiah stepped out from the darkness and under a streetlight, giving us a single wave to approach him. Without speaking, we walked around to the back of the building and spotted a door.

Josiah spoke in our minds, *The witches are here. Can everyone sense them?*

Zac looked frustrated. He was the only one that didn't have some form of psychic ability. The werewolves didn't have much, but could sense that something wasn't right, something evil permeated this area. Not only that, but with their heightened senses, along with Josiah's, they could pick up distant sounds and scents indicating the ritual was being performed as we stood there. Dom was trying to focus on Lexy, not able to read her mind but snatching up a word or image every few seconds. I sensed dread and fear pulsing through Lexy and was able to pick up what sounded like an incantation.

I grabbed Zac's hands. Josiah immediately understood what I was doing and placed one hand on Zac's arm. By doing this we created a powerful mind link with Zac that about knocked him off his feet. Daniel and Isaac steadied Zac so he wouldn't collapse. Josiah and I opened our minds and fully shared with Zac what we were feeling and hearing from inside the building and clued him in on what type of situation we were about to walk in on for his own knowledge and safety. Everyone needed to be on the same page, to work as a team. Zac was at a bit of a disadvantage, let alone his emotional turmoil over Tessa.

Josiah stiffened. *I smell human blood. Free-flowing. They must be cutting themselves and using their own blood for the sacrificial offering. We need to move now!*

The door was locked. Dominic gave it one quick look and used his telekinetic ability to slide the deadbolt open. Josiah held up one hand in a warning gesture to prevent us from charging inside and touched a finger to his lips reminding us to stay quiet and use telepathy to speak.

Daniel questioned him, *Is there a boundary spell? Will we trigger an alarm?*

I think there is one but it's weak, Josiah relayed. *They need tremendous concentration for the resurrection and aren't able to effectively maintain other spells.*

I had an idea. *How about using my quartz? It's supposed to disperse negative energy. Right now it's very warm and glowing. It senses danger and is warning me, I think.*

Toss it across the threshold, Josiah instructed. *As you do, envision a spell dissolving and a safe passage. Your grandmother was a witch, maybe you inherited a little of her talent.*

I crouched down two feet outside the entrance. I mentally reached out to the team, to draw on their additional strength. I did as Josiah said, picturing a wall that I literally wished away, breaking the spell so we could enter unharmed and undetected. With a shuffle-board motion, I zipped the necklace through the entrance, over the threshold. It settled on the floor fifteen feet away and the steady radiance had now paled in brightness to a dim glow, which to me was a good sign.

Satisfied that the spell had dissipated at our point of entry, Josiah gave one nod that signaled we were clear to go. He sensed a positive change in the atmosphere surrounding the door and believed the quartz did the trick. Dom and I brought up the rear, making sure to stay several paces behind the rest of the team and to remain in the shadows while they confronted the witches, the demon and whatever else we walked in on.

The building appeared to have once been a small, neighborhood grocery store. Remainders of shelving units, leftover milk crates, three rusty shopping carts and signage items littered the area on both sides of us. Luckily, a few night lights were on which helped to illuminate the interior and saved me from tripping or kicking something. With incredible stealth, we crept through a stock room and an office like professional burglars. The next area revealed the huge, wide-open space where groceries would have been found when the store was in operation.

That's where the resurrection ritual was taking place. The chanting reverberated in my ears and sent chills down my spine. I smelled herbs and burning candles and a revolting odor of decay. We stayed hidden in the darkness for another moment, gathering our bearings as we observed the witches. Dom and I wouldn't leave that spot when the others decided to raid the scene. The only electrical source of lighting came from one fluorescent fixture hanging on the far left side of the store. The front windows had been covered with sheets of brown paper. Many, many shelving and display units were shoved to the front of the store to create plenty of floor space for the ritual and to add another layer of concealment from the outside world. There must have been fifty candles lit around them.

The witches were totally oblivious to our presence while they recited the incantation. They stood within a large circle that had been traced on the floor along with other painted symbols and letters. We were looking at their right sides, although they were turned enough for us to see some of their backsides. That was an advantage as opposed to trying to rush them face on.

A cold wind whipped through the building. The candles flickered; a few went out. The air sizzled and a section of the floor cracked. A vaporous outline was taking shape in front of them but the chanting never stopped, instead it grew in volume and intensity. My pounding heart and rapid breathing seemed compelled to match the rhythm of the chant. Josiah shook my arm when he noticed the signs that I was slipping into a trance.

Daniel and Isaac stripped off their clothes and tossed them to me. Silently they transformed into the true werewolf shape of the beast and were ready for action. My quartz necklace that I was wearing once again, felt hot on my skin. Not burning, but it got my attention. I peeked at it under my shirt and it emitted a solid glow.

Blood dripped from several of the witches' hands. All wore black, hooded robes that covered the length of their bodies and brushed the tops of their feet, making it impossible to identify who was who. Then one witch stepped forth from the rest, but did not leave the protection of the painted circle. This particular witch seemed to be the leader, as the others followed any commands given in conjuring the demon. Suddenly, all the hoods were pulled back, revealing each individual.

The leader was a man, not a woman.

We were shocked. Josiah held back gasping. He mentally fed us information, *Logan. A powerful wizard and a necromancer. I thought he died years ago.*

Logan sliced his hand with a blade letting a stream of blood mingle with the still-forming demon. This entity, although not solid yet, resembled a werewolf in beast form, only taller, more massive in bulk, very gruesome…and murderous. The demon looked around at the witches, the room, its own claws, not sure what to make of it all. Logan prompted the witches to continue the incantation as they were so close to completing the resurrection and conjuring a complete, physical body.

I turned to Daniel and Isaac who stood side by side, ready to charge. *Why does that thing sort of look like you two?*

No time for talk. Let's do it, Daniel ordered and Josiah agreed.

Josiah, Daniel and Isaac swooped in at super-human speed. They had to remember that the idea wasn't to kill the witches, but the demon. Although, if the witches attacked and tried to kill them, then the war was on and anything could happen at that point. Kill or be killed.

Dom and I didn't move a muscle in the dark. No worry about exposing ourselves as we were too terrified to budge. We desperately tried to access the witches' minds with no luck besides sensing their confusion and fear. Even Lexy, who we'd contacted at the magic shop, was closed to us as far as reading her mind to learn anything that might give The Liaison team an edge in this predicament. The witches freaked out when two werewolves and a vampire appeared out of nowhere, interrupting their ritual, and that fact alone overwhelmed their thoughts.

In his mind, I told Dominic, *Put your arms around me. The quartz might include you in warding off negative vibes and help hide our presence here.*

I didn't have to tell him twice. Dom slid snugly behind me and encircled his arms around my waist, staring over my shoulder at the scene unfolding before our eyes. Daniel would have to understand that Dom was holding me to try to absorb any protection my quartz could provide us.

Josiah's outer persona changed to fit the situation as he portrayed the classic vampire ready to take a bite out of someone's neck if they didn't do as he wanted them to do. But it was difficult, if not impossible, for him to compel thirteen witches, which included Logan, to do his bidding. Josiah only put forth a basic compulsion to stay back and to not interfere, hoping he could gain extra seconds for Daniel or Isaac so they could get close enough to kill the demon. It worked on the majority of the witches.

Except on Logan. He was a super strong necromancer and waved off Josiah's compulsion like a fly.

I heard Logan mutter, "Josiah. Well, well. What an unpleasant surprise."

Dom and I saw a flash of the violent images bursting forth from Logan's mind and his intention to kill Josiah. Dom's arm flung out, but kept to the darkness, as he used his telekinesis and knocked over two large candles in front of Logan which made him jump to the side to keep his robe from catching on fire. The quick-thinking move on Dom's part prevented Logan from piercing Josiah's heart with the ancient, carved sword that he gripped firmly in his hand and had concealed under the robe. This move wouldn't have killed Josiah, but would have immobilized him, allowing Logan to go for the kill by cutting his head off or setting him on fire.

Immediately I forced myself to focus on entering Logan's mind. To try to manipulate his thoughts and redirect his actions and emotions before someone, someone I cared for, was killed. Mistake. Logan paused. And he looked right in our direction even as we remained hidden in the shadows. Dom realized then what I was trying to do and shook me as he squeezed tightly against me, making me pull away from Logan's mind before I was caught. I had hit a mental block that actually gave me a sharp pain in my head. Dom caught up my hands with his and reached for the quartz so we both held it, hoping for some kind of protection.

And now Logan suspected someone besides Josiah had tried to mess with his mind. Josiah knew this, too, and redirected Logan's attention to the fight at hand, away from Dom and me. Most of the other witches scampered out of the battle zone, so completely in shock and scared to death, never expecting to have three supernatural beings crash their secret demon resurrection. We didn't think any even had their wits together to conjure up a spell to aid their side of the fight. Luckily.

My eyes shifted to Daniel who wielded a long, wicked blade; perhaps it was considered a medium-length sword. Isaac brought along a similar weapon. Both were capable of cutting the demon's head off in one fast swoosh, thus killing it. Afterwards, Josiah had intended to cart off the head and burn it to prevent any further attempts at a resurrection.

Daniel and Isaac were a few feet away from the demon that now appeared to be in solid form. Daniel didn't hesitate as he charged the creature, swinging his razor-sharp blade with perfect accuracy aimed at the neck. At the exact same time, Isaac ran up behind the demon and ripped his sword horizontally through the back and spine. Between the two of them, that thing was going down with the sweet sound of blades singing through the air.

And air was all that they encountered. Daniel and Isaac were anticipating the impact on their swords when making contact with the demon's body, but instead met with no resistance and pirouetted in a full circle. Both lost their balance but righted themselves before hitting the floor. Their werewolf agility came into play and readied them for the next move. The only problem was the demon had not truly materialized after all, so they couldn't kill it.

Everyone had assumed, while we watched in the shadows as it took shape, that the ritual had succeeded and that the men needed to swarm in right then while they still had the upper hand. Kill it before it was at full strength and could move freely about. But, the resurrection seemed stuck in limbo. Something was missing or was not performed precisely right, and would not allow the demon to take a solid form. From our viewpoint it looked substantial enough to make us believe it was alive and existing in our world.

I had all but forgotten about Zac. He stood a few feet from me and made a forward motion out of the shadows and towards where the action was taking place. Daniel and Isaac took another swipe at the air where the demon's ghostly figure still lingered. Logan and Josiah ceased fighting for the moment to comprehend what was happening... or not happening.

Zac lost it. He recognized one of the witches. All of a sudden he was running the distance to get to them, toting his gun, bellowing, "You killed her! It was you that killed Tessa! Now it's your turn to die!"

A major life-changing tragedy struck within seconds. And it wasn't for the witch.

As Zac moved in to fire his gun at Tessa's murderer, Daniel intercepted him and they fell to the ground in a struggle. Daniel was still in full beast form and had to try subduing Zac without hurting him with his supernatural strength. Zac's adrenaline was flying sky high and he managed to escape Daniel's grasp. Before Zac made it one step, Daniel lunged at his leg and caught it with one of his claws which unintentionally dug deep into Zac's flesh.

Zac kicked with his free leg in an attempt to break loose and then spun his body around and pointed the gun at Daniel...and fired. The bullet penetrated Daniel's arm. Being so mentally linked with him, I felt the searing pain the moment he was shot. I knew he'd live and heal quickly from this wound, but I couldn't help the terror that ripped through me.

This whole thing was so falling apart! The Liaison didn't want to gain a reputation as being killers or terminators. We'd have to change our name! Our goal was to intervene, mediate and neutralize paranormal situations or disputes in as non-aggressive ways as possible. To try to save the ones who hadn't yet turned wholly evil. If that failed, then remove the evil in any way necessary. In Zac's mind, that witch, who I didn't know her name yet, *was* evil. She killed Tessa. You know, maybe he had a point. With her black magic, she had broken Tessa's neck.

Daniel released Zac's leg and both jumped up on their feet like ninjas. Zac started to turn once again on the witches, primed to kill, but Daniel had him in his grip and knocked the gun from his hand. Zac reared his clenched fist and punched Daniel in the face...a very, very bad move on Zac's part.

Zac didn't want to fight Daniel. That was not his intention at all. He only wanted Daniel to let go of him. That witch was a cold-blooded murderer and he wanted vengeance over Tessa's death. His memory of Tessa's neck snapping that night as he held her and to look up into the face of her killer...one he now recognized standing not too many feet away, it was asking too much of him to just let it go.

Zac's knuckles hit Daniel's jaw square on...and grazed Daniel's sharp, pointy teeth. Werewolf teeth, let's not forget, as Daniel was in the shape of the beast. Teeth that can turn a human into a werewolf from a bite or even a mere scratch.

The knuckles were definitely cut as blood trickled down Zac's hand. Everybody in that room knew what chain of events had been put into play and things were close to erupting. Many witches decided it was time to leave and ran from the room in fear. No one wanted to be near Zac with what was about to happen.

But the icing on the cake was still to come.

As Zac and Daniel staggered apart, Zac stumbled into what remained of the demon's apparition. It dissolved and faded into nothingness when Zac fell through it...but before it completely disappeared, a small wisp of the demon's specter drifted into Zac's body. He collapsed on the floor and started having a seizure.

The few remaining witches who witnessed this last catastrophe were on their way out of the building by now. The demon resurrection had failed. No need to hang around while a newly transformed werewolf possibly mixed with a dash of demon was about to make his grand appearance and could turn lethal on everyone in his path.

Logan recognized that this party was over. It never really took hold. He left the developing scene with a cheesy flash of smoke concealing his exit. With the immediate area concealed in a haze, his voice thundered and echoed in the room, "This isn't over yet! The King will rise!"

Everyone waved away the smoky air and rushed to aid Zac. He convulsed on the floor and tried to fight the werewolf conversion.

Chapter 11
Transformation

Josiah firmly held Zac's head to keep it from smashing onto the hard floor as the convulsions continued. I tossed Daniel and Isaac their clothes so they could quickly dress after they transformed back to human shape. Before Daniel shifted, he dug out the bullet in his arm with a long dagger-like fingernail. A shiver ran through me as the spent bullet fell away, and in the next instant, a human, naked Daniel was dressing in front of me in record time. Blood trickled down his arm but it didn't seem to bother him, just an inconvenience for the moment. Daniel joined Isaac where he knelt on the floor and both grabbed Zac's arms and legs in an effort to keep him from hurting himself.

Dom and I bent down to be near Zac but Josiah threw his arm out and yelled, "Stay back! Zac's dangerous right now! We're having a hard time just keeping him still."

Daniel stressed, "He's just begun the conversion process…" Zac thrashed his head violently from side to side in Josiah's hands. "And some element of that demon absorbed into his body. We have no idea what Zac might be capable of or what the transformation will do to him. Dom, Kara - don't come near him."

Josiah's solid black eyes locked onto mine then Dom's for a few brief seconds. Suddenly, we felt compelled to follow his exact command. In fact, we found ourselves stepping backwards about fifteen feet. Josiah glanced at Daniel to gauge his reaction and both looked at me with concern. Daniel nodded in silent agreement. At first I was angry that Josiah took control of my mind and that Daniel seemed okay with the compulsion…but as I helplessly watched Zac's involuntary movements, I understood Josiah only wanted to protect us.

And all because Dom and I were human. The supernatural beings constantly had to look out for us. We were a liability to them and to ourselves by being involved. I kept telling myself over and over to not make a big deal of this. But the way Daniel, Josiah and Isaac had looked at us when we walked too close to Zac...they didn't want us to complicate the situation or make matters worse by having Zac scratch or attack us.

Inwardly I sighed. Dominic sensed my confusion and hurt as he picked up on my thoughts. He sent a mental message that felt like a slap, *Stop with the guilt trip. Now's not the time to let your thoughts wander. Stay focused.*

I snapped out of my daze just as Daniel threw the truck keys to Dom and said, "You're driving."

Daniel, Isaac and Josiah carried Zac out through the back door; the same way we had entered the building. Dom and I ran ahead to unlock the truck. They managed to get him across the street and hoisted him and themselves into the bed of the truck, all the while Zac twisted and fought in their arms. Dom slammed the tailgate closed and lowered the camper shell window. I clambered into the back seat while Dom fired up the truck. We didn't have any options but to return to Josiah's house and let Zac ride out the conversion.

Daniel tapped on the slider window of the cab. I fumbled with the latch and opened it. He asked, "Can you work with Josiah to calm Zac's mind? Distract him somehow. We don't want him to fully convert into a werewolf until we're able to get him safely inside the basement."

I sat on my knees, peering into the bed of the truck and held on to the back of the seat to keep from falling. Zac's hands were already partially transformed into claws. Daniel had removed Zac's shoes to keep them from bursting apart and to lessen the feeling of being confined. It appeared that his feet couldn't decide whether to transform or not and were in a state of flux. He screamed in absolute agony.

When Daniel turned into a werewolf - beast or wolf form - it always happened in the blink of an eye. This was not the case for Zac, since this was his actual conversion from human into a werewolf plus mixing in whatever demon traits he may have absorbed. He was becoming a different species/being/kind/race/creature...whatever you wanted to call him; it all meant the same thing. And this was his first transformation...it was terrifying.

I sought out Zac's mind to soothe him and in horror, I cried to Josiah, "I can't make a connection! I can't get in!"

Josiah answered telepathically, *I will compel him...force him to surrender to me and obey my command. In his state, he isn't going to like that and it won't last long. That's your window of opportunity to shine, Kara.*

Dom could not help me as his attention was centered on driving us back to Josiah's as fast as possible. Daniel and Isaac were doing everything in their power to restrain Zac. Neither could concentrate enough to lend me any real mental backup support. Josiah had a grip on Zac, too, but since psychic power was one of his specialties, he had the capacity to physically and mentally overpower Zac. Josiah was the strongest, even if it was just for little fragments of time during Zac's conversion. So, it was just Josiah and me.

I closed my eyes and linked with Josiah so I would know the exact moment Zac's defenses were down. Josiah packed quite a punch. An explosion of pain ripped through Zac's skull and stunned him to the point that his back arched upward and dropped to the bed of the truck with a heavy thud. With his mental block down, I plunged deep into Zac's mind, calling out to him...

Zac, it's Kara. I want to help you. Zac...can you hear me?

Nothing...I placed my hand over the quartz necklace, but couldn't hold onto it and the backseat at the same time.

Zac, focus on my voice. Listen to me and nothing else. Let me calm you and quiet your mind and body. I kept surrounding him with comforting thoughts: warm spring days lounging under a shade tree; the feel and smell of a gentle breeze; the sound of birds tweeting over his head; a light rain shower ending with a vibrant rainbow; leaves in the fall changing to brilliant shades of red, orange and yellow; the taste of freshly-made pumpkin pie with a dollop of whipped topping; snuggling under cozy blankets on a cold winter's day; fluffy snowflakes sprinkling on his head; and our friendship that overflowed with the love and concern I felt for him.

I visualized, projected and implanted these images, thoughts and emotions with so much intensity that I felt tears running down my face. Josiah and I upheld this strange suspended state of conversion for Zac as best as we could, simply by distracting him for the approximate ten minutes it took to get to Josiah's house. At least it was the middle of the night, the streets were empty, and Dom was able to floor it all the way. But the conversion would happen no matter what and we could not stop it. We had only bought us, or Zac, a little time until we could conceal him in the basement and let all hell break loose for his full blown transformation.

Then I heard him...*Pain...everywhere...like I'm exploding...scared...don't know what's real anymore...*

"Did you guys hear him?" I hysterically questioned the guys as we rushed out of the truck. Everyone acknowledged that they had heard Zac's mental plea for help and his total anguish.

Daniel, Josiah and Isaac captured Zac's body as he started thrashing around again and loudly moaning. Zac's ears and portions of his face were changing into that of the beast or a wolf; I couldn't tell for sure which. There wasn't much time to spare so they moved him with preternatural speed into the house and down the basement steps.

Dom and I raced after them, trying to catch up. We made it to the basement and discovered most of Zac's clothes had been removed. They glared at Dom and me as if we shouldn't be there. Again, I'm sure they felt a need to protect us, the humans, both physically and psychologically, from any danger or ghastly display that we needn't witness.

They weren't kicking me out. Or Dom. I stood my ground, speaking softly to all of them, straight from my heart. "After everything we have been through, do you really think you have the right to tell me to leave and go sit upstairs? To wait it out? Did everyone forget I just played a huge part in keeping Zac calm out in the truck? And Dominic drove like a race car driver and safely got us back here? We are The Liaison. We're a team and we'll handle this together. Dom and I will stay back but we're not leaving."

On as private a mental path as I could create, I pleaded to Daniel, *Don't make me go, Daniel. I love you and I need to see this, especially if I choose to become a werewolf.*

He flinched and explained, *But this <u>isn't</u> exactly how a normal conversion happens. We think there are traces of demon mixed in him. Remember that.*

And then I heard an awful crunching sound.

All eyes darted to Zac as he hunched over on his knees on the basement floor. More sounds of cracking and popping...like ice-coated tree limbs that cannot bend anymore under the weight and simply snap off to release the pressure...you tend to wince when you hear that distressing, splintering crack as it echoes in the still winter air.

Zac's bones were breaking and reshaping. His hands were no longer hands but resembled monstrous claws, flexing and straightening with long, razor sharp fingernails as they scraped the floor. His bare feet contorted and took on the form of a wolf's padded paws with splayed toes complete with lethal toenails that curled down just a bit to aid in his balance. These paws still retained some humanistic qualities that enabled him to stand upright, although Daniel's feet seemed more of a balance between human and wolf.

Josiah, Daniel and Isaac surrounded Zac, preparing for the full transformation to take effect and whatever violent behavior came with it. We needed to keep him confined to the basement and prevent any opportunity of escape. And if he didn't pounce on Dom or me, that would be a mighty big plus. We didn't know yet if "our" Zac was with us anymore or if something else was taking him over. Besides painful screams, he hadn't spoken a word. No one had been able to read his mind since before we brought him into the house. We felt his terror but no specific thoughts.

Zac reared his head back, as if stretching his neck, but stayed in an odd crouched position on all fours. I did not recognize him anymore. His head magically enlarged and supported a huge, grizzly, sinewy muzzle with a black nose and whiskers that poked out in all directions. And the teeth...sharp, deadly, "rip your throat out" weapons...which could so easily pass on the werewolf curse with just the teeniest little scratch. The pain of the conversion was evident as his lips curled back from his muzzle and a gooey drip of saliva hung from the corner of his mouth, not quite able to swallow yet.

A high-pitched whine, a desperate cry, surfaced from his throat. I absently took one step forward and Dom jerked my arm to stop my motion. Daniel looked at me for a split second and mouthed, "No." As long as Zac wasn't attacking anyone or totally destroying the house, we knew it was best to not interfere with this painstaking transformation. But did someone hit a slow motion button? The punishing torture to his body and mind was a nightmare to watch as it just lingered on and on.

Zac's ears were tall, rigid and alert like a wolf or a German Shepherd. They twitched trying to capture any sounds of predators… or perhaps prey…I hoped we wouldn't be targeted as such.

Zac's head dropped down as his spinal column erupted with more vertebrae to support the larger frame. Muscles rippled and expanded while the skin stretched and adjusted onto its new powerhouse of a foundation. His human body had already been at peak physical condition from years of strict Navy SEAL training and he had kept up the grueling workouts after leaving the service. And so, if this transformation into a werewolf, especially the beast form, was based on his current athletic build, we were due to have a muscle-bound monster on our hands.

The men had not removed his underwear since that part of the torso usually didn't undergo a major change. Sometimes when Daniel shifted into the beast, he'd leave his pants on if they were loose fitting to begin with. Well, the briefs were nearly bursting their seams as Zac grew in size…everywhere. A guttural growl released from his mouth, followed by more cries as he panted and struggled to draw in air.

Thick, wavy fur several inches in length sprouted and covered most surfaces of Zac's body. The colors were a mixture of black, brown and white. Daniel's fur was all black; another difference between them, but I didn't think the color symbolized anything special, although I could've been wrong. With the addition of the fur on top of his already bulked-up beastly form, his underwear had now become way too constricting. Gee whiz, *I* could see that! And as the realization dawned on Zac that he could easily resolve his discomfort, he grasped the briefs with one claw and tore them off, flinging them through the air. They landed a few inches in front of me. I sucked in my breath…and his head cocked to the side, hearing my gasp.

Then he stood up. The transformation was complete.

Zac was a foot taller than his human self and his head brushed the ceiling which forced him to duck down a bit. He towered over everyone. He was much taller, larger, stronger and scarier than Daniel's beast form. This was another distinguishable variation which we believed stemmed from the influence of the demon.

He sniffed the air and faced Dom and me. All of his attention seemed specifically focused on us: the humans. Oh my God - his eyes were yellow! Intense, haunted, vivid yellow eyes stared at us. They should've been black, like Daniel's, not yellow! Some normal wolves had yellow eyes...but nothing like Zac's had turned. What did that mean?! My quartz responded with a pulsing heat. From what I was learning, that wasn't a good sign.

I couldn't stay quiet and meekly asked, "Zac? Are you okay?"

He growled and for the first time acknowledged Daniel, Isaac and Josiah with a defiant, challenging stance. I supposed that was a stupid question to ask Zac. Gee, he just turned into a werewolf. No, he really wasn't "okay". Was there nothing I could say that did not have a double meaning?

Daniel asked a more direct question. "Zac, can you talk? Try. It'll feel awkward and like your tongue is in the way, so speak only one or two words at a time."

Zac had a crazed look in his yellow eyes. Agitated, he flexed his arms and chest, making the muscles jump about in a disturbing manner. You could see every engorged muscle in his body; it didn't matter that he was covered with fur, with the exception of his private parts that were basically non-furry. He was obviously still naked and that, in itself, was extremely distracting.

His eyes dropped to what used to be his hands, but now were lethal claws. He glanced down at the rest of his body, inspecting it, and growled again shaking his head in disbelief.

Zac garbled and coughed out one word, "Angry."

We waited in silence to see what he would do next. It was hard to tell if he was going to cry or punch the living daylights out of someone.

Another word tumbled from his mouth, "Eat."

He looked at Dom and me as he said that. Zac took only one

stride in my direction when Daniel burst through his clothes while shape shifting into the beast. Isaac ripped through his clothes, too, following Daniel's lead. Daniel, Isaac and Josiah created a blockade to prevent Zac from attacking us.

"There's lots of meat in the frig!" Dominic yelled out to anyone listening. "I'll get it! Zac, please don't eat anyone - just give me a minute!"

Dom ran up the stairs to the kitchen. We could hear him above our heads, his feet pounding on the floor, snatching as much meat as he could carry from the refrigerator. I backtracked half way up the stairs so I wouldn't be in direct sight of Zac but could still see what was going on. When the guys confronted Zac face to face, he momentarily froze his movements. Probably all the commotion of seeing two werewolves shifting in front of him and a vampire's clout had knocked a little common sense into him concerning his actions.

I couldn't believe what Daniel did next to buy us more time. He stepped closer to Zac and mumbled to him, "Let it out."

And with Daniel's go-ahead, some of Zac's confusion, frustration and anger were given an outlet to vent; a target to direct his emotions at. It was not the time for sweet, consoling talk or using mental manipulation on him. I didn't know if that would even work, but I could experiment later. Daniel allowed himself to be Zac's personal punching bag, with Josiah and Isaac as backup, all in agreement that Zac needed to release his emotions. What he really needed was the chance to run outside, to feel the earth, smell the air and experience nature with his newfound, heightened senses. Well, that wasn't going to happen within the city. Although, Josiah's house was next to Middlesex Fells Reservation, but…Zac was far too dangerous and unpredictable and he hadn't transformed to an actual wolf yet! He could not go gallivanting off through the woods looking like a monster!

Daniel, Isaac and Josiah teamed up against Zac and kept the severity of their individual injuries to a minimum. They could calculate his moves and keep alternating who he fought, avoiding any serious or possible (although highly unlikely) mortal blows. Also, this acting out gave us an idea of what Zac was capable of and the amount of power he possessed. Which was unbelievable! It's important to mention that they weren't provoking Zac or trying to increase his frustration, but reminded me of sparring partners. Letting Zac blow off steam and wear himself out was the intention. If he fought one on one with any of them, I believed Zac could win, even against Josiah, unless Josiah dissolved into mist or could force a compulsion on him. Maybe then, Zac could be defeated. It was scary.

Daniel was definitely putting himself out front more than Josiah or Isaac, taking on the brunt of Zac's aggression. He felt guilty for Zac's conversion. Turning Zac into a werewolf was not part of the plan. That unfortunate accident forced us to retreat from chasing witches and immediately deal with a major life changing event. I'm sure once I started digging into Zac's mind, I'd probably discover that he blamed Daniel and considered it Daniel's fault that this happened in the first place.

Dom plunked down next to me on a basement step, arms overflowing with ground beef, steaks and pork tenderloin. With a house full of men, the refrigerator had been fully stocked to keep them fed. Josiah didn't eat the meat, but everyone else needed actual food and Dom was more than happy to be our grocery shopper and chef. It appeared Dom had grabbed every package of meat he purchased.

He whispered, "Should I tell them I've got the food?"

"Not yet. They're letting Zac release some aggression, which could be to our benefit and survival," I explained. Dom swallowed hard, understanding our dangerous predicament.

We watched in shocked amazement and flinched whenever Daniel, Isaac or Josiah took a hard hit that knocked them off their feet or made them stumble backwards. If one needed recovery time, the two remaining would step up, taking his place. This went on for fifteen minutes. Punch, spin, hit, fall, clobber, turn, duck, grunt, swing.

Then Zac bent over from the waist and placed his claws on his knees, panting for air. That seemed like a positive sign. Either he was taking a time out or he was seriously tired from the relentless fighting. I decided to touch at Zac's mind, taking a more personal approach, hoping I could soothe his inner and outer beast. And to understand what his transformation had done to him. Before I made that attempt,

I mentally sent out the message to the others of my intentions, and instantly received dirty looks, but I needed to try regardless of their worries.

Using my mind, I called to Zac, *It's Kara, Zac. We have food for you. Do you want to eat now?*

He collapsed on the floor in a huff. He nodded a yes, but he mentally responded, too. *Yes.*

In the beast form, using his mouth - his muzzle - to talk was difficult and hard for us to decipher. Since Zac was now a werewolf, he had his own psychic abilities like the rest of us; something he didn't possess before the conversion. The werewolves were not superior with psychic skills, but could adequately read minds. With the demon essence a part of Zac, I wouldn't be surprised if his telepathy was superior to Daniel's. It would be easier for everyone to speak with our minds when Zac was not in human form, as I did most of the time when Daniel shifted.

Daniel retrieved the food from Dominic and tore the plastic wrappings off the packages. He tossed the meat directly to Zac or slid the Styrofoam plates across the floor. Once Zac smelled the raw meat, his saliva glands kicked into high gear and globs of drool dripped out of his mouth. He crouched on the floor and crammed the food into his mouth. He ate like a starved animal, greedy and possessive, devouring everything given to him. No one disturbed him out of fear he'd mistake any of our moves as a threat to try and take his food away. It was not a pretty sight to watch him gobbling up raw meat. In fact, it was rather disgusting. He ate the last morsel by licking it off the concrete floor and wiped his face with the back of his arm.

He had visibly relaxed, looking exhausted. Daniel coaxed him, "Zac, try to concentrate on your human body and shift back to that form now."

Zac answered using telepathy, *Why? Are you going to kill me?*

"No!" Every person firmly stated out loud at the same moment. We needed to reassure him of our concern and keep his aggression at bay.

Seconds passed and Zac returned to the body of a man, drawing his legs up in an effort to conceal his lower region. He had a full belly and was totally beat, all which brought his anger and anxiety level way down and helped him transform back. Daniel and Isaac also transformed when it appeared we were in the safe zone with Zac's violent, animalistic side. I informed the clothes-shredding werewolves that I would go find new clothes from upstairs right away so they'd have something to wear. Again.

By the time I returned, Zac had moved to Josiah's bed and was covered with a blanket. I handed out the clothing and turned around to be respectful to Zac's privacy while dressing. I was getting more accustomed to Daniel, and even Isaac's, nakedness during transformations when clothes weren't on hand and to their total lack of shyness.

"I assume you and Zac will switch sleeping quarters?" I asked Josiah to break the awkward silence.

He responded, "Yes, it would be for the best. If he transforms and gets out of control, at least he'll be confined to the basement - a safety measure for him and us. And we'd hear him before he could make it out the front door."

Zac flopped on the bed, tired and defeated. His mind mulled over the events of the evening and he spoke in low tones, "I'm sorry for my actions during the raid on the witches. The whole evening snowballed…it had a domino effect, didn't it?"

I interrupted, "No one is at fault. Remember that."

He mumbled, "Yeah, right. If I hadn't charged across the floor after Tessa's killer, in the middle of a demon resurrection no less, which is what started this entire ordeal, then I wouldn't be lying here trying to control my newfound werewolf behavior now, would I?!"

I sat next to Zac on the bed, surrounded by Daniel, Josiah, Isaac and Dom. I touched his arm and with every bit of psychic power I could muster, flooded his mind with reassuring and calm thoughts. He had started to get agitated again as he reflected on the evening's ordeal and we needed to have a conversation without him transforming.

I pleaded, "Look around, Zac. We are here for you."

Josiah peacefully commented, "Let's review a few points in an honest, open and non-threatening manner as possible, okay? Zac, you'll stay in the basement. If you come upstairs, you'll be accompanied by Daniel, Isaac or myself. We have to confirm that you have your new abilities under control and won't run out the front door as a beast and go on a mass killing spree. Do you understand?"

"Yeah...I understand why I have to stay down here."

I soothingly rubbed Zac's arm and quizzed him, "Why were you so famished? Why did you stare at Dom and me like *we* were your supper?"

Totally out of character for him, a single tear slid down his cheek. "I don't know. I wanted to eat something so badly. But it makes me sick to think I was really craving human meat above all else. That's not normal, is it Daniel?"

"No, it's not," Daniel sighed, filled with concern. "When my pack members and I went through our conversions, we never had the urge to feed on humans and still don't to this day. Sometimes our aggression has led to the loss of human life, but we don't seek out humans as a food source. Maybe werewolves who've turned evil would favor the taste of humans, especially in their beast or wolf forms. When we've taken the shape of a wolf, not a beast, we hunt other *animals* in the wild for food. As you know, in our human form, we eat the same food as Kara and Dom...just much larger portions."

No one liked to hear the word evil in relation to Zac's conversion but we had to voice our worries and discuss what to do next. There were several differences between Zac and the other werewolves, both physically and psychologically. Could he be trusted? Would he switch sides - from good to evil?

Isaac pondered, "I wonder why you never shifted into a wolf? During the initial conversion, a human transforms directly, you could say almost naturally, into a wolf. The beast is the in between stage and tougher to maintain without practice. And, no offense buddy, but you smell different, too. Like a werewolf but not exactly. And you wouldn't know this unless you looked into a mirror, but as a beast, your eyes are a spooky yellow!"

Dominic piped in, "And you are one freaking gigantic fighting machine! Dangerous, dude! Note to Self: Make sure I never tick off Zac!"

Zac smiled weakly and snickered a bit at Dom's accurate but comical outburst which lightened up the tension in the room and soon had everyone chuckling. It was a relief to see Zac's personality was intact and had not been blown to smithereens. But we needed to help him quickly learn to accept his fate and gain control of and maximize his supernatural abilities. And fast...since we were clueless as to when the witches would try another resurrection.

It was 2:30 in the morning. We were beat and Zac's eyes kept fluttering closed. Thankfully.

Josiah made a motion and suggested, "It's time to sleep. Later, we'll research something Logan, the wizard, declared before his disappearing act. He shouted, 'The King will rise!' I think I know which demon they were attempting to resurrect by connecting the dots: the demon's physical appearance in its ghostly form, Logan's mention of a King and toss into the mix Zac's oddities from his transformation, including his cravings. Daniel and Isaac, how much do you really know about werewolf history?"

CHAPTER 12
KING

Zac was so exhausted physically and mentally that he slept well into the afternoon. That was a huge bonus for the rest of us if we didn't have to worry about Zac's whereabouts or his emotional state. I crawled out of bed around 9:00 due to Daniel's gentle shaking and his insisting that we had important things to take care of; especially if Zac *was* sleeping and didn't need a babysitter to watch over him.

Dominic prepared breakfast. He showed signs of anxiety when he mentioned that there was no meat at all in the house. Zac would need to eat again and would most likely want to do so shortly after waking up…just like us, he'd be hungry. And if the previous night was an indication of his new eating habits, meat was his number one food of choice. Raw meat seemed to be preferred in his beast form, although I'm sure he'd eat it cooked, too.

Daniel recommended, "Josiah, you mentioned doing research on this demon. Dom could go to the store and load up on groceries while Kara starts checking the internet for information. Does that sound like a plan?"

"Good idea," Josiah stated. "Dominic, I'd recommend leaving now and buy plenty to stock up the house but don't dawdle. I want everyone to be involved in and informed about our discoveries, including Zac. We'll try to let him sleep until he wakes up on his own, unless it gets too late in the day. In the meantime, we'll learn what we can about what kind of demon was trying to be resurrected and how I believe it has direct ties with werewolves."

Dom went to the store, Isaac quickly washed dishes and I turned on the computer, waiting for instructions from Josiah on what exactly

I should be performing a search on.

"Look up Lycaeon. I've seen it spelled a few ways," he directed me and spelled out one version of the name. "Daniel, obviously you know about the Lycaeonia curse, since that is what turned you into a werewolf. But, are you aware of the actual origin of werewolves?"

And I quietly wondered why the curse tended to have "ia" stuck on the end. The search results on the internet pulled up a few differences in the curse's name. Why not call the curse --

"*King* Lycaeon..." Daniel answered, filling in the next words of my thoughts.

As Daniel's face lit up in horror with his own comprehension, Isaac said, "What does that have to do with the witches' demon?"

Josiah looked like he wanted to smack Isaac upside the head but instead chose to spell it out for him. "Logan threatened that 'The King would rise'...?! Doesn't it all add up? He is a highly-skilled sorcerer and necromancer and he and his little coven want to resurrect King Lycaeon as the Demon Werewolf."

Isaac's understanding, his realization of who and what Josiah was referring to, sunk in and stunned his brain. "That explains why the ghostly image resembled a werewolf...because it *was* one! The first one ever created!"

"I'm not sure if King Lycaeon would technically be a demon. When he died, he was just a werewolf, albeit an evil one," Josiah thought aloud. "But that in itself, and the fact that Logan is the epitome of black magic and is attempting to summon Lycaeon's spirit, wishing to give it solid form, probably would result in a demon creation. Hmm..."

Telepathically I sent this information to Dominic while he was grocery shopping. I didn't want him to miss anything. It wasn't a time to chit chat, just knowledge being forwarded. I hated that Dom wasn't there to directly hear the conversations, but I did my best to include him. In fact, to hold off some of the demon and werewolf connection revelations until Dom returned, I quizzed the guys about necromancy.

In Logan's case, his justified title of being a necromancer meant he used black magic to communicate with the spirits of the dead, either as an apparition or to resurrect them. Many times the ultimate goal was to predict the future or to gain power in some form or fashion. The act of performing necromancy involved several methods we had witnessed Logan using; such as, drawing circles on the ground and drawing within them other shapes and symbols. He also employed the reciting of incantations with the aid of his witches, burning magical herbs and candles and the blood sacrifice. The sacrifice was like a payment or an offering for summoning the demon or spirit.

After my thorough education on necromancy and black magic, Dom returned from the grocery store. We paused to help him unload and put the food away and then it was back to business.

As it turned out, Josiah was a walking encyclopedia. He had a personal interest in learning all he could get his hands on pertaining to the supernatural. I might as well have taken my laptop and thrown it out the window, which, of course, I would never actually do. I did locate on the internet a lot of other critical details about King Lycaeon that sparked conversations and filled in many of the missing pieces in the puzzle. Daniel had a fair amount of knowledge on werewolf history and folklore and added in his two cents worth, but Josiah ruled with the juicy particulars. It made sense - he had also lived much longer than the werewolves in our group and traveled extensively, whereas Daniel's pack rarely ever left the vicinity of their home in Hamlin, Kentucky. It was a bit ironic to think that their best way to learn about their past was the darn internet. Supernatural beings didn't frequent their locale very often, so they weren't likely to sit around a bonfire socializing. That meant little outside contact to hear about any gossip or to simply learn from others of their kind.

There are several myths and legends about who was the first (or earliest) werewolf on record and when "he" came into existence. Through Josiah's vast encounters with werewolves, vampires, wizards and who knows what else, add to that Daniel's experiences (somewhat limited even though he IS a werewolf) then ice the cake with the extra fluff I plucked off the internet, well, we believed we had pulled together a reasonably accurate account of how the first werewolf was created.

Josiah recapped, "King Lycaeon was the first king of Arcadia in ancient Greece. The King of the Mt. Olympus Gods, Zeus, decided to visit King Lycaeon after he heard rumors of cannibalism, human sacrifice and great despair rising from the people of Earth. Lycaeon was forewarned that Zeus was on his way but he remained skeptical that Zeus was an actual god. He chose to put Zeus to a test. A feast was held in Zeus's honor where he was presented with wonderful dishes of food but one plate contained human flesh. Lycaeon's theory was that only a real god would be able to tell if the meat was from a human. Zeus was not fooled and in his anger over the cannibalism he turned King Lycaeon into a werewolf.

"The King fled into the countryside, in the shape of a wolf, but Zeus made sure he retained his human mind so he'd always remember his fate and what terrible deeds he'd done. Zeus alleged that a wolf form better suited the King's lifestyle since he liked to eat human flesh."

Daniel continued with the story, "From that point, we're not positive what happened to Lycaeon. Not long after that incident, Zeus released a great flood that wiped out much of humanity. He felt it was time to start fresh with the world again, as he was not pleased with human behavior and their lack of respect. Who knows how many years after Lycaeon was turned that this flood occurred and how many people actually died? Lycaeon did have descendants, though, stemming from the Anteus Clan and many of them were werewolves. Lycaeon is dead, perhaps from the flood or by someone's hand; otherwise a resurrection would not be possible."

"And werewolf history ties in with witchcraft and magic simply because of their connection to Zeus and his other-worldly powers," I concluded. "Mt. Lycaeus was a place in Arcadia where a cult called Wolf-Zeus would gather every year. Sacrificial feasts included bits of human flesh and if you tasted it, you turned into a wolf."

Dominic added, "It seems there was another werewolf from ancient times, Moires, who was married to a Fate goddess named Moera. I don't know how he became a werewolf exactly…if King Lycaeon was in wolf or beast shape and bit him or Zeus turned him or that cult…Well, anyway, Moires learned from his wife about magic and how to raise the dead. Gee, sound familiar, as in Logan trying to raise the dead? As time passed, very powerful witches and wizards were able to conjure up spells that could turn a human into a werewolf. Most of the time, it worked best with a coven of witches, instead of an individual trying to cast the spell. Power in numbers."

"Curse," Daniel corrected Dom. "I know it is a spell, but it has permanent, life-altering effects. I'd use the word curse instead. Luckily my pack and I have thrived over the years and fought the threat of evil that never ceases to nag at our minds. I'd like to think that besides a few blips on the radar, we've done well for ourselves. Still, to have everything you know ripped out from under your feet, and no one to guide you or explain what was happening to your body, was confusing and horrible. And then to accidentally turn your loved ones into werewolves was unbearable. I suppose it might be different if we were born werewolves, but we started life as human beings. And now to have Zac's life changed forever…because of me. I can't believe this! First, he loses Tessa and then I turn him into a werewolf! Yes, I'd definitely say it's a curse."

Dominic glanced at me, as did several others. Daniel's frustration over the whole situation had surfaced, exposing his guilt and bringing up long ago, painful memories. Everyone knew I had serious thoughts about converting into a werewolf. After hearing Daniel's declaration, they wondered if it might influence or sway my future decision on the matter.

Dom mentally took a jab at me, *And you want to be a werewolf? Or, excuse my assumption, you are considering this? Oh, happy days.* Sarcasm and bewilderment flowed into my mind with the push of his words.

Daniel was aware of the silence in the room and let his gaze travel over our group. Realizing how his ranting could be interpreted, or misinterpreted, and the influence it could have on me, he locked his eyes on mine in utter panic. He started to speak, but I decided to cut him off before he dug an even deeper hole.

I shrouded him with love and support and doled out a good, old-fashioned pep talk. "Daniel, it may be a curse, in principle, but you stated how you've survived it. The early years were terrible, from what you've said, but you are alive and well, as is your pack, hundreds of years later. And you've blended into society and made a good life, including financially, for yourself. That's something to be proud of. And you're one of the *good* guys in all of this with me standing by your side. Ain't that something in itself?! Remember, we are here as a team to kick the baddies' butts. We'll get through this."

Well, that was enough to cause an emotional stirring from everyone in the room. It was one of those "awww..." moments. My psychic senses absorbed the warm, fuzzy ambiance the guys projected. Even Dom couldn't, and wouldn't dare, counter my response to Daniel. They witnessed my devotion to Daniel and to my commitment with the whole affair. Daniel reached out, hugged me tightly and rubbed my back and whispered in my ear, "I love you."

The time as usual had flown by and we needed to break for lunch. Our research, including Josiah & Daniel's knowledge database in their brains, and in depth discussion over the material, had proved to be incredibly helpful and rewarding. Zac was still sleeping but we knew that couldn't last much longer.

"I have to do what I can to help Zac," Daniel vowed. "I won't let him be alone in this. At least he has the advantage of knowing about werewolves firsthand, whereas I did not when I was first turned. But, he is *different*. Very dangerous."

Josiah agreed, "Yes, Zac is not your average werewolf. That small portion of demon mixed with werewolf could make things quite interesting. We have to watch for any signs of evil or malevolent behavior. I hope we can control him. In all actuality, that's not what I should be saying, as that in itself sounds evil. He has to control himself and his actions. But, Daniel, don't shoulder all of this on yourself. I do believe I speak for the majority when I say that we will help guide Zac."

Heads nodded in agreement. We prepared for Zac's awakening... it was eerie how the entire lot of us possessed varying degrees of telepathic ability. Zac gained that ability the moment he became a werewolf. For the next two hours, we touched on his state of mind to determine when he was fully awake but made sure not to distract him or force him to wake up. It was amazing how long he had slept - 12 hours! We sensed him moving restlessly on the bed in the basement, still in human form, but becoming more alert as the seconds ticked by.

Dom fetched the extra meat he had cooked during the day and additional packages of raw meat from the refrigerator. We didn't know what form Zac would be in once we saw him, as he could decide to shift into the beast again, and preferred the raw meat in that shape.

Zac, as a man, was pacing the basement floor. He looked up and simply said, "I'm starving."

I walked over to him with an upbeat attitude and smiled, "Well, I would be hungry, too, if I had just slept 12 hours."

Zac's attention immediately darted to the food that Dom held in his arms. Showing no restraint at all, he started to transform. We groaned, anticipating what we'd have to deal with, and watched Zac burst out of his clothes. Very fast. Not like the "don't blink your eyes" type of fast that Daniel could do, but it took Zac about ten seconds as compared to his first grueling transformation which lasted thirty minutes or more. I found myself standing a foot in front of one wicked looking creature. Who was starving. With sharp teeth and claws that were used as deadly weapons. And I was blocking his path from getting to the food.

Dominic tossed the meat in Frisbee fashion across the floor to get it closer to Zac without having to directly hand it to him, keeping his distance. Also, he hoped the action would draw attention away from me. The problem - I was frozen in place. I should've stepped to the side and gotten out of Zac's way. A package had burst open when it had impacted the floor, sending the aroma of raw meat and blood drifting through the air. He inhaled deeply and it became his intended target. His left arm swung out to push me aside so he could get to the meat in the fewest steps possible. He was totally unaware of how immense his strength was and how easily I could be injured.

When Zac's arm rose to shove me out of the way, everyone moved so fast I felt a rush of dizziness. Dom created a little force field around me to keep me safe, specifically from Zac. But I swear I felt the air swoosh from the momentum of Zac's arm. Suddenly Daniel grabbed me and literally tossed me to Josiah, who caught me in mid air and plunked my trembling legs near the stairs, away from danger and next to Dom.

I was untouched, but Zac's arm didn't exactly bounce off the invisible shield like we had expected. Instead, his arm had partially sunk into the force field, as if it had hit a pillow in slow motion or a wall of Jell-O, and stopped within an eighth of an inch from where I had been standing. Everyone realized Zac had penetrated the safety zone Dom had attentively created. Not a comforting thought as that was another indication of how powerful he was against supernatural elements. By that time, Zac was devouring the meat, not taking notice of the fact that Daniel, Isaac and Josiah had formed another barricade to protect Dom and me and to prevent any possible notions Zac could have of escaping. If they stepped too closely to Zac's personal space, he growled and snapped at them. He didn't want to be bothered while he ate, but as long as they stayed a respectable distance away from him, he was content tearing into the meat.

Even though Zac was in his beast shape, so far, Daniel and Isaac had not transformed. If Zac became too violent, they could always shape shift at any given moment. They wanted to work with Zac in their human shape, if possible. It would be a calmer, less threatening atmosphere for him and they could maintain some sense of normalcy in speaking with and helping Zac cope.

But, shame on us...we let Zac go too long without eating something and should've awakened him hours earlier to prevent such a ravenous appetite from developing. We had dreaded the time when he would inevitably wake up and so it was a relief to just let him keep sleeping. An avoidance tactic that backfired. Hunger and anger triggered his transformations. He'd have to eat every few hours to maintain a full feeling and we'd have to be careful to keep any negativity to a minimum. That last part would be nearly impossible.

Zac gorged himself with an insane amount of meat. And most of it was raw. After fifteen minutes, he slowly licked his clawed hands, careful not to cut his tongue on the sharp talons that were his fingernails. He stood up, towering over Daniel, Josiah and Isaac. His beastly features were as fear-inducing as ever, but his yellow eyes had taken on a sparkle of contentment and his muzzle had partially closed, covering his ghastly teeth. I touched at his mind without trying to be intrusive or agitating him. In fact, I tried to go in undetected by slithering near the far reaches of his thoughts, to just grasp a tiny clue of what to expect next from him. His awareness of his own psychic powers was growing...he knew the second I started poking around in his head. Zac's eyes flew to me, although he had a difficult time looking at me directly, since the guys blocked his view.

"Zac, shift back. It's okay," I encouraged him and attempted to walk closer.

Daniel, Josiah and Isaac remained rooted to the ground and would not allow me to pass by them. Until he returned to human form, he was unsafe to be near. Zac's head dropped to his chest and swung slightly from side to side while he tried to get a grip on his current shape.

He let out a long sigh and just like that, he transformed back to a man. Then he turned away from us and walked into the bedroom.

The guys loosened up their stances and within moments, Zac returned with clothes on. Once fed, he regained self-control over his body, as hunger was no longer in the forefront of his mind.

"Now what?" he grilled, crossing his bulging forearms, not pleased, but not threatening. "And I'm going to need more clothes soon if I keep destroying them all."

Daniel chose to respond first. "We'll get more clothes tonight. While you slept today, we researched werewolf legends and history and reviewed what knowledge we had learned over the years. Be prepared for an onslaught of information."

"No problem. Lay it on me. I'm familiar with being briefed from my time in the service," Zac countered, all business-like.

Josiah suggested, "I believe it's safe for us to go upstairs and sit comfortably in the living room. You've eaten, Zac, which helps relax your mind and body. I can sense your seriousness and desire to understand this entire situation. There's no point in standing around in this uncomfortable basement trying to have this conversation."

Once we settled in the living room, each of us took turns explaining to Zac everything we had discovered and discussed throughout the day. Several of the oddities between Zac and regular werewolves (Daniel and Isaac) were thrown on the table. The reasons for the differences stemmed from the fact that Zac was turned into a werewolf but seconds later fell into the apparition of a demon that had not been able to take a solid form. Some tiny essence of the demon entered his body. That was obvious.

The specifics of that demon, though, gave a deeper explanation for what Zac was experiencing. The knowledge helped us to comprehend what we were up against both in helping Zac to cope and in fighting the witches. The resurrection had been performed with black magic by an evil wizard and powerful necromancer, Logan, who was trying to summon the evil King Lycaeon, *the* first werewolf, resulting in a perfect storm for a demon creation. And because a bit of that particular demon's essence had entered Zac's body, it then became a part of him and went along for the ride when Zac converted into a werewolf.

Zac craved meat. In beast form he had hungrily licked his chops while gazing at Dom and me because he had picked up King Lycaeon's fondness for human flesh and meat. We had to keep him distracted with animal meat and hope he would never get the chance to eat humans. He would have to be destroyed if it came to that. Zac's taller size, bulkiness and strength and even different coloring to his fur were all due to the mixture of King Lycaeon's genetic makeup and Logan's black magic influence. The eerie yellow to his eyes was an indication that evil existed within him and if not controlled he could very easily slip to the dark side. Zac would need to overcome any evil and violent urges, especially during transformations when he was most vulnerable.

Zac was a ticking time bomb. He was a live grenade with the pin already pulled and just a finger was holding down the safety lever to keep him from exploding.

"Gee, I've got so much to look forward to," Zac scowled sarcastically.

I interjected, "We will help you get through this. Now that you've heard all the background on what's what, we can move forward. Right?"

Daniel jumped in, "Tonight you need to try shifting into a wolf… which you haven't done yet…and that's strange. But Isaac and I will guide you through it and help you visualize the process."

"It's time for supper. Zac, you should eat again with us. If we can keep you from feeling hungry, that should alleviate part of the problem with spur-of-the-moment transformations," Dominic recommended. He snickered and added, "You've always loved food, so I'm guessing I won't hear any complaints."

Zac agreed, determined to stay in control. "I'm not really hungry yet, but I will eat. Can I stay up here? I don't feel any urge to turn into a beast this time."

We looked to Josiah for an approval or a denial to Zac's request.

We were the guests in his house plus he had the most experience to judge Zac's present state of mind and well being. Was Zac being truthful? Was there an underlying, evil presence waiting for the opportune moment to consume his thoughts and take over his body?

Josiah approached him in a cheerful manner and placed a hand on each of Zac's shoulders. He made sure he did this in a non-threatening way to prove that their friendship was intact and to soothe his nerves. I believed Josiah was also reading Zac's mind, seeking out his intentions, but didn't announce that he was doing such a thing. He may have tried to place a compulsion on Zac to stay calm, but I wasn't sure.

"Yes, you need to eat regular meals with everyone. You must concentrate on blending in. And time is not on our side," Josiah urged Zac.

We joined Dominic in the kitchen and sat around the table while he placed an array of food in front of us. It looked scrumptious and smelled enticing, making my mouth water in anticipation, which then made me wonder how Zac would react to all of it. Josiah lingered near him as a visual reminder that he was being watched and to keep his inner beast leashed.

I wasn't going to mask the fragile situation and gently asked, "Zac, do you need any help reining in your emotions while you eat?"

He hesitated. Everyone sat perfectly still and waited for his answer. No one placed any food on their plates or took a drink from their glasses. Zac roughly scratched his head and ran his hands through his hair, not sure of himself anymore. Josiah was still standing off to the side of Zac and gave us a look indicating to be patient. Zac propped his elbows on the table and held his head in his hands, staring down at his empty plate. The speed of his breathing increased as did the guttural noise escaping through his lips.

Zac kept his eyes closed, realizing the food was tempting his taste buds more than he had expected. He was making a valiant effort to hold back transforming. He wanted to prove that he was strong, that he was trying his best to adapt to his new circumstances. He also knew when it was time to ask for help. That time had arrived.

CHAPTER 13
MELTDOWN

"Kara..." Zac gasped my name. And then he switched to telepathy. *Help me. I want to control myself, but the scent and sight of food is driving me crazy. I don't know how much longer I can hold out before I turn. Please, go ahead and work your magic on me.*

Okay, Zac. I'm going to walk up behind you now, I forewarned him so he wouldn't swat me like a fly.

I stood up but Daniel stopped me and stated, "No, you're not going within an arm's reach of Zac. You can help him, but do it at a distance."

I could understand not touching Zac when he was in full beast or wolf mode, but with Daniel, Josiah and Isaac protecting me and Dom's slick telekinesis moves, I felt safe enough to enter Zac's personal space. I held my ground and said, "No time to argue. I'm going in. Stay close."

Daniel bristled with my dismissive attitude but stuck to me like glue as I walked behind where Zac was sitting. I sensed a force field pop up around me that Dom had instantly created for my protection. It was a wonderful gift - to have my own security blanket in the blink of an eye. Although, his last force field didn't quite hold up against Zac like we had hoped, which was unnerving. Also, I wondered if it might actually block or lessen my psychic powers and how I needed to access Zac's mind.

"Dom, drop the shield," I insisted. I sent him a mental message, *Thanks, but hold off. Keep on your toes if he transforms.*

I touched Zac's back firmly with the palms of my hands. His body tensed; his instincts told him to prepare for an attack, especially since I had approached from behind. His back muscles tightened and were hard as rocks. He was ready to react.

What do you do when someone needs relaxation? How about a massage? I started to knead the tight areas in his back. And since I always achieved better psychic results when I had direct contact with the person that I was mentally manipulating, the back massage was a perfect combination.

"Zac, stay still and relax. This probably seems weird...but work with me here. Slow your breathing. You are in control. We're here to help you through this," I used my best hypnotic voice that I could fashion.

Everyone was afraid to talk as we didn't know what could set Zac off on a wild rage or induce his shape shifting. The other guys gave me strange, confused looks with the sudden, brisk rubdown I was giving Zac. Daniel and Isaac cocked their heads and raised their eyebrows. Their hilarious display resembled identical, inquisitive dogs. Dom crossed his arms on his chest, clearly thinking I had lost my mind to get that physical with Zac when he was in the midst of fighting a transformation. Josiah rubbed his chin and a corner of his mouth lifted with a knowing grin.

My quartz necklace warmed a smidgeon as it hung on my chest. I noticed, as did Daniel, that it emitted a slight glow, but nothing warning me that my life was in immediate danger. Another idea struck me.

Dom...Music! I psychically told him. I implied he should use his telekinesis to turn on whatever was available in the house that could play music. But definitely not head-banging, heavy metal music that could pump up or excite Zac. Something soothing and toned down is what Zac needed. After all, isn't that what we've always heard? Use music to calm the beast. Duh!

As the music played in the background, I repeated to Zac numerous times that he was in control of himself. Then without any barriers from him blocking my path, I freely entered his mind. I implanted images of normal eating behavior, of the team gathered around a table laughing and enjoying a meal, of remaining in a human form while eating and understanding it was not necessary to transform every time he felt hungry. I was concerned that he might get defensive, so I added that transforming was perfectly acceptable but there was a time and place for it. I told him he had to seek out a neutral zone, a stable platform within himself. Find a balance. He had been a kickass Navy SEAL and he had the stamina, willpower and skills to succeed on this new mission. The mission was to adjust to his new life. Quickly.

Zac had gradually lowered his hands and forearms to the table and he appeared to be unconscious, but I knew that he was establishing his perimeters - his frame of mind. His muscle tension had eased dramatically as his head leaned to one side.

"Open your eyes, Zac," I encouraged him. And then to get the ball rolling, I said, "Dom, Isaac - why don't you have something to eat? Zac, what would you like?"

"That pork chop is calling my name. And so is that baked potato," he smiled and picked up his fork. His hand trembled slightly as it hovered over the meat, but his self-control kicked in and the shaking stopped. He placed the food on his plate and appeared content.

I glanced over to Daniel and Josiah with relief pouring off my face. At the moment, everything was under control. Zac began cutting into the meat like a normal person and I motioned for Daniel to sit down to eat, too. He paused, observed that Zac seemed harmless and joined the others at the table. Josiah preferred blood for nourishment, but vampires could eat some fruits and vegetables once in a while. I was impressed when he casually walked over to the pot of green beans, speared a few with a spare fork and ate calmly. Josiah wanted to help create an enjoyable, orderly dining experience for Zac.

But what about me? I wasn't eating, yet. Should I take my hands off Zac's back and assume he could maintain this level of normalcy? I wasn't giving him a full-blown massage anymore, but my hands were still gliding over his shirt and I hadn't completely withdrawn from his mind. I felt like I was holding down the fort.

"Zac? Do you want me to walk away or should I stay and help you while you finish eating?" I didn't mind at all if he truly needed my help. I could eat after he was done. Not a big deal.

He held his knife and fork in midair while in mid-thought. "Can you be...on patrol within my mind and go eat at the same time?"

The way he asked me was almost child-like, filled with

uncertainty and a dash of embarrassment. He didn't want to rely on someone else. He thrived on independence and was a survivalist. But he had entered new, unchartered territory. He realized the importance of testing the waters before diving in head first and that when a comrade was unconditionally offering their hand to help him with a sticky situation, he should take it.

"I can do that, Zac. Let's try. I just don't have as strong an influence on you as when I have the physical contact. And you're so darn powerful that you could block me entering your mind anyway. You've done that before," I openly admitted but agreed to have a seat at the table.

Before I moved away from him, I patted his shoulder and rubbed behind his earlobe, remembering that a part of him was a wolf, and they loved their ears scratched. I knew that from my time with Daniel. There was nothing lovey-dovey or goofy-obnoxious about it - just a friendly gesture like I would have given to my dog, Nicky. Once again, it was comical watching the facial expressions of the other guys when I did it.

With my constant presence in Zac's mind, we managed to get through the meal with no further incidents. Josiah discreetly provided backup, masking himself under my presence, and adding a slight compulsion on Zac to be at peace and enjoy a pleasant meal. Actually the entire team, with their psychic abilities, was in some form monitoring Zac's mental state and would be alerted if something was out of kilter.

Supper talk was kept light, generic and brief. Hopefully Zac would swiftly gain more and more control over his super-charged emotions and spontaneous shape shifting. None of us had forgotten that Logan and his witches were still out there probably preparing for another demon resurrection. Our mission was not over just because of what had happened to Zac. We chose not to have a discussion about any of that during supper in order to keep Zac's mindset as neutral as possible. Josiah presumed we had approximately a week before Logan could find another location and be ready to re-enact the resurrection ritual. One week, if even that long, for Zac's crash course on werewolf basics. And we had no idea what to expect with the dash of demon in him.

Zac flopped on the couch, looking sleepy and gratified from food euphoria, and flipped on the television. Hmm...his behavior and looks were so normal that it was eerie because he was anything but normal. He was an anomaly.

Since Zac was currently in control of himself, it was my chance to make a break for it. I needed to buy clothes for Zac. We didn't trust his ability to interact with the public yet so I had been promoted to be his personal shopper. Daniel mentioned he and Isaac could use extra clothes and volunteered to take me shopping. I knew the guys wouldn't let me go alone and had guessed Daniel or Dom would end up as my chauffeur.

Josiah chose that moment to step outside and find someone nearby that he could feed off of for his own nourishment. He explained that he'd be back in five minutes. Extremely weird to think he was seeking out his victim, or food source, and would be drinking their blood and be back before Daniel and I even left the house. Of course, Josiah didn't think anything of it, as that is what he'd been doing his entire life.

I asked Zac what sizes he wore in shirts, jeans, shoes and underwear and if he had any preferences in styles or brands, scribbling the information on a piece of paper. Dominic handed over a wad of cash that Eli had provided for the benefit of the team. Eli was rich and generous with his money. He supported us and paid for any expenses incurred on the missions. He was the man behind the scenes.

As Daniel and I walked out the front door, Josiah was returning from his blood feast. It was evening and his eyes twinkled from the light on the porch. I noticed how after he had fed, he appeared even more vibrant, handsome and alive. When he was hungry, the whites of his eyes almost disappeared being consumed by the color black and his aura was doubly intimidating. But now he had satisfied his thirst, leaving the person oblivious to and unharmed from his supernatural requirement. His fingers quickly brushed against my face and tingled with warmth on my cold cheek. His normal body temperature was lower than humans but after feeding it warmed significantly and stayed elevated for many hours as I experienced from his tender touch. And did I say how sexy he was...?

"Don't keep our girl out too late," Josiah teased in a singsong voice, amused with being able to stop me in my tracks.

Damn! He had used his mesmerizing charms on me again! And read my thoughts, too. He really got a thrill out of flirting with me which infuriated Daniel to no end. And bristling Daniel's fur was the icing on the cake which elicited massive snickering from Josiah. He playfully punched Daniel's arm, rather forcefully, but of course Daniel could take it; then Daniel followed up with a retaliating slug to Josiah's arm and a growl. Boys must be boys...I sighed.

"Zac will get restless in a few hours and both of you should be here to assist him," Josiah reminded.

Daniel and I agreed to make haste and left to begin our shopping adventure. We finally had some time to ourselves with no one else hovering around us. The stores were a short drive away and we calculated we'd be back within two hours.

Daniel realized our alone time lately was few and far between and considered it precious. Even if the time had to be spent doing something most men hated - clothes shopping. He didn't waste a second of it as he pulled me across the seat to sit right next to him during the drive. I sensed his emotions and thoughts were all over the place, like he didn't know where to start talking or what to say first.

"Kara, you know I love you, right?" Daniel was warming up for his big speech.

I exclaimed, "That's a silly question. Of course I do and I love you. I can tell you need to talk before you explode. It's just you and me. I'm listening."

The floodgates opened up and he let it spill.

"I'm upset, confused, jealous and feel guilty. I've been trying to conceal, although not always successfully, how troubled I am over the shocking turn of events during the last week. If I weren't in love with you and constantly worried about your safety, maybe my emotions wouldn't be so intense. It's horrible enough dealing with Tessa's death and Logan and his minions with their possible demon resurrection planned and to top if off - I turned Zac into a werewolf! But to have you so deeply involved in this...I don't know...it feels like I'm having a meltdown."

I calmed his mind by pushing in feelings of hope and reassurance. I reached up to kiss his cheek and snuggled close to him on the seat of the truck. I couldn't deny that I was afraid and freaking out, too, but with all my will, I blocked that from Daniel. If he really knew how terrified I was, he'd drive that truck right back to Hamlin, Kentucky to get me away from any danger and to protect me. I had locked up, as best I could, the overwhelming urge to panic. In truth, I hadn't had a chance to process everything with the never-ending commotion.

Daniel and I could not leave The Liaison members to fight this battle against Logan without us. And Zac needed our help with his transition into his new life as a werewolf. I was scared and anxious, but I felt I had a purpose in life. A destiny to fulfill. My psychic powers combined with the abilities of our team could do some major damage. In a good way. Daniel's love for me, and the dear friendship of the others, was a plus that bolstered my confidence and enabled me to shove aside most of my fear. What better way to kick butt and save the world than with the very people you loved?

I let Daniel hear those thoughts - my inner ego rambling on about all the "do good" stuff but making sure to block anything negative. I didn't block all my worry from him; he'd think I'd gone off the deep end if I thrived on danger. But I did downplay it and focused on the positive.

He sighed loudly and continued, "I miss home and the relative security there. Isaac isn't as affected as I am. To him, this is an adventure and he has no girlfriend to look out for. Which brings up the fact how you are the only female in our tightly knit group. I thought Dominic was my main contender in trying to win your heart. Now, Josiah has been sleazing his way into your mind and who knows what his intentions are for you. Even Zac might take a sexual liking for you with his new demon-charged, unpredictable werewolf senses and all the mental and physical contact he needs from you to maintain control. I have no idea what the future holds for him. His conversion is my fault."

We arrived at the shopping mall and intermittently continued the conversation while making the purchases. Daniel's practical approach in choosing clothes for Zac surprised me. All I did was rattle off the sizes as he efficiently located items that would best suit a werewolf and tossed them into the cart. He grabbed a number of new clothes for himself and Isaac, too.

I reinforced, "It is not your fault for converting Zac into a werewolf. He could have jeopardized the raid on the demon resurrection because of his impulsive urge for vengeance on Tessa's killer. You stopped him from shooting that witch and tried to keep the chaos from escalating. Well, as it was, the demon never took solid form and we scared the living daylights out of the witches."

"But Kara, the consequence can't be reversed. The fact remains - Zac is a werewolf."

"That's right - it can't be changed. So now we deal with it. Don't forget that *he* shot your arm and punched you in the face! Has everyone forgotten that? It is not your fault! Do I need to slap you or something?!" My voice had risen and several people glanced in our direction.

"Maybe choose the 'something'," he tried to divert the attention off of us and feebly smiled.

It was critical that Daniel climb out of this hole he had dug for himself. I remembered his story about when he, Isaac and their friend, Stephen, had been turned into werewolves from a witches' curse in 1693. Within days they had accidentally turned several family members and friends into werewolves and eventually turned a few others. It was a disaster. They fled from their homes. Daniel became the pack leader, ridden with guilt, but vowed to shoulder the burden to provide for and protect them, to understand their supernatural abilities and to keep their existence hidden in order to survive. The only additional werewolves added to the original pack came from a few births and two humans who chose to become werewolves in order to stay with their loved ones. Daniel and his pack *didn't* haphazardly run around in beast or wolf form converting people.

I started feeling guilty for yelling at Daniel after I replayed his history in my head. He and his pack had been so disciplined, so careful for hundreds of years to never allow such an accident to occur again. To turn an unsuspecting, innocent person into a werewolf. To turn someone without their permission. Like it had happened to them back in 1693.

And then there was Zac.

Daniel felt failure and humiliation. He was the leader of his pack.

He was immensely strong and intelligent and his common sense was rarely questioned. To be *the* one to have had the misfortune, the mishap, an "oops" if you will, in converting a human was inconceivable to Daniel's mind. No wonder he was nearly having a mental breakdown from the turmoil clashing around in his head.

We were quiet as I paid for the clothes at the register. We carried the bags to the truck and I reiterated, "You are not at fault. Do not compare what happened to you and your pack against what happened to Zac. It is different."

We climbed into the truck and he started the engine. I cranked up the heater and we were on our way back to Josiah's house. I pleaded, "You desperately needed to vent and to let your concerns be heard. I am always here for you, Daniel. But now, I need my big, furry boyfriend to come out of his doldrums and step up to the plate. If you're a good boy, I can reward you later with treats."

A broad smile cracked on his face as he fantasized what exactly I meant by my statement. I was freezing on that January night and let that be known. He tucked me under his arm, driving with one hand on the wheel. His body heat flooded outward, warming me within seconds. I couldn't imagine what he'd be like in the dead of summer if he could emit that much heat in the winter. I had a feeling I'd be kicking him to get away from me as I'd be sweating bullets from the overwhelming heat. Midwest summers were already too hot and humid as it was. For the moment though, I relished his warmth and snuggled as close as I could get to him, glad for our brief time alone.

We arrived at Josiah's feeling a renewed sense of determination and ready to tackle the next obstacle. Daniel and I strolled up the porch steps, hand in hand, carrying shopping bags in our spare hands. Just as I was reaching for the door, it opened for us, but no one was on the other side of it. Dom. That was a nice gesture so we didn't have to fumble for the knob.

Dom waved two fingers in a salute. "You're welcome," he had read my mind.

I tossed a bag to Zac and Isaac. Both inspected their new clothes and nodded with approval at what Daniel had picked out for them. Zac sat perched on the edge of the couch, alert and ready for action. His foot tapped impatiently and he kept opening and closing his fists.

I teased him, "Have you been good while we were gone?"

"After I stuffed myself eating, I chilled in the living room. I was wiped out. But the last few minutes I've been hyper," Zac explained and stood up to stretch his back.

Curious, I asked, "Did you know or sense that we'd be walking in the door soon?"

Zac closed his eyes and tipped his head to the ceiling. He answered, "Hmm...yeah, I think I did know. I was wondering when you'd get back...then I felt that you were actually very close. And I...I recognized the sound of Daniel's truck...before he even had it in park."

"No offense, Zac, but it reminds me of dogs that literally know when their owners are pulling into the driveway. Your senses are growing by leaps and bounds. Aww...you missed us and were all excited to see us again!" I gave him a wide-mouthed, goofy smile showing all my teeth and displayed a big thumbs-up.

Then Zac growled at me! His head tilted down, his lips curled and there was a tiny flicker of yellow slash through his eyes. He did not transform and I didn't think he would attack; although my quartz suddenly grew warm, but he wanted to remind me who and what I was really talking to. I guess he didn't like being compared to a dog in his sensitive frame of mind. Well, his behavior made me mad when I was just trying to have a little fun. The entire room went silent except for the blare from the television set. Dominic used his telekinesis to turn it off before someone threw something at it. Daniel and Josiah moved into defensive positions to better protect me if Zac chose to become aggressive.

I stomped up to Zac with my hands on my hips. Daniel and Josiah were on either side of me, about ready to snatch me away from any danger. I felt Dominic's force field flare up in front of me. I shot him a look and screamed, "That's okay, but just let me be able to move freely."

I shoved abruptly into Zac's mind with enough impact to make his head jerk back. *Listen up, mister. And don't you dare change into a beast right now!* Zac was stopped in his tracks, not sure what to do next. I went on. *I wasn't implying that you're a dog. And I love dogs, as a matter of fact! So my little teasing words should be considered quite the compliment to you. I thought it was sweet that you were waiting for us. What's wrong with that?*

I poked my finger as hard as I could into Zac's heavily muscled chest. Three times. *That* should show him I was not going to be growled at! All I wanted to do was help and try to lighten up the tension that all of us had been under and then of all things, I got growled at by Zac! The old Zac could shed his serious business façade and take and dish out a joke with a snap of your fingers. I knew he had been through hell lately but what I said wasn't anything terrible and he took it the wrong way. My feelings were really hurt. My eyes brimmed with tears and my mouth scrunched up tight.

Even though I wasn't speaking telepathically to Zac anymore, those remaining thoughts flowed into Zac's mind as his own psychic talent took over. Everyone had listened in and held their breaths to see who would make the first move. Dominic snickered and I turned my head to see what the heck he thought was so funny. Just as I brought my teary-eyed gaze back to Zac, I caught him winking at Daniel. Then he picked me up off the floor and twirled me upside down.

"What are you doing?" I gasped, as he held me by my ankles.

A switch had flipped in Zac's mind. Between my finger poking antics on his chest and the threat of tears, he was both amused and dumbfounded. At my expense. And with my coat and shirt falling to my armpits while I attempted to keep myself covered! But I'd gladly take him horsing around than with a foul attitude.

Zac cleared the air. "Like you said Kara, I guess I'm just excited to see you!"

He handed me over to Daniel like a sack of potatoes, still upside down. Everyone was laughing and snorting. I twisted to get loose, with no such luck, then Daniel grasped my waist and cartwheeled me to an upright position, but held me off the floor.

Exasperated, he said, "What am I going to do with you? One of these days you're going to push someone too far and get hurt."

I had to get one more dig in. After all, I was still in Daniel's grip, looking quite hilarious and completely non-threatening, I'm sure, plus I think he was afraid to put me down. So with feet dangling and arms crossed, I reprimanded Zac. "Always remember that you don't bite the hand that feeds you!"

Zac paused and appeared to let that sink in, with a slight bob of his head. With understanding, he said, "You're right. I'm sorry I growled at you...which was very strange having that come out of me...and getting angry. That was pretty brave poking me like you did. And cute," He snorted. "The whole incident was a much needed slap in my face. I know you want to help me. Thanks. I mean it."

Dom cleared his throat, held up one finger, ran into the kitchen and emerged with a bag of beef jerky. He threw it to Zac and stated, "Just to clarify: I do believe *I'm* the one that feeds you!"

Groans and laughter echoed throughout the room. Daniel plunked me on my feet, feeling that it was safe to do so. Zac tore open the bag, pleased with the offered snack, and seemed happy as he started to eat. It had been about two hours since he had last stuffed his face with the rest of us. Keeping his body from getting hungry was a key to stabilizing unwanted transformations, at least at this early stage of his conversion. Daniel assured us that as time passed, Zac's cravings should decrease and his control would increase, lengthening the time between feedings, too.

Josiah brought up what we had all been thinking about and planning to do for the evening. "Zac, are you ready to shape shift into a wolf tonight? You will need to master that ability."

Zac spoke with a mouthful of jerky, "Definitely. So, I guess this time it might be a good idea to strip off my clothes *before* I shift instead of destroying them, huh? Should I put on those new boxer shorts now or later? Man, I'm used to briefs. Daniel, I can't say I ever saw you as a wolf with your underwear on. How's this issue with clothes supposed to work, anyway? This is going to take some getting used to!"

Everyone visualized entertaining images of Zac having underwear problems in all the forms a werewolf was capable of taking and the chuckling broke out again. Rolling my eyes, and vividly recalling Zac's previous episodes which were extremely revealing, baring all of his enlarged, heavily muscled, naked body during his beastly transformations, I quickly fetched his shopping bag and flung a pair of boxers at his head.

CHAPTER 14
LEARNING

"Let's skip the boxers for now," Daniel suggested. "They tend to get in the way and become a distraction. Get your clothes off and wrap a towel around your bottom half. When you transform into a wolf, the towel will either fall off or be draped over you. If you're stuck in the beast form, the towel will still be there to cover your privates."

I chimed, "All for my benefit, I assume?"

Zac mischievously added, "It depends on what you consider a benefit! If only men were watching, I doubt I'd bother with a towel. Kara, I'm sure it's awkward for you when I'm standing here naked. But if you insist, I can forget about the towel for your viewing pleasure."

"No, no…Use the darn towel, hotshot," I struggled, somehow becoming the center of attention. "When you're in control and it's not an emergency to transform, then the *proper* thing to do would be to remove any clothes so you don't rip them apart and put on something looser or cover yourself up."

Daniel approved of my response to Zac's impromptu tease. Having a naked man or beast fully displayed for my perusal was at the top of Daniel's jealousy list. Even Dominic seemed pleased that I wished for Zac to try his best in regards to covering up during shape shifting.

Zac returned from the bathroom with a large towel wrapped around his waist. Josiah recommended we move the experimentation to the basement to keep the situation in a more controlled area. The basement was still a wreck from Zac's earlier transformations. Between his acts of violence and messy eating behavior while in beast form, someone, probably me, would have to dive into cleaning it.

Josiah placed two folding chairs several yards away from where all the action would take place. Those chairs were designated for Dom and me. Keeping us at a distance from Zac's practice session was done in an attempt to keep us safe...or safer. A few other chairs were scattered around, creating a bit of an obstacle course, in case Zac's self-control disappeared and he decided to make a run for it. Not that a few chairs would have much of a chance in slowing down a large, powerful wolf or a menacing beast. Daniel, Josiah or Isaac might actually use those chairs simply to sit on because we planned on working with Zac for many hours that night, if he'd allow us to and if he'd be able to handle it.

Daniel explained to Zac, "We'll create a calm atmosphere for you." He glanced at everyone in the room to relay the seriousness of the matter. "Try to relax and breathe deeply and slowly. Close your eyes if you wish. Let your mind be free of other distractions. Focus your mind on the image of a wolf. That wolf is you. Concentrate on yourself and your body shape shifting into that wolf. If any part of your body starts feeling pain, zone in on those spots, relax those muscles and welcome the change. Embrace the transformation."

Zac squeezed his eyes shut and concentrated. His mouth grimaced in pain as he hunched over grasping his knees. "It hurts. The image of the beast keeps popping up."

I sat on the edge of the chair, almost tipping it over. Telepathically I sent Zac images of the wolf that he needed to focus on. I flooded his inner being with warmth, encouragement and positive emotions.

Daniel instructed, "Picture yourself as a man then the beast then the wolf. In a fast-forward motion, see all three forms *ending* with the wolf. Do not drag it out. Imagine it happening within seconds. You can do it."

Again I pushed into Zac's mind and sensed a tinge of evil trying to influence him to take the form of the beast instead of a wolf. Obviously that little essence of the Demon King Lycaeon that had absorbed into Zac's body did have a negative effect on him. The demon himself may not be possessing Zac, but that fragment of Lycaeon was inside and attempted to sway him towards evil, especially during transformations.

Zac's face and ears sprouted hair and his fingers elongated, turning into claws. He dropped to his knees from the burst of pain rippling through his tortured body. His last transformation happened within seconds when he had shifted into the beast. But he didn't want the beast to emerge now; he needed the wolf to surface. His breathing was fast and sweat was beading on his skin. He managed to keep the beast leashed, but he was struggling.

I crept closer with Dom by my side. I pleaded aloud, "I'm trying to help. The demon glitch in Zac prefers his beast mode. He needs an extra push...from everyone."

The psychic power generated in that small basement was electrifying. The entire team linked our minds together and concentrated solely on Zac. Josiah and I could compel and manipulate Zac's thoughts and feelings while Dom, Daniel and Isaac could speak in Zac's mind with support and prompts to take the shape of a wolf.

I gripped my quartz necklace for added strength. In a hushed, firm voice, I gave an order, "Zac, become the wolf. Shift *now*!"

And with a quiver of his muscles, he morphed into a monster-size wolf. He swung his head to each side trying to view his new form. His eyes saw the towel loosely hanging around his mid-section and with his mouth he pulled it off and whipped it through the air in my direction. I laughed and sighs of relief could be heard from everyone. I stepped closer still, but Dom held me back and pointed to his own teeth as a reminder to me of the risk of coming in contact with a werewolf's mouth.

Zac sat on his haunches, excited but exhausted, trying to slow down his rapid panting. Just like his beast form, his coloring was a mixture of brown, black and white. His eyes were unique - gleaming black with eerie yellow streaks. His size was larger and bulkier than Daniel's wolf shape, keeping in mind that Daniel was larger than a regular wolf as it was; with Zac, he resembled a wolf, but his size was closer to that of a grizzly bear.

Dom had the foresight to bring a chunk of ham downstairs and retrieved it from the bottom step where he'd kept it wrapped and hidden. Dom tossed the ham to Daniel. He removed the wrapping and casually laid the meat on the floor for Zac. We suspected Zac might feel hunger pangs since that seemed to be the norm whenever he transformed. Better be prepared and just feed him right off the bat rather than have him stare hungrily at Dom and me as his next meal. We were trying to wean him away from the idea of eating human flesh as King Lycaeon had a hankering for it and that seemed to be affecting Zac's taste buds. Thankfully, Zac was never introduced to human flesh so we'd been able to sway his thought patterns towards animal meat.

Zac gobbled up the ham in lightning speed. He sent out a mental message to me, *Water. You give me salty ham but no water!* He barked, which startled him of his ability to make the sound.

Everyone was on high alert, listening for any telepathic chatter, and heard Zac's request. I ran upstairs and fetched a pitcher of water, a bowl and removed a wall mirror hanging in the bathroom. I carried everything downstairs and set the mirror aside where no one saw it. Daniel filled the bowl with water and set it in front of Zac who greedily slurped it all up.

"Zac, would you like to see what you look like?" I asked. All heads turned to me wondering what I was up to now.

Two peppy barks were my answer along with a psychic mind push, *Yes!*

He was fed, thirst quenched, nothing threatened him, all his friends surrounded him with support and he had eventually made a successful transformation into a wolf. Things were in balance, so far. And he was accepting his fate and wished to see himself as we saw him. I grabbed the mirror and walked to where the others stood, barricading me from getting any closer. I frowned but handed over the mirror to Isaac, while Daniel kept a wary eye on me.

Isaac faced the mirror towards Zac, holding it against his own chest. Zac paced back and forth and swished his furry tail to and fro. He growled, exposing his deadly and life-altering teeth as he continued looking at himself in the mirror. Isaac narrowed his eyes and took a step back when Zac growled.

I asked, "What's wrong?"

Zac peered around Isaac and said to me, but letting everyone's mind hear, *Just want to see what I look like as a badass!* He play growled again but it turned into a goofy howl and he snickered in my brain. If he were in human shape, I'd have given him a mighty hard flick to his shoulder with my finger.

To boost his already huge ego, I said, "You look ferocious and any enemy would think twice going up against you. But my opinion is biased towards werewolves as I've had some experience with them, you know." My eyes rested a moment on Daniel and returned to Zac. "I also know the real Zac inside. And in my eyes, I'm looking at a miracle. An amazing creature with incredible abilities."

Zac's muzzle drifted down and his paw scratched at the floor a few times as if he were embarrassed from the compliment. I had hit a nerve, in a good way. I hoped his future shape shifting could retain the traits that brightly shone through to the surface at that moment. I thought of mentioning how proud Tessa would be of him, but her death and the events following it had led to Zac accidentally becoming a werewolf. And mentioning her might upset or enrage Zac, and we surely didn't need that when he was doing so well right then.

Josiah moved things along suggesting, "Zac, try transforming several times tonight to become as familiar with the process as possible."

Daniel said, "If you can increase the speed, it will virtually eliminate the pain you're experiencing. It will be an advantage in battles and secure your safety. You can't be taking minutes to transform when the enemy is seconds away from attacking. The more you practice shifting back and forth will make you aware of what you need to concentrate on when choosing which shape you want to take. You need to contain the essence of the demon or use it to your benefit. But don't let it call the shots. Werewolves tend to be aggressive by nature and that's something we'll deal with, but we can't let anything *evil* take root and grow in you, Zac."

With his huge wolf head, Zac nodded in agreement.

Isaac draped the bath towel over Zac and prodded, "Now change back to a man. Don't get stuck at the beast stage."

Zac transformed, lingering a little too long in the shape of the beast, as we feared he might, and the pain overwhelmed him. He cowered on the floor, gripping the towel, and with a mental boost from the rest of us, managed to force his body to shift into a man again. A bit unsteady, he stood up, stretched and walked the length of the basement to shake out the tightness in his body. As he was allowed freedom to move in human form, I squeezed his arm as he came near and I let him know I had complete confidence in his skills. He hugged me, which caught the guys off guard, almost making them jump out of their skins, fearing for my safety. I immediately signaled I was fine and they should back off. Zac thanked me for helping him and I sensed he was holding back tears. He regained his tough-guy composure and was back to serious business.

Over the next few hours, Zac practiced transforming numerous times into a wolf and back to a man, taking breaks after each transition as it did take a toll on his body. At one point, he ate another snack and downed a 24 ounce bottle of water. To test his control, Daniel instructed Zac to maintain the beast form for a period of ten minutes and then turn into the wolf. Zac needed very little of the team's consolidated psychic assistance as it approached the midnight hour. Everyone was tired and Zac no longer stood up to transform but stayed plopped on the basement floor, physically and mentally exhausted. In a way it was funny watching him sprawled out on the concrete floor and shifting into different forms, just lying there. Josiah was the only one standing, while the rest of us slouched on chairs. Dom and I were not allowed to approach the werewolf zone and remained at a distance next to the staircase.

Zac was in his wolf shape, resting his head on crossed paws, back legs kicked lazily off to one side. Sleepy eyes peered at me and slowly blinked. He sighed. Not moving a muscle, his gaze switched to Daniel and he mentally asked him if he could finally shift back into a man and collapse on the bed to sleep for the night. We were pleased with Zac's progress and Daniel agreed it was time to call it quits for the night.

I hopped off my chair and took two steps forward and begged, "Zac, before you shift back, I'd like to come closer and touch you. These guys won't let me do that if there's a chance you'd forget to be careful with your teeth and end up scratching me. You're so tired I figured it's safer now…I had an idea…Would you let Daniel drape a towel around your mouth? As a reminder for you about your teeth? And a safeguard for me so I can come over to you?"

For some reason, I got all choked up and had tears in my eyes and trouble swallowing. I had felt very out of the loop sitting so far away all night, even if I was able to enter his mind at any time and help him with transformations. I liked to be up close and personal and use my hands to touch the person I was aiding. Zac raised his wolf head, tilting it sideways and absorbed my thoughts, realizing I wasn't trying to be mean by asking if he'd let a towel be placed around his mouth. I just wanted to make physical contact and give him affection, friendship and comfort.

Zac understood and nodded his head, sending Daniel the message, *Do it. But use a belt to keep my mouth closed. Make it tight.*

Daniel paused. Emotions of jealousy and concern for my safety flared up but faded when he witnessed the determination on my face and my true reasoning behind the request. Josiah handed over his belt and Daniel gently and respectfully placed it around Zac's muzzle, cinching it tight so it would not slide off. Once again, Daniel asked Zac if he was okay with being restrained and if he was feeling any aggression with the situation. Muzzling a werewolf was a surefire way to bring on violent behavior and the fight or flight reaction. Zac mentally told us that he did not feel threatened, especially since I was near him and he understood the need to protect me.

Zac remained lying down and I squatted on the floor, with Daniel right next to me, in case something went wrong. I rubbed Zac's wolf head, scratching behind his ears. Instantly he closed his eyes and melted under the touch of my hands. He was so tired. I petted him and ruffled his fur exactly like I would have done to my dog, Nicky. It bothered me to see the belt holding his jaws shut when I had recommended a soft towel. He picked that thought from my mind and playfully shoved me with his head, knocking me onto my butt.

Zac reminded me, *I told him to use a belt. I'm fine with it. Don't stop the massage! This is a whole new experience! And dig in with your nails. Ahhh...*

Since everyone was allowing free access to each other's minds, Josiah and Isaac heard Zac's delight from my petting him like a dog and laughed hysterically. Zac rolled over on his side, exposing his belly so I could thoroughly rub it, too.

Daniel narrowed his eyes, grinned and cautioned me, "Watch how low you go rubbing on his belly, my dear."

Dominic came over and got in on the action, too, but kept the scratching to Zac's head or back. Rarely does one have an opportunity to touch a werewolf in wolf form without wondering if they were going to suddenly bite you. Dom commented how silly and freaked out he felt knowing this was his friend and could hardly believe what we were doing! Zac was enjoying himself and was at peace, loving the attention.

After another ten minutes of indulgence, it was time for Zac to shift back to a man. The belt fell off his mouth with the change in body shape and he snatched the towel to cover himself. Dom asked Zac if he wanted anything more to eat before going to sleep, but he was too exhausted to think of food. That was a good thing. He yawned and shuffled into his bedroom, crashing onto the bed, instantly entering dreamland.

* * * *

9:00 A.M. - Breakfast. Staying up late and sleeping in later had become the norm. Zac was famished and needed food without delay in order to prevent a transformation. He fought the beast within wanting to emerge. I flooded him with soothing thoughts and imagery. I noted that his self-control had improved and once Dom started shoveling food in his direction, he had stabilized.

Daniel and Isaac commented on how that tiny demon essence floating around in Zac definitely had a yearning to eat, especially meat. Werewolves normally have a high metabolism and consume massive quantities of food but they tend to quickly burn up excess calories. Even though Zac was eating more frequently than the other wolves, we didn't believe he'd gain unnecessary weight because we kept him so active and he was muscle-bound before the werewolf conversion. Muscles burn calories. Daniel added that being hungry didn't usually trigger a transformation, not like it did Zac. Anger or another intense emotion could entice Daniel to shape shift and the transition was always man to wolf, not beast. The beast shape was difficult to sustain, often taking years of practice. Werewolves naturally preferred the form of a wolf. It was…natural! Zac was different, no doubt about it.

Daniel, Isaac and Zac moved into the living room and dove into a deeper discussion on the lifestyles of werewolves. The talk centered on maximizing all of Zac's heightened senses to his full advantage. They reminded him that he had yet to try out his supernatural speed and agility. They had witnessed a sampling of his phenomenal strength during the night of his conversion when he vented his frustration by punching the daylights out of Daniel, Isaac and Josiah. But Zac's ultimate power and strength had not had a chance to be tested, to see what he was truly capable of achieving…which they firmly believed, once he honed his skills and mastered control, he would be a superior warrior. Previously being a Navy SEAL was a major benefit he could draw upon.

I trotted down into the basement to clean the horrific mess left over from Zac's transformations, the fighting episodes complete with blood splatters, sloppy eating habits courtesy of Zac when in the shape of the beast or wolf, and the general crud of a house being lived in. With five men and me. To be precise: two humans, three werewolves and a vampire.

After two hours of tedious cleaning with not a peep from anyone offering to help, Dominic braved entering the basement in hopes that I was finished. Amazing how he happened to show up when I was about done. Obviously he had read my mind and knew that bit of information in advance and that it was unlikely I'd hand him any cleaning devices at that point.

"Hey, it looks like you're done," Dom stated slyly then switched gears. "Josiah said we should try to pick up on Lexy's thoughts - without her awareness, of course. It's been several days since we busted up the demon resurrection. The witches never saw you and me there and Lexy hopefully hasn't figured out we're involved. Since we had contact with Lexy in the magic shop, maybe we can capture images from her mind again. And Zac is quickly learning about and adapting to his new life as Super Werewolf. We need to prepare for when Logan and his coven attempt another ritual. Josiah feels positive that Logan hasn't given up."

I agreed and propped the mop in the corner while Dom positioned two chairs to face each other. We sat with our knees touching, held hands and created a strong mental link, picturing Lexy in our minds. We had to be ultra cautious that we didn't tip her off with our invasion into her thoughts. Neither of us really got anywhere. Perhaps if we surged into her mind with our combined power, but that kind of defeated the purpose of being stealthy. I caught a blip from a conversation she had…something about the moon. And she seemed to not know the location of the next resurrection yet. Dom gathered the same images from our light, elusive mind read on Lexy. We didn't push any further and withered away from her mind, confidant that she had no clue of our tapping into her thoughts.

I zeroed in on Josiah and telepathically sent him what little info we had discovered. He relayed back, *That's actually helpful. I believe they'll try the next resurrection when the moon is full. We've got about five days. I'll inform everyone.*

Dom and I hadn't moved from the chairs. He held one of my hands, not wanting to let go, and stroked his thumb over the back of it. Dom's crush on me, his love for me, had not died. Things had been a tad crazy of late. There weren't many breaks or occasions for him when Daniel was not around to show his affection to me. Or else Zac needed my help. Or Josiah was shamelessly flirting with me. Everyone's emotions were all over the place.

Dom asked, "After seeing what Zac went through with his conversion and the ongoing changes he's forced to make in his life, are you still considering becoming a werewolf?"

I groaned. He continued, "Zac hasn't talked about his future yet. He can't be left completely alone this early in his transition. And he can't be over Tessa's sudden death. Don't forget that he's not your average werewolf with that mix of demon in him. Have you honestly thought through what your future would be like if you turned into a werewolf?"

"I don't want to talk about the pros and the cons now. I can read your mind and that's what you want us to do. It's time for lunch, especially for Zac." I stood up from my chair. Dom rose, too, and reached to hug me, kissing the top of my head. I hugged him back, resting my face on his chest, and not stopping myself from letting thoughts of appreciation and love pour into his mind. I did love Dom…just not quite the same way as I loved Daniel.

"You know, Dom…I'd think by now you would've given up

badgering me about converting," I confessed, still hugging him. "I know you're worried about me but when I hear the same lecture from you over and over, it gets old. I start to tune it out and get frustrated."

We separated and walked to the stairs. I giggled and remarked, "I'm surprised you haven't come up with new tactics instead of using the old ones on me all the time. Sheesh! Men!"

"Hm..." Dom stopped in his tracks for a second, considering what I had said. Maybe I shouldn't have made that offhand comment. It fueled his fire and could string him along with the possibility that he might be able to sway my attention in his direction. I wasn't going to invade his thoughts and hastily blanked out my mind.

Lunch and the afternoon passed. I proceeded with more mindless cleaning. Dom researched maps of the area and witchcraft information. Daniel and Isaac took Zac outside for the first time since his conversion into a werewolf. They stayed on the back porch and wouldn't let Zac venture any further out into the yard. Josiah remained tight against the door, steering clear of the sun's direct rays. If Zac flipped out and took off, Josiah could still assist Daniel and Isaac in the sunlight, but there was no point in purposely subjecting himself to sunburn if he didn't need to. So, shade was his best bet.

I dipped into their thoughts now and then and poked my head out the door to confirm that things were under control outside. That morning they had discussed Zac's heightened wolf senses. He was testing his abilities and marveling at the experience. Touch – regulating his body temperature and walking barefoot on the cold ground; feeling the sensitivity of the earth on the soles of his feet. Scent – deeply inhaling all the aromas around him and being able to identify specific things from the mishmash, including a dog that had urinated next door. Taste – well, we already knew his fondness for eating but some of the smells he picked up outside affected and enhanced the reaction to his taste buds. Sound – people talking from a distance, vehicles hitting a pothole down the street, a deer rustling leaves in the woods that couldn't be seen but he could hear it. Sight – he was able to see the individual colors of the feathers on a bird sitting high on a tree branch. His mind was soaking up the overload of information to his senses. The fact he was psychic could be labeled a sixth sense, which he made use of at that moment, as he tapped at my mind asking for a dose of my comfort and to help quell the anxiety overwhelming him. He was overly excited, and worried a transformation might be triggered. I administered my mental chill pill to Zac and all was well.

    Several hours later, after supper and once darkness consumed the night, the team decided to move forward with Zac's "Werewolf 101 Class". Josiah estimated we had five days before the witches' next attempt at a resurrection ritual. We wanted Zac to help with the raid and he had to be prepared to handle his newly acquired abilities, both physically and mentally. Fortunately, strict discipline and the desire to gain knowledge were ingrained in his psyche.

    We were not totally confident with his self-control yet and concerned about how his werewolf/demon instincts might influence his choices in decision making. Daniel and the others planned to test him. Time was not on our side, as usual, but we needed to see him in action. That could get interesting.

CHAPTER 15
BLOOD

Josiah's house was situated next to Middlesex Fells Reservation. His back yard connected to wide open ground, a pond and a large wooded area. Josiah intentionally chose to rent that house because of those amenities and the added privacy of not being surrounded by other houses.

It was dark, the middle of winter and cold, with no people in sight and perfect to allow Zac freedom to run. Dominic and I kept our eyes open for anything suspicious or any observers who might happen upon the scene. Zac, Daniel and Isaac stripped down and shifted into their wolf shapes. Zac's wearisome practice had paid off as his transformation was almost flawless, showing only a slight falter as he passed through the beast stage en route to turning into a wolf. He only lagged a mere second or two behind the shifting speed of Daniel and Isaac. Zac playfully barked at me but Daniel nudged him with his nose to keep quiet and his stance warned Zac not to approach me. They looked in the direction of the trees and with eagerness sprung forward using the tremendous strength in their hind legs.

Josiah was torn between transforming and taking a run with them or hanging out with and guarding Dom and me. I told him, "Go already! It's painfully obvious you want to be with them."

"I won't be gone long. Just a little jaunt," Josiah barely got the last word out of his mouth and he had shape shifted into a large, brownish/black wolf. His size was closer to that of a normal wolf, not as big as the werewolves. He circled around my legs, brushing against me.

Can I get rubbed behind the ears like Zac, too? He teased, pushing the thought into my mind. Dom heard it, too, and rolled his eyes and sighed. I bent over and gave Josiah a good scratching and rough-housed his fur. He suddenly licked my cheek and took off at a dead run to catch up with the others.

As I wiped the slobber off my face, I telepathically sent Daniel a message, although I'm sure Josiah did the same to forewarn him. *Daniel, Josiah is on his way...as a wolf. He didn't want to miss out on all the fun!*

To keep warm, Dom and I paced back and forth in front of the spot where the wolves had disappeared into the woods. They would return the same way they went in and we needed to stay in the near vicinity. It was cold enough that we could see our breath. My toes were numb and Dom's ears felt frozen even with a cap on. We switched our pacing to light jogging, covering about one hundred feet of distance.

After twenty minutes, Josiah dashed through the gap in the trees. Another ten minutes and the others would return, he told us in our minds, remaining as a wolf. He explained that Zac had learned to catch prey and was feeding on a rabbit. He noticed how cold we were and encouraged us to keep jogging as he bounded alongside of us. At a certain point I had to stop to blow my drippy nose. I felt something bump the back of my leg and realized Josiah had found a rather large stick and wanted me to throw it. A game of fetch ensued which kept our thoughts off of freezing. He even gave Dom a few chances to throw the stick.

Josiah liked to tease me by not letting go of the stick and would play tug-of-war nearly knocking me off my feet. I could not play rough like that with the real werewolves for fear of their teeth. If Josiah accidentally nipped me with his wolf's teeth, it might hurt, but there was no threat of being converted since he was a vampire in wolf form, not a werewolf.

Just as Josiah and I were playing and tussled with the stick, the werewolves emerged from the tree line. I was facing them while Josiah remained facing me, relentlessly tugging the stick to and fro as I held the other end. Daniel and Isaac clearly understood Josiah's antics were basically harmless with me. Zac *misunderstood*, terrified that Josiah was hurting me or that his teeth would cause a conversion if I was scratched. He momentarily forgot that Josiah could not turn me into a werewolf. When Zac first came upon the scene, his initial thoughts were to rescue me from an attack. But in reality I did not need to be rescued at all.

He reacted.

Zac charged in our direction and transformed from a wolf into the beast on the fly. In terror, I let go of my end of the stick as I stared at Zac while Dom pulled me backwards. Josiah (still in wolf form) turned to see what was causing my reaction. Josiah was well aware when the wolves had made their appearance. His superior senses had alerted him to their arrival and he had no reason to be on guard against Daniel, Isaac and Zac. The entire outing with Zac in the woods was quite successful. Until then.

Zac's preternatural speed was too fast for my human eyes to follow. In the blur, he had jerked the large stick from Josiah's mouth and tackled him to the ground. Even though Josiah was in wolf form, Zac remembered that he was dealing with a vampire and used his natural instincts and knowledge to subdue him.

Zac accurately staked Josiah through the heart.

I started to scream, but Dom placed his hand over my mouth. We could not draw attention. Josiah lie immobilized in the body of a wolf; blood soaked into his fur and pooled under him on the ground. Daniel and Isaac, already transformed and dressed, rushed to Zac's side to drag him away from Josiah. They immediately explained his misguided judgment of the situation and that Josiah wasn't trying to hurt me. Zac crumpled to his knees in shame and shock.

I dropped next to Josiah's side. His eyes locked onto mine. One paw tried to move but it was too difficult and he gave up. I rubbed his head, desperate to help but not sure what to do. I remember him telling me that being staked would not kill a vampire. But it stopped them in their tracks. And the loss of blood would greatly weaken them. I got my answer...

Pull it out. Now. Josiah begged me. His frail voice in my mind was a mere whisper.

My hands trembled as I touched the stick, a.k.a. the stake at that moment. The urge to vomit or gag was overwhelming and I hadn't even yanked it out of Josiah's chest yet. Tears spilled down my cheeks, burning my raw skin in the frigid night air. Daniel, Isaac and grief-stricken Zac were just turning their attention to Josiah and me. After Zac had attacked Josiah, the goal was to move Zac away from doing any more damage or causing harm to anyone else.

Before the others had a chance to comprehend what I was about to do and react to my move, I jerked the stake out of Josiah as fast as I could. I heard Dominic gasp in awe at such a bold undertaking on my part. Daniel or Isaac assumed that one of them would have the task of removing the stake once they had distanced Zac from Josiah. They certainly didn't expect me to do it.

Josiah automatically transitioned to human form and placed his hand over the gaping wound. The blood flow stopped within seconds as his body healed itself. He went to stand up and staggered. To see Josiah fragile and barely able to walk was disheartening. He was normally so powerful and confident. He had lost a massive quantity of blood and the injury was severe. Daniel offered to help Josiah into the house and hooked his arm over his shoulder.

I entered Josiah's mind, putting up a block to all others. *Do you understand why Zac attacked you?*

Yes, Kara. He thought he was protecting you from me. I completely understand. I'm not angry. He was confused. I'll be fine, but I may need something from you once we're inside. Josiah left it at that. Vague.

Thankfully, we didn't have far to walk until we were all safely back in the house. Josiah was taken to his room and gently eased onto the bed. Zac shuffled in, eyes downcast and apologized.

"Josiah, I'm sorry. I thought you were..."

"Zac," Josiah reassured him. "It's all right. I know why you came after me. Your fearless instincts told you to save the girl! Daniel explained to you the scene that you happened upon, which I'm grateful for. I realize you misinterpreted the playful tug-of-war with Kara as an act of violence. And to clarify, when I transform into the wolf shape, *my* teeth cannot convert humans. I just need to rest and regenerate. By tomorrow, I'll be back to normal."

Along with Josiah's forgiveness, I flooded Zac with encouraging thoughts and emotions to boost his depressed mood. He seemed relieved and nodded in respect, leaving the room. Daniel followed

Zac out, not wanting him to get too far from his sight. Dom and I lingered near Josiah, fiddling with the blankets and wondering what to do.

Dom reached for my arm and mentioned we should probably leave him alone. Josiah muttered, "Kara, can you stay and sit in the chair for a bit? I wondered if you could try implanting in my mind images of healing and maybe use the positive energy from your quartz necklace to speed my recovery time?"

Dom yawned and shrugged, agreeing that it seemed the logical thing to do. It was late so he left the room to go to bed. I was standing two feet from Josiah and looked towards the chair, ready to walk over and get it. He shackled my wrist with his thumb and middle finger. He wasn't in the least bit hurting me with his handcuff technique, as there was no tightening of his grip, but I wasn't going anywhere, either.

"Please sit next to me, Kara," he was very weak and I suspected it took a fair amount of effort to restrain me.

"I have every intention to help you. Why are you holding my wrist as if you're afraid I'll leave?" I asked with my suspicion growing.

Josiah switched to telepathy and created a direct link to my mind, blocking out others from listening in. *Your healing images and the magic of the quartz can only help so much...I need human blood more than anything else. If I don't drink blood, it will take me much longer to heal and to regain my full power back. We don't have that kind of time with Zac going through his learning curve as a new werewolf and witches preparing for another resurrection. And I don't think it would be wise for me to be stumbling around outside in my pathetic condition, searching for a human to feed off of.*

I erected a mental block against the others in the house, as Josiah had, to keep our conversation private. My heart pounded loudly in my ears. I was terrified and curious. *Josiah, you'd normally put a compulsion on some stranger so you can feed off them – blanking out their minds and then erasing their memories. I'm sitting here completely aware of your intentions. I do want to help you...But what am I supposed to do? Offer up my neck? Here, have a sip while I wait?!*

Without hesitation, he responded, *Yes, precisely. I'd greatly appreciate it. I won't hurt you, I promise. I can make the puncture marks disappear with my saliva. I'd take the same amount from you as if you were making a generous blood donation. If you wish, I can erase the incident from your memories.*

I did want to help Josiah and it seemed that replenishing his lost blood was the fastest method. I thought of all the clueless victims he had drunk from over the years and assumed they had walked away from the incident unharmed, just a bit short on blood. He answered all my questions before I even asked them. He was convincing. And my quartz necklace was not warning me that my life was in any danger, which was encouraging.

I don't want to feel pain when you bite me. And do not remove my memory of this...I want to remember...go ahead...do it. I closed my eyes and took a slow breath, trying to calm my nerves.

Josiah moved into a sitting position on the bed. His fingers grazed my neck, brushing my hair back and away, and cupped his hand at the base of my head. He pulled me closer to him; his mouth was an inch from my skin. He spoke in my mind with a sultry, mesmerizing voice that melted any worries I had. *Thank you, Kara. I will do as you wish.*

I opened my eyes and gazed into the black depth of Josiah's eyes. *I think it's more like I'm doing what you wish.*

Amused, and with a devilish grin, he sunk his teeth into my neck with staggering speed. As he promised, there was no pain. Instead, I instantly felt like I was floating. Dream-like. He was comforting me; speaking but not speaking; revealing emotions instead of using words. The mind control he commanded over me during his feeding dissolved any fear and anxiety. There was no denying a deeply intimate emotion rushed through my body. I gave of myself and sensed I was truly helping him.

And then he was done. As his mouth pulled away from my neck, his tongue licked over the puncture marks, which felt tantalizing. Any tell-tale signs that he had drunk my blood disappeared. I felt a little woozy from the amount of blood taken by Josiah; but I trusted he had known when enough was enough. If he didn't, I'd probably be collapsing to the floor or already dead.

Josiah appeared refreshed, energized and healthier. His eyes sparkled and he smiled gratefully at me. He lifted his shirt to check where he'd been staked. No mark was evident. His hand cradled my face and felt warmer than usual. He leaned in to kiss my cheek. And then he made a try for my lips, but I bent my head down and he missed his target.

Still using telepathy, he admitted, *Relax. I'm not forcing myself on you. Can you hold my hand and let the quartz work any additional magic healing me? Your blood strengthens me more than other humans. I doubt the quartz is even needed. Very intriguing. Kara, you have a unique combination of traits that draws supernatural beings to you, as it does me.*

I lifted my head, reached to hold his hand and asked out loud, "Such as?"

As I said, your blood is potent. And you're a beautiful, powerful, psychic female that can manipulate thoughts and emotions. You show courage and an acceptance when facing werewolves and vampires. I'm not trying to frighten you, but staying human is very dangerous. Something will happen to you one day...like it did to Zac. You are too involved, too close, literally, with supernatural beings. If you choose to become a werewolf, all those magnetic traits will be enhanced, not lost. Have you thought about turning into a vampire? Josiah's words echoed in my mind.

My eyeballs popped out and my mouth gaped open. A response he expected and found an enormous amount of amusement in watching.

Josiah chuckled, *I'm joking...hmm...I think. No, no, I'm just teasing you! Another thing...it's obvious Dominic loves you, too. Even if you chose him over Daniel, I imagine you'd still be involved in covert missions with The Liaison, confronting vampires, werewolves, etc. The danger will continue to hover over you...getting killed or being converted. With Dom, you'd have breaks from all the action and live a human life, just taking your chances when you needed to deal with...us. Although, as a human, you have weaknesses and are vulnerable. Not that being a vampire or werewolf doesn't have its own problems, but your advantages, safety and success in those situations would significantly improve if you converted into a werewolf...or a vampire.* His advice was persuading.

Josiah brought my hands to his mouth and kissed them. I sensed he had regained his full power and I knew my blood aided in the swiftness of his recovery. I can't imagine how Daniel or Dom would have reacted if they walked in and witnessed Josiah drinking from my neck. I wasn't sure yet if I would tell them.

To push the issue, he arrogantly added, *Kara, I adore flirting with you. If you're ever looking to have some fun, with no strings attached, I'm quite available. Just call.*

Josiah! I blushed and stood up, as did he. It was late and I was tired. I couldn't help myself but to hug him, which he thoroughly took advantage of by running his hands down my back and settling them on my hips, not ready to let me go. He winked and I lightheartedly hit him in the gut, which of course didn't knock the air out of him, but prompted him to let me go.

* * * *

The next morning I called my parents to fill them in. They freaked out. I tried a little mental manipulation to ease their stress. They knew I would try something like that and it irritated them even more. Regardless of their worry and warnings, Mom had a great piece of advice. We should visit an old witch named Claire who lived in Salem and had known my grandmother. Dominic located her address and driving directions on the internet. She might be able to help us in bringing down Logan and his coven.

With some time to kill (not the best choice of words with the latest events), Dominic called Eli. He needed to be kept in the loop even if he didn't physically help out in the field. At Daniel's invitation, Eli had agreed to stay at the resort and keep an eye on Daniel's business and the other werewolves. Dom talked for nearly two hours. A great deal of the conversation covered Zac's conversion. Because of Zac's heightened hearing, he could tune into everything Eli said on the other end of the phone. And seemed agitated from what he overheard.

Dom's call to Eli had pushed lunch later than usual, which probably added to the tension in the house. Zac stayed in human form while he ate but tore at the food like a barbarian and remained quiet. The rest of the team discussed the conversations with Eli and my parents. A road trip was planned for the following day. Zac would stay with Josiah in the house and continue to improve on his self-control, transforming and amplified fighting skills.

Suddenly, Zac spun around and glared at Dominic, roaring in defense, "I can't hold this in anymore. I heard you whisper to Eli that you were worried about Kara being near me. You're afraid I'm going to hurt her. I can't believe you don't trust me. I would never hurt Kara."

Dom couldn't stop the next words from flying out of his mouth. "How can you be so sure about that?"

As if on cue, Zac burst through his clothes into the beast, growling in outrage. Dom had blatantly questioned Zac's capability in containing himself and if Zac was truly aware of the constant danger he put me in when he took the form of the beast or a wolf. It had angered Zac beyond his current threshold. The tough guy attitude combined with the werewolf aggression dominated his mood and actions.

Hopefully soon he would remember to remove his clothes before transforming, as another outfit was ruined. Daniel, Isaac and Josiah cautiously moved around the living room to better positions in case they needed to wrestle Zac to the floor. That was another bad thing as we were not in the basement, it was broad daylight and we had a live beast stomping about that could decide in a split second to bust down the front door and terrorize the neighborhood. I sighed to myself and attempted to enter Zac's mind to calm him but encountered a mental block. I don't think he even realized he shut me out, but I guessed he was so overwhelmed that some type of self-preservation mode kicked in.

Dom's protective force field whipped up around his own body. Dom couldn't seem to keep his mouth shut and went on to say, "Case in point, Zac. Look at yourself right now."

Dom's words, even if they were the truth, and the act of creating a shield as he feared for his life, were the last straws that broke the camel's back. Zac charged towards Dom. I took one step to place myself between Zac and Dom, praying that Zac would stop in his tracks when he looked me in the eyes. And whatever his intentions were would then be derailed and he'd have a chance to prove himself to the team…that he really wouldn't hurt me. Daniel read my mind and didn't want me to take that chance with my life.

That one step I started to take, I never finished. Daniel shoved me back onto the couch and tackled Zac as Zac's claws swiped at Dominic's force field. We had witnessed before that Zac's strength and power were able to penetrate through Dom's invisible, protective shield, albeit at a slow motion speed. But the shield did at least allow a small amount of time to escape from Zac's threat.

Daniel was in human form while Zac remained as a beast. Josiah and Isaac acted as referees and tried not to interfere. I knew Daniel was the Alpha male in his pack back home. Before Zac's conversion, he was a natural leader, independent and a survivalist. Turning into a werewolf, he'd have the tendency to want to be an Alpha. Two Alphas have an extremely difficult time living in such close quarters. Fighting would be expected. Besides werewolf, Zac had the essence of demon mixed into his DNA. Everything we had seen so far proved that Zac was stronger and his powers were superior to that of your average werewolf.

When Daniel tackled Zac, he managed to propel him backwards, causing Zac to lose his balance and trip over his own two beastly-shaped feet. He crashed flat onto his backside. The impact rumbled the house like a mini earthquake. Daniel sat on top of Zac, pinning him to the ground with his legs. Zac swung at Daniel first; then the punches alternated back and forth as they each took turns pounding on one another. At times the movements were so fast it was beyond what my human eyes could follow. The supernatural speed and strength was amazing and terrifying all at once. Chunks of Zac's fur whizzed through the air.

Zac whacked Daniel hard in the stomach which gave him the edge he needed. Daniel's legs lifted off the floor enough from the force that Zac rolled out from under him. Both jumped up onto their feet like ninja warriors, ready for the next round. Daniel had turned his hands into claws to gain some advantage but resisted turning fully into a beast. There wasn't much space in the living room for two beasts to be duking it out. And Josiah and Isaac would only step in if the outcome for either looked grim or if Zac tried to escape the house…or to prevent Josiah's house from getting totally destroyed! So far, the living room was intact, although the recliner and an end table had seen better days.

Zac bared his teeth and snarled savagely at Daniel as thick drool dripped out of his mouth. He attacked and slugged Daniel's jaw, making blood spray the wall. Daniel fought back and the action went into super-speed. I couldn't tell what was happening until Zac knocked Daniel off his feet and pounced on him once he hit the floor. Claws ripped at Daniel's neck, close to the jugular vein but missing the target thanks to Daniel's arm deflecting the aim. Blood trickled from the countless cuts that could be seen on both of their bodies. I had to keep reminding myself that all of the wounds would heal within a day or so...none were fatal.

Only minutes had passed since the fight began and I knew Josiah wouldn't let it go on much longer. Aggressive behavior was deeply embedded in the genetic code of werewolves. Zac was still a newborn and learning to adjust. Overhearing the phone call between Dominic and Eli discussing how dangerous he was to everyone did not please him. It made Zac feel like he was the enemy. Daniel was allowing him to blow off steam but had to redirect Zac's anger off of Dom and keep me out of harm's way. During the fight, Dom had moved to my side and encircled us with his force field. Isaac stood next to us as extra protection from Zac.

Just as Josiah and Isaac decided to move in to help Daniel subdue Zac, Zac bit down with his sharp teeth into Daniel's shoulder. Hard. And he didn't let go right away. Daniel screamed out in agony, which was a rare occurrence, and violently kicked with his feet and swung both fists at Zac's head trying to force him to unclamp his teeth. Josiah and Isaac grabbed Zac by his arms, yanking him off Daniel. Massive quantities of blood gushed from Daniel's mutilated shoulder as he threw his hand up to lessen the flow. Zac continued to thrash about while Josiah and Isaac held him tight.

Furious, I screamed at the top of my lungs, "Stop! STOP!" And the room fell silent.

I raced over to Daniel as he squirmed on the floor in pain. Zac, still in beast form, still being held by Josiah and Isaac, panted loudly but no longer fought them. I was in a panic, not sure what to do.

I pleaded for Daniel's sake, "Can't anyone help him? Why is he in such pain?"

"It's okay...don't worry," Daniel's voice cracked. It was apparent that he was not healing as fast as he normally would, though.

Josiah commented, "Kara, he'll be all right. His body might need longer to heal this time as that's a major chunk of flesh missing from —"

"Okay!" I cut him off. "You don't have to describe the grisly details. I can see with my own two eyes the damage. This is ridiculous..."

I cut myself off at that point as I was about to blame Zac and tear into him for once *again* hurting someone. Instantaneously I erased that thought from my head and prayed Zac hadn't had the chance to pluck it from my brain. If he had, he could go on another blind rage thinking everyone was ganging up against him or flee the house or who really knew what he might do?!

I realized my hand was grasping the quartz necklace in desperation. I removed it from my neck. My voice shaking, I said, "Daniel, get your hand out of the way. I have an idea."

I placed the quartz stone directly onto Daniel's bleeding shoulder – or what there was of it. I could see the white bone glistening through all the blood with the muscle and skin ripped to shreds around it. I had that sick feeling in my stomach. I closed my eyes, entered Daniel's mind and created our strong mental link. He followed my lead as I visualized calm, serene, beautiful settings back in Hamlin, Kentucky. I implanted positive thoughts, my love for him, and images of being completely healed. I channeled all of my energy through the quartz, focusing to aid his body in its own rapid regeneration capability, eliminating the pain and removing any negative demon side effects from Zac's bite.

Opening our eyes, we noticed the quartz was glowing brightly and was not hot, which indicated danger, but cold. And Daniel smiled. His shoulder was not wholly healed yet but had significantly improved and he reached out to hug me. I felt much better and knew the quartz had made a difference. Daniel's fight with Zac had taken place in order to protect Dom and me. At least I was able to do something to help him in return for his sacrifice and his efforts. Everyone was amazed with the healing qualities of the quartz and my psychic power to control it. As was I.

By then, Zac had transformed back into human form and sat slumped on the floor, exhausted and confused. He realized how many times in the last few days he had hurt people or had near misses. Daniel – minutes before. Before that, he had threatened Dom. He had staked Josiah. Several times he had come much too close to me during his transformations, forcing the others to guard my safety. And the fighting bouts that kept occurring with Josiah, Daniel and Isaac. Guilt and sadness beat at his brain and soul.

Any danger from Zac didn't exist at that moment. I took a blanket off the couch, walked to where Zac remained sitting naked on the floor and covered him with it. Daniel followed me, wary of any surprise moves on Zac's part. I also felt the security of Dom's force field surrounding me again.

"Zac, I have another idea," I did my best to lift the harsh atmosphere in the room. "And maybe it will keep you from destroying so many of your clothes!"

His eyes looked vacant, like he might be on the verge of losing his mind. I slowly touched his hand, turned it over and pried open his fingers, which were covered in his own and Daniel's blood. I laid the quartz in the palm of his hand and closed his fingers over it…hoping for another miracle.

Chapter 16
Allies

The mental and physical torment to Zac was evident. We could not keep having disagreements and be looking over our shoulders to see if Zac would betray or fight one of our own team members. We had enough problems to worry about and other battles to focus on. The team absolutely had to pull itself together. We needed to solidify our goals and plans and take action. Zac was destroying the bonds of trust and friendship within our team. How were we going to take down Logan and his witches when we couldn't control the chaos in our own group? That was why I tested Zac with the quartz.

Zac's eyes glazed over as he attempted to keep tears from slipping out. With one hand still clutching the quartz, he reached for my arm with the other. A rumbling sound was heard from Daniel; his warning to Zac. The protective shield that Dom erected around me stopped Zac's hand from touching me. It was plain to see that Zac was no threat to anyone at that time. I glanced at Dom indicating I wanted him to dissolve the force field. With a grunt, he nodded.

Once again sensing the distrust from the others, Zac felt defeated, let his hand drop and stared at the floor. His emotions had flipped from raging anger to wallowing in misery, face down in the gutter. He peered at the quartz in his shaking hand and brought it to his forehead, praying in sheer desperation that it could help him. I cautiously entered his mind and discovered an odd stillness emerging.

I rejoiced, "Zac! The quartz is working! Open yourself to its magic. Focus on it giving you peace."

I decided to see what the quartz by itself was capable of without my added psychic manipulation to Zac's mind. My awareness was tuned into his mental state but I did not intervene. The quartz was relieving his stress and dispelling the negativity in his body. I was ecstatic that Mom had given Grandma's necklace to me as it was a true gift. Zac rose from the floor, tightening the blanket around his waist and feeling that a huge weight had been lifted off his shoulders. He held the quartz gingerly, gazing at the sparkling beauty of it.

"Keep the quartz for now, Zac," I insisted. "When I go on the road trip tomorrow, I want you to wear it around your neck while we're gone. If you need to, transfer the quartz to a different chain or string that fits your neck as you practice transforming."

Zac's confidence had returned and his control was intact. He regretted his previous behavior and wanted to break the ice. "I'm sorry. And I'm sick of saying that so often. Kara, I think you're onto something with this quartz helping me."

"Just don't eat it, crush it, toss it into a tree or lose it!" I teased. "And a little jewelry will look rather sexy on you, Zac!" Everyone groaned. As if beefed-up, looking-ready-for-an-action-movie Zac needed any extra compliments to gloat over.

* * * *

I awoke to another cold, dreary morning. At least I had gotten to bed before midnight, unlike the majority of my evenings of late. I snuggled up to Daniel's immense warmth and peeked over his chest at the clock. His arm circled my shoulder and he pressed his nose into my hair, taking in my scent.

Daniel whispered, "Love you. We have ten minutes until we have to get up."

Daniel, Isaac, Dom and I were heading to Salem for a visit with the good witch, Claire. But we did have those ten minutes to kill.

"Love you, too," I slurred and rolled on top of him, running my hands over his ribs and kissing his chest.

He never slept in a shirt and that allowed me the luxury of instant contact with his glorious skin. I, on the other hand, wore my trendy but sloppy winter sleeping clothes. My hands, head and neck were the only exposed body parts. I stretched up to kiss his freshly healed shoulder and Daniel chose to take full advantage of my bare neck. He drew me up closer to his mouth and ran his tongue along the outside of my neck, stopping at the earlobe, which he ever so lightly nipped. I found myself gazing into his dark eyes and wondered how much longer we could keep up this act.

We loved each other but always made sure to stop fooling around before things went too far. We lived with the fear of Daniel hurting me or accidentally converting me if he transformed. I was 21 years old and Daniel was, well, depending on how you counted, turned into a werewolf at the age of 26…add to that a few hundred years…you get the point.

"I need to make up my mind soon," I admitted, passionately kissing him.

He muttered into my mouth, "About what?"

"You know!" I pulled back and propped myself on his gut. "I need to decide if or when I want you to turn me into a werewolf. This dancing around the fact is driving us both insane. If I choose no, or choose another year from now, can we handle that? Or do we try experimenting more with the make-out sessions and hope for the best? And if I say yes, when the heck do we find time for my personal lessons and learning curve as a newbie? Look what Zac's going through now. You don't want to babysit two new werewolves."

He sighed and said, "Baby, this will be continued at a later date. I promise."

One extra-long kiss as his hands crept up under my shirt then he flipped me over onto the bed and lovingly pecked my nose. Our ten minutes had passed. Time to get up.

He read my mind and chuckled, "I'm already up."

That he was as my eyes dropped down in appreciation.

* * * *

On the drive to Salem, I decided to fess up about Josiah drinking my blood on the night he was staked. I realized that eventually, with all the mind readers in the bunch, I could not keep the experience locked up in my head without the chance of randomly thinking about it and someone latching onto the thought.

"I have an announcement," the passengers in Daniel's truck stopped their conversations in mid-sentence. "The other night when

Josiah was staked I helped to speed up his recovery. Everyone knows that."

Dom interjected, "You placed soothing images in his head and used the healing qualities of the quartz. Right?" His suspicion increased.

Daniel replayed that evening in his mind and with a creased forehead glared at me. "I'm drawing a blank...I can't recall anything from your thoughts during the time you were with Josiah. I don't remember you reaching out with your mind to me...it's a big void. Kara, what happened?" His teeth were clenched and the muscle in his jaw jumped erratically.

Isaac broke in with his recollection of that night. "We left Kara with Josiah. Dom, you went to bed. Daniel and I stayed with Zac, talking with him until he could relax and fall asleep."

"I did use the quartz and my psychic power on Josiah...a little," I swallowed and cleared my throat. "But I also gave him what he really needed more than anything to heal. My blood. He didn't physically force or compel me. It was my choice."

All three of them blurted, "What?!"

"It only made sense, you over-protective, jealous goons! He lost buckets of blood from Zac's stake job. Without fresh blood, his body's ability to regenerate would have taken days. In the condition he was in, he couldn't exactly take a stroll outside to find some willing victim. I was there and could help him. He doesn't kill or hurt humans when he feeds. Nothing else happened, besides his normal flirting. I'm fine." I said my confession and was relieved to get it out in the open.

The atmosphere in the truck sizzled. No one knew how to respond. Josiah didn't harm me and he didn't turn me into a vampire or a servant. They couldn't argue the fact that the best, quickest way for Josiah to regain full power was to replenish his body with blood. What they didn't like was that it came from me. Now, as long as I did not think about Josiah's suggestive invitation, which was difficult since I just admitted he had flirted with me, perhaps we could move forward.

"I don't like it," Daniel argued. "Don't worry. I won't let my feelings affect the team. Josiah has a dominant personality that irritates me to no end, but having a vampire with his strength and abilities who is on our side is priceless. Zac's conversion is more than enough for everyone to handle. I'm not going to pick a fight with Josiah. That doesn't mean I won't have a few words with him, though."

Boys will be boys. And Daniel was ferociously protective and possessive of me. Between being an Alpha male and having the werewolf trait of marking his territory, I'm sure he was imagining all the ways he would enjoy kicking Josiah's butt, even if he said he wasn't going to. Of course, they'd still be friends afterwards. Pardon me, I'm going to beat you up now and then we'll shake hands and all is well. A lot of men were like that. I held grudges. Of course, Daniel had no intention of seriously injuring or killing Josiah, but a good old-fashioned scrimmage was most likely up Daniel's sleeve.

When we entered Salem, Massachusetts, Daniel and Isaac absorbed the changes to the city they had once lived in...and fled from in 1693. Dominic and I remained silent out of respect for their emotions and memories. Sadness and a sense of awkwardness overwhelmed them. Daniel drove for twenty minutes trying to locate where his and Isaac's house had been. He believed he was in the correct vicinity, but the original structures had been torn down ages ago. Everything was completely different and foreign to them.

Daniel stated, "I don't know what I'm looking at or for anymore. Let's move on. What's Claire's address?"

I had called Claire the night before, briefly explaining who I was and why I wanted to talk with her. Thankfully, she agreed to let us visit her. We were on a fact-finding mission to gain knowledge about the witches and any other problems with the supernatural. I read the directions to Daniel and before long we were pulling up in front of her very old, tiny house.

The four of us stepped onto her porch and she opened the door, anticipating our arrival, and welcoming us into her home. I hurried through the introductions and told Claire that my grandmother considered her a dear friend. Claire hugged me and started crying. She pulled away and dabbed at her eyes.

She was about 70 years old, colored her hair red, wore red glasses, was medium in height and thin in a healthy, youthful way. She wore khaki pants and a black sweatshirt that said: "I'm easy to please. Just do it my way." She was not simply some old lady, out of touch with reality and withering away, but instead a modern, vibrant, gently aging woman.

She apologized for the tears, but my grandmother's death was very traumatic for her as they were close friends. Claire smiled and said how I resembled my grandmother. She exclaimed, "I understand you're psychic. How wonderful!"

She shook Dom's hand, pausing before letting it go. "And you're psychic, too."

Dom proudly added, "And telekinetic!"

"Hmm, I have a trick or two…that I can teach you!" Claire gushed in spell-rhyming fashion.

Excited, I mentally tapped Dom's mind, *This could be awesome!*

Then she approached Daniel and Isaac and crossed her arms on her chest, with one foot off to the side, tapping. Sizing them up. Speculating that something was different with them. I should have forewarned her they were werewolves.

Using proper manners, Daniel offered his hand to her. "Pleased to meet you, ma'am."

She grasped his hand, tilted her head and questioned, "You're not human, are you?" And she looked at Isaac next who also offered his hand to her, which she shook. "Neither are you."

"We are werewolves, Miss Claire," Daniel answered bluntly. "We were men cursed in 1693 by black magic witches."

She stumbled and looked like she would faint. Daniel caught her and she regained her balance. Fear and confusion radiated from her wild expression while she made an effort to connect the dots. She was a witch and Daniel a cursed werewolf; she assumed he wanted revenge.

"I…I'm not from that lineage of witches," she stuttered and stepped away. "I'm not involved with evil witchcraft."

I dove into her mind to calm her when she jumped to the wrong conclusion about Daniel and Isaac. I signaled to Daniel what I was doing and that he needed to further explain himself.

"We're not going to hurt you." Daniel extended his hand again. "Did you sense danger when you touched my hand?" She shook her head no. "We intend to take down a malicious coven masterminded by a necromancer named Logan. Several of the witches are descendants from the original coven that turned us into werewolves. They are trying to resurrect a demon."

Claire reached for Daniel's hand. She wasn't a true psychic but with her skills in witchcraft she could read Daniel's aura and determine if he was telling the truth. She brought his hand to her cheek when she realized she had made a mistake in judging him. She knew Daniel was truly a good person.

"I should not have condemned you so swiftly," she let go of Daniel's hand and motioned for everyone to sit down. "It's not often I'm face to face with a werewolf…in my own house!"

I proceeded to tell Claire our story, with the guys assisting, keeping it as condensed as possible, and concentrated on the crucial points. Daniel would reel me back in when I rambled on about insignificant details, which happened often. Claire listened intently and asked only a few questions. It was a lot for the woman to process.

We finished and asked her if she had any advice, knowledge or information to give us that could be of benefit or aid our situation.

She let out a long exhale. It was our turn to listen as she fed our minds with her words. She began:

"In the early 1800's, most of the bad, evil witches and psychics had been killed, moved away or had chosen not to practice black magic. The families that stayed in the area focused on witchcraft spells that were of a positive nature, not for despicable purposes. Some simply stopped practicing it. By the way, I'm not immortal, so I did not personally witness any events that long ago.

"Over the last ten years, I've noticed that very slowly the use of witchcraft was growing and becoming more popular. I am aware of the witch resurgence and of the alarming, increased interest in black magic. I've heard rumors of the coven you're dealing with but I didn't know for sure that Logan was involved and in charge. He is a legendary sorcerer and necromancer who has survived many battles and should have died a long time ago. His talents are incredible; and as such, he was able to cast a non-aging spell upon himself. I have no idea how old he actually is, but believe me, he is very old.

"Kara, your grandmother, as you know, was a combination psychic and a witch. She did amazing things! I am a witch but have developed skills and tricks that enhance my intuition, coming close to being labeled as psychic abilities. She was, and I am, a 'good witch.' From what I've heard, these talents skipped a generation in your family – your mother. She had a little of that sixth sense here and there, but nothing more."

I confirmed her information. "Yes, that's what I've been told. Recently. I didn't know anything about my ancestors being witches and psychics or that werewolves and vampires existed until a few months ago. Dominic stumbled across me with his own telepathic ability and opened my eyes to an entirely new world."

Dom pressed her to teach him something new he could try with his telekinetic skills. She had ensnared him with curiosity during their introductions. She laughed with delight and we followed her into the kitchen wondering why we needed to go into a different room. She placed a paper towel in the sink, muttered a few sentences which must've been the spell, and the paper towel burst into flames.

Not to be outdone, Dominic turned the faucet on using his telekinesis and squelched the fire just as Claire was reaching for the knob. She was quite impressed.

"I can create a force field, too," Dom was tickled to show off what he could do and loved to experiment. "Walk at me with your hands straight out. Go slow!"

She did as he requested and bumped into an invisible wall. Thank goodness he told her what to expect so she didn't crash into it and injure herself. Again, she was pleased with his talent.

"Dom, you should have no problem creating your own fires with what you're capable of doing now." Claire proceeded to teach him the spell. Even if he wasn't a wizard, his telekinesis could interlace with the words and cause the friction in the molecules that would make fire. I think that's what she said. It sounded like mumbo-jumbo and science stuff that I couldn't comprehend. Daniel, Isaac and I politely let Claire and Dom work out the kinks to the fire trick while we watched, sitting on the kitchen chairs, scratching our heads. After five attempts, Dom had a nice little fire going in her sink, which he doused with water before he set her curtains ablaze. Hopefully Dom wouldn't be practicing inside Josiah's house, as I had a feeling that wouldn't go over too well.

Daniel inconspicuously waved at Dom when Claire had her back to us, indicating we needed to keep moving along. Dom asked if he could return some day to learn more spells from her that she thought could be blended with his use of telekinesis. She beamed with enthusiasm and agreed to help any way she could.

I asked her what she recommended I do about the quartz. We had told her how it soothed Zac and helped to bring some peace to his mind and body. I was torn in two directions: let Zac keep it to provide some calming effect and to help guard his soul or take it back for my own uses. I didn't want to lose it or give it up…and yet I felt Zac needed it more than I did. And I knew his life had been ripped apart. His sanity was on the line and if he couldn't control his anger and transformations, we were all in trouble.

Claire paced the floor of her kitchen where we had remained after Dom's fire-making lesson. She finally spoke, "If Zac is part of your team, someone you care for, your friend, someone you believe still possesses those worthy qualities he had before his conversion and can recognize what is good and what is evil…then you need to let Zac have the quartz, Kara. It sounds like his werewolf aggression or the demon gets out of hand once in a while, but otherwise he is still Zac. Basically, giving him the quartz may save his life. The only catch is you'll need to embed it in his body. Preferably the back of his neck."

"Holy cow! Why can't he wear it as a necklace?" I screeched.

Claire explained, "He transforms. One of those times, it will fall off when he's in beast or wolf form and he'll lose it. Or else during a fight it could get ripped off his neck or he could yank it off accidentally. The base of the neck is perfect. It's close to the brain to help ease stress and will offer greater healing benefits, plus it's out of the way and out of sight."

Daniel pondered, "His skin will heal within minutes of cutting and embedding the quartz under it."

We added that project to the To-Do List. I wasn't looking forward to telling Zac that he could keep the quartz but first we needed to slice his neck open and shove it under his skin. Ta-da…you won't lose it now, Zac! I had some concern about his reaction to our upcoming surgical procedure.

Claire had one more suggestion. She dug out a little black book and wrote a name, address and phone number on a piece of paper and handed it to me. Thomas and Bridget Dustin. Husband and wife werewolves that lived about an hour away. She said we should visit them. She didn't know them well, hadn't seen them in years, but through mutual friends had kept their contact information current. They, too, had been cursed by witches not long after Daniel and his pack fled Salem.

"How many people did those witches turn into werewolves?!" Daniel fretted.

Claire said, "They should tell you their own story."

"We have half a day left and shouldn't pass up this opportunity," Daniel made the decision. "Kara, call them."

I made the call to the Dustins, introducing myself and our situation as I did when I first called Claire. They were eager to meet with us. We prepared to leave and thanked Claire for her generous advice and helpful information. She hugged each of us as we made our way out of her house, insisting we watch our backs and to take care of Zac immediately.

It was midday and we were starving, which made me worry about Zac's eating schedule. I homed into Josiah's mind, *Hello, it's Kara. Just a quickie...make sure Zac eats so he doesn't get irritated.*

Josiah answered in his usual sultry tone, *A quickie? Interesting choice of words as my imagination takes over...But back to Zac...he ate a hearty meal and is behaving. He's been working out and practicing maneuvers. And my dear, you don't have to identify yourself when you enter my mind. I will always recognize it is you just as you will always know my psychic signature.*

Well that took a lot of words to say Zac ate lunch! I kidded and relaxed with the news. *Thanks. I'll see you later in the day.*

Daniel zipped through a fast-food drive-thru and we stuffed our faces on the way. We discussed our apprehension and excitement to meet other werewolves, as that was not a common occurrence. At least going into it, we knew they were civilized, that they followed the unwritten law to blend in with society, and had no conflicts with us.

Thomas and Bridget opened the door, just as Claire did, before we could knock. They had similar characteristics as Daniel and Isaac – healthy, strong, confident and didn't look any older than about thirty.

Bridget guided us into the living room and everyone made their introductions.

We didn't waste any time with idle chit chat. Daniel said he remembered their last name from the time he had lived in Salem but didn't know them personally. Thomas recalled Daniel & Isaac's family, too. They rode the wave of emotions as each summarized what had happened to them back in 1693 and beyond.

Thomas explained that not long after Daniel and his pack of werewolves fled Salem, another hunting party was formed to find and kill the witches. The coven was evil and had continued to wreak havoc on innocent people and needed to be stopped. The majority of the town didn't understand that the black magic witches were casting a spell, a curse, turning the hunters into werewolves. Any oddities in behavior were attributed to witchcraft. But in many cases, those individuals or families had actually been turned into werewolves and were not using witchcraft at all, but were merely withdrawing from society to not be discovered for what they had become.

Thomas was a member of the second group of hunters. And the exact same thing happened to him and his comrades as it did to Daniel and Isaac. The witches turned them into werewolves with the curse.

But this time, the curse backfired on the witches. Thomas and the other victims of the werewolf curse had gone into hiding for several months to stay away from humans and to adapt to their new form of life. And then they sought revenge. They devised a plan and followed through with precision. Thomas and several in his pack killed the majority of the black magic witches. They did not go after their children or other family, just the individual witches directly involved in the coven. After that, for the most part, reports and problems concerning evil witches faded away.

Until the last several years...and that's when they observed the reappearance of a group of witches in the local area practicing black magic.

Bridget informed us, "With the use of modern technology, we are part of a worldwide, underground network of werewolves. We write in a secret code to update and warn our members about anything that threatens our existence or of possible troublemakers to look out for and how to deal with them."

Thomas asked, "Daniel, did you say you're living in Kentucky?"

"Yes, although a main facility for our team is in Highland, Illinois, which is near St. Louis, Missouri. Kara is from that area and Dom moved to the site."

Bridget gasped, "Umm...We've heard a rumor...it's pretty solid...that werewolves and maybe vampires are being caught and are undergoing experiments in some lab..." she paused to swallow then finished, "in St. Louis."

Dominic jumped out of his chair and shrieked, "Are you kidding me? How could I not know this?! That's only about 30 miles away from our headquarters! Wait – what do you mean by *experiments*?"

CHAPTER 17
EMBED

After the shocking news that alleged experiments were being conducted on werewolves and vampires somewhere in St. Louis, Dom decided to call Eli. First, we wrapped up our visit with Thomas and Bridget Dustin and expressed our sincere gratitude to them. We exchanged email addresses for further communication, as having allies in this line of "business" could prove beneficial. It was an hour's drive back to Josiah's house and we needed to hit the road. Everyone felt uneasy and repulsed at the horrific images that kept materializing in our minds. We needed to confirm if the rumor was true. Chances were high that the scientists worked for the government, since they did know of the existence of werewolves and vampires. Dominic had been an FBI agent in that particular department, similar to *The X Files*, before Eli approached him to help form The Liaison. But Dom had no knowledge of any lab experiments on other species.

The phone call to Eli was a dead end. He didn't know anything but promised to discreetly look into our findings and try to discover what was going on. Dom highlighted the most critical points of the last few days for Eli in an attempt to keep him informed. The conversation between Dom and Eli ended a few blocks from Josiah's house and when Dom hung up, he looked disturbed. He pursed his lips together in frustration as he stared at the phone. Daniel, Isaac and I had stayed quiet to let Dom speak to Eli and now we wondered what was bugging him. He shrugged his shoulders and mumbled not to worry, that he was probably over-analyzing the different scenarios that kept popping up in his head.

Josiah and Zac were expecting us and sat eagerly awaiting the updates from our day. I relayed what we had learned, with Daniel and Isaac tossing in their comments and Dom shouting his remarks from the kitchen while he made supper. We had gained some valuable friends that day – Claire the witch and Thomas and Bridget the werewolves.

We finished supper with no aggressive outbursts, making sure Zac was full. Then I cautiously mentioned to Zac that Claire suggested we embed the quartz in his neck. Immediately. For his sake and sanity. And ours. And everyone's safety. He looked at me as if I'd completely lost my mind.

"No way," Zac countered. "I'll just wear it since it does help keep me calm. But I'm not having a stone stuck into my body."

And with that, he pushed his chair away from the table and stood up. He chose to walk away from the discussion instead of getting into a heated debate. He headed down into the basement where his bedroom was located. He had stood his ground on the issue and avoided a conflict of interests. Then he made his escape before his aggression overpowered his self-control and what comfort the quartz that he wore could provide. Not necessarily a bad move. He didn't display any rage and managed to not transform into a beast or wolf, so in some ways, you had to pat him on the back for his actions.

But we knew better. It wouldn't last long. He was probably already seething as he hid out in his room. I tapped at his mind, *Zac, one reason we want to implant the quartz in your neck is so you won't lose it whenever you transform.*

All I got from him was the equivalent of a grunt. And he created a flimsy mental block to indicate not to bother him. I withdrew and shadowed just the outer edges of his mind, which let me monitor his emotions and random thoughts to know what was happening to him. I did not try to knock down his shield. I sensed his natural instinct for survival kicking into overdrive. The idea of allowing someone to literally slice into his flesh while in a vulnerable position and stuff a foreign object under his skin was not setting too well with him. Zac thought by removing himself from the scene, to walk away, he had everything under control.

But he paced the floor and his anxiety exploded as he became more agitated and paranoid. He suspected that we would gang up on him. He was trapped in the basement with no way out except back up the same way he went down. Zac was angry with himself as he should have known better than to seek refuge in a place with no alternate escape route. (Although, if he had chosen to stomp out the front door alone and in his current state of mind, we would've stopped him. Or at least tried to.) His avoidance technique was not going to work.

"Zac is freaking out. He's having a breakdown," I warned the others. Josiah and Daniel had linked into my brain from the moment I telepathically reached out to Zac. They knew what I knew and had made a unanimous split second decision. Daniel, Josiah and Isaac flashed past, stirring up a breeze, while Dom and I scrambled to the basement stairs trying to catch up with them.

By the time my feet hit the basement floor, an all-out battle was in full swing. Zac vs. Everyone Else. He was in beast form as were Daniel and Isaac. Sadly, it reminded me of a previous dilemma Daniel had dealt with in his pack. I was brought on board with The Liaison to help Daniel neutralize a rogue werewolf, Stephen, before he turned completely evil. The decision was clear – if we did not succeed in helping Stephen regain self-control and calm his aggression – he would be killed. Thank the stars, good won over evil and Stephen emerged a new man, or werewolf.

I was stumped. When our team had hunted down and restrained Stephen, I had used the art of distraction to tear down his mental block which allowed me inside to manipulate his thoughts and emotions. It worked. But Zac was different. The situation was different. Tessa was killed then he got converted into a werewolf within the span of a week. He had a soldier's mentality, was a true survivalist and had superb fighting skills. Don't forget that blip of demon inside that was fighting tooth and nail to keep from having my quartz implanted in his neck. In comparison, Zac's power, physically and mentally, was far superior to that of Stephen's. I managed to help Stephen but how would I ever make a crack in Zac's mental block to help him?

A chair flew across the room, smashing into the basement wall. I knew from reading Daniel's and Josiah's minds that if they could not get the quartz into Zac's neck and he continued to fight them or if they did embed it but the quartz had no effect, then their plan switched to killing Zac. The Liaison, if we were to survive and do any good, could not tolerate arguing and fighting within our team. Zac could destroy us in more ways than one.

Zac snarled over and over with a vicious display of razor sharp teeth. Drool dripped from his muzzle and white foamy spit collected in the corners of his mouth. Those terrifying yellow eyes showed no signs of weakness, no backing down. A savage, frenzied animal that was in major defense mode glared at us.

The brotherly bond between Daniel and Isaac allowed them to fight in perfect unison. They surrounded Zac and charged at him. Daniel grabbed his arms and Isaac tackled his legs, causing the trio to tumble onto the concrete floor. Josiah pounced onto Zac's stomach, trying to knock the air out of him and to keep him from getting up. Fists and claws were flying through the air as one of Zac's arms escaped Daniel's hold. Zac twisted and kicked hard, trying to free his feet. Isaac held tight as Zac's legs raised him a few inches off the floor and slammed him down.

"Where's the quartz?" I screamed. My eyes darted left and right, scanning the floor and Zac's body.

Zac's bizarre laughter echoed in the confines of the basement. It was uncanny and gave me goose bumps. Didn't anyone notice he wasn't wearing it? The whole point of this was to embed the quartz into his skin and we didn't have it! My grandmother's mystical necklace that was handed over to me by my mother was now missing! I had willingly chosen to give it to a friend who needed it more than I did in order to basically save his life.

Zac was messing with us…with me, since the quartz was mine in the first place. I was beyond outraged. Dom and I ran towards his bedroom to search for it. It had to be in the basement somewhere. As I edged my way around the mass of supernatural beings tangled up on the floor, somehow Zac renewed his efforts to free himself from Josiah, Daniel and Isaac. He didn't want me snooping around and locating the quartz. His arm swiped out at me, partially slipping from Daniel's grasp, with his claws extended into my path. Several of the talons ripped through my jeans. And sliced into my leg.

Oh. My. God! I doubled over from the pain and shock, reaching for my calf and falling to the floor. In a panic, Dom pulled me away from Zac's proximity. Daniel couldn't let go of his arms to come to my aid and the guilt in his eyes made my own pain even worse. Josiah slugged Zac so hard that his head flung to the opposite side and blood seeped from his open mouth. Zac stopped thrashing about, stunned from the trauma to his brain.

The wound on my leg throbbed with the beating of my heart. I'd have to have stitches. I knew the cuts were deep and lengthy from Zac's ultra-sharp nails. The blood had instantly soaked through my jeans and was flowing onto the floor. I couldn't stand up. It hurt way too much and I felt dizzy. We didn't have time to deal with this now. I couldn't just up and leave and have Dom take me to the hospital. We had to find the quartz and make an attempt to save Zac. How ironic that sounded…Zac had attacked and injured me and yet I still thought to save him while I sat bleeding…in serious need of help myself.

All of a sudden, Josiah was kneeling in front of me and ripping my pants leg open to expose my injury. He held my calf gently, bent his head down and ran his tongue over the slashes several times. He licked all the excess blood off of my skin. His dark eyes met mine with a mixture of concern and desire…and then he was gone. I had almost forgotten about the healing agents in his saliva! The gaping wounds on my leg were no longer visible and I felt restored.

No one had said a word as Josiah healed me. After he punched Zac in retaliation for hurting me, he had time to come to my aid while Zac remained dazed. Josiah's action, the entire episode, spanned less than ten seconds, and he once again sat back on top of Zac holding him to the floor.

Thank you. I linked to his mind, grateful but feeling a mixture of emotions from the incident. I felt his warmth flow through me; his way of saying, "you're welcome."

I wiped the tears off my face and Dominic offered his hand to pull me up. He had watched as Josiah performed the miraculous, impromptu triage, turning into my own personal doctor. Dom wasn't about to say any offending words to a vampire when he could observe firsthand that Josiah was the one who had the ability to help me. No harm done. Daniel couldn't argue or get mad at Josiah, either. Was Josiah supposed to let me suffer, possibly bleed to death, when he knew, even the werewolves knew, a vampire's saliva could fix me?

Time was of the essence, my leg was fine now and I was back on the hunt for the quartz with Dominic. And *really* ticked off at Zac now.

Before Zac regained full consciousness from Josiah's blow, I dove into his mind while his guard was down and plucked some clues on where he had probably hidden the stone. It didn't take long and I found it hanging on a nail behind the dresser mirror. Removing the quartz from his neck and hiding it had been a spur of the moment idea on his part.

I approached Zac but kept a safe distance. Holding the quartz in my open hand, I announced, "I found it. Zac, why can't you get it in your thick head that all we're trying to do is help you? Don't you think if we wanted you dead, between two werewolves and a vampire, we'd have already killed you?"

He snorted at me and started to struggle under the guys again. *Maybe I'd be better off dead.* He replied in everyone's minds.

Josiah, Daniel and Isaac needed to flip him over on his stomach in order to access his neck and embed the quartz. That would not be an easy feat as any movement could allow his escape or result in someone getting injured. Again. The situation with Stephen surfaced in my thoughts and how I had used distraction to gain the advantage over him. I knew what I was about to say to Zac would be a low blow. But, hey, Zac had clawed up my leg…would he have tried to actually kill me if given the chance?! It was time to play dirty.

I looked him straight in the eye without flinching. I focused on his mind and any weak spots. "You know, Zac, if you really want to die, I'm sure we can accommodate you. And if you haven't figured it out, if you don't let us embed this quartz into your neck, and you keep fighting us, you will be killed. I'm sure if *Tessa* were alive she would not approve of your behavior."

Silence…his panting stopped as if what I said took his breath away.

"Flip him now!" I urged Daniel, Josiah and Isaac and they obeyed with lightning speed.

Zac was face down on the cold, concrete floor which had numerous cracks running through it from the violent smack downs. He was in shock from my harsh, but truthful words. I had used the memory of Tessa as bait, as the distraction to break him. As his chin ground into the floor, he transformed back into a human and I heard muffled sobs coming from him.

Josiah lengthened one of his fingernails into what resembled a thin blade and sliced into the base of Zac's neck. He cried out but the three of them held him tightly. The cut would heal rapidly with his werewolf DNA. No one worried about the wound or his bleeding.

Josiah instructed, "Kara, toss it to me."

I took aim and lobbed the quartz at Josiah, who didn't remove his eyes or one hand from Zac, and he effortlessly caught the stone in midair without looking. He raised a thick layer of skin on Zac's bleeding neck and pushed the quartz deep into the flesh. Then he pulled the skin together over the quartz to aid in the speedy werewolf healing process.

Within seconds of embedding the quartz, Zac cried out again. "It burns! Get it out!"

He writhed under them, shaking, breaking out into a sweat, moaning and transforming back into the beast. Daniel and Isaac had remained in their beast form throughout the whole ordeal since they needed their full strength to restrain Zac. He was trying to reach back with his claws to dig the quartz out of his neck and Daniel had to grasp his arms to prevent him from mutilating himself with the sharp fingernails. As it was, Daniel and Josiah had suffered many cuts from Zac's claws and teeth, but most had already healed or were in the process. Isaac stayed at Zac's feet and received the least amount of injuries from him. With Daniel, Josiah and Isaac united against Zac, he wasn't able to concentrate on pummeling one single person nonstop, which thankfully lessened the severity of everyone's battle wounds.

Zac's demon essence and all natural instincts fought the power of the quartz. I had a feeling we were in for a late night again. In a swift strategic move, Zac shifted into a wolf and managed to push himself off the floor onto his front legs. The maneuver made the guys scramble to keep him restrained. In the wolf's body, he was rather agile and hard to hold still. Dom and I retreated to the stairs to stay as far away as possible without actually leaving. Josiah yanked Zac's tail to prevent him from lunging in my direction. He yelped and twisted around to bite Josiah's hand but Isaac clamped Zac's jaws shut while

Daniel knocked him off his feet. All three wrestled Zac into a submissive position, each assuming responsibility for controlling a different section of his body.

Daniel grunted from the exertion and without speaking suggested, *Why don't you and Dom go upstairs? Please. It's too dangerous with three werewolves in such close quarters. The longer you're near us, the higher the chances become you could get hurt. Again. You've done your share to help. We've got the quartz in his neck and we'll let him settle down. You had one close call tonight and I don't want to have to worry about another.*

"I agree," Josiah piped in. "We can handle it. Zac's system just needs time to adjust. He is unpredictable with the sudden transformations and almost squirmed away from us heading straight for you. Get some sleep. We don't need to sleep as much as you do."

I objected, "But he might need me—"

No, Daniel interrupted. *Just pretend as if Zac got stung by a bee and he's having that initial reaction of pain and the urge to get the stinger out. He'll get through this.*

"Uh, huh," I wasn't too convinced. "Must be a really big bee."

Josiah nodded in approval at the comparison and urged, "Go on. I healed your leg, but your body and mind are still exhausted and need time to recover. Dom, get her out of here."

And just at that moment, Zac shifted back to the beast shape. Another frantic wrestling match followed in the attempt to keep him down. Dom yanked my arm and we skedaddled out of the basement.

* * * *

Dom and I trudged into the kitchen to find something to drink. We were dehydrated and as Josiah accurately diagnosed – exhausted. From the depths of the basement, a lone wolf's whimper resonated through the entire house. How could we ever fall asleep when every few minutes we heard the sounds of a brawl or Zac's growls and haunted cries?

Ten minutes passed and Dom made the first move. "Kara, there's no point standing in here when we're both ready to collapse. Let's go to bed...and I don't mean it the way that came out of my mouth. Well, it doesn't sound too bad...although I don't think Daniel would approve finding us in the same bed wrapped in each other's arms. I'm so tired I'm rambling on like an idiot."

We paused in the living room and listened for noises coming from the boys in the basement. Both of us concentrated our weary psychic skills on reading anyone's thoughts for an update on Zac's progress. We hesitated to go upstairs where the bedrooms were, two floor levels away from all the action.

Daniel felt my mental prod and picked up on my last thought, *Two floors of distance would be fine. Nothing new to report. Would you just go to sleep?!* He immediately redirected his attention to keeping Zac contained. Zac continued to struggle from the quartz's effect but I sensed a tiny, itsy-bitsy calming sensation trickling through him. Finally. And I sent that information back to Daniel, Josiah and Isaac – just in case they weren't able to sense it themselves like I did.

Dom and I shrugged our shoulders and went upstairs, each going to our separate rooms to change clothes and get ready for bed. As I crawled under the blankets, Dom softly tapped on my door and asked if he could come in. It was a little weird having him in the bedroom that Daniel and I shared, but I didn't want to tell him that he couldn't come in to talk to me.

He approached me and sat on the edge of the bed, looking at the floor as I leaned against the headboard. "Kara, we have been through so much together. When Zac sliced open your leg tonight...I knew it was bad. Everyone knew how severe the damage was. I felt your pain in my mind and seeing the blood everywhere...and I couldn't do anything to make you better. I'm not going to deny it, but Josiah freaked me out when he licked your leg and poof! You're healed! I'm sure Daniel was completely shocked, too. Regardless, Josiah was a lifesaver. Hmm...you helped speed up healing him when he drank your blood after Zac's stake job and tonight he returned the favor and healed you. Although he would've tried saving you no matter what. He, too, has a 'thing' for you. Just something to be aware of...he's tasted your blood twice. I don't know if that means anything at all. Just rambling again."

I grinned. "That's okay. I'm usually the one doing that!"

I jabbed him in the arm playfully. He turned to face me with a tender, serious look. "You told me that you get frustrated every time I bring up a certain life-changing situation that you're considering and to find a new tactical approach. So, I'm taking your advice and I'd like your input."

"Huh?" I said, baffled.

Dominic knew Daniel was heavily engrossed in dealing with Zac at that moment; pre-occupied with restraining him, as were Josiah and Isaac. They had to keep an eye on Zac's adjustment and acceptance to the quartz.

Which meant that Dom had me all to himself for several hours.

CHAPTER 18
EVALUATE

Dominic's new ploy to sway my feelings and future decisions surprised me. He boldly treaded a fine line that could've crashed at the bottom of a ravine. I had told him days before, half-joking, that he needed to come up with a different tactic, a new approach, to changing my mind about staying with Daniel and of the likelihood I'd choose to convert into a werewolf. Dom definitely decided to take me up on that suggestion and made his move. I couldn't blame him for his actions as I had spurred him on.

He reached for my hand and brought it to his heart then bent his head to kiss my fingers, one at a time. He scooted closer to me on the bed, still holding my hand to his chest. Using his free hand, he pushed my hair off my left shoulder and with gentle fingers, circled my neck. Dom gazed into my eyes with such love and need that it took my breath away where I couldn't swallow. I closed off my mind to Daniel in as tactful a way as possible without drawing any attention to look suspicious…as if to him I'd fallen asleep.

Dom smiled, aware that I had blocked off my mind to everyone except him. And he had done the same, where only I could read his thoughts, in order to keep our time together private. I'm sure Josiah could have easily broken through either of our mental blocks, but he didn't have a reason to at the moment. Josiah, Daniel and Isaac had their hands full with Zac.

Dom released my hand and I kept it where he'd placed it on his heart. Both of his hands held my head and he leaned in to kiss me, but an inch from my lips, he went motionless. I had closed my eyes, anticipating the kiss, not stopping him. He switched destinations and kissed one cheek then skimmed across my lips, teasing my mouth with a light touch, on his way to kiss the other cheek.

"You haven't told me 'no'…yet," He whispered into my ear. "Kara, I love you."

I tried to explain. "I love you, too, but I love – "

His mouth planted forcefully on mine, cutting off my next words. I started to question myself as I responded to Dom's kisses. Especially since there was *no* fear or worry about pushing *Dom's* desire beyond the limit of self-control. He couldn't transform and accidentally convert me or forget that his supernatural strength could hurt me….Like *Daniel* could.

The lack of restrictions equaled freedom as I wrapped my arms around Dom. He used his telepathy to toss the blankets aside while his hands and mouth continued their exploration. I slid down onto the bed and Dom instantly covered me, being thoughtful to support his own weight and not crush me.

Needless to say, Dom and I fooled around for a little while. He caught me off guard and in a moment of weakness, both mentally and physically. I loved both Dom and Daniel. But the love was different for each. I'd met them at nearly the same time, only a few months earlier, for heaven's sake! It's not as if I'd been dating Daniel for years; I wasn't married to him; and I was only 21 years old. Wasn't that supposed to be the prime age to socialize and get your life figured out? Or try?

Well, we did not have sex…

At a certain point, I exclaimed, "Dom, we have to stop. And you know that. I can't deal with this. Not now. Not here in this bed. Not with Daniel and all the others in the house. Not with Zac turning into a werewolf and his aggression issues. And gee, let's not forget the witch hunt and the demon resurrection any day now. I'm not going to complicate matters within our small, fragile group any worse than they already are by being caught making out with you and causing total chaos! Yeah, that would go over real well. Or if it was up to you, I'd march up to Daniel and tell him I'm breaking up with him and hooking up with you now. Uh-huh. Let's create a wee bit more pandemonium around here. I don't think so."

Dom knew I was right. But he felt he had made progress with me and was flying higher than a kite. I could have told him to stop right off the bat when he first kissed me. He didn't force me to do anything. I was a willing and active participant…and wanted to see and feel this other side of Dom. No holding back until I came to my senses before we had gone too far. It was not the time or place. And I wasn't positive if there ever would be any of that with Dom. Sheesh, love was complicated. I wanted to slap myself as some doubts about my future choices churned in my brain.

Dom put his shirt back on that had been feverishly flung off. He paused to focus on the location of everyone in the house. I did, too. We were safe from discovery. Of course, Dom couldn't leave it at that and head off to bed. No. He still had to get the last word in, but I noticed it didn't come across as nagging anymore.

Dom covered me with the blankets and sat by my side. His final plea tugged at my heart. "This will probably sound goofy, but I've dreamt of running off with you…distancing ourselves from this dangerous lifestyle. Or if you wanted to stay with The Liaison, I'd promise to find ways to protect you better so you're not putting yourself into such life or death situations. I do know that I want you with me. But if I can't have you, I hope you don't decide to become a werewolf. I don't want you to go through the torture and completely change your life. If you choose Daniel, well, I just don't know, Kara. Remember that you don't have to turn into something else for *me*. I want you just the way you are."

* * * *

I was the first to wake up around 9 A.M. The house was silent - an excellent sign. I was anxious to see how Zac was doing with the quartz embedded in his neck. He didn't want it in his body and had put up a good fight. I hoped his opinion had changed about the quartz after he had time to adjust to it overnight.

I darted to Dom's room and whipped back the covers. No shirt, but shorts on. What was it with guys not wearing shirts all the time? It was the dead of winter in Massachusetts and bitterly cold. But I have to admit, I paused to admire his eye-catching chest. "Rise and shine! Let's check on Zac."

Dom did a swift mind scan to locate the whereabouts of everyone in the house and verified that they were in the basement. He grinned with his male smugness and abruptly grabbed my arm to pull me down onto his bed. In a split second, he had tossed the covers over us, which were toasty-warm from his body heat and enveloped me in his arms. He took advantage of any opportunity to flirt and shower me with his attention.

"So you like my chest, huh?" Dom had read my thoughts and his ego was soaring.

I couldn't deny it. I felt comfortable lying next to him and it was cozy, especially since the house was chilly. After a few minutes of his harmless hugging, I poked him in the gut and dashed off his bed. We really needed to check on the guys in person to see how everyone had survived the night.

By the time Dom and I had dressed for the day, our curiosity on Zac's progress was about to explode. Daniel had never made it to bed. He, Josiah and Isaac decided it would be best to stick it out the whole night with Zac. Dom and I hurried down two sets of stairs, bypassing Dom's domain (the kitchen). He planned on making breakfast, but not until we confirmed that everything was stable with Zac. We reached the basement, out of breath, and surveyed the crime scene. I recalled what harm had been done – to the interior of the basement and physically to the guys. Most of the damage had occurred before Dom and I were told to leave. Another good sign. Zac's urge to lash out had lessened overnight.

Our human feet pounding down the steps, the gasping for air and our scent had alerted the supernatural foursome that we had arrived. By the bedraggled looks of it, we had just awakened them. Isaac was plunked on the floor guarding the stairs while Daniel slumped on a chair in Zac's room and Josiah was leaning haphazardly inside the doorframe to the bedroom. Escape would have been near impossible.

Josiah moved out of the way as Zac emerged from his room. Dom and I were amazed at the difference in him compared to the last time we had seen him. It was obvious how much he had improved during the night and into the mid-morning hours. I tentatively stepped towards him and the others moved to position themselves between us. For a few moments, the three (Josiah, Daniel and Isaac) respectfully and with no threatening motives, read Zac's thoughts and tried to gauge his emotions. I imagined they had developed stronger mental links with Zac during his adjustment to the quartz. I touched at Zac's mind for my own knowledge and precaution and felt no hostility. I sensed gratitude for our desire to help him, shame and guilt for slicing my leg open and a renewed determination to fight evil. And he absolutely oozed with a Steven Seagal coolness.

Everyone was satisfied that Zac was under control and stepped aside. Josiah looked at me and filled in the gaps. "A few hours after you and Dom went upstairs, Zac reverted back to human shape. When he finally recognized how the quartz could neutralize his aggression and the demon part of him, then his mind and body gradually accepted it and stopped fighting against the power of the quartz. He understands why we embedded it under his skin...so now there is no chance that he'll lose it. And he even slept a little, too. I've been monitoring his mind all night and I am quite pleased to present to you...the new Zac."

Josiah patted Zac on his bulging shoulder and the atmosphere in the room had become one of solid camaraderie. As usual, my eyes welled up with tears at this revelation. Zac looked directly at Daniel and glanced at the others alerting them that he was fine and could be trusted. Little nods of approval came in response.

Zac approached me and begged, "Kara, once again I find myself apologizing. I'm sorry I..." He closed his eyes and swallowed to regain his composure. "I wasn't myself. It was all a haze what happened last night. I didn't mean to hurt you. Josiah said he healed your leg."

I stretched out my arms and jumped at Zac to give him a big, tight hug and he easily swung me off my feet, hugging back. "It's okay, Zac. I'm fine. Except I need some air, though. Loosen your grip!"

He chuckled and once I could breathe again, I started laughing, which made everyone loosen up and laugh, too. He put me on my feet and said, "So, when do we eat?" And in a brotherly way, he slung his heavy arm around my shoulder and annoyingly shoe-shined my head.

* * * *

Zac tested his self-control while Dom prepared brunch. With the addition of the mystical quartz embedded in his neck, he had a calmer attitude. He was learning to focus on and draw from the positive energy it offered him. And he definitely had a challenge ahead as meat was his weakness and Dom chose to fry up bacon among other complimentary items. Zac's affirmation: no drooling, no aggression and no transforming. That was the goal. The scent drifted through the house making everyone's stomachs growl in anticipation. *I* was close to drooling; but Zac held his ground.

Dom called us into the kitchen and plopped a heaping plate of food in front of Zac. And quickly backed away…just in case Zac flipped out. He sniffed several times and closed his eyes to inhale one long, appreciative breath. It looked like he was meditating. All was good when he opened his eyes and cheerfully said, "What?!" We had a nice, normal meal and Zac behaved without any help from us.

During the afternoon everyone dove into practicing for the upcoming battle against the witches. Lately, we had been obsessed and distracted with Zac's conversion. Now the time had come to review and fine-tune our supernatural skills along with hand-to-hand combat moves. If we were not able to stop the resurrection and the demon materialized, we would have to try to kill it. The guys needed to prepare and strategize and coordinate their attack.

The witches' demon resurrection was looming on the horizon and could happen any night. We had no definite clues where the ritual would be performed. I hoped my short encounter with Lexy at the magic shop would pay off, giving us a lead or direction on a location. Dom and I had not been successful when we discreetly touched at her mind, but assumed she had been told by Logan to block out the details in case anyone tried to snoop into her thoughts. My belief was that Lexy would be so mentally consumed, anxious and terrified with the resurrection that I would pick up on her extreme emotions and read her mind. Dom had been able to read her mind at the store, too, and he continued as I did to focus on her every few hours.

Dom desperately wanted to improve on his new skill that Claire had taught him. He had not used his telekinesis to create a fire since we had visited her. Josiah recommended that he go outside as he didn't want his house burned to the ground. Dom didn't argue. We bundled up and followed behind Josiah, Daniel, Isaac and Zac. They could regulate their body temperatures and the cold air didn't bother them much, but they still wore jackets to start out and to keep comfortable. If or when the jackets became too restrictive or felt too hot, they could toss them off. And I reminded the werewolves to please make an attempt to remove their clothes *before* transforming. We were running out of clothes that hadn't been ripped to pieces.

Josiah's property flowed out into the Middlesex Fells Reservation which consisted of 2,575 acres. Plenty of wooded area that allowed three wolves and a vampire room to roam and to practice fighting maneuvers without being seen.

Josiah lucked out and could join the outdoor activities because the sun wasn't visible due to the heavy, gray clouds. He planned on spending his time in the woods. The thick trees, even with no leaves, would provide added protection from the sun's rays. He didn't want to be exposed to sunlight for too long and end up getting sunburned. Although I didn't see how that would happen with the lack of sun on that cold, gloomy afternoon. Josiah's other weakness during daylight hours was a decrease of his supernatural abilities and strength. He was at a disadvantage to spar with them so the plan was to talk strategy while Daniel, Isaac and Zac concentrated on their moves. It would be dark by 5:00 and by then Josiah would be at full strength and ready to practice his maneuvers in his best form.

Zac was put through another self-control test. It was critical he pass the test as it could mean life or death to his comrades. He had to distinguish between friend and foe. During the practice sessions and choreographed tactical exercises with his friends, he had to realize when to stop, when to pull back, and to know that he could not follow through with a deadly strike. Zac had already injured Daniel, Josiah, and me because he wasn't able to control his aggression and to comprehend that we're not the enemy.

Zac knew that everyone was keeping a close eye on him and he expected to be tested such as he was. Daniel and Isaac worked through moves with Zac. Josiah, in his daylight weakened state, observed and would step in and help if things went wrong. If necessary, he could try using compulsion on Zac and was still able to fight and aid in restraining him.

The whole lot of them had given me strict instructions to not come near where they practiced. I was allowed to stand behind a tree some 175 feet away. Dom had approached and stood next to me, although I knew he wished I would follow him to another clearing where he had been experimenting with starting fires. He was having problems creating an instantaneous combustion but I figured in no time he'd have the skill perfected and be able to snap his fingers and have fire on the spot.

Dom and I remained silent and still. We did not want to be a distraction as the werewolves played out possible fighting scenarios. They were in human form but the action had intensified as Daniel and Zac took greater risks using knives and small swords. We watched Zac smoothly knock Daniel off his feet and straddle him, thrusting his knife at Daniel's throat, but holding back at the last second from slicing him wide open. His hand trembled as his adrenaline raced and his breathing was wild.

Daniel praised Zac, "Good job. Now help me up."

Zac removed himself from Daniel and offered his hand to yank him up from the ground. The edge of the knife had nicked Daniel's neck and a tiny trickle of blood formed, but to a werewolf, that was nothing. What mattered was Zac's willpower. He stayed in human shape, as a test to controlling his transformations, and he was aware of the situation and knew Daniel was not a true threat. And didn't attempt to kill him. That was the final test and he passed it. Even if he *was* sweating, shaking and making strange noises in his throat at that precise moment. He knew when to stop while practicing with a friend.

Zac looked at Isaac, "You're up next. Let's do it." He was elated with his progress and on a roll.

I tapped at Dom's mind while he leaned against the tree next to me. We thought it best to not talk out loud and disturb the others. And I only wanted Dom to hear my words. *I feel useless standing here. I'm thrilled that Zac is doing so well, but I'm not sure I need to hover over him to help with his emotions or thoughts as I had been. And I'm freezing.*

Giving him your quartz was the right thing to do, Dom consoled. *And if you feel useless, I have many suggestions on things we can do...* He grinned slyly and I shook my head. He opted for another idea. *Okay, but I can dream, right? We could go inside and make supper? I need to do that soon anyway.*

I psychically sent a message to Josiah, as he was not currently involved in the sparring match, and I didn't want to interrupt the others. *Josiah, My Miracle Healer...have I thanked you yet today for saving my life? Oh gee, I can sense your ego just skyrocketed higher than normal.*

You are more than welcome. Josiah slithered through my mind. *I will gladly offer my assistance to lick any future wounds. Your blood is exquisite.*

I have a question, I asked. *Why could you heal me but not be able to save Tessa's life?*

Josiah clarified, *Tessa's neck was broken. She was dead instantly. I cannot reverse that kind of internal damage. External cuts, like you experienced, I can heal with my saliva. Sometimes the effects can go deeper, but not to the degree of fixing a broken neck <u>and</u> bringing her back to life. Well, technically I could have brought her 'back', but she would be a ghoul: a reanimated corpse.*

Yeesh. We wouldn't want that. I wish I had a dictionary or encyclopedia set on the supernatural, I mentioned.

Josiah was quick to offer his services. *I can teach you everything you need to know, my darling.*

I had to admit it was fun flirting with a vampire. And to be able to get away with some of the teasing and sarcastic things I said to him was outrageous. He could crush me with one finger. His ancient, superior power commanded respect and I did have great respect for Josiah, but enjoyed our playful connection. Moments before, I had Dom toying with me. And poor Daniel working his butt off, so focused on trying to help Zac deal with his conversion and still wanting to do what's best for us. Of course, Daniel and I hadn't 100% decided on what *was* best for us. Or for me.

I recognized Josiah's presence had never left my mind. Great. He heard everything I was thinking. He chuckled and said, *My, you've got an active mind which I find fascinating! Ah, decisions, decisions. I've already told you my feelings on this the night you let me drink your blood so I could heal faster. Hmm...since then it appears Dom has upped the ante to persuade you.*

Great, again. Josiah nabbed up my memory and thoughts on Dom and me making out. Was he my own personal counselor now?! Flustered, I announced, *Anyway...Dom and I are going inside to make supper. Pass that along.*

He laughed in my mind that he so easily breached. *I will inform the others that supper will be prepared.*

Dom and I hurried to get inside to soak up the warmth of the house; although it wasn't that toasty since the wolves and Josiah liked cooler temperatures. *And I'm turning the heat up!* I announced loudly in my brain...positive Josiah heard that, too.

* * * *

An hour and a half later, supper was over and the dark of the night was upon us. Daniel, Josiah, Zac and Isaac returned to the great outdoors to practice their skills and to learn from Josiah how to try blocking the witches' spells. Dom and I layered up our clothes to go back outside for a short time. We looked silly with our eyes peering out through slits in the scarves and waddled when we walked, but we did gain some extra warmth.

Dom and I piled fallen limbs into a pyramid shape in an open area and he practiced creating a bonfire with his mind. His first attempt was a slow smoking spark which would eventually ignite the whole stack of limbs, but he strived for that instant ignition. His second attempt was a massive flash of fire that set it all ablaze. The heat radiating off the fire made standing out in twenty degree temperatures not seem so bad and it felt comforting. It reminded me of Daniel's fireplace at his resort. Gosh, I missed that place and hoped we would take care of business here and head home soon. I assumed that was still my plan...but Dom had me questioning myself...

I reached out to Daniel's mind to make sure everything was fine and rammed into emotions of jealousy and frustration. By concentrating harder, I could hear the conversation he was having with Josiah. They were acting out what to do in an ambush and the drill had turned into something more than that. Daniel decided it would be a perfect opportunity while out in the woods to confront Josiah about drinking my blood. On the way to Salem, I had told Daniel, Dom and Isaac that Josiah needed human blood to heal faster when he was staked by Zac. I offered him mine. Daniel was not pleased, but promised that he wouldn't kill Josiah. When he had a chance, though, he wanted to have a few words with him about it. And that time had come.

I glanced at Dom over the flickering bonfire. "Come with me. Daniel is having his little chat with Josiah now."

We found them quickly and carefully approached. Their heightened sense of hearing clued them in to our whereabouts. Daniel was not bothered with my appearance as he warned me he would vent on Josiah at some point. The bantering had gotten past the fact that Josiah drank my blood...

Daniel grilled Josiah, "Why didn't you *tell* me you took Kara's blood?"

Josiah calmly answered but readied himself for an oncoming punch to the face. "I didn't have to. She made the choice to tell you herself."

"Then you're licking her leg in front of everyone. Tasting her blood once more with a look of pure ecstasy on your face," Daniel tackled Josiah in the mid-section.

Josiah landed with a thump and rolled to the side avoiding Daniel's lunge. He added, "Did you want me to let her bleed, possibly to death? You know my saliva heals wounds such as hers was. Oh, and I won't lie. Her blood is ecstasy to my taste buds."

Daniel roared and attacked Josiah, swinging like a madman. After taking a few of his hits, letting Daniel blow off some steam, Josiah dissolved into mist. Sneaky move. And he popped up behind Daniel, immediately putting him into a headlock.

Still restrained in Josiah's arms, Daniel yelled, "What are your intentions with Kara?"

"I can ask you the same – what are *your* intentions? I am a free spirit, a nomad. I am not looking for a long term romance or to settle down," Josiah let Daniel go as he had Daniel's full attention and stepped back. "Maybe someday I will find someone...I have no harmful intentions for Kara. I have no plans to turn her into a vampire unless she seriously asked me to do so. I won't deny that she stimulates me to no end. And I might fantasize about her and impulsively tease her. But you have my word on this: I wish to protect her. And to help her and The Liaison in whatever way I can."

Daniel scratched his head. One second Josiah was admitting he has sensual thoughts about me but then he vows to protect me and gives his allegiance to The Liaison. Daniel couldn't decide whether to slug him again or shake his hand. Either way, Daniel had the chance to voice his opinion on the matter which made him feel better.

And of course Josiah had to shake things up a bit more and add to Daniel's confusion. To take some of the heat off of himself, he vaguely said, "Maybe you shouldn't be worrying so much about *me*."

That could be taken a few ways. He could be telling Daniel to worry about or pay attention to me. Or, what I'm sure Josiah actually meant, was for Daniel to worry about Dominic snatching me up.

Suddenly, Zac and Isaac appeared from the trees. They had been practicing moves elsewhere. Zac blurts out, "Something doesn't feel right. It's okay; I'm in control of myself. But I sense a stirring in my mind. My guess is that Logan must be prepping for the demon ritual or starting it. I…I think the demon part of me knows what's coming."

CHAPTER 19
LEXY

Zac's news of his foreboding feelings, the uneasiness within his mind, put us on edge. We were in agreement that the tiny blip of demon in Zac's genetic makeup had somehow tipped him off that soon, if not already, Logan intended to perform the resurrection. The team decided to go back inside the house for the night.

Zac's warning, his strange sensations, were directly tied to Logan and whatever he was doing to prepare for resurrecting King Lycaeon, the Demon Werewolf. That little piece of demon essence in Zac perceived Logan's intentions and a faint anticipation had been triggered. Zac assured us that he was in complete control of his mind and body. He explained that with the quartz embedded in his neck, he now recognized the speck of evil within him and kept it corralled. He also reminded us to not forget that deep down, he was still a warrior. The evil was contained, but when it came time to fight, he didn't plan to sit idly by, twiddling his fingers.

Dom and I attempted to tip-toe into Lexy's mind for the umpteenth time, trying to be an invisible presence. Nothing. Maybe Lexy hadn't been told anything yet. Logan probably wanted to keep the time and location of the ritual a secret for as long as he could and wouldn't tell his coven of witches any specifics until that day. He realized we wanted to stop him and he didn't want us plucking any information from their minds. I wasn't feeling any high strung emotions emanating from Lexy, so we were fairly confident that the ritual was not occurring at the present time.

We felt lost and wanted to do something, but didn't know what we could do. We had no leads. It was late. Everyone was tired and the guys had exercised their butts off during the afternoon and night. We would get a fresh start the next morning.

* * * *

Mid-morning Dom and I sat on the couch and touched at Lexy's mind, hoping she had been told some information about the ritual. Josiah's calculations indicated if Logan wanted to achieve the ideal environment for his demon resurrection then it had to be that night or the next night.

We sensed a peculiar vibe from Lexy. It felt like another presence or force…something that didn't originate from her but from an outside source. I bumped against it lightly, not wanting to draw attention to my own presence in her mind. The poor girl – if she knew how many times Dom and I had scanned her mind lately, she'd have to be medicated from the shock. Dom and I couldn't penetrate the mental block without giving ourselves away, if we hadn't already. And that block wasn't a normal one. Logan, or one of the other witches, must've divulged pertinent details about the demon ritual and didn't want outsiders – us – crashing the party.

I called my grandmother's friend, our new witch associate, Claire. We were dealing with witches, so why not call a good witch to help us in our fight against the bad witches and one nasty sorcerer?

Claire willingly voiced her concern, "The way you have described Lexy, meeting her at the shop and what you find when you slip into her mind, leads me to believe that she isn't wholly evil and could be unsure of her place in that coven. Logan more than likely placed a compliance spell on Lexy so she would do his bidding and follow orders. He'd 'mix' into that a reverse deception spell and then she wouldn't even realize that she was being tricked - being used to help him gain power. If you're suddenly ramming into a mental block with Lexy, she must have knowledge about the ritual now. You are sensing Logan's spells on her. Either one of them could be keeping you out of her thoughts."

I added, "We haven't pushed into her mind. We don't want her to know what we're doing."

"I wouldn't doubt that she or Logan knows that someone is

poking around in her mind. They may not know *who* it is, yet. Beware, Kara. You are treading into dangerous territory and could fall into a trap. I have a bad feeling..." Claire cautioned. I couldn't help but jump into her mind and try to soothe her anxiety and fear for us.

She was instantly aware of what I had done. It was as if I could see her smile over the phone when she said, "That is amazing what you're capable of doing...I felt a calming sensation flow through me. Kara, your psychic abilities are immensely powerful. Use them well and to their full extent during your entire life. But you can't stop me completely from worrying about you and your friends. Call if you need anything. I will do whatever it takes to help you."

After the goodbyes, I hung up the phone and announced, "Well, that does it. Dom and I have to go to the magic shop and see Lexy in person."

"Why?" Daniel argued. "We could 'hear' everything Claire told you. I think you should stay away from Lexy."

I explained, "She's our only link to Logan and this ritual. She didn't see Dom or me during the last failed attempt at the resurrection when we raided them. So, she shouldn't connect us to werewolves or a vampire...or Zac. We are running out of time. We don't know where the ritual is to be held. Are we to aimlessly drive up and down the streets hoping beyond hope that we luck out and just happen to enter an area that gives off a bad vibe and then cross our fingers that it's actually the location? According to Josiah and Zac and Lexy's sudden mental block, we could have a full-fledged werewolf demon materialize within the next two nights. If Dom and I can get physically closer to her, maybe we can read her mind better and find out something. Anything. And remember, she should be expecting us to stop by anyway. I told her I'd come back in a week to see what she found out about Dom and me attending the witchcraft meetings."

I clearly made my point. Besides worrying about my safety, which there was always that to worry about, they couldn't argue my case. Lexy was our best bet. Everyone knew it.

Dom made a fast, simple lunch for the crew and then he and I prepared to leave. Daniel kissed and hugged me in desperation, clearly not liking the plan to visit Lexy at the magic shop. Dom could sufficiently protect me with his telekinesis skills and physically he wasn't a wimp. But he was only human...as was I, making us vulnerable to an attack. It was only Lexy; I kept telling myself.

Daniel tossed the keys to his truck at Dom and we were on our way to the magic shop. Tension filled the truck. It would've been nice to take Daniel or any of the others along as our safety net. But the witches knew what they all looked like and Dom and I could not be seen with them or it would blow our cover.

I sighed, "So, we go in and try *not* to act like spies. We talk sweet to Lexy and ask if she found out any news, like she was supposed to, on upcoming witchcraft meetings with her group that we could attend. Meanwhile, we take turns like a ping pong match zeroing in on her mind, but distracting her so she doesn't catch on to our intrusions. We sponge up any info on the demon ritual and make a cheerful exit."

"Yep. That's the idea," Dominic tried to instill confidence, but he had his doubts. "I'm worried that our conversation with Lexy will sound unnatural as we bounce back and forth - you talk, I talk, you talk, I talk - hoping she doesn't figure out what we're up to as we try to penetrate deeper into her mind. We should keep our minds open to each other so we're aware of what we've extracted from her. And we'll know the exact moment to switch and let the other one infiltrate her thoughts."

We arrived at the magic shop around 3:00. An older woman was making a purchase at the register when we walked in. Lexy glanced up and smiled at us in recognition. Dom sent me a closed mind message, *So far, so good. She hasn't turned us into toads, yet.*

I pinched his arm. *Don't be too quick to jump to conclusions. Hold my hand. Remember: we're a couple...that's how Lexy remembers us as.*

The only customer left the store and we had Lexy to ourselves. Dom and I strolled up to her and immediately took turns discreetly spreading our mental tendrils into her mind. She stood behind the counter and gave us a warm greeting. "Hi! Nice to see you again! How are you doing?"

I answered her, giving Dom his chance to gently scope out her thoughts, while I hung back, but kept linked to him. "We're still arranging our place from the move here. Such a mess! But, otherwise we're fine. I thought I'd pop in to see if you found out anything new about our chances to join your witchcraft group?"

It was difficult carrying on a conversation about one thing and secretly filtering her thoughts on another level. Dom squeezed my hand letting me know that what I had said did seem to weaken her mental block temporarily. He fed the images he snatched from her thoughts into my mind: something written on paper that resembled an address, Logan's imposing face and blood dripping. Not much to go on.

Lexy frowned in response to my question. "I'm sorry. It's been crazy lately and the person I need to ask has been…um…working on a personal project."

"What do you need to ask the boss, Lexy?" Dom and I jerked our heads in the direction of the voice, startled by the extra person entering the shop space from a separate room. We thought we were alone with Lexy. This woman must have just arrived and walked in through a back door and overheard part of the conversation. I sensed she was a witch and not anywhere near as nice as Lexy. Her image flashed through my mind – she was one of the suspicious women that the employee at the Humane Society had described to me. I had committed the image I saw in the employee's mind to my own memory. And I remembered seeing this witch while I had stayed in the shadows during the failed resurrection.

Lexy stuttered, "Oh, hey, Nicole. This is Dom and Kara. They're interested in witchcraft and want to attend a meeting – "

Lexy didn't get any further than that. While she introduced us to Nicole, I tried a quick scan of Nicole's mind, hoping her defenses were down and that I could pick up some clues from her, too. I felt pure, unabated evil. If I had to guess, this chick was Logan's second in command. The flashes I gathered – she was responsible for Tessa's broken neck, involved with the slain dogs and cut her hand as a sacrifice at the last ritual and the witch Zac had meant to kill but was stopped by Daniel. The shock of being face to face with Tessa's murderer hit hard and I lost my concentration to remain stealthy. That was a bad thing.

Nicole's eyes darted to me as she felt a disturbance in her mind and confirmed her suspicions. She cut off Lexy's introduction using the hand signal for "stop." She was not a true psychic but with her witchcraft senses she could detect me probing her thoughts and witnessed my reaction to them. She mumbled what I assumed was a spell and instantly a mental block came slamming down. Thankfully she was not aware of the extent to my psychic abilities as I had dampened them to read her. Regardless, our cover was blown. She put two and two together and got a big, fat four.

She placed one hand on her hip and leaned the other against a display unit. Nicole was not fazed; instead, she stood glaring at Dom and me like we were idiots. No one moved.

She clucked her tongue and stated, "You'd like to be involved with our little coven, huh? Lexy, should we let them in?"

Nicole turned to Lexy to get her opinion. Our gazes shifted to Lexy, wondering what she would say.

Nicole didn't give her a chance to reply, obviously running the show, and told us, "I can grant you that wish…"

I should've seen it coming. Nicole had used one of my best strategies – distraction: when we had taken our eyes off of her and looked at Lexy, she moved with lightening fast reflexes and threw the contents of an open vial at Dom and me. Moments before, she had placed her hand on the display shelf, knowing what inventory sat on it, found the vial and twisted off the cap with her fingers. As the powdery, glittery dust was ejected from the vial, she blew hard at the air and yanked off the long scarf from her neck, using it to fan the particles into our faces. Nicole muttered several singsong sentences which turned out to be a spell to enhance the dust. Dom had attempted to use his telekinesis to reverse the direction of the dust back at Nicole but she immediately waved it away, one step ahead of us, knowing how critical it was for her to keep from breathing it in.

Yes, magical, mystical, enchanted dust. Powder has a nice ring to it, too. We didn't suck every speck of it into our lungs, but a sufficient amount to create the result Nicole was looking for.

Dom and I collapsed onto the floor. We were incapacitated. Nicole was pleased and cackled with glee. As Dom and I started to feel the influence of the dust, we latched onto each other's minds, seeking deep within ourselves for the focus and power to stay mentally linked. It wasn't easy and our telepathic skill of communicating was terribly fuzzy. Besides the weak connection to each other, we were not able to use any of our other psychic abilities. We verged on total unconsciousness and fought to hang on to reality. We could hear and smell but we could not see, talk or move. Besides killing us, what better way to disable a psychic than to knock one out?

Dom? I clung to the battered pathway into his mind. He didn't answer. *Dom?!* Panic was rising fast in my body, even though I couldn't move, I still felt it inside.

He chose his words wisely, trying to conserve his energy and to not lose our link. *Relax. Use senses that work. Focus. Don't let go. Love you.*

I think tears were running down my face, but the magic dust had me so out of it, I wasn't sure. Dom told me to use my senses. Okay...I heard Nicole's shoes tap down on the floor with each step as she circled Dom and me. A slight breeze from her movement passed over my hands and face. I could smell her perfume or deodorant or some other aroma drift by.

She stopped walking and I heard a thump followed by a whoosh of air coming out of Dom's mouth. She kicked him in the stomach. And he was helpless against her assault.

Lexy nervously questioned Nicole, "What are you going to do?"

Nicole replied, "You mean, 'what are *we* going to do?' This girl, Kara, right? She's psychic, which you should have already known. And the man used telekinesis. But, of course, you're too trusting and friendly and didn't think to test them or look into that before, did you? And *you're* supposed to have some psychic power? Hm. Anyway, I'm guessing they're either chummy with the crew that ruined our last ritual or are being controlled by that vampire to scope us out and report back with any news. And it's possible they have nothing to do with them. I don't remember seeing these two during that raid, but the memories she touched on in my mind makes me wonder...With little Kara being psychic, she could be useful at the resurrection."

"How?" Lexy's voice rose and she shuffled from behind the counter.

Nicole explained, "The demon resurrection would have a much greater chance at success if we offered a real sacrifice. And since no one is going to volunteer, I think we've stumbled upon a perfect opportunity." She nudged me with her foot. "Cutting ourselves and offering our drops of blood to summon a demon just ain't the same as a full-blown sacrifice. And with her paranormal skills thrown into the mix, she should be quite an enticement for King Lycaeon."

Oh my God! ME! She wanted me for a sacrifice! I couldn't scream or run or do anything but lie on the floor. I felt my mental link to Dom quiver and slacken and I almost lost him. Realizing the need and importance to remain connected, I reached for him in desperation.

Don't give up. Fight. I'm here. Dom encouraged, although he could not conceal from me his anger and fear. He fell silent and concentrated on strengthening our psychic bond.

As far as we could tell, neither Nicole nor Lexy had any idea that Dom and I spoke to each other telepathically. Our motionless bodies made them believe we were completely oblivious to what happened to or around us. Lexy was a smidge psychic, but her power and skills thrived in witchcraft. Dom and I weren't chatting back and forth and if Lexy tried to probe our minds, we would sense it and act comatose. She'd come up empty-handed and not realize the slight amount of awareness that Dom and I still clung to.

Nicole instructed Lexy to grab Dom under one arm and she'd take the other. "We'll drag him outside to the alley because he can't stay in the store when we leave. We can't handle two people in the condition they're in and we need her more than him. We'll lock up and take Kara with us. The dust and my spell will eventually wear off and I want to get her to Logan before that happens. In fact, I'm taking another vial just to be safe."

Dom was dead weight and Nicole and Lexy had their hands full trying to pull him outside. I heard them gasping and groaning from the effort. I had deeply embedded myself into Dom's mind for self-preservation, as he did mine, so when the witches dumped him on the hard, cold ground, I felt it rock his system. I was terrified he would freeze to death before help arrived. I heard Nicole enter the building again, but Lexy remained behind a few seconds with Dom.

Through him, I heard her whisper, "I'm sorry. I don't want anyone to get hurt. But I'm in too deep…I can't walk away. They need me. I have to help…"

Lexy hurried inside the shop, leaving Dom propped up against the building. She had hesitated leaving him. Evil had not taken her over. Yet. She seemed trapped, confused and afraid. It didn't help that Logan had his spell on her and may have threatened her, too.

I heard Nicole locking the front door. Lexy approached and drummed her fingers on the glass countertop. Nicole ordered, "Grab her legs. I'll take the upper part. Let's go."

I was carried outside and placed into the trunk of a vehicle. Nicole was rough with me as she let my head bonk down inside the trunk; and if I could, I would've screamed in pain. Lexy was by far gentler with me and tucked my legs and feet into a more comfortable position. Her hands had been touching me non-stop for several minutes – from carrying my legs to arranging me in the trunk. My concentration to maintain contact with Dom had been so strong that I almost didn't notice how Lexy gave me a feeling of familiarity, like someone I should know. I couldn't ponder over that at the time and let it slide since my brain was so foggy I very well could have been reading her wrong.

She paused before closing the trunk lid and said nearly the same to me as she did to Dom, "I'm sorry. I don't know how I got so involved in this mess."

The vehicle's engine started and I was on the move. I sent an urgent plea to Dom, *We need to send an S.O.S. to Josiah. He should hear us. But I'm afraid we'll lose our own link if we try to draw him into our minds. It's hard to hold onto this connection. You'll freeze soon! And I'm to be sacrificed!*

Dom agreed. *Don't let go of me, Kara. We'll both picture Josiah and scream 'Help!' Ready, now!*

HELP!!! We simultaneously sent the telepathic message to our vampire friend, holding his image in our minds. Our own connection weakened when our focus had to divert to the S.O.S. call. We frantically grappled to restore it.

Josiah heard our call for help and responded, *What's wrong?*

Dom and I had no energy to answer him and we did not want to jeopardize losing our fragile mental link. The guys knew Dominic and I were going to the magic shop and they would start there first.

Josiah tried again, *If you can hear me, we'll be <u>driving</u> to the magic shop. The sun hasn't gone down yet, I'm not at full strength and none of us can take the chance of being seen in a different shape.*

We're on our way.

Silence. Dominic and I felt the presence of each other, but said nothing more. We waited.

Perhaps fifteen minutes passed and the vehicle that I was stuffed into stopped. I was still incapacitated and could not see, move or talk. When the trunk lid popped open and Nicole and Lexy reached in to hoist me out, I tried to open my eyes. I managed to catch a glimpse of the ground as my head rolled forward onto my chest. Each draped one of my arms over their shoulders and lugged me to the new witch hideout. Too bad I didn't have an inkling of where I was being taken.

During the same moment, Dom's saviors had arrived. Through my mental link with him, I was aware that Josiah, Daniel, Zac and Isaac had found him in the alley. They picked him up off the ground and instantly recognized how cold he had become. The three werewolves, staying in human form, enveloped Dom within a huddle to raise his body temperature.

Dom never let go of our connection. He, too, remained incapacitated under the spell. With the close proximity to Josiah, it was easier to alert him to the situation. In as few words as possible, Dom telepathically prompted Josiah, *Read my memories.*

Josiah carefully entered Dom's mind so as not to shock him with his power. Through Dom, I heard Josiah declare, "They've got her."

CHAPTER 20
SACRIFICE

Dom and I were still under the influence of the magic dust and Nicole's immobilizing spell. Josiah slipped into Dom's mind to strengthen the delicate mental link to me with his own power but remained quiet and listened to our conversation, not wanting to derail my concentration.

I described to them what few things I could about my surroundings, which I mostly gathered through my senses. *Lots of grass. Concrete. Door. Another door. Going down steps. Dark. Stuffy. Moldy like a basement. Enclosed. Flickering light...candles or lanterns maybe. Nothing else.*

Nicole and Lexy deposited me onto a filthy, cold, concrete floor and I conveyed the information to Dom. Nicole spoke to Lexy, "We wait for Logan. He won't be here for another hour or two. He mentioned he would drop by some items for the ritual tomorrow night. I'm starving and I doubt you've eaten supper either. Be a sweetie and go to the nearest drive-thru and get us something to eat."

Whew! I wasn't being sacrificed that night! *Resurrection tomorrow night.* I sent the message to Dom.

Dom responded, *We heard. We will find you. Josiah is at full strength. Merge your mind with his now.*

Dom didn't need to say anything further. I had full confidence in Josiah and trusted him with my life. Josiah knew the dire need to keep the fuzzy threads of my mind intact with one of them at all times and with his superior psychic power, he would latch onto me with ease. He would know everything that my mind processed.

Dom temporarily released our deeply rooted, although weak,

connection and I felt a slight free-falling sensation. But Josiah swooped in and with tremendous skill gathered up the frayed pieces of my drained mind.

He instructed, *Kara, you're in good hands with me. If you doze off, I'll still be merged with you. Don't worry. This doesn't take much effort on my part. Just as long as you don't block me out, I will keep a solid link with your mind. And even if you did block me, I'm fairly sure I could penetrate it. Relieve yourself from maintaining the merge. Try to regain your energy. I won't let you go. My mind is open to you so you will know what's happening on our end, too.*

I wanted to speak with Daniel. I knew I didn't have the strength to connect to him and normal werewolf telepathy was limited when they had to be the one to create and uphold the link. But the prevailing love between Daniel and me might give him the ability to make the connection. I asked Josiah, *Can Daniel talk to me?*

Now that I'm holding this merge together, he should be able to. Don't try it yourself as you're too drained, Josiah offered. It was strange how I was able to hear him tell Daniel to reach out to me but to keep it brief. Josiah reminded both of us that he could hear everything we said to each other since he had to stay locked onto me.

Daniel shimmered into my mind. *Kara, are you hurt?*

No. Can't move. Like a coma. Thoughts are foggy. Love you.

Daniel's heart ached for me. *I love you, too. Hang in there.* His voice echoed and he slipped out of my mind. He knew I was weak and didn't want to upset me with his own frustration and vengeful feelings towards my abductors. Hearing him and feeling his presence kept my anxiety level tolerable. The magic dust and Nicole's spell were drugs to my body, forcing me into a disabled state, with my emotions and thoughts distorted. Knowing I had little to no control, panic would rise then fall in a haze.

Josiah's hold on me was impressive. My mind floated, securely anchored to him, but no longer straining to support my end of it. I could listen in to the conversations he was having or tune it out like a radio and concentrate on what was going on around me. At times, he projected images of what he saw through his own eyes to me, giving me an understanding of what progress they made or what they were doing.

Daniel carried Dominic to his truck and placed him on the passenger seat. Josiah stated that he could instantly remove the spell and counteract the effect of the magic dust. But if Dom chose to let the effects wear off naturally, he wasn't sure how long Dom would remain incapacitated...definitely several more hours, possibly up to two days!

Dom spoke telepathically to Josiah and asked, *How can you fix me?*

Josiah bluntly answered, "Vampires are not normally vulnerable to spells or magical herbs that attack physically or mentally as you're experiencing. You need to swallow a few drops of my blood. It won't hurt you or convert you. It's like an antidote."

Dom urged, *Hurry up and do it.*

Josiah slashed his wrist with his teeth, just enough to make blood drip from the cut. He lowered Dom's jaw and brought his wrist to Dom's mouth, allowing several drops of potent vampire blood to flow into his body. Josiah sealed Dom's lips closed with two fingers and tilted his head back.

Josiah confidently said, "Give him a few seconds..."

While they waited for Dom to emerge from his comatose state, Zac inquired, "Josiah, I'm confused. You couldn't go into the magic shop or read the witches' minds because of spells. But now you tell us spells don't work on vampires. What gives?"

Dom groaned and moved his head in a circle as he regained full use of his body. All attention was on him. Josiah caught him before he fell off the seat of the truck and suggested, "Your feet are numb. Sit still a little longer. Let my blood circulate through your body."

Josiah returned to Zac's question and elaborated, "If the spell or substance is meant to directly affect a person's *body* or *mind*, as in Dom's and Kara's case, normally it is *not* a problem for vampires. The magic shop has a spell on it to keep me out. The spell was not placed on me but on the entrance to the shop. The same thing with my inability to read the witches' minds: a blocking spell was placed within their minds to keep me out, but the spell was not placed on me. It's tricky but someone of Logan's caliber could manage it. I knew from early on that someone of immense power had to be in charge to conjure such spells."

Dom slowly slid off the seat and out of the truck, stretching his body. Josiah's blood had reversed the spell and purged the magic dust from Dom's system. He appeared vibrant and energized. Josiah chuckled, letting me see the image of Dom in my mind.

In the meantime, at an unknown location, I remained out of action on the floor, awaiting Logan's appearance. Lexy had returned with fast food and she and Nicole were eating. From the scent of food and sound of their voices, I judged they were a fair distance from me. That meant the room wasn't small. As Lexy apprehensively spoke with Nicole, I sensed she kept glancing in my direction. Her voice was clear and loud when I assumed she was looking at me; then as her head turned, the volume decreased and the words were harder to hear. I noticed that sounds echoed in the room, too.

I switched back to Josiah's thoughts, reminding myself he held our merge and no exertion was needed on my part. He silently acknowledged any new bits of information I had experienced in captivity and forwarded it on to the others.

Dominic was ready for action now that he could move and talk once again. Grateful and out of immense respect, he shook Josiah's hand, thanking him for breaking the spell. Dom noted, "Logan's mind blocking spell isn't holding up 100% on Lexy, though. The fact that I was able to snatch an image or two from her mind tells me the spell has weakened. Or her own doubts about her place in this are causing cracks in the spell. She is basically a good person and has not been entirely swept up by evil. She said she was sorry for what was happening to Kara and me and didn't want anyone to get hurt."

Daniel commented, "In the wrong place at the wrong time…"

I prompted Josiah to review my memories and tell the others what I had absorbed from Nicole back at the magic shop. I wasn't positive Logan had a blocking spell on her, though, since I had been able to see images of her snapping Tessa's neck and killing the dogs, among other things. Of course, she slammed down a mental block the moment she realized my invasion. Maybe Logan's spell really had weakened. Either way, Nicole was evil and beyond our help. But Lexy…

Josiah imparted my incident with Nicole. Everyone agreed that Lexy could be the swing vote. We had to figure out how to bring her on board, to our side. Zac bristled at the mention of Nicole killing Tessa. Josiah warned him to keep his cool as we needed clear heads to win this battle. The quartz embedded in Zac's neck had indeed been a blessing and gave him a new perspective on things; his self-control had improved by leaps and bounds. But that didn't mean highly emotional events wouldn't take its toll on him, as it would anybody.

Dom fretted, "The images I caught from Lexy's mind are useless. I pictured her writing an address on paper…but I can't decipher any of it. I'm not even sure it *was* an address. I saw Logan's face. And an image of blood dripping…which I'm sure that has to do with the sacrifice."

Daniel said, "She's scared. Fear can make you do many things you would not normally do."

Through Josiah's mind, I speculated, *She can't leave the coven without Logan's backlash.* I switched my focus to my present situation. I heard a door open then close and heavy footsteps heading towards me. *Logan is here.*

We are with you, Kara. We will find you. It was a boost of strength and comfort hearing those words. Especially since the words filtered into my mind as one united voice: Daniel, Dom, Josiah, Zac and Isaac. Josiah must've signaled them to say the words out loud, all at the same time. He didn't want them to overwhelm me by having everyone individually linking to me at once, so Josiah made sure I heard through *his* mind all the spoken voices.

"Well, well. Who do we have here?" Logan taunted.

Nicole proceeded to quickly explain the events leading up to that point, including the use of the magic dust and her spell to incapacitate me. Logan was impressed, but reprimanded, "Good work. But why isn't she tied up and blindfolded? You should have taken care of that as an extra precaution."

Nicole didn't hesitate with his indirect order. I heard her promptly walk away, objects being shuffled about, then she approached me. She told Lexy to hold my head up so she could get the blindfold wrapped around me. Next, my wrists were brought to the front and tied with some kind of material. My anxiety rose with being bound. It was bad enough I couldn't see, move or talk but to add to that being tied up sent my heart racing. My mind was screaming for help. Josiah cautiously spoke, *Kara, breathe. Stabilize yourself. We are here with you.*

Only in my thoughts...! I shrieked. *But you are not actually HERE!*

Josiah paused. *We will be. Do not let them know you are telepathically speaking to anyone. Focus on your situation but do not close your mind to me. Do you understand?* Josiah directed with authority.

Yes. I answered and concentrated on my surroundings.

Logan, content with my restraints, recited an incantation which appeared to dissolve part of Nicole's spell. My whole body was tingling with sensation and I could feel again. Although my wrists were bound, I could wiggle my fingers. I bent my knees and brought them closer to my chest. With great effort, I pushed on my forearm and leg and swung my torso up until I was sitting on my rear. A hand pressed down on my shoulder to keep me from standing. At least my face was no longer plastered against the cold floor. I felt incredibly weak and sore but I could move. My brain was still mush. Logan was no fool and would not let a psychic regain full mental capabilities. He intended to keep me drowsy.

Logan's reason for removing part of the spell was made clear. He wanted to ask me questions and I needed to be able to answer and I couldn't do that if I couldn't talk.

"What is your name?" he pressed.

That seemed harmless. I responded, "Kara McBride."

"What are your parents' names?" he continued.

I didn't like bringing them into this. I said nothing. Logan muttered another incantation. He scratched on the floor and swished something through the air. With my blindfold on, I could only guess he had conjured up another spell. My brain was zapped with a sharp, severe pain. It felt like having a migraine and being super sensitive to light and sound.

And I found myself answering him. "Tanya and Adam McBride."

Josiah whispered in my mind, *Truth spell. You have to answer him. I don't know if I can guide your choice of words or not.*

Logan asked, "What are your grandparents' names – dead and alive?"

I started listing my grandparents' names on my dad's side and then my grandparents' names on my mom's side. The second I mentioned the name of my grandmother who had been a psychic witch, Logan laughed. One of those mean, spiteful laughs that isn't at all funny to the person being laughed at or about.

"So, Margaret Edwards was your grandmother...Tsk, Tsk. It appears you inherited some of her psychic power. Oh, yes, I knew her. She interfered with my plans one too many times. I'm the one who killed her."

WHAT!? I swear it felt like a knife pierced through my head, heart and stomach all at the same time. I thought I was going to vomit and shook violently. I was angry, sad and sickened. This monster had murdered my grandma about a year ago! Not only was Logan cackling but Nicole had joined in, too. Lexy was quiet. The realization that they had captured the granddaughter of a powerful psychic witch had made them euphoric, filled with delight. Nicole would get a big blue star for this accomplishment. Capturing me.

"Kara, you will be the perfect sacrificial offering for our demon resurrection tomorrow night. Your pathetic goodness and potent blood will attract and please Lycaeon. I can't wait!" Logan sounded like a child antsy to open his birthday presents.

He had another question or two for me. "Are you involved with the group who derailed my last ritual?"

"Yes."

"What are the plans for your wretched group of do-gooders?" He pushed.

"To stop you and kill the demon," I blurted. *Come on, Josiah. Help me out here.*

It's okay. You haven't said anything to jeopardize the situation. It's not like he didn't already know that, Josiah comforted.

Logan bellowed with laughter and mocked me. "That would be a little hard to do with all the additional preparations I've included this time. Plus we have *you* now. And your pathetic friends have no clue where we are. My blocking spells should've helped keep out any nosy mind readers from discovering our whereabouts. I'll be sure to refresh that drowsy spell on you to dull your mind before I leave. As long as you don't try to escape, I won't completely incapacitate you. Aren't I nice?"

He walked right in front of me and squatted to ask the last question. "Your friends *don't* know where we are, do they?"

I told him the truth. "No." I whimpered and tears soaked into my blindfold.

He stood up, satisfied with the results of his truth spell and recited a mouthful of sentences that sent another sharp pain jarring into my brain. The truth spell had been withdrawn; but in its place came the reinforcement to my already fuzzy mind. I recognized the sound of Logan blowing the air which meant that I was inhaling more of that damn magic dust. I quickly moved my fingers. He kept his word and didn't restrict my movements...but I was really, reaaaaaaallllllly sleepy...

* * * *

I had slept a very long time. I touched Josiah's mind, *How long have I been out?*

About twelve hours, he answered.

Holy cow! That magic dust knocked me out. My mind was so incoherent and my body moved but felt like dead weight. Exactly what Logan had wanted. While I slept, Josiah explained that he never let the mind merge between us dissolve. Dom and Daniel helped to support the mental link to allow Josiah to go out and feed (drink blood). Several times the other guys wanted to assist with keeping the connection to me solid and to share in the responsibility so the task didn't weigh 100% on Josiah. During those hours I had slept, they reviewed the scenario and what they currently knew, researched possible places I could be and scouted the town for buildings with basements. Dom had tried probing Lexy's mind to no avail.

I floated in Josiah's mind, or perhaps he floated in mine, with no real exertion on my end. I feared that in my weak, unclear, spell-induced, psychic frame of mind that if the connection to me was ever lost, I would be lost. They may never find me. We tried to restrict how often others entered into a separate mental link with me so as not to drain my energy in needing to focus and hold a telepathic conversation. Josiah kept promising that he wouldn't lose his hold on me, but I was still scared.

Daniel cautiously and briefly spoke, with urgency in his voice. *Work on Lexy. Flip her to our side. She's our best hope to find you and stop the ritual.*

He *failed* to say, "She's our only chance to save you from imminent death and to prevent the demon from causing mass chaos." The words hovered in everyone's thoughts. I knew they did.

Speaking of Lexy...I heard footsteps, felt the breeze stirring and sniffed her familiar scent with her arrival. A cup was pressed to my lips and she pleaded, "Please drink this. It's just water and you've got to be dehydrated by now."

My blindfold hadn't been removed and my hands remained tied, so I had to rely on her to hold and tip the glass so I could drink from it.

Lexy offered, "I have leftover pizza. Try to eat...here it comes." Her voice trembled, whispering as she hand fed me.

I was starving and I loved pizza. And oddly, I trusted Lexy not to try poisoning me. Even with Logan's mind blocking spell protecting her from me reading her thoughts, (not that I could with a drowsy spell cast upon me), I had sensed something was about to give. Her wall had cracks...I sensed her powerful flow of emotions and she was near a nervous breakdown. I also sensed a boost of strength from Josiah and the other guys. They prodded me to talk to Lexy and convince her she was heading down the wrong path. Through Josiah, my team was aware of my situation. And I needed to be alert enough to have a conversation with her.

"I have a little time to spend with you. People will be coming and going all day preparing for the..." Lexy paused, not wanting to say the words.

I finished, "Demon resurrection."

"Yeah..." Lexy showed no enthusiasm. "Right now, there's no one down here but us and that's why I wanted to sneak you water and food. I don't know if anyone would actually be mad about that or not. But no one suggested getting you anything, either. So...I decided to do it."

I continued eating the pizza as she brought it to my mouth. Her fingers skimmed across my skin when she wiped my face clean with a cloth. Her physical contact seemed familiar. Confused, I said, "I feel like I should know you."

Lexy muffled her sobs. She stunned me when she revealed, "That's because we're cousins. This whole thing is insane! I swear I didn't know until you told Logan the names of your family members. Your grandmother and my grandmother were sisters. And I was shocked when he admitted that *he* killed your grandma. I had no idea!"

"Help me then. You don't belong with them." I begged, still reeling from the revelations and a woozy mind.

"Logan will kill me, and I mean literally kill me, if I leave or if he thinks I'm a traitor. If he kills me, how can I help you if I'm dead? I don't know what to do!" Lexy panicked.

Several sets of footsteps were walking down the steps and Lexy backed away and fell silent. Nicole approached and told Lexy to work at the magic shop for the day and return by 6:00. Nothing would happen until the evening. Logan wanted the shop to be open for business so all would appear normal. Lexy had to leave. Any arguing with Nicole would look suspicious.

And I still didn't know where I was. I supposed if she told me right then where our location was, and The Liaison team stormed in shortly afterwards to save me, Logan and the witches would suspect her of defecting. She was the last person seen with me. Logan would be enraged and kill her. Not only that, but we'd ruin our opportunity to kill the demon and destroy Logan since neither was present at that moment. If his hideout was discovered, he wouldn't turn around and attempt the ritual tonight for fear of another attack. Or perhaps he would push forward with the ritual, just not in the current location, and without me as the sacrifice. And we'd be hunting for Logan all over again.

I couldn't be saved yet. It would have to all go down at once. Rescue me during the process of killing the demon. Oh, joy.

The day passed without event.

My team was searching the city, trying to figure out where the hideout was on their own and without any knowledge or help from Lexy. Especially since we weren't positive if she eventually would or could help us. I sensed their frustration and worry. Time was running out. I wished Lexy would return and prayed she had decided to help me...in some way.

Logan arrived. The evening was upon us. His voice rumbled with authority and echoed eerily in the room. More people entered. The aroma of candles grew thicker and intermingled with funky smelling herbs. I heard scratching sounds on the floor; probably symbols etched in chalk. I decided it was best to play up the drowsiness factor and to appear as non-threatening as possible in hopes Logan wouldn't zap me with more magic dust.

The final preparations for the demon resurrection were in progress. Logan swooped down to gather me off the floor and placed me on another hard object...a table? a slab of concrete? I couldn't see anything so I wasn't sure at that time.

"Lie down. If you don't follow orders, I will force you with a spell. I want you conscious and responsive during this ceremony," he instructed.

I did not want to be under any spells if I could avoid it. I did as he told me. The magic dust was bad enough; I didn't need him controlling my will and actions, too. Logan–so many spells he was trying to uphold...you'd think that would weaken him. And where was Lexy?

Logan removed the binding around my wrists and pulled each arm out to the sides and strapped them down. Nicole commented that everyone was present and all things were accounted for. Oh no...that meant that Lexy *was* there but would I get another chance to talk to her? Would she tell me where we were which would then allow Josiah to "hear" the location? Before it was too late?

I screamed out in pain and terror as a knife sliced through my flesh. First one wrist, then the other. A slow drip, nothing meant to kill me. But a perfect amount for the sacrifice.

CHAPTER 21
POW

Logan began chanting. The witches followed his lead. I heard my blood dripping into bowls on the floor. The scent of burning candles and herbs was overwhelming. I twisted and rubbed my head against the surface of my sacrificial altar, trying to slip the blindfold off or adjust it to see something. It had moved up on one corner and enabled me to view a concrete ceiling. A regular basement would not have a ceiling made of concrete. The witches surrounded me in a wide circle, blocking my view of the interior walls. If the room used modern electricity, I saw no evidence of it. Lanterns, candles and archaic torches supplied the lighting which cast creepy shadows that flickered from any movement.

Daniel entered my mind, *Kara, we are going to empower you with our strength. Josiah swears he can keep the merge with you. You and Dom will shove at the mind blocking cracks in Lexy's mind to get through to her. Tell Lexy that Logan has spells on her. Ask her where you are. Ready?*

Hurry! Do it now! I mentally shouted.

The rush of adrenaline and strength flowing into my mind and body caused me to shudder and queasiness rippled through my stomach. But I didn't feel quite as drowsy and my drunken brain had perked up. None of that would last long with blood dripping from my wrists, though.

Dom was linked to me and knew the second I had adjusted to the surge of power. We acted like a battering ram, pushing into Lexy's mind. I sensed she flinched but no one noticed with all the focus centered on the incantation. Witches chanted with Logan, reciting memorized words to resurrect the demon. Logan scrawled more symbols and markings on the floor.

Lexy! I begged her. *Listen to me – Logan has spells on you...a mind blocking spell and probably a compliance spell. Fight it. Help me! Please before it's too late. Just tell me where we are. That's all I need. Where am I?*

Dom surprised her with his presence and pressured, *Lexy, this is Dom. Please help her. She's your cousin. You're a good person. You don't belong here. <u>Where</u> is Kara?*

I lifted my head again to get a glimpse of her from under my slipped blindfold but it hurt my neck to keep doing so. It seemed that the reality of her involvement, influenced by Logan, and what the horrific outcome of the demon resurrection actually meant, hit her like a brick. She was fighting to break through the spells that Logan had placed on her...an internal struggle she tried to conceal from the other witches as she pressed one hand to her temple and took a step back.

Cemetery. Mausoleum with underground crypt. She did it! Lexy had switched sides. But in the meantime, she had to be extra cautious not to give herself away.

Thank you! Now don't act suspicious. Play your part. My friends will be here soon. I was so grateful to her.

Dom shouted the location to all the guys, even though through the mind merge, each one had heard it. They had previously gathered and loaded the truck with weapons and anything else that could be advantageous for the battle.

They were on their way!

Dom was driving Daniel's truck and sent me a message, *Claire is with me.*

What? I mentally yelled. I didn't like the idea of 70 year old Claire going head-to-head with Logan or a demon even if she did look like she could run a marathon.

Dom heard my opinion and pointed out, *That's why we didn't tell you today. We called her for guidance and she insisted on driving to Josiah's this afternoon to help.*

Josiah informed me, *I'm flying to the cemetery as an owl. I'll be there first. If a demon materializes, I will disrupt the ritual until the others arrive.*

Daniel anxiously announced, *Zac, Isaac and I have shifted into wolves. We'll get there faster and just moments after Josiah.*

Dom added, *It'll take about fifteen minutes for me to drive there.*

Each of you, remember, you can't charge in until the demon has taken a completely solid form so you're able to kill it. I will tell you when. Josiah held the mind merge with me and forwarded my words of caution to the others.

Logan, along with his witches, continued reciting the incantation to summon the demon. He noticed my blindfold was falling off, but by then, he didn't care. His confidence soared and he leaned over and pulled the blindfold off my head. Finally, I could see everything around me with both eyes.

I glanced at my wrists that consistently dripped the sacrificial blood to lure the demon, King Lycaeon, and hated to admit it, but my strength was beginning to dwindle again. I wasn't a doctor, but I believed it would take a while to lose enough blood to die. The blood dripped every so often; it wasn't flowing out of me, as whoever did the cutting made sure not to go too deep with the knife. Otherwise I'd be dead before the demon was resurrected and Logan had strongly stressed he wanted me alive and kicking for the demon's personal enjoyment. I assumed since Lycaeon had a hankering for human flesh when he had been alive, I would be the main course.

From what I'd read on the internet concerning this type of ritual used to summon a spirit (King Lycaeon's in our case), it could carry on for hours, even days. I didn't suspect it would last for days. Logan planned to complete the ritual and conjure up a demon that night.

I'm here, Josiah announced. *It wasn't hard to find. Large mausoleum. Crypt. Numerous cars parked close by. I can sense you are near. Do you see anything yet?*

I raised my head off the concrete slab. It dawned on me that I was strapped to an old coffin made for crypts, as I noticed two other coffins situated within the room. A swirling breeze whipped through the stuffy air. The numerous candles and torches flickered violently; the flames almost being extinguished. I circled my head around, searching for any signs of a demon materializing. And there it was off to my right side! It was a ghostly apparition, not at all solid yet as I could see through it. But it was forming. The concrete floor rumbled and cracked in a reenactment similar to the first failed ritual. Josiah cautioned not to wait too long to shriek for their rescue. What if it decided to attack me the moment it had a physical body?

Daniel acknowledged that he, Isaac and Zac had arrived. They transformed into the beast shape and waited outside for my signal. Zac would enter first. The quartz embedded in his neck should dissolve any spells that would alert Logan to intruders. It had worked for me with a door entrance on our first raid. Dom and Claire were on their way...several minutes out. I was weakening. I did not have the strength to mentally carry on conversations with anyone other than Josiah who remained locked into my mind. The surge of power I had received from the guys was only temporary to help me push into Lexy's mind. Between the drowsy spell, the loss of blood and my anxiety, I didn't feel too great.

I turned my eyes to the right to get a better view of the demon. He was milky in density, no longer see-through. Logan encouraged the witches to concentrate on the words to the incantation. It appeared a protection circle had been drawn on the floor and all the witches including Logan stood within it.

Josiah sifted into my thoughts to tell me Dom and Claire made it. Everyone was there. I just had to say the word "now" and they'd attack Logan, the witches and the demon. And rescue me. I had a bad feeling. There were so many separate battles within one big war, all needing to play out at the same time or within minutes of each other.

Josiah read my thoughts and encouraged me, *Kara, we have strategized. Each of us has a specific objective. Be strong. Stay alert and tell me if that damn demon is solid yet!*

I looked once again at the demon. Logan stepped forward and as an added bonus, sliced his hand and let his blood drip on the floor near the demon and quickly stepped back into his protective circle. The demon definitely resembled the werewolves, after all that was what he was before his death. The huge difference was the evil aura gushing forth from him. His form appeared solid until he moved his arms and I saw a tiny bit of blurriness. The demon, King Lycaeon, saw my blood filling the bowls on the floor and bent over to scoop one up in his immense claws. He tipped it back and gulped with pleasure. Uh, oh...if he could pick up that bowl and drink, then he *was* physical enough to kill.

NOW!!!!! I shouted to Josiah in my mind, with as much strength as I could muster. I could barely keep my lips closed so as not to ruin the surprise attack on Logan, but my entire body went rigid with the force of my internal cry for help. And when Lycaeon reached for me, I could no longer be silent. It didn't matter how weak and drowsy I felt, I screamed at the top of my lungs.

And I was right. So many things happened at once. It's difficult to describe who did what to whom, where, when and how! Okay…try to follow along…

In a microsecond of my yell for help signaling my team to attack, Josiah streamed in as mist and popped up on my left side, the opposite of where Lycaeon stood. With a flick of his wrist, he broke the straps holding me to the coffin and ran his tongue over both wrists to instantly heal the cuts. Lycaeon cocked his head and stood motionless. He didn't quite understand what his role was in the scene playing out all around him. He was utterly confused…

Josiah turned his attention to Logan…

Dom and Claire were the last to enter the crypt and rushed to me. Josiah started to fight Logan. Dom held his ground and formed a force field around us. He knew I was weak and not able to fend for myself. Claire took my arm and helped me to sit upright instead of staying in such a vulnerable position lying flat on my back.

Claire began to recite verses to a holding spell. She hoped it would prevent the other witches from attacking us or from casting any spells to gain control of the chaotic situation. Three less powerful witches turned tail and ran out of the crypt terrified. Six witches remained close to the demon. Claire's holding spell seemed to be effective. They failed in their ability to cast new spells. Their ridiculous, feeble attempts to save, protect or assist Lycaeon were a joke. Nicole was part of that little group.

She didn't last long…Zac attacked Nicole, Tessa's murderer. I saw her hands swirl frantically, trying to conjure up a spell, but there was no time. Zac's supernatural speed and power were no match whatsoever to any mortals. Even witches. Especially when werewolves and vampires were not susceptible to spells directed onto their physical bodies. He broke her neck, almost ripping her head off her body in the process. Nicole had broken Tessa's neck and it seemed fitting to Zac to kill her in the same way.

As Nicole slumped onto the floor, Lexy ran to her and searched her clothes. She triumphantly found what she was looking for: the extra vial of magic dust Nicole had taken from the magic shop. When Logan had reinforced the drowsy spell on me, I don't know if he borrowed the same vial from Nicole or had his own. Regardless, Lexy had it in her hand now. And she smiled wickedly waiting for her chance to use it.

Daniel and Isaac charged Lycaeon about two seconds after Josiah released and healed me. The underground crypt was an unusually enormous size, I could understand why Logan chose it, but space was still limited. Daniel and Isaac used their swords that Dom had brought along in the truck. Lycaeon's strength was growing by the second as he rediscovered his body's supernatural abilities. He had no style or grace and was a bit clumsy, but his speed saved him several times from a death strike. Daniel's sword stabbed his arm; Isaac's blade swished past his face. Lycaeon clawed out at their bodies every chance he got.

After Nicole was killed, five witches lingered near where Lycaeon was fighting Daniel and Isaac. One proud witch announced, "My ancestors ruled in casting the Lycaeonia Curse. And now we will rule this demon – who was once King Lycaeon – the original werewolf. Nothing will stop us. He will help us take--"

And she never finished. Her neck was severed with a flash of Daniel's sword. She was one of the descendants of the evil witches who had turned Daniel, Isaac and their friend, Stephen into werewolves.

Apparently Lycaeon didn't like hearing he would be "ruled", and lashed out violently at three witches who stood closest to him. Their deaths were so swift; I barely witnessed what had happened. All of a sudden, they were slashed and dead on the floor. With his speed, he must've used his claws and swung his arms out, cutting the backs of their necks all in one fell swoop.

The last witch from that cluster started screaming at Daniel, Isaac and Zac in a psychotic manner, blaming them for interrupting the resurrection and enraging Lycaeon to the point he killed her friends.

She charged at them. What she thought she could do against three werewolves, who knew. It was a suicide move, for sure. Zac took one step and struck her with his clawed fist...she died instantaneously.

With no witches causing any interference or distractions, Zac joined Daniel and Isaac in the battle against King Lycaeon. The brawls on the floor using hand-to-hand combat resulted in terrible gashes and blood flying in all directions. It was possible Lycaeon had already received a lethal wound that was slow in killing him. He continued to fight ruthlessly and no one was going to take time out to check the severity of his injuries. They would not stop until he was dead.

Claire collapsed from the exertion to maintain the holding spell. She sat on the floor, clutching her chest and trying to catch her breath. Dom bent down to her and gave me a worried look. Claire kept saying she was fine and that she'd make it...she was upholding the spell on the last few witches, concerned they might come after me to use as a bargaining chip to get what they wanted.

Logan and Josiah fought in a slightly different way than the werewolves fought. Their actions were smoother, more graceful movements, and had a mystical quality to them. Logan attempted many times to cast spells onto Josiah or to his surroundings, but realized it took too much time to recite the words, and Josiah kept distracting him, ruining the spells, with brutal punches and kicks. Logan had even used one of his precious witches as a shield to protect himself. I supposed he didn't care if she survived or not. The demon resurrection was a success, in his mind, and perhaps he didn't need all of them now. He grabbed and placed that one witch in the direct path of Josiah's deadly, sharp fingernails as they sliced the air with the intended target being Logan's throat. Her scream was cut short, as Josiah's nails cut deep into her throat and part of her face. She died.

A second witch had come to aid Logan in his fight against Josiah. She knew martial arts and had thrown off her cumbersome robe to allow her full range of movement. She barely had a chance to show off her fighting skills, as Josiah deflected all of her hits as if she were a pesky mosquito. Logan attempted to stay behind her in order to concoct another spell, forcing her to fight Josiah. During an intricate karate move, Logan forcibly shoved her into Josiah, a move that propelled her skull firmly into Josiah's fist. She died from either a broken neck or head injury.

Logan managed to create a fireball and whizzed it at Josiah's head, nearly setting his hair on fire. A second fireball followed in quick succession that Josiah wasn't as prepared for. He leaned to the side but somehow Logan placed a tracker on his blazing projectile and it followed Josiah's movements, plowing into his stomach.

Dominic extinguished all remnants of both fireballs with his telekinesis and newfound talent in working with fire. Josiah glanced at his stomach, pleased that he and his clothes were no longer ablaze. Logan was totally blown away by Dom's ability to control fire. He glared at Dom with a non-verbal threat that indicated Dom would be next on his chopping block. Josiah recovered, dissolved into mist and reappeared on Logan's left side, and kicked hard at the most damaging area possible on Logan's knee, breaking it. Logan stumbled, but shifted his weight to his good leg. To keep the odds in his favor, Josiah knocked Logan off his feet with a roundhouse kick which sent him flying.

Logan's flight path was headed towards Lexy. Dominic created an invisible barrier to protect her that Logan crashed into and slid helplessly to the floor, near Lexy's feet. She knew this was her time to shine. Determined, she tossed the magic dust at Logan, furiously blowing the air, exacting her own revenge. Dom was able to read her mind, knew her intentions, and used his telekinesis to help move the magic dust through the air, right into Logan's face. He went down, his eyes on Lexy the whole time, astounded with her betrayal to him. The magic dust sapped Logan's strength, especially with the massive dose he had inhaled.

All the many spells Logan had erected were starting to crumble and fail. With his loss of control, Josiah was finally able to push into his mind. Logan was furious; and in his confusion and drowsiness, he vowed to kill all who stood in his way of attaining ultimate power. Even as Logan's eyes drooped with sleepiness, he ranted how he and King Lycaeon planned to rule humankind and how all the riches of the world would be his. Yep, delusional. He obviously wasn't paying attention to how his magnificent demon was presently getting his butt kicked.

Josiah tore into Logan's throat with his elongated vampire teeth, drinking some of his powerful blood, before punching through Logan's chest and ripping his heart out.

Logan was dead; all his spells ceased to exist. My drowsiness was lessened, but the effect of the magic dust was still in my system. And, my body was weak from blood loss. I wasn't sure if I could even walk across the room.

Claire asked Dominic to bring me down to where she sat on the floor, propped against the concrete coffin where I had been strapped. Her skin had paled to ghostly-white. Her breathing was heavy and slow; and she had difficulty drawing in enough air to fill her lungs. Lexy approached and we huddled close as the battle raged on between King Lycaeon and our guys: Daniel, Isaac and Zac. Josiah stood at attention in case they needed his help. He had done his part and eliminated Logan as a threat.

Claire grasped my hands and brought them to her forehead. Tears flooded my cheeks. She was dying. Most likely from a heart attack or stroke due to over-exertion and stress. As she held my hands, she uttered, "I give you my last remaining strength to aid in saving yourself and your friends. I'm glad to have known you, Kara. When I next see your grandmother, I will tell her what a good person you are and what wonderful talents you have…"

And she took one last breath…And her hands fell to her lap, still clasping mine…And her head dropped onto her chest…And she died.

And suddenly I felt her essence pass through my body. A small, but beneficial, burst of what had been her last ounce of strength, handed over to me. Maybe she could have held on another hour until we could have gotten her to a hospital. Or maybe not. But she chose to let go of life at that moment, and not wait to see if she could be saved. Instead, she gave to me a form of healing. My blood loss from the sacrifice had severely weakened me and now I suddenly felt renewed. I still wasn't ready for a jog around the block, but I felt like a 7 on a scale from 1 – 10.

I stopped my sobbing and wiped the tears from my face. It was time to end this. I hated to distract Daniel, Isaac or Zac as they fought Lycaeon, but it was vital they coordinate their attack on him with my plan. I telepathically sent them my brief message. Josiah, still linked with me, winked and nodded.

I called out, "King Lycaeon! What do you think of this?"

I implanted images of tables heaped with food. If he was basically a werewolf under all that demon resurrection crap, then he should be starving, especially since you could say he was similar to a newborn again. No one moved a muscle. I had gained strength, thanks to Claire, to mentally manipulate him and we didn't want anyone to distract him while I worked my magic. Within his mind, those tables held massive quantities of various types of meat, all mixed with human flesh. Something he craved. It sickened me to create such imagery, but I focused on some of the horror movies I'd seen over the years and could come up with some pretty gruesome stuff. I swamped him with feelings of hunger and thoughts of snatching some of the meat off the table, tossing a handful into his mouth and tasting the tantalizing flavors passing over his tongue. I visualized bacon and sliced human flesh, for Lycaeon's delight...[barf!]...sizzling in a skillet and concentrated on its potent smell, then shoved that into his brain. He actually faltered in his stance. Complete sensory overload.

A distraction. I seemed to favor that type of attack. And it was what we needed. I nodded in approval.

As Lycaeon briefly fantasized about the meat, Zac ferociously socked him in the head to keep him fully dazed and defenseless against his imminent death. Isaac calmly stepped in front of Lycaeon and stabbed him through the heart. At the exact same time, Daniel approached Lycaeon from behind, gripped his sword tightly and with perfect aim and grace, cut off Lycaeon's head. It tumbled to the floor. Isaac moved out of the way as the body fell forward.

King Lycaeon's vice, or sin, that originally turned him into a werewolf by Zeus is what killed him now. Eating human flesh. Only this time, it was the images of such a vile act that distracted him in mid-fight and gave his enemies the upper-hand.

Lycaeon's head rolled in Josiah's direction and he picked it up by the hair, staring at it in fascination. The eyes unexpectedly blinked, startling Josiah as he held the head at arm's length, and not too pleased to see it still appeared to be alive.

"Dom, a little fire, please?" Josiah prompted.

Josiah tossed the head near Logan's body and Dom instantly set the ghastly sight on fire.

Daniel, Isaac and Zac dashed out of the mausoleum to Daniel's truck. They transformed, dressed in clothes they had previously stashed, then returned to the crime scene. Now that the action was over, I surveyed the sight. Bodies were everywhere. It was shocking. Daniel immediately ran to me and hugged and kissed me. Even though I felt much better and could walk on my own, he wouldn't let me. He carried me out.

Isaac carried Claire's body. We would respectfully take her to a mortuary and Josiah would have to place false memories into the attendant's mind of the incident.

Before leaving the cemetery, Zac and Josiah tossed tree limbs and other ignitable items into the crypt and Dominic set everything on fire. We didn't want the remains of anyone or of any items to be discovered - especially the body of a demon. I felt guilty burning the inside of the crypt, but Daniel reminded me that almost everything in there was concrete, except for the demon, Logan, the witches and all the paraphernalia they had brought in with them.

It was near midnight. Lexy was quiet while we trudged to our vehicles. She was one of four witches who survived out of the thirteen total, which included Logan. She commented on how we shouldn't worry about the other three, as they were less powerful witches who tended to be skittish and were never thrilled about the demon resurrection in the first place. It seemed that Logan had placed a compliance spell on many witches to get them to conform to his wicked desires and plans.

It had snowed about three inches. I was glad Daniel insisted on carrying me after all. We would go to the mortuary with Claire's body next. Josiah said he'd fly there in owl form as Daniel's vehicle was a tad crowded. Afterwards, he needed to go feed before he came back to his house.

Lexy timidly asked, "So, could you guys use another team member? Having a witch around could be pretty helpful, you know!"

Silence.

We were stunned. Our thoughts raced. How do we answer her? She was a bit psychic, too, and we hated to stand in front of her and have a telepathic conversation amongst ourselves about do we or don't we let her join. That would seem rude.

Lexy's eyes glazed over and she didn't blink, holding completely still in her thoughts. I noticed it and nudged Daniel who stared at her, too. We wondered why she behaved like she was in a trance with a faraway look in her eyes.

All of a sudden, she snapped out of it. She looked up at Zac with tears in her eyes and gently said, "Tessa wants me to tell you, thank you for avenging her death, do good with your life…she loves you…but now she has to go…"

Well, *that* would definitely help Lexy's case.

CHAPTER 22
COPING

"Wait!" Zac grabbed Lexy roughly by her shoulders. Josiah placed his hand on Zac's arm as a warning to be careful or else he could crush Lexy with his strength. He didn't let her go, but loosened his grip. "Tessa's here? Can you talk to ghosts and see them?" Zac grilled her.

Lexy stuttered, "I...I've had a few experiences."

"Tell Tessa I'm sorry I couldn't save her," Zac released Lexy and dropped to his knees in the new fallen snow. "And I miss her..."

"She can hear you, but is quickly fading from us. She sees the light now and it's her time to move on," Lexy informed him, barely able to speak the words as her voice broke with sorrow.

Zac cried out, "I love you, too!"

By then, most of us were bawling. In between sniffles, Lexy whispered, "She smiled and said 'Goodbye, Zac.'"

After taking a few moments to absorb the fact that Tessa's spirit had spoken to Lexy in order to relay a message to Zac, I stated, "She has *my* vote to join The Liaison."

Everyone agreed with me and welcomed Lexy to the team. With complete sincerity, Zac thanked her for delivering Tessa's message and apologized if he had bruised her.

Lexy shrugged it off and asked, "Now what happens?"

I gave Josiah's address and my phone number to Lexy. I reminded her how we could communicate telepathically, too. I told her to pack and make preparations to leave the state of Massachusetts. She'd be heading to Hamlin, Kentucky. We gauged that if we worked our rear ends off to wrap things up in Winchester, we could be on the road in two days.

She suggested, "I have the key to the magic shop. If someone has room in their vehicle, we should swipe as many witchcraft items as possible. With Logan dead, it's a free-for-all!"

Zac offered the use of his vehicle. We decided it was beyond time to leave the cemetery, take Claire to the mortuary and then call it a night.

* * * *

Two days later, four packed vehicles, three psychic humans (one a witch), three werewolves (one with a dash of demon), and one vampire - we put the pedal to the medal and mashed it to Kentucky. Josiah drove his sports car with the heavily tinted windows and kept his body almost completely covered to avoid too much sun exposure. Zac and Isaac were in Zac's SUV. We remained cautious with Zac's emotions and anything that might set off his werewolf aggression. The embedded quartz was doing a fine job on helping his self-control. But Isaac rode with him just in case...especially since driving a vehicle in traffic can cause road rage. Lexy drove her car. And Daniel drove his truck with Dom and me. During one day, I kept Lexy company for several hours and it gave us a chance to talk. With Tessa gone, it had been weird being the only girl on the team. Tessa would always be missed. But Lexy filled that empty spot and had wonderful talents to benefit The Liaison.

It took about three days to travel to Hamlin. All of the vehicles stopped at Isaac's resort first to drop him off along with his one lone bag. The rest of us rolled in to Daniel's resort, ecstatic to have arrived. We clambered out of the vehicles as Eli rushed to greet us. He shook his head in sadness and wonder when he looked upon Zac, knowing how Zac had lost his wife and been turned into a werewolf.

Lexy introduced herself to Eli and asked, "Should I call you Boss?"

He chuckled. "No, Eli is fine. I'm just the crazy scientist with the money! When I can, I try to counsel or mediate. The team is quite capable without me."

I noticed Dominic narrowed his eyes as he peered at Eli. Dom wasn't smiling. He was in deep thought. I poked his mind, *What's wrong?*

I'm not sure. Don't worry for now, Dom stated.

It was dark when we reached the resort so Josiah was in his element and comfortable. He and Eli shook hands and exchanged polite introductions. Eli seemed truly shocked with all the changes to our little Liaison team. It's one thing to hear events unfolding on the phone, but when it's in your face, the reality sinks in.

Daniel suggested, "I'm assuming all the cabins are vacant?" He looked to Eli.

"No one has checked in." Eli confirmed. "And all has been quiet while you've been gone."

"We won't be taking any guests for a while. There are plenty of cabins for everyone. Let's go inside where it's warm, get the keys and figure out who wants which cabin. Then we can unload the vehicles and finally get settled in," Daniel took charge.

We lumbered into the main entrance of the resort. Ah, it felt nice to be home. Or at least I considered it one of my homes. I quickly took Lexy by the arm and pulled her to the lounge area with its heavenly fireplace. The others followed us; Daniel nabbed up several keys from behind the counter that belonged to the other cabins before walking in. Lexy, Dom and I huddled close to the crackling fireplace to soak in the warmth.

Daniel again looked to Eli and asked, "Is there plenty of food here?"

Eli grinned, "After your call the other day to forewarn me when you'd be back, I dialed up your niece, Abigail, and desperately asked for her help. We went grocery shopping and are fully stocked up."

Dom piped in, "I'll resume my alternate role as Head Chef. Especially if Abigail was involved in picking out the food choices, we'll be eating like royalty."

"I can help cook, too. That's if you need any help..." Lexy offered, trying to butter up Dom. He nodded, although not as enthusiastically as he should have.

Lexy still felt awkward with the team. After all, she had been our enemy. Although it was clear she had been influenced by Logan and the other witches and truly didn't believe in their desires and actions. And I kept forgetting she was related to me – we were third cousins.

Daniel handed out keys to the cabins. He gave Lexy keys to a small cabin where she'd have her own privacy. When she left Massachusetts with us, she knew she no longer had a permanent residence. We hadn't discussed living arrangements, as our main goal was just to get back to the resort. Now the question and concern was evident on her face as she stared at the keys.

She fretted, "I can't stay *here* forever. Should I find an apartment? What do I do?"

Daniel explained, "When we, The Liaison, need to be in this area, everyone will stay here or at one of the other resorts I own, and which Isaac and my sister, Rebecca, manage. You don't need to look for a place to live."

Eli continued, "The werewolves and Josiah are financially set for life. I imagine, or hope by now, that the others have told you that I have more money than I know what to do with, too. I fund the missions for The Liaison and provide the team with an expense account. Within reason, you can purchase items to provide for yourself and your needs. Dom's name is included on all the paperwork, so in case something should happen to me, then The Liaison has access to the money and can continue on. That should answer your money question, Lexy.

"Also, we have a private facility near the towns of Marine and Highland in Illinois, which is about 30 miles from St. Louis, Missouri. It has living quarters and I suggest you live there during those times that the team is in limbo or researching for the next mission. Traveling appears to be a big part of the job description, so I don't recommend renting an apartment," Eli finished. Lexy smiled and seemed content with his answer. She had two places where she could stay: the resort and the secret facility.

After a nice warm-up in front of the fireplace, we marched back outdoors to fetch our luggage. Eli already had his cabin and would remain in it. Josiah was given his own cabin, as was Lexy. Dom and Zac would share a large cabin which allowed someone (Dom) to be near Zac throughout the night and keep an eye on him. Daniel and I had our normal room in the main building of the resort.

Dom didn't waste much time fiddling around, settling into his cabin. We were starving and he was chomping at the bit to whip up one of his specialties in the abundantly decked-out kitchen of his dreams. Now that we were on Daniel's turf, Dom had toned down his advances on me. Really, he hadn't had any opportunities lately. We'd been a bit busy, I'd say.

I was on my way to the utility room to wash clothes and paused in the kitchen. I asked Dom, "You're acting strange with Eli. What's up?"

He said, "I think he knows something more about that lab in St. Louis than he's telling us. Those other werewolves, Thomas and Bridget Dustin, told us experiments were being conducted on werewolves and vampires. I can't fathom how Eli would not have any knowledge about it. He lives in the area and the entire subject matter is right up his alley. I'm going to confront him at some point..."

Suddenly, Lexy popped into the kitchen and asked what she could do to help. Not wanting to alarm Lexy with Dominic's doubts about Eli, Dom and I ended our conversation. Thankfully, Dom was friendly to her and gave her a few basic tasks to assist him with supper.

Lexy liked Dom. Heck, I could tell that without reading her mind. She playfully flirted with him. She was innocent and sweet, not at all vulgar or possessive, with her teasing. I had a little streak of jealousy race through my system, realizing what it must feel like for Dom when he sees me with Daniel.

Dom overheard my thoughts and clarified, *I don't think you truly know the depth of my jealousy and pain, Kara. But I'm glad to see and hear your reaction to her flirting with me.*

Oh, Dom...Just ease up on Lexy. She's trying to be nice and to help. Enjoy yourself. I advised him.

I wandered to the next room with my load of laundry. I did feel jealous. But I liked Lexy and I wasn't upset that she liked Dom. Back in Winchester, she had figured out during the resurrection that Daniel and I were actually together. She originally met Dom and me at the magic shop and I had lied to her when I introduced Dom as my boyfriend. In her eyes, I was with Daniel and Dom was fair game. I should be thrilled Lexy had an interest in Dom. And I was...that's what I wanted, right? I planned on staying with Daniel...right? Then why was I recalling the make out session Dom and I had in Josiah's house? No, no, no. Perhaps his obsession with me would lessen if

Lexy flirted with him and gave him the attention he deserved.

Nope, Dom snuck into my mind once again, firmly planting his response.

Annoyed, I flipped the knob on the washing machine and tapped my fingers on the lid. I really needed to get in the habit of blocking my mind during any deep thinking about relationships.

I mentally heard him snicker.

* * * *

The next day Daniel invited all of his pack over to give them updates on the turn of events in Winchester, which included checking out the new Zac and meeting Lexy. As expected, they were wary of Lexy but not outwardly unkind. It helped that I introduced her to each werewolf individually and mentally soothed each one, reassuring all of them that she was good.

Zac was the hot topic. He was now a werewolf and officially belonged to Daniel's pack since Daniel had converted him. The wolves had known Zac from previous trips to Hamlin. He was respected, trusted and liked and had proved his loyalty by aiding them more than once. And now he was one of them.

It was a cold but beautiful day. Daniel wanted to take Zac outside, in familiar territory, and simply run free in the woods with some of the other wolves. Eli, Lexy, Josiah, Dom and I stayed inside. Josiah lounged on the couch, away from direct light, yawned and searched for something to watch on the television. It was freaky to see him, a vampire, so comfortable and chilled out considering the number of werewolves around, but Josiah had built an excellent relationship with them. At the moment, he was finally able to relax and not worry about anything as compared to the situation in Winchester. Over his 886 years in existence, seeing werewolves run around in wolf form was nothing new or special. Whereas Lexy and I had our faces plastered to the frigid sliding glass door, waiting for the upcoming, spectacular show.

Two of the female werewolves chose not to go on the run. Rachel was pregnant and concerned there would be too much roughhousing for her while carrying a baby. Rachel's mother, Lydia, stayed with her and kept an eye on the piles of clothing. I was not a witness to the massive strip down. I can't imagine what it must've looked like! And to observe so many transformations happening at one time!

I telepathically called to Daniel, *Please bring all the wolves out into the open so we can see you before you tear off into the woods! I love watching everyone together. And Lexy is about to explode in anticipation!*

He laughed in my mind, extremely pleased with my excitement. *Okay. Everyone has shifted. Zac is much faster with his transforming now. But he's wound up and nervous with so many of us...check in on the state of his mind for me. I'm so glad we embedded that quartz in his neck. It helped. I'm rounding up the gang. Here we come.*

I focused on Zac. *How are you doing?*

Nervous, he bluntly replied.

I giggled. *You are nervous?* The wolves came into our view. What a fantastic, magical sight. I spotted Zac easily with the yellow streaks in his eyes, multi-colored fur and larger size. *Zac, don't be. You are among friends. Don't worry about accidentally nipping or biting any humans for now. We're safely inside. You are in control of your body and your mind, Warrior Wolf.* With his history in the military and his current status, I think he appreciated the meaning of the nickname I had made up out of the blue. I smiled and filled him with positive, encouraging emotions and slipped in, *I order you to go have fun.*

In response, he barked in my direction and pranced in a circle. He paused, holding a regal stance, turned his nose to the sky and howled. The other wolves joined in howling a harmonious chorus. Amazing. Even Josiah was captivated enough to get his butt off the couch and take a glimpse of the wolves in action and nodded with approval. Dominic grabbed a marker and paper and scribbled "10" then held it against the glass for the wolves to view. It was his score on their howling effort. Everyone roared with laughter. The wolves barked with enthusiasm, happy to entertain us.

Lexy was completely, joyfully mesmerized. She had seen the werewolves in their horrifying beast shape, but I didn't think she'd seen them as actual wolves. Very large wolves. Including Zac, I counted thirteen wolves chasing one another, wrestling and frolicking up to the sliding glass door so we could get a closer look. When you added Rachel and Lydia, there were fifteen werewolves in Daniel's pack.

Daniel informed me, *We need to run off some energy. And I want to test Zac's speed and agility. See you in a while.*

I acknowledged him and gazed at the beauty and phenomenon of the wolves as one by one they disappeared into the dense woods.

Dom tapped at my daydreaming brain, bringing me back to the present situation. He telepathically alerted me that he would confront Eli while we waited for the wolves to return. I didn't care for the idea. But Dom's suspicions had grown and we needed answers.

CHAPTER 23
BETRAYAL

If Dom discovered anything important while interrogating Eli about the St. Louis lab, he'd tell Daniel and Zac when they returned. Using telepathy, he asked for Josiah's assistance in retrieving information from Eli. It felt like we were ambushing him. And I hated to have a conflict in front of Lexy when she was so new to the team and still trying to find her place. We shouldn't keep her in the dark, either.

Eli was the man behind the curtain…he funded this whole operation. But what if he did know something and wasn't telling us?

"Eli, I've got to ask you a few things that have been bothering me," Dom looked directly at him. I could tell Dominic really wasn't at ease putting the spotlight on Eli, but he had his suspicions and was going by a gut instinct, an intuition. "As you answer my questions, Josiah and I are going to read your mind. Josiah can compel you to respond if you try to clam up. If you attempt to mentally block us, Josiah can effortlessly get around it, especially since you do not have psychic skills. We can extract the information, but I'd like to give you the chance to speak for yourself. I don't like doing this to you, but for the safety of our team and for the entire reason The Liaison was created, I must question you."

Eli was stunned by Dom's initiative and appeared nervous, giving the impression of a trapped animal. "Wh-What are you talking about, Dominic?"

"Did you know about the lab in St. Louis conducting experiments on vampires and werewolves?" Dom got right to the point of the matter.

Eli staggered and dropped onto a nearby chair. He ran his hands over his head and rubbed his jaw. He was well aware of Dom's mind reading skills. And a vampire as old as Josiah could completely control him with extreme supernatural power. Eli was no match against either one. With Dom's and Josiah's combined abilities, Eli was doomed if he thought to lie about anything. I wondered what was taking him so long to reply. His hesitation raised my own suspicion, whereas before the interrogation, I had felt little or no misgivings. I chose not to read Eli's thoughts. I didn't want to interfere while Dom and Josiah invaded his mind, already working their magic.

Josiah provided evidence of his power as Eli was mildly compelled to answer questions honestly. Josiah could completely take over Eli's mind and will, but wanted him to have an awareness of the discussion and give him the chance to reply without being harshly forced.

Eli choked up on his words. "Yes, I know about the lab in St. Louis."

Tears rolled down my face as I fought to stay quiet. Lexy touched my arm, confused and concerned.

Dom made sure his questions were specific. "Okay. That answers the first half of my question. But are you aware of the experiments? I asked you about this when I was in Winchester and you told me you knew nothing. Give me details."

Under duress, Eli told the truth. He struggled with his explanation, realizing how it made him appear to us. "Several years ago, I worked at the lab you're referring to. We were toying with the idea of capturing werewolves. Vampires were a possibility, but it would be difficult to trap one." Josiah nodded in agreement.

Eli continued, "Few humans know about the existence of such supernatural beings and the government wanted to keep it that way to avoid mass hysteria. But we started to notice an increase in the number of disturbances, sightings and deaths due to werewolves and vampires. As you know, the government has always wanted to co-exist with them, as long as they kept their existence hidden from society. If things got out of hand, humans would step in and eliminate the ones causing problems (or attempt to). Cover-up stories kept their reality unknown, for the most part."

"Keep going," Dom prompted. Eli had paused and was massaging his temples. Either stress or Josiah's compulsion had given him a headache.

Eli nervously cleared his throat. "Well, the reason the lab – the government – wanted to capture werewolves, and perhaps a vampire, was to study them. We thought we could create an anti-aggression drug or maybe some kind of medication that mellowed their killing instincts. I know it sounds crazy! I didn't need the income and so I resigned around that time. And I didn't like the idea of capturing and performing experiments on werewolves or vampires. Shortly afterwards, I made the decision to strike out on my own and that's when The Liaison was born. I wanted to help neutralize problems with the supernatural beings before the government chose to step in."

Frustrated, Dom said, "Are they presently doing experiments or not?"

Eli pleaded his case, "Dominic, you wanted the details and I'm giving them to you."

Josiah already knew the answer. He had sifted through Eli's memories. His eyes were a dead giveaway as they turned solid black. But Josiah and Dom wanted to hear Eli *say* the truth out loud and so Josiah psychically forced him to confess.

"Yes," Eli broke down. "Experiments *are* being conducted. I have contacts at the lab who've told me only *evil* ones were captured, though. Also, I have shared some of my theories and my notes that you've seen me type into my laptop. They don't have any names or addresses. I was trying to help, in my own way. I didn't agree with the experiments."

I erupted from my silence, "How do those scientists know for sure they've captured werewolves or vampires that have completely turned evil? What if one of them isn't, Eli?! Remember Stephen? I was brought on board to help determine if he was actually evil or if he could be saved with The Liaison's help…with *my* help using mental manipulation. And he *wasn't* bad…just lost and confused. He's fine now, thankfully. But to those scientists who work for the government, they would have mistaken him as an evil werewolf. So picture, if you will, Stephen getting abducted, locked in a cell, maybe chained up, and who knows what kinds of creepy tests the scientists would be conducting on him. It makes me sick to my stomach."

That wonderful feeling and joy I previously experienced when watching the wolves romping to and fro outside had totally dissolved. No. Dissolved was far too gentle a word. My peaceful morning had completely been smashed into a thousand pieces. Someone I trusted and admired had betrayed us. Eli knew about the St. Louis lab. He knew about the experiments. But he never told us.

Daniel felt my mental anguish while out running with the wolves. He pressed into my mind, *What's happening? Something is wrong.*

I wanted him and all the wolves to enjoy their freedom and have fun out in the woods. I wished I could join them. It was good for Zac to familiarize himself with wolf pack conduct and to test his full range of supernatural skills and their limits concerning speed, strength, agility and his heightened senses. I hated to be the bearer of bad news.

I'm not in any danger. But don't stay out as long as you intended. I have news about the lab in St. Louis, I explained to Daniel, trying hard to conceal my imploding emotions. I sensed he had signaled the wolves to return to the resort.

I announced to Eli, Dom, Josiah and Lexy, "Press the pause button on this conversation. The wolves will be here soon."

Within ten minutes, the wolf pack had returned, dressed and gathered inside the lounge. It was crowded and we should've gone to the conference room, but no one seemed to mind the closeness... Except Eli, who was sweating up a storm by then.

Dom and Josiah took the floor, recounting word for word Eli's statements. I had to witness the shock and anger over Eli's betrayal all over again, only this time it was on the faces and in the minds of the werewolves. He should not have kept the lab experiments a secret. The restless wolves were worried about their future safety and if they would be targeted for capture. They wondered if innocent victims had been abducted. And how would the results from those experiments affect all of them in the long run? Zac twitched in his effort to keep from transforming and I felt the atmosphere in the room turn hostile.

I looked to Daniel, Dom and Josiah. Dom sensed the urgency to keep control of the situation. He looked to Eli and said, "You are going to St. Louis and will weasel your way back into working at the lab. I'm sure with your knowledge and genuine hands-on experience, they'll welcome you with open arms. Eli, your goal will be to find out what is really happening there, who and how many are being experimented on, and if the captives are truly evil."

Everyone continued to fume, wanting to kick Eli's butt, but with his new task outlined for him, he was of value. Eli slipped off to his cabin, away from the hateful glares, and started to pack his suitcase. The whole group stuck around and discussed the turn of events. Eli felt ashamed for having worked at the lab and kept it a secret fearing if we knew, we'd think he had underlying motives. Or we'd want nothing to do with him. He wanted to be helpful and had never caused harm to the werewolves. He loved working with them and cared for their welfare. His crime was not telling us about the laboratory from the start; it seemed there *wasn't* any other twisted, underlying motive on his part to sabotage the werewolves. Josiah had compelled him to answer truthfully.

Regardless, feelings had been hurt. Eli didn't want to abolish The Liaison or break ties with the wolves. But he needed to prove his loyalty and mend frazzled relationships. He could do that by going undercover at the lab for us. It was odd how Dom more or less took charge of the team from that point forward. Eli didn't go out in the field anymore. We had rarely consulted him while in Winchester. His gobs of money supported us, but we really didn't even need that because the werewolves were loaded, too. As was Josiah. If Eli split, The Liaison could carry on.

Before some of the werewolves left to go home, Josiah announced he had a surprise due to arrive the next night. While we were picking apart Eli's betrayal, Josiah put out a mental call to his vampire friends, Mizar and Serena.

Jaws dropped. Including mine. Holy cow!

* * * *

Mizar and Serena made their grand appearance during the evening hours as Josiah predicted. Well, there wasn't anything to predict when they could telepathically tell him, "We'll be there in ten minutes."

They did not slyly sneak in through the woods on foot, although I assumed that was an option with their preternatural speed. Hmm...I wondered which method of travel was faster for them: racing along on their own feet or driving the big, black, wicked-looking machine, with the acres of shiny chrome, which they whipped into the resort's parking space. I gawked and commented to Josiah and anyone else listening, "Gee, that's not exactly low-key. But it's so cool!"

Josiah rattled off, "It's a '57 Chrysler 300. Take note of the fitting blood-red interior."

The vampires stepped out of the car to a full audience. The werewolves had not seen Mizar and Serena in 180 years. Not since they had formed a truce, hunted an evil vampire in the area and Serena aided the wolves with a boundary spell – preventing the locals from noticing that the wolves never aged. A huge amount of respect and trust existed between these particular vampires and werewolves. Greetings were genuine and warm. Josiah introduced The Liaison members to them, including me. So cool.

Mizar looked at me, having read my mind, and grinned, "You've expressed that comment twice now. Thank you, Kara, I'm pleased to meet you. I've heard snippets about you from Josiah. Believe me, it was all good."

I shook their cold hands…which if a vampire was cold to the touch, they usually needed to feed. Serena, also reading my thoughts, smiled and commented, "I'm impressed. Correct diagnosis but I can wait till later. Daniel, shall we go inside your charming resort to discuss our plans?"

This time, we invaded the conference room. No lounging in the lounge.

Mizar and Serena were briefly filled in on our recent trip to Winchester, since that was when we met Thomas and Bridget Dustin, the werewolves, who officially told us about the alleged experiments in St. Louis. We explained in greater detail what Eli's confession revealed concerning this lab. It was agreed Eli would finagle his way back into the lab, offering them his experience and knowledge, but secretly report to us his findings. Eli advised us not to expect this to happen overnight. The head scientist in charge most likely would not give him full access to the entire laboratory right off the bat. We needed to give him at least a month to infiltrate the top secret areas to learn as much as possible.

Mizar and Serena took up Daniel's offer to stay at his resort for a week or so and then they'd drive up to the St. Louis area, find a quaint little motel to hunker down in and start their own surveillance of the laboratory. They'd contact Josiah with any intel.

Zac, Dom, Lexy and Josiah would remain with Daniel and me at his resort. With eight cabins available, he had the room for them. And why not stick together for now? A plan had been formed. Eli would leave the next morning. According to his timeline, we had approximately one month before heading to St. Louis and diving into our next mission.

I had a very important decision I wanted to make well before one month was up.

CHAPTER 24
DECISION

My mind flipped and flopped. Do I or don't I? I paced the bedroom floor. I stopped and stood in front of the mirror and brushed my hair. Whenever I was nervous my scalp itched; and it was driving me nutty that night. My heart pounded with a deafening beat which resonated in my hyperactive brain. I went to the bathroom. I brushed my teeth. As I peered out the window, I fogged up the glass with my heated breath.

Finally, I flopped onto the bed and stared at the ceiling. And waited.

One day (or night) had passed since the arrival of Mizar and Serena. They fascinated me with their stories and vampire quirkiness. Eli had left for St. Louis. Everyone settled in and for the most part, enjoyed the company of one another. Peaceful for the time being.

It was close to midnight. Daniel entered the bedroom. He had just completed a favorite routine that consisted of transforming into a wolf and doing a perimeter check of his property. All was secure. Lord, with as many supernatural beings in the area, how could it *not* be secure! But in his words, "you can never be too careful."

He tossed off his shirt, fell onto the bed and hungrily gazed at me. I snuggled up to him, feeling his warmth radiate off his body as he planted kisses on my head. After one minute, I pulled away, sat cross-legged and wrapped the blankets around me. I gave him my "serious look" so he knew I meant business.

Daniel pestered me, "Uh-oh...I sense I'm about to be besieged with a lengthy, heart to heart discussion. Perhaps it should be called a speech as I'm sure you'll be doing most of the talking."

He winked. I groaned at his insinuation that I ramble. Hmm... "I'm going to make my decision whether to have you convert me into a werewolf or not. I'm making up my mind tonight."

Daniel sat up, alert and listening. I had his full, undivided attention.

"So, let me talk...This choice is mine, unless some unforeseen accident occurred as it did with Zac. At this moment, it is my decision and it could change my life forever. Watching Zac go through his conversion was awful. I could feel the pain and confusion he experienced. Learning how to gain self-control and dealing with his aggression was difficult and grueling.

"But Zac is doing well now. He endured the conversion and is thriving. Just as you and all the members in your pack did, Daniel. If I became a werewolf, we wouldn't have to worry about a lot of injuries I'm susceptible to while dealing with the supernatural. I would heal quickly. I could help fight and not have to cower behind you...I know my human weakness is a distraction to you – don't try to deny it – any time you fight an enemy and have to worry about my welfare at the same time. I could inadvertently be putting you in danger.

"Speaking of danger, when we're alone and making out, you're always having to control your urges - your wild animal nature, for fear of hurting me. I really can't see maintaining a relationship as a couple, with the obvious desires we both have for each other, and never, ever attempting to have sex because you're afraid for my human safety! And another major thing is that you don't age. As a human, I do. I'm 21, you're 26. So, we'd be okay for many years yet, but eventually, the fact remains that I will continue getting older both physically and mentally. Yuck! I don't want to get old if you're not! Totally unfair!" I waited a few seconds to let Daniel absorb everything I was throwing at him.

I continued, "Claire told me something that stuck in my mind. She said, 'Kara, your psychic abilities are immensely powerful. Use them well and to their full extent during your entire life.' And so, if I were a werewolf, my psychic powers would increase and be an even greater benefit during our battles against the bad guys or in helping those with emotional turmoil. And when she spoke of 'my entire life', it would no longer be limited to a human life span, but to the lengthy, almost immortal life of a werewolf. I believe I can do a lot of good with that much time on my hands."

Daniel was nearly exploding from his impatience and anticipation. "Well, spit it out. Don't make me work for it!"

I exhaled slowly, "I have a premonition, whether it's real or not, that what we discover about the lab in St. Louis will be horrifying. I sense it's going to get messy. It would be nice if I could be in top form with additional skills and enhanced power when we hit the road for St. Louis."

Daniel knelt on the bed in front of me, pushed off the thick blankets surrounding my shoulders and gently grasped my head. Inches from my face, he pleaded for a direct answer, "Please, Kara! What precisely are you telling me?"

It felt right. With a mischievous grin, I answered him with complete honesty, "Daniel, I want you to turn me into a werewolf."

He kissed me with such force and vigor, it knocked me backwards on the bed. I added, "I'm not asking you to convert me *tonight*, but within the next day or so. I imagine we'll want help from some of the others during my conversion and dealing with the transformations. We'll have one month for you to help me adjust before the St. Louis mission."

His mouth drifted across my neck as he breathed in my scent. He whispered, "One month…Baby, I'll mold you into the perfect werewolf. You'll be in good hands."

I already was. I giggled, "And I'll be joining the ranks of the unknown."

THE END

© Black Rose Writing